PENGUIN BOOKS

Death or Glory III

Highroad to Hell

Michael Asher has served in the Parachute Regiment and the SAS. With his wife, Arabist and photographer Mariantonietta Peru, he made the first west–east crossing of the Sahara on foot – a distance of 4,500 miles – with camels but without technology or back-up of any kind.

He is a Fellow of the Royal Society of Literature, and has won both the Ness Award of the Royal Geographical Society and the Mungo Park Medal of the Royal Scottish Geographical Society for Exploration.

He has written many books, including *The Regiment: The Real Story of the SAS* and the first two books in the Death or Glory series, *The Last Commando* and *The Flaming Sword*, which are also published by Penguin.

Death or Glory

PART III

Highroad to Hell

MICHAEL ASHER

PENGUIN BOOKS

PENGUIN BOOKS

Published by the Penguin Group
Penguin Books Ltd, 80 Strand, London WC2R 0RL, England
Penguin Group (USA) Inc., 375 Hudson Street, New York, New York 10014, USA
Penguin Group (Canada), 90 Eglinton Avenue East, Suite 700, Toronto, Ontario,
Canada M4P 2Y3 (a division of Pearson Penguin Canada Inc.)
Penguin Ireland, 25 St Stephen's Green, Dublin 2, Ireland (a division of Penguin Books Ltd)
Penguin Group (Australia), 707 Collins Street, Melbourne, Victoria 3008, Australia
(a division of Pearson Australia Group Pty Ltd)
Penguin Books India Pvt Ltd, 11 Community Centre,
Panchsheel Park, New Delhi – 110 017, India
Penguin Group (NZ), 67 Apollo Drive, Rosedale, Auckland 0632, New Zealand
(a division of Pearson New Zealand Ltd)
Penguin Books (South Africa) (Pty) Ltd, Block D, Rosebank Office Park,
181 Jan Smuts Avenue, Parktown North, Gauteng 2193, South Africa

Penguin Books Ltd, Registered Offices: 80 Strand, London WC2R 0RL, England

www.penguin.com

First published 2012
001

Copyright © Michael Asher, 2012

Set in 12.5/14.75 pt Garamond MT Std
Typeset by Jouve (UK), Milton Keynes
Printed in England by Clays Ltd, St Ives plc

ISBN: 978-0-141-04721-8

www.greenpenguin.co.uk

MIX
Paper from
responsible sources
FSC™ C018179

Penguin Books is committed to a sustainable
future for our business, our readers and our planet.
This book is made from Forest Stewardship
Council™ certified paper.

ALWAYS LEARNING   **PEARSON**

If you can force your heart, and nerve and sinew,
To serve their turn long after they are gone,
And carry on when there is nothing in you,
Except the will, that says to you, 'Hold on.'
If you can fill the unforgiving minute,
With sixty seconds' worth of distance run,
Then yours is the earth, and everything that's in it,
And what is more, you'll be SAS, my son.

– SAS selection poem; adapted from 'If'
by Rudyard Kipling

Dispatch

From: Advanced HQ, First Army, Tunisia
DMI, Allied Forces HQ, Constantine
To: MEHQ, Cairo, Egypt
30 January 1943

From: 2/Lt. M. Sadler 1st SAS Regiment
To: OC G(RF) GHQ, Cairo

Stirling's and McDermott's parties attacked by Germans reference Z.0755, 24 January. All jeeps taken & all personnel captured except Sadler, Cooper & Taxis . . . two men left at Ksar Ghilane 22 January waiting to be picked up. Co-ordinates NE Africa purple grid . . .

From: Col. Gen. Erwin Rommel
GOC Panzer Army
To: Lucy Rommel
2 Feb. 1943

Dearest Lu,
. . . At the end of January a number of our AA gunners succeeded in surprising a British column in Tunisia and captured the commander of 1st SAS Regiment, Lieut.-Col. David Stirling. Insufficiently guarded, he managed to escape and made his way to some Arabs, to whom he offered a reward if they would get him back to British lines. But his bid must have been too small, for the Arabs, with their usual eye to

business, offered him to us for 11 pounds of tea — a bargain which we soon clinched. Thus the British lost a very able and adaptable commander of the desert group which has caused us more damage than any other British unit of equal strength . . .

From: GHQ, Middle East
RAMC Depot, Cairo
Medical Centre
1st Feb. 1943

Subject: Captain Thomas Edward Caine DCM DSO

1st SAS Regt

This officer was evacuated from operations in the Western Desert with a shrapnel wound in the thigh. Last November he suffered severe concussion as a result of a motor accident: the vehicle went out of control while proceeding along the Nile Corniche in darkness, and plunged over the barrier into the river, just short of the MP checkpoint. It is believed that the accident resulted from a struggle between the driver, identified as an enemy agent, and the passengers — the above-named officer, and a female staff officer, Hon/Capt. Elizabeth Nolan, GM and bar, of G(RF). Capt. Caine surfaced after a sharp blow on the head, but continued to dive down into the water in search of his companion until pulled out of the water by the crew of a police patrol boat. The other two occupants of the vehicle are missing, presumed dead.

Capt. Caine is now physically fit, but still, in my opinion, displaying symptoms of trauma. He has been in action almost continuously since 1941, first with 2 Field Sqn Royal Engi-

neers, then with 52 Middle East Commando, and most recently with 1st SAS Regiment. He has commanded two strategic special operations behind enemy lines, and has been twice decorated for bravery. He has been captured twice, subjected to physical abuse, and escaped both times. He has suffered a total of twenty-six wounds, some of them serious. This incident was particularly disturbing for this officer: his fellow passenger, Capt. Nolan, was the G(R) officer whom he had previously extracted from behind enemy lines, and to whom he had formed an emotional attachment.

Capt. Caine was prevented from deploying with 1st SAS Regt on recent postings: he remains restless for action. He has asked me repeatedly to pass him fit for active service. This I have refused to do, not because his physical condition is deficient, but because I continue to have doubts about his mental state.

Signed:
Dr G. R. Healey Lieut.-Col. RAMC

I

They came for Captain Thomas Caine at three o'clock on a Sunday morning, as he lay asleep in his hotel room in Ismaeliyya. Caine heard them coming: he leapt out of bed and flattened two of them with his bare knuckles as they stepped through the door. He'd just had time to register that they were wearing battledress and black berets, when he felt a sharp jab in his right thigh: he collapsed like a limp fish.

When he came round minutes later he was being hustled into the back of a jeep. He was fully dressed: they'd pulled a sandbag over his head and cuffed his hands behind him. 'Just sit quiet, Captain,' a gruff voice said, 'or we'll be obliged to use rough stuff.'

Caine knew better than to ask what it was about. He was aware he'd find out soon enough, and doubted if he'd be surprised. Since he'd lost Betty Nolan, almost five months earlier, nothing much surprised him any more. He couldn't remember clearly what had happened that night: one minute they'd been sitting in the back seat of the taxi, happy as Larry, the next, Nolan had been struggling with the driver: the car went out of control, crashed through the safety barrier, slamdunked into the Nile. Caine's head must have hit something hard: he'd been out a few seconds. When he'd come to,

5

the vehicle was still lodged half on the surface: oil-coloured water was gushing in. It was pitch dark, and he couldn't feel Nolan's hand.

He was certain that the driver had been Eisner: the Nazi agent was known to be a dab hand at disguise. They'd thought he was out of the picture since Field Security had chased him from his Cairo base. He must have come back, watched them, planned his move carefully, waited for his chance. Whatever his plan had been, though, Caine didn't give a toss any more. Eisner had taken Nolan from him: everything else, even the war, dwindled to insignificance beside that fact.

The jeep hummed on into the darkness: none of the men spoke. Caine felt groggy: the dope that had knocked him out, whatever it was, had left him with a hangover. He tasted sandbag hemp, heard matches strike, breathed cigarette smoke through the sack. It seemed an age before the wagon crunched to a halt on a gravel drive and they bundled him out. He sensed that it had grown lighter but couldn't be sure. He was hustled up steps: a door groaned, footsteps rang on flagstones. He smelt incense, heard music from a gramophone far off. They nudged him up a staircase, shoved him through another door, pushed him into a chair. Caine felt fingers working on his handcuffs.

'*Not yet,*' a voice said.

There was a sound like the creak of bicycle spokes: Caine was trying to work out what it was when a fist lumped him hard in the jaw. He gasped, tasted blood.

'*I say, steady on, Roger.*'

'*Piece of dogshit put me in a wheelchair.*'

The hood was whipped off: Caine found himself staring into the indignant face of Captain Roger Glenn, the officer he'd kneecapped during the *Sandhog* scheme. Glenn's splitshovel teeth were bared in a snarl. His broad swimmer's torso seemed to burst out of the wheelchair he was sitting in.

Next to him stood Major Jasper Maskelyne, Royal Engineers, the ex-stage magician whom Caine had last seen as an ever diminishing dot on the vast canvas of the Sahara. Maskelyne was more neatly dressed than he'd been last time, but his tailored BD suit only emphasized his oddness: snakeskin features, carrot nose, littlebird eyes, hairless skull that seemed attached to his body by a spring.

A third officer sat in a sagging armchair on Maskelyne's left: a dwarf of a man with half-colonel's insignia on his shoulder-straps. He had a head like a cannonball, beady eyes magnified by thick lenses, a barrel-sized mouth and the leathery skin of a Barbary ape. In a competition for peculiarity, Caine thought, the jury was out as to whether Monkeyface or Maskelyne would win first prize.

He surveyed the room, took in wood panels, patterned carpets, leatherbound books, battered table, shapeless leather armchairs, massive stone fireplace: a blackboard with a sheet over it. There were brass candlesticks on the mantelpiece, an ivory crucifix, paintings of saints with gilt halos. The room was lit by gaslamps: the first glow of dawn was creeping through mullioned windows set deep in stone walls.

Maskelyne drew a .38 Webley from his holster – an action so deft that Caine hardly caught it. He suddenly recalled the conjuror's sleight of hand, the deceptive speed and strength of those stickinsect limbs. Maskelyne pointed the pistol at him. 'I'm going to have them release you,' he said, 'but try any funny stuff here, Caine, and I swear I'll shoot you down. Do I have your word?'

'Let's see,' Caine drawled through thick lips. 'Your men jump me in my hotel room in the early hours, shoot me up with some sort of dope, handcuff me, stick a sandbag over my head and cart me off to some unknown location, and you expect me to give *you* my word? If you wanted me to join the party, why not send me an invitation? Even a phone call would have done the trick.'

'Same old clever dick,' Glenn snorted. 'You don't look so clever now.'

'What about belting a blindfold man in handcuffs? How clever is that?'

'You deserved it. You shot me in the kneecap.'

'If I remember rightly, you were going for your weapon at the time . . .'

'That's enough, gentlemen, please,' the apefaced colonel cut in. 'You've had your moment, Roger. Let's put that regrettable incident behind us.'

Caine squinted at him. 'There's still a weapon pointing at me.'

'Give us your word you won't try anything,' Maskelyne said.

'All right, you have my word.'

Maskelyne slid the pistol back into its holster, nodded

to the invisible soldier behind Caine, who unlocked the cuffs. Caine massaged his sore wrists, wiped blood from his lips, caught Glenn's eyes watching him. He detested Glenn, had done ever since the chap had caused the death of his friend in commando training. Still, he wouldn't have shot him if there'd been a choice.

'Sorry, Roger,' he said quietly, 'but my scheme was vital. You and Major Maskelyne were about to compromise it.'

Maskelyne's nostrils flared. '*Compromise?* Do you realize how much planning went into *Bertram*? You might have messed up the whole show.'

Caine decided not to argue: *Bertram* was stale news anyway. Montgomery's advance had succeeded. Tripoli had fallen. Rommel's Panzer Army had been pushed all the way back into Tunisia, and the Axis was currently threatened by both the Eighth Army in the east, and Anglo-American forces encroaching from the west. The Huns' days in North Africa were numbered.

The little colonel faced him. 'I apologize for the rough treatment, Caine,' he said in a matchpaper voice.

'What about the dope? How did they do that?'

Caversham beamed. 'It's called a ballistic syringe – a handy little invention of ours. It's a weapon that shoots a dart with a dose of tranquillizer in it. You got the minimum dose.'

'Am I supposed to be grateful?'

'You have a reputation for truculence, Caine.' The colonel clucked impatiently. 'Had our men simply asked you politely, you would probably have kicked them downstairs and crippled them for life. You once killed three Brandenbergers armed only with a rusty blade.'

'That was the *enemy*.'

'Yes, and we all know what you can do to *friends*. You knocked down the Deputy Provost Marshal of Cairo. You lost your commission for threatening to shoot the CO of an infantry battalion. You're a thug, Caine. An intelligent thug, but a thug all the same . . .'

Caine was about to observe that the C-in-C hadn't seen it that way when he'd pinned the DCM and the DSO on his chest. It occurred to him, though, that General Alexander might have been thinking the same thing.

'. . . but then, in our line of business,' the colonel went on, 'intelligent thugs are just what are required. I am Caversham, by the way, Lieutenant-Colonel. Miles. Our little outfit here is known as MO4. This is our base – St Anthony's monastery, Sinai. It's good cover. It has the odour of sanctity, and it keeps us away from the gaberdine swine at GHQ.'

Caine's gaze was drawn to an odd painting on the wall behind Caversham's chair. It showed a saint with a long white beard split into two wearing a monk's habit, apparently suspended over a pale sea. The monk was being attacked from all sides by spiny fish-like monsters and demons with bats' wings and chicken feet, some wielding cudgels, others tearing at his clothes. The monk seemed to be trying desperately to remain unperturbed by the assault. Caine knew just how he felt.

The little colonel caught his glance. '*The Torment of*

St Anthony,' he remarked. 'St Anthony was a monk who lived in a cave here two thousand years ago. Had regular tussles with demons and monsters, apparently. He was a healer, known for curing a whole bouquet of plagues, collectively called St Anthony's Fire. Anyway, he left his bleached bones in the desert, and later they built this place on top of them.'

Caine shifted impatiently. 'Could we get to the point, please, sir? I don't think you've brought me here to discuss ancient history.'

'I say, I *do* like a man who gets down to business.'

Caversham lumbered over to the blackboard, whipped off the sheet, revealed a map of Tunisia.

'What I am about to tell you, Caine, is top secret. You will not breathe a word of it to anyone. Is that clear?'

'Crystal, sir.' Caine was on his guard: just a moment ago they'd been pointing a loaded gun at him: now they were offering him secrets. It wasn't a healthy combination, he thought.

Caversham picked up a ruler, tapped the map. 'In the early hours of this morning, General Montgomery launched a frontal attack on the Mareth Line . . . Are you familiar with the Mareth Line, Caine?'

'Not exactly, sir.'

Caversham turned to face him. 'It's an impregnable wall of defences, twenty-two miles in length, guarding the whole eastern approach to Tunisia. It is currently being held by thirty-two Axis infantry battalions and a Panzer division, all of which have been ordered to fight to the death . . .'

He paused for dramatic effect, rapped the map again. 'As I was saying, our assault on the Mareth Line this morning was repulsed with heavy losses – the first reversal we've sustained since the breakout from Alamein. The GOC is now stuck. If he keeps throwing his forces at that line, he's likely to lose thousands. He can't easily go around, either, because the left flank is protected by the Matmata Hills. The whole area is described on French maps as *terrain chaotique* – it's like hell's back door.'

He sucked in grizzled cheeks. 'However, there *is* a way round. It's called the Tebaga Gap – a narrow pass on the western side of the hills that gives access all the way through to Gabes. If a large enough force can squeeze through there, Monty can encircle the Mareth Line, and thus avoid what might turn out to be the nastiest punchup of the entire campaign.'

He rasped a breath: Caine sensed a climax.

'A week ago, Monty dispatched General Freyberg's New Zealand Corps with orders to breach the Tebaga Gap. Their advance was compromised. Not only have the enemy dug in at the mouth of the gap, but three crack Afrika Korps divisions are also on their way to reinforce the position. When they get there, there's going to be a hell of a brouhaha.'

'Very interesting, sir,' Caine said, 'but what's it got to do with me?'

The colonel cleared his throat. 'Your part in it, Caine, is simple. There's a disused highroad through the Matmata Hills south of the Tebaga Gap. Only a track, really, but it passes over a bridge at el-Fayya gorge.' He pointed at the map with a squaretipped finger. 'Our latest int. is that a reconnaissance battalion of the Totenkopf Division is being detached to cross the el-Fayya gorge, traverse the Matmata Hills by the old highroad, and knife Freyberg from behind. That could put the kibosh on our chances of getting through Tebaga. It would mean Monty getting stuck at Mareth: it could turn the tide of the war, just when things were going so well.'

He paused to make certain that Caine had taken it in.

'One battalion?' Caine queried. 'That wouldn't be much of a threat to New Zealand Corps, would it?'

'It's a recce battalion: two Panzer divisions are moving up behind it. We don't know which way they're going to jump, but there'll be hell to pay if *they* turn up in Freyberg's rear.'

Caversham paused again, scrutinized Caine from behind thick lenses. 'What would you do in this situation, Caine?'

'Take that bridge out, sir. Sharpish.'

For a moment Caine thought the colonel was going to clap. Instead, he winked at Maskelyne.

'Jasper, please give Captain Caine a cigarette.'

Maskelyne pursed dry lips, stood over Caine with hands raised, as if he were about to conduct a choir.

Caine flinched as the conjurer's fingers probed inside his left ear. 'What's this?' Maskelyne demanded. With a theatrical flourish, he held up a squashed Victory cigarette. 'Mind you, I don't think I'd want it after where it's been.'

'Now you see it, now you don't.' Caine shrugged. 'Got a light, sir?'

He stuck the cigarette in his mouth.

Maskelyne opened his other hand, displayed an empty palm. He closed it, made a pass, opened it again, showed Caine a chrome Ronson lighter that had appeared from nowhere. He lit the cigarette, eyed Caine as he took his first puff.

'Thank you,' Caine said.

Caversham cleared his throat. 'Your job, Caine, is to go in with a small patrol and blow up the el-Fayya bridge. You will drop in by parachute the day after tomorrow, pick up motor transport and demolition gear from Captain Fraser, now commanding a composite SAS unit made up mainly of Frogs and Bubbles – Free French and Greeks, that is – on Freyberg's flank. You will follow the old highroad across the hills to the bridge, destroy it, and withdraw the same way. Simple, you see.'

Caine regarded the colonel with steady, stoneground eyes. 'Let me get this straight, sir. You're asking me to go in behind enemy lines and undertake a vital sabotage operation under the noses of a Jerry battalion, scouting ahead of two Panzer divisions. If the timing's out, I'm likely to get squashed.'

'Don't be ridiculous,' Maskelyne scoffed. 'Speed is the key. You'll be in and out well ahead of the enemy.'

'Just how many men will I have with me on this little jaunt?'

Caversham looked as if he were toting big numbers

in his head. 'Six,' he said at last. 'Seven including yourself. Special Service troops are hard to find.'

'Yes,' Glenn added. 'We really had to scrape the bottom of the barrel to get *you*.'

Caine dropped his cigarette butt on the stone floor and ground it out underfoot. He was officially on sick leave, but he knew he was fit, whatever the quack said: he'd been anxious to get back into action for some time. He had no objection to a mission behind enemy lines: blowing a bridge was certainly an SAS task. But why hadn't he been tasked by the SAS or by the raiding forces planning cell, G(RF)? Why hadn't orders come down the usual channels? He didn't trust Glenn or Maskelyne, and he'd never even heard of MO4.

He raised his blacksmith's shoulders, drew in a deep breath. 'Thank you, gentlemen,' he said. 'The scheme sounds interesting. I'd like to help you, but I'm going to have to turn it down. I'm serving in the 1st SAS Regiment. I can't do anything without orders from my CO.'

Maskelyne made a scoffing noise. 'Which CO would that be, Caine? Stirling's been in the bag since January. Jellicoe's only acting depot chief, and Mayne's in Lebanon with 'A' Squadron. Of course, you know that, don't you? You weren't invited to accompany them, because your medical officer declined to pass you fit.'

Caine glared at him. 'You seem extraordinarily well up on my fitness record, Major. You know I'm considered unfit for active service, yet you reckon I'm in prime condition to carry out some dizzy bloody scheme for you.'

15

'Admirably so,' Caversham cut in. 'You see, Caine, this op – *Nighthawk* – has to be kept tight as a duck's derrière. We need personnel whose absence will go unnoticed by enemy agents. As you are on sick leave, you qualify.'

Caine shook his head. None of it made sense: if they wanted to blow a bridge at short notice, why not use Desert Air Force bombers? If aircraft couldn't be spared, there was Fraser's Bubble and Frog squadron, already in the field. Why go to the trouble of parachuting in a special unit?

There had to be more to it than they were saying. There always was.

'I've already played Aunt Sally twice, sir,' he told Caversham. 'I got away with it, but I lost some good men in the process. I don't fancy being set up a third time. No, I'll pass on this one, thank you. It was very kind of you to offer, but no thanks.'

He stood up, watched Maskelyne's deft fingers caress his pistol butt. 'I don't think you're going to shoot me, Major. Not in cold blood, not in the back.'

Maskelyne's fingers crept away from the weapon. He licked his thin lips. 'No, I'm not going to shoot you, Caine. But you're not going to walk away from this either.'

'Oh?' Caine said. He tilted his head. 'And why would that be?'

'Sit *down*, Caine,' Caversham ordered, his voice sharp as a hacksaw. 'I will explain *exactly* why.'

Caine hesitated, sat. Caversham stood facing him.

'On 6 November last year, you were involved in a motor crash, when a taxi, driven, you claim, by a Nazi agent, plunged into the Nile. You got out, but your companion, Captain Elizabeth Nolan, was lost, believed killed. Is that correct?'

'*Believed?*' Caine repeated the word under his breath. *Believed?* For an instant he was back there, in the Nile, fighting the treacle water, kicking out in the wet darkness with what felt like a ball and chain on his legs, struggling out of the clutches of the demon that wrenched him down, his lungs bursting, his head burning with pain. He was floundering his way to the surface, smashing through the river's dark skin, sucking in mouthfuls of air, shrieking out her name in the great empty cavern of the night. He would not let her go, no matter how many times he had to dive back down into that terrible black pit, no matter if he had to plunge into the stinking bowels of hell itself. He'd kept on diving and surfacing and yelling her name, until the patrol boat arrived and other hands dragged him out: even then, he'd clawed, kicked, punched at his rescuers, trying to get back into the river, beating at them like a madman, screaming her name until the darkness had covered him like a hood.

Caversham was staring at him. 'Yet you *don't* believe it, do you, Caine? That's why you've spent every spare moment since then tramping the streets of Cairo, visiting every place Nolan has ever been, hanging about in every bar, every nightclub, talking to every cabaret girl, every barman she'd ever met.'

'How do you know that?'

Caversham whipped off his glasses, started to clean them with a handkerchief. 'It's my job to know. *That's* why the doctor wouldn't sign your medical release, isn't it? Not because of the shrapnel wound you sustained on desert ops, but because he considered you unstable: you refused to accept Nolan's death. You still don't believe she's gone.'

Caine's skin was suddenly clammy: his pulse went up a notch. 'It was pitch dark that night,' he said. 'They dredged the river but never found any bodies. They said she'd got dragged down, but Nolan's a strong swimmer. She could have swum to the opposite bank or got out somewhere else. It's not impossible. Maybe . . .'

He stopped himself. He couldn't tell Caversham about the mysterious phone calls in the night: Eisner's voice gloating, *She's not dead, Caine. She's alive. She's mine now. Mine to do whatever I like with.* Of waking up later to find that his room had no telephone – that he'd been talking to a ghost. Or the times he'd actually *seen* Betty Nolan on the streets, spotted her in the shadows of a nightclub: of the time he'd glimpsed her walking arm in arm with another man – a man looking suspiciously like Johann Eisner. About the time he'd sighted the two of them necking in a doorway, and had approached them, only to confront a blonde FANY and a resentful young lieutenant.

Caversham replaced his glasses, lowered his orangutan head nearer to Caine's. 'What if I were to tell you that Captain Nolan is *not* dead?'

18

Caine fought to control himself: his face turned white, his breath jabbed. 'This isn't funny, Colonel. Nolan has nothing to do with this.'

'Oh, I assure you I am quite serious,' Caversham said. 'You see, Caine, Captain Nolan is alive. I have conclusive proof of that.'

2

Dawnlight poked gilded shafts through the mullioned windows. Maskelyne turned off the gaslamps. Caversham spread photographs on the table, handed Caine a magnifying glass. He lit a pipe, stood back, watched him with quiet satisfaction. The shaftlight caught little explosions of smoke from his pipe, transformed them into swirling mandala shapes.

Caine had to admit the photographs looked genuine: Nolan in a dark skirt, white blouse and light jacket, outside a Cairo cinema: *Now Showing. Gone with the Wind: 26 December* 1942. That was more than a month after the crash. Nolan reading a newspaper: the headline could be discerned through the lens: *Tripoli Falls to Allies – 23 January 1943*. That was seven weeks ago.

Caine used the glass to check for trick photography: he examined the Nolan in the pictures minutely – the almost boyish haircut, the peek-a-boo wave that fell over her left eye, the slender legs, the vivacious breasts, the tiny blemishes – the scar on her neck, the freckles, the mole on her wrist. He studied her face – the full lips, the enticing overlap of her front teeth and, most of all, that dreamy, faraway look, the oceansoul eyes under lowered lids, that used to drive him mad. Every detail seemed right, but still he couldn't be certain. He'd believed that Nolan was alive with no real evidence: now he was being offered evidence, he was reluctant to accept it. He didn't want to have her snatched away a second time.

Caversham gathered the snaps and laid the stack back on the table. Caine watched him. 'All right,' he said. 'They look like the real thing. God knows how much I'd like to believe that it really is Nolan, but . . .'

'*But,*' Caversham cut in, laying his pipe in an ashtray, 'certain questions need to be answered. First, if this *is* Captain Nolan, why hasn't she contacted you? Why, for that matter, hasn't she reported back to GHQ? As a serving officer, that makes her a deserter, doesn't it?'

Caine nodded reluctantly: Caversham had hit the nail on the head. If he'd expected categorical answers, though, he was disappointed.

'All I can do, ' the colonel said, 'is offer two tentative explanations. First, that she has been suffering some sort of disorientation, and is no longer aware of her identity . . .'

Caine nodded again. Nolan hadn't returned to her lodgings, and, come to think of it, he hadn't recognized any of the clothes she was wearing in the snaps. If it *was* true, though, how was she living?

He shivered.

'The other possibility is that she has been prevented from making contact, either by friendly forces, or by the enemy.'

A thought popped into Caine's head: he knew it should have occurred to him earlier. '*Eisner?*'

21

Caversham gave him a thick grin. 'It's certainly on the cards. You survived the accident. If Nolan survived, why not Eisner too?'

Caine tried to stop himself thinking of Nolan and Eisner together, took a mental step back, tried to observe the three MO4 officers from a different standpoint. Could this be an elaborate hoax? Deception was, after all, Maskelyne's game: he was quite capable of orchestrating the illusion that Nolan was alive. At the very least, Caversham and his crew must know where these photos had come from.

He took in a deep breath. All three of them gawked at him.

'Of course,' Caversham went on, 'you're thinking that we must know the source of these photos and, if so, we could trace Nolan through it. After all, *somebody* took them, didn't they?'

'It had occurred to me.' Caine forced the words out.

Caversham shook his head. 'You must believe me: we do *not* know Nolan's whereabouts, nor who, if anyone, is controlling her. It is true that we might be able to track her down through the source of the photos, and we are willing to do so . . .'

Caine's eyes widened in anticipation.

'. . . but only on the condition that you carry out the little job that we talked about.'

Caine saw red. He bunched his fists, flexed ironclad pectorals, took a step towards Caversham. Maskelyne's hand streaked to his holster, but not even the conjuror could match Caine's speed when he was riled. In a greased movement he grabbed the magician's right wrist, twisted his arm back, shook the pistol out of it. It clanked on to the stone floor. No one made a move to pick it up.

Maskelyne stared at him coolly. 'You gave your word.'

'Oh yes, my word – I remember. With a pistol in my face.'

Glenn stayed rooted to the wheelchair: Caversham didn't budge an inch. 'This is quite unnecessary, Caine. You can walk out this minute, and no one will lift a finger to stop you. You can comb Cairo till your beard is grey, but you won't find Captain Nolan. You will only find her with our help, and that help is dependent on your accepting this mission.'

Caine knew they'd got him. He could leave now, report to the SAS depot at Kabrit, tell them he'd been abducted. He could report Caversham's actions to the Provost Marshal. None of that would get him an inch nearer to Nolan.

'Even if I get back in one piece, how do I know you'll help me?'

'You don't,' Glenn crowed. 'You'll have to trust us.'

'Accepting the mission means accepting my orders,' Caversham cut in. 'In particular, you won't carp about the chaps I assign you. Is that understood?'

Caine eyed him. 'Why? What's wrong with them?'

Maskelyne handed him a sheet of paper with a very short list typed on it. Caine read:

Fiske, Richard	Pte Royal Army Ordnance Corps. 3 years, theft.
Jizzard, Mitchell	Gnr Royal Artillery. 5 years, extortion.
Quinnell, Dominic	Pte Royal Irish Fusiliers. 4 years, conduct unbecoming.

He looked up, mystified.

'Convicted offenders,' Maskelyne grinned. 'Serving time.'

For a moment, Caine couldn't believe it. 'You mean you're sending me into the field with a bunch of ex-detainees from the *glasshouse*?'

'You should feel at home with them,' Glenn interjected. 'That's just where you ought to be.'

'Oh, do shut up, Roger,' Caversham barked. He eyed Caine solemnly. 'Look, Caine, these men were all we could get at short notice. Of course they aren't SAS, but on the other hand, they *are* all ex-commando, all parachute trained, and all volunteers.'

Caine swallowed. 'Colonel, on a scheme like this, you need men you can trust. These chaps will be liabilities.'

'I doubt it. They've been offered the choice of an honourable discharge or a chance to soldier on if they acquit themselves well. So they have every reason to toe the line.'

Caine choked down an expletive. He was convinced now that Maskelyne, Glenn and Caversham had cooked this up between them with something untoward in mind. He again considered turning on his heel and marching out. It hit him suddenly how much he despised them. The army had been his home since the age of sixteen, and he'd always felt solidarity with his comrades. It was the brass he couldn't stand: the arrogant, incompetent blunderers who thought themselves entitled to make men jump through hoops on command – who would use his feelings for Nolan to control *him*.

The image of Nolan was too fresh in his mind, though. He'd accepted the job, and that meant taking any lemon they handed him. He squared his deep chest, took a breath, clenched his fists.

'You agreed not to quibble about your team,' Caversham reminded him.

'I did, sir, but I wasn't expecting this. If these men do anything to endanger the mission, you're responsible.'

'I accept that responsibility.' Caversham's eyes didn't flicker. 'Now, if that's all done, I want you and your team assembled in the briefing room after breakfast, at 0900 hours sharp.'

He was about to turn away when Caine stopped him. 'Wait a minute, sir. How come there are only three names on this list? Where are the rest?'

Caversham turned back. 'Oh, sorry, I forgot. Your friends have been here since yesterday.'

'Excuse me, sir?'

'Your SAS comrades . . . Sergeant . . . no, Second

Lieutenant now ... Copeland, Trooper Wallace, and Corporal Trubman.'

Caine gaped. 'You mean you're dragging *them* into this? But they're on active service.'

'Actually, they're not. Copeland was en route to OCTU. Wallace was under arrest for knocking down his OC and Trubman was awaiting transfer back to a signals unit. So, as luck would have it, they fitted the bill. In any case, it means you will have at least *some* men you can trust not to shoot you in the back.'

Caine glanced at him sharply, taking in the simian face, the blackball eyes. He resisted the urge to demand what the hell he'd meant by that.

3

Fiske, Quinnell and Jizzard were sorting equipment in the refectory corridor: they stood to attention when Caine and Maskelyne approached. Maskelyne told them to stand at ease. 'Let me introduce your patrol commander,' he said. 'Captain Thomas Caine, 1st SAS Regiment. You'll take your orders from him: I don't want any backsliding, men. Do a good job and you'll come back with a clean slate.'

'Aye, if we come back at all,' Jizzard grunted.

'That's enough,' Maskelyne snapped.

The three men had prison-style crewcuts, and were wearing starched fatigues and ammunition boots they'd obviously been obliged to spend hours bulling. Caine told them to stand easy, shook hands. They eyed him without enthusiasm, emanated a sort of resentful silence, as if they'd been volunteered for yet another pointless army task, like painting black coal white.

Jizzard was a heavy Scotsman with red hair, shifty brown eyes, a doorstep chin and an intimidating expression. He was an ex-gunner who'd come to Egypt with Layforce, and had spent his leisure time running a protection racket among Cairo shopkeepers: until the MPs had got wind of it. Quinnell was shorter, with a head like a bloodhound and features that seemed to change abruptly from the responsive to the ferocious: broad lips, intense brown eyes, bull shoulders. He looked strong and confident, but his voice was almost girlishly soft: he blinked when he talked. A self-confessed IRA man in Civvie Street, he'd gone AWOL in Cairo when they'd tried to arrest him for subversive activities. Both he and Jizzard had holed up for a while with deserter gangs in the Delta before the Redcaps had nabbed them.

Fiske was the odd man out. An ex-officer in a past life, he'd been caught redhanded with his fingers in his unit's till. He was tall, gaunt and stiff-faced, with grave eyes, tight lips, a toucan nose and ears like dockleaves. Caine felt there was something inert hidden in his frozen gaze and wirestrip mouth. He looked fit, but his movements were stiff and jerky: he reminded Caine of a mechanical toy.

Caine's first impression wasn't favourable. The job of blowing the el-Fayya bridge seemed uncomplicated, but he knew that Murphy's law always applied behind enemy lines. Copeland, Wallace and Trubman had proved themselves in combat: he wondered how the three tenderfoots would hold up. He hoped that all would go according to plan. Then he wouldn't need to find out.

'All right,' he said. 'I don't know you, but I'm taking you on the word of Colonel Caversham. You've all had commando training, and you've all seen action. Just keep your noses clean, do what you're told and you'll be all right.'

He left them to their new kit. Maskelyne showed him into the refectory, where men of all ranks were sitting at trestle tables or queueing for plates of eggs, bacon and sausages at a cookhouse bar. 'Your chums are here,' Maskelyne told him. 'Don't forget, briefing 0900.'

Caine looked around, saw his mates sitting at a table on the far side of the room, tucking into breakfast. They weren't exactly exuding an air of camaraderie. Fred Wallace was hunched over his plate, glowering like a grizzly, his lantern jaw working like a trap as he forked in bacon. Perched next to him, Harry Copeland looked as though he'd turned out for church parade. His BD suit was immaculately pressed, SAS wings up over his double MM ribbon, his newly acquired pips a flash of blue on his shoulders. Taff Trubman sat slightly aloof from the others, wearing his wrinkled leather jerkin, his face inscrutable, eyes dim under steelrim glasses. Caine knew the signaller had finally completed his SAS parachute course. He didn't have his wings up, though, and he wasn't wearing his corporal chevrons or medal ribbons either.

Caine got his plate filled, drew a halfpint of tea from the urn, went over to join them.

'Well, well,' Wallace guffawed, 'look what the cat dragged in.'

Trubman nodded to him. Copeland got up, clapped him on the back. 'I've got a present for you, skipper,' he said.

He pointed to a bulging kitbag on the floor. It had Caine's name stenciled on it. Propped against it was the Thompson sub-machine gun that was Caine's pride and joy – the weapon he'd modified to take 50- and 100-round drum magazines securely, and had fitted with a bayonet-lug.

Caine picked up the weapon, cradled it, proved the works. 'Where did you get my kit?' he asked Cope.

'Maskelyne gave it to me.'

Caine pulled on the tight flesh of his chin, wondered how Maskelyne had managed to get hold of his personal weapon and equipment. He'd left it at the SAS depot at Kabrit when he'd gone to Ismaeliyya on a 48-hour pass. 'This weapon was locked in the armoury,' he told Cope. 'How did he get it out?'

'Used 'is magic wand o' course,' Wallace chuckled.

Caine laughed.

He laid the Tommy-gun on the floor next to Cope's SMLE sniper's rifle: he seated himself at the table.

'They hauled me off a lorry two days ago,' Cope told him. 'They said you'd requested me for a special job. When I arrived here there was no sign of you. I was starting to think you weren't coming.'

'Same story with me, skipper,' Wallace grunted through a mouthful of sausage.

'*You*, you big dollop,' Cope smirked. 'You were in the cells at Suez: they marched you out in handcuffs.'

Wallace looked abashed. 'All right, maybe they did. But if they 'adn't mentioned your name, skipper, I'd have skittled 'em, wouldn't I?'

'What's this about you chinning Paddy Mayne? That must have been a first.'

Wallace's forehead rimpled, the pitbull eyes went dark.

For a second, Caine had a vision of the Wallace he'd once been forced to fight under the influence of a disorienting drug: an ogre from hell. He put the image aside, reminded himself that the real Wallace was a man whose heart matched his giant's frame, who liked children and animals, and who was as loyal to him as a brother.

'It weren't Paddy's fault – it were the rozzers, *wannit*? See, after I lamped him, there was a bit of a kerfuffle. The Redcaps moved in to break it all up, and I'm the one that cops it. Always happens: they go for the big bloke. They slam me up in the chokey: next thing I know some morons are marchin' me out, saying Captain Caine wants me for a job. When I get here, of course, there ain't no Captain Caine – just like Harry said. There's only that creep Maskelyne yakking on about how he's sendin' us off on some scuzzy scheme in Tunisia. Almost throttled him. They locked me up in the cellar. I'd of rotted if his majesty here hadn't ordered 'em to let me go.' He rumbled with laughter. 'Should of seen him handin' it out, skipper. Second Lieutenant weren't in it.'

Copeland brushed imaginary dust off his shoulder-straps. 'From now on, Trooper Wallace, you will address me as *sir*.'

'Course I will, *sir*. You can kiss my hairy arse, an' all.'

Caine chuckled, attacked his bacon and sausages: he felt a surge of gratitude that his mates were with him. He squinted at Trubman. 'What about you, Taff? I heard you got RTU'd.'

Trubman reddened. 'They said I wasn't SAS material, see.'

'Those pisspots,' Wallace butted in fiercely. 'You survived two big schemes: you got medals. What the hell do they want, Santa Claus?'

Trubman sighed. 'They don't twig signals, see. Stirling did, but after he got bagged it all went to pot. Jellicoe calls me in and says that 'A' Squadron's retraining for mountain warfare. Says I'm not the *right stuff*. So there I am at the transit camp, waiting for RTU, when a couple of bruisers arrive and say you've requested me. Not a dickie-bird about what the job is. I thought it must be all right, seeing as it was with you.'

It was more than Trubman usually said. Caine warmed to him, felt privileged that these men trusted him. He hoped he was worthy of that trust: everything he'd heard about the way they'd all been dragooned into *Nighthawk*, though, left him in doubt.

'Did you apply for a movement order, Taff?' he enquired.

The signaller shook his mole head. 'Nope. They said it was all on the QT.'

Caine peered sideways at Copeland. 'What about you, Harry?'

'Same story.'

'You, Fred? They show you any paperwork?'

'Not a damn thing.'

'So there're no orders, no plan, nothing written down. And if you're wondering about me, they snatched me from a hotel in Ismaeliyya early this morning. First heard about *Nighthawk* two hours ago.'

There was a tense silence as they took this in.

'I thought it might be a tit-for-tat thing for *Sandhog*,' Copeland said quietly, 'but no one in their right mind would go to this much trouble to get rid of us. There's got to *be* an Op. *Nighthawk*, even if they've been short on details.'

'*Nighthawk* shitehawk,' big Wallace poled in. 'Watch yer backs, boys.'

Cope passed around Player's Navy Cut. Caine cracked his Zippo, lit the cigarettes, wrapped the lighter away in its rubber condom.

'Any news of Brunetto?' he asked Copeland.

For a second, Cope's face caved in. His sweetheart, Angela Brunetto, an Italian defector who'd saved their lives more than once, had been missing since February. She'd been working in the DMI's office as an Italian translator. One day, she'd simply failed to turn up for work. She'd vanished without trace.

Caine watched Copeland, feeling for him. He recalled the photographs Caversham had shown him: for an instant he wondered if it could have been Brunetto in them, not Nolan. After all, the two girls were near looka-likes. It wasn't possible, though – not unless Brunetto had been deliberately got up as Nolan. Even then he'd have known the difference. Brunetto didn't have Nolan's waiflike look: her features were smouldering and sultry.

'The Field Security lads claimed documents had been nicked,' Cope said. 'Papers she had access to, that kind of thing. They reckoned she was a spy. Said the whole business – you know, her and me – was a set-up to plant her inside GHQ.'

'*Never*,' Wallace thundered. 'Those dipsticks don't know their arses from their elbows. She skewered her old man in front of us.'

'That's what I told them, but they didn't want to know. She was an Itie, they said, and Ities are the *enemy*. That didn't make sense either, because they must have vetted her before they gave her that job. They made a big deal of pointing out that it was *her* letter that drew us into Rohde's trap on *Sandhog*.'

'Yeah,' Caine said. 'Except that Rohde was really being drawn into *our* trap. They must have missed that.'

'They missed a lot of things. I saw Stocker – you remember, the Field Security chap? He knew about Brunetto from the start: helped her get the job. The blighter threw me out of his office.'

Which didn't sound like Stocker either, Caine thought. The major had made his mistakes, certainly, but he was normally as keen as mustard. Caine mulled it over uneasily: a cold finger touched his neck. He had the same dreamlike feeling he'd been experiencing on and off all morning, ever since Glenn had swung for him. Only six people had returned from the *Sandhog* mission, two of them women. Now, the two girls – first Nolan, then Brunetto – had gone. The four male survivors – himself, Copeland, Wallace and Trubman – had been pressganged into accepting a hazardous mission. Not only had the scheme been planned by officers who had every reason to hate them, but no one else in the world knew where they were.

4

They were only minutes off target when the Bombay's pilot spotted the Messerschmitt hanging like a dark mosquito over the dawn-shaded peaks of the Matmata Hills. His heart dropped. He cursed the delays that had prevented him from reaching the drop-zone in darkness. He spoke on the interphone, told the dispatcher to abort the *Nighthawk* drop.

Caine was braced at the fuselage door, head aching from the tightness of his pudding-bowl helmet, shoulders raw from the weight of his parachute kit. He watched the desert waft past, a weave of amber and black a thousand feet below: he waited edgily for the order to jump. The flight had been an endless hell of booming aero-engines, gut-wrenching turbulence, cold, puke, gasoline fumes. He knew they were late, knew that jumping in daylight might leave them exposed: whatever lay in store for them out there, though, it had to be better than this. He glanced round at the faces of his patrol, illuminated in the first pale flush of light. All of them – even Big Fred Wallace – looked as sick as pigs.

The dispatcher, a brawny flight-sergeant in RAF battledress with an outlandishly long moustache and

Brylcreemed hair, touched Caine on the arm, leaned over to yell in his ear.

'Drop's cancelled, sir.'

For a moment, Caine thought he hadn't heard right. '*What?*'

'We've got trouble. Me 109F. Pilot's about to take evasive action.'

Caine looked round furiously at Harry Copeland, found pinpoint eyes darkcupped beneath his helmet. 'You hear that, Harry? They're bottling out.'

Copeland's mouth tightened. Before he could speak, though, the aircraft banked viciously. Thrown against the dispatcher, Caine grabbed at the doorframe to steady himself. His face was only inches from the sergeant's. 'Listen, you tell that damn' air-jockey that we're going to jump, I don't care if the whole bloody *Luftwaffe*'s out there.'

The aircraft shuddered, dipped, rattled: the dispatcher clutched at the interphone-bracket, shook his head. 'Can't do it, sir. Pilot's the boss.'

Caine felt white-hot anger churn his guts: he shot out a broad hand, seized the sergeant's collar, heaved the upper part of his body through the door into the slipstream in a single fast movement. He held him there. 'Tell him, or you take a nose-dive. It's a bloody long way down.'

The RAF man squirmed in Caine's iron grip. '*We'll lose the aircraft.*'

'Bugger the aircraft. Get us on the deck.'

He shoved the man's body further out into the slip-stream, saw the slicked hair whipped up in the wind.

'*All right. All right. Let me go.*'

Caine yoiked him back, dekkoed the patrol, saw pudding-bowl heads waggle, saw uneasy hands gripping strops, saw harness-trussed bodies leaning into the yaw.

'But, sah,' Jizzard wheezed. 'You cannae do . . .'

There was a low *lub-dub-dub* of machine-gun fire: a fat 20-mil round jounced through the fuselage, skimmed the Scotsman's helmet, greased the fuel tank, snapped out the other side.

'*Jesus fucking Christ*,' Jizzard screeched.

'*Shut up*,' Copeland snarled.

The Bombay listed: the men were almost thrown off their feet. Caine clung on to the doorframe, heard an engine splutter, smelt smoke. The big bird dropped altitude: Caine felt his stomach lurch. The men swayed on her strops until she righted herself. The flight-sergeant hung on the bracket, lifted the interphone with quivering fingers, spoke into it. He put it down shakily: his face was peacoloured: sweat trickled down his cheeks. 'Port engine's hit, sir. She's still cranking, but Jerry's coming round for another run.'

'*Blow her out of the sky*,' Big Wallace roared: the giant was leaning almost horizontal, all his colossal weight on his strop. 'Ain'tcha got no bleedin' guns on this crate?'

'Vickers "K" mounted in the nose-turret. No gunner.'

'You flamin' great *dickhead*. We're SAS, ain't we?'

The giant was already unshackling his static line: Caine stopped him.

'I'll do it,' he growled. The aircraft wobbled, skipped, porpoised. Caine detached his line from the bar, shuftied Copeland: his mate had braced himself against the fuel tank: the fingers that gripped his webbing strop were white. 'As soon as I give the all clear, take the stick out, Harry. I'll be right behind you.'

Cope swallowed. 'Got it, skipper.'

Caine leaned back against the fuselage, stared at the dispatcher. 'I'm going to the nose. Tell the pilot to stay on course.'

The sergeant nodded uncertainly. Caine squeezed past his men, felt Wallace's chip-pan hand on his shoulder. 'Good luck, skipper.' With the parachute on his back and the container on his legs, it was impossible to move fast: he shuffled along the cabin to the nose, felt the plane buck under him, saw wan light spill in through the turret's Plexiglass. The space was confined: too much of a squeeze with his parachute on: he released the catch, dumped it on the floor, dropped his container. A second later he was sitting in the gunner's chair with the Vickers 'K' in both hands. He checked the pans and the big aero-sights, wrenched the cocking handle, lifted the weapon on its mount. Below him to the right lay a moonscape of hills: the wasteland of stone and rock Caversham had called *hell's back door*. To the left lay the opal plains of the desert.

He peered through the sights: at first he didn't see the Me109: then he clocked her, a flea-sized blip coming

straight at him. He felt a spasm of panic, fought it down.
The Messerschmitt was a sleek thoroughbred – the fastest thing in the air: compared with her, the Bombay was
an outdated, lumbering bear. He'd blown up enough
109s to know that the latest versions carried two remotely
fired .20mm cannons mounted in wing-pods. The Vickers was a first-class weapon, ideal for aerial shooting, but
he'd never fired one from an aircraft: it seemed an impossible dream to hit anything travelling at almost four
hundred miles an hour.

The Bombay pitched. Caine ground his teeth. *For
Chrissake, keep her steady.* His eyes locked on the Jerry: she
was bigger now, growing visibly in his sights. Suddenly,
threads of scarlet tracer leapt out from her wings: light-
beams converging on a point somewhere in front of him.
A shell smashed through the Plexiglass, scattered fragments, whined past his ear. Caine gasped, ducked, blinked,
sloughed a breath, focused on the 109: he waited until
she was dead centre of his sights, pulled iron. At that
moment the Bombay juddered again: Caine watched his
own tracer-lines go wild. He swore: his heart pounded:
the Messerschmitt loomed nearer. Something went *click*
in his head: for a second it seemed he was no longer
breathing. His heartbeat slewed to a murmur, the roar
of the Bombay's engines faded, time itself seemed to stop:
the Me109 seemed motionless in his sights. He squeezed
the trigger: even before the muzzle-cone spurted fire,
even before he saw red tracer-lines scintillate, he *knew*
he'd done it, *knew* he'd hit her fuel tank. The Jerry's
wings tipped almost imperceptibly: then her fuselage

blowfished out in swelling knuckles of crimson: she blew apart in three broad stabs of smoke and fire.

Caine didn't wait to see where the wreckage fell: he'd already spotted something else: a couple of miles away to the north, tiny squares of purple, standing out against the pastel skin of the desert. It was the drop-zone, where Fraser's reception committee would be waiting, with their jeeps and demolition gear.

Caine scrambled out of the turret, struggled frantically with the parachute and container. He heaved himself to the main cabin, clocked expectant faces, hooked up his static line. He gave a double thumbs-up. '*What are you waiting for?*' he bawled. '*Get the hell out of it, now.*' The patrol were almost on each other's backs as they fell out into the sky.

5

Caine halted the convoy on the rise looking down on the el-Fayya gorge: he surveyed the position with binos. The bridge was a structure of stone arches spanning forty yards across the ravine: a walled blockhouse stood on a limb of the escarpment, set way back from the bridge's western end. There was a copse of tamarix trees at the base of the limb – strange, twisted treetrunks, entwined around each other like vast serpents. Marbled scarps rose out of shattered tufa on both sides of the track – rock faces razored into terraces and scallopings, pocked with caves like dead eyes. Flights of small birds made spirals and veronicas along the clifftops.

On the opposite side of the gorge, the old highroad disappeared over the rim of a hill. There were hard black peaks in the far distance: Caine couldn't see the barren plain he knew lay between here and there. The sky was pewterglass, fleeced with cotton: it was hot, but not desert hot. Here in the hills of Tunisia, it felt like a different game of soldiers: even the air smelt different.

Caine lowered the glasses, waited for reaction. There was no movement – the whole place seemed deserted. He examined the track ahead, looked for disturbed ground that might give telltale sign of mines. The road was scattered with pebbles sifted by recent rains: his

41

best guess was that nothing human had been here in weeks.

'It's gonna be a sod blowin' them buttresses,' Wallace remarked. Standing up in the driver's position, he looked more like some wild partisan than a regular soldier, Caine thought. He wore a rawhide jerkin over his patched and faded smock, and was hatless, his hair an unkempt tangle, his slab of a chest slung with bandoliers. His Purdey sawnoff hung from one side of his web belt, alongside a bayonet and a brace of grenades: a .45 Colt was holstered on the other. Wallace scratched the wirebrush bristle his chin, peered down through pindot eyes: his unassisted vision was keen as a kite's.

And he was right, Caine thought. He took another shufti at the arches. The bridge and its defences had been constructed by the French before the war, ready to hold this part of Tunisia in the event of an Italian invasion. It had been built to last: they would need every ounce of Nobel 808 they had to knock it down.

'Let's get on with it then,' Copeland's voice cut in from behind them. Cope was sprawled against the twin Vickers machine-guns mounted in the jeep's rear, cracking his knuckles with nervous impatience: a cigarette dangled from his lower lip. 'What are we waiting for – *Christmas*?'

Wallace spat sideways, sat down so heavily in the driving seat that the vehicle rocked. 'His imperial majesty speaks. You'd think 'e were a bleedin' field-marshal. 'E ain't even done his officer trainin' yet.'

'I'll have you on a fizzer, watch out.'

Caine slid back into his seat, chuckling. He knew Wallace didn't begrudge Copeland's new rank: it was just that Cope struggled so hard to conceal his pride that the big gunner couldn't help needling him.

'Nah.' Caine grinned at Wallace. 'He was world champion bighead even when he was a buckshee Tom.'

'Oh yer, I forgot.'

Caine half turned, waved to Trubman and Fiske, behind them in the W/T jeep. To the rear of Trubman's vehicle, Jizzard and Quinnell manned the third jeep, laden with explosives and demo kit.

'Let's move it, ladies,' Caine bawled.

They descended the slope cautiously. Copeland trained the machine-guns on the blockhouse, pivoted muzzles. They ran the jeeps into loops of shade under the tamarix trees. The patrol sprang out in all-round defence: Cope stayed aboard, braced the Vickers, scanned areas of possible threat. For a few minutes there was dead silence, broken by the cawings of crows on the escarpment above.

'All right,' Caine growled. 'Scrim 'em up.'

'Is that *really* necessary, Captain?' Fiske enquired. 'We've got these nice trees as cover.'

Caine gave him a long glance. He'd only known Fiske three days, but had already noticed his fondness for mouthing off. He might have been an officer once, but he was in the habit of forgetting he wasn't one any longer. Caine was about to say something cutting when Trubman beat him to it. 'If the captain says scrim up, you scrim up, man. Get on with it.'

43

Caine raised an eyebrow, clocked Trubman's fish-shaped face. The signaller had recovered from the bayonet wound he'd taken on their last op, but close up you could see a trace of fatigue in the eyes, a hint of resignation that made him look older. It was the long-distance stare of the battleweary: Caine also saw it when he looked in the mirror.

'Fiske, go with Wallace,' he said. 'Clear the bridge, and any other defences you find. Work out how we can lay the charges.'

Fiske and Wallace slunk off, weapons at the ready, five yards apart. Caine helped Jizzard and Quinnell stretch a cam-net over their jeep, noticed a dark stain in the sand beneath the front end of the wagon. He knelt down, touched the dampness, smelt his fingers. He inspected the condenser slung across the radiator grille. 'You've sprung a leak,' he told them. 'Didn't you notice?'

Jizzard shook his head. His face had a coarse, parboiled look: his eyes were haunted. 'Never saw a thing, sah, but then ah wasnae driving, was ah.' He nodded at Quinnell. 'What idjit would put a Paddy behind a steerin' wheel?'

Quinnell's eyes blazed. For a moment Caine thought he was going to hit Jizzard.

'The *idjit* would be me, Jizzard,' Caine snapped. 'In future you report all mechanical problems *at once*.' He stared the Scotsman out, his slatepolished eyes hard, his massive shoulders bristling. 'You want to take me on, Private?'

Jizzard's gloating look vanished. He dropped his eyes. 'No, sah.'

'Right. You two clear the blockhouse. And keep your eyes peeled. If you miss a booby trap like you missed that leak, you'll be riding home with your legs in a basket.'

The two of them sweated up the slope towards the blockhouse: Caine made safe his Thompson, helped Trubman set up the wireless antennae. Copeland cleared his .303 SMLE sniper's rifle, strolled over to Caine, bracing it under his arm as if he were on a pheasant shoot. He was a lean figure with the sharpbeaked face of a trawling bird, cornstubble hair, snowblue eyes, prominent Adam's apple. Though his smock and overalls were as worn and washed out as Caine's, they looked almost smart. Copeland owed his commission to the fact that Caine had taken a shrapnel wound on desert ops the previous December. Caine had been evacuated: OC Paddy Mayne had promoted Cope, then a sergeant, to fill the vacant troop officer's place.

Copeland gave Caine a V cigarette, stuck one in his mouth. Caine lit them both with his Zippo lighter – his talisman ever since it had saved his life on the *Runefish* op. That seemed a heck of a long time ago. He'd found Nolan on that scheme – and lost her twice since. How could a man be so careless with the person in the world he most cared about?

Copeland seemed to catch his thoughts. 'You reckon Nolan's alive?' he asked softly, the cigarette still in his mouth.

Caine shrugged, not ready to talk about it. He stubbed out his fagend hard. 'Stand stag, Harry, will you? I've got a condenser to fix.'

45

He took the toolkit and went to patch the leak. It required welding, but he had some stuff that would do the trick for now. Lying on his back with his head under the cylinder, his broad hands caressing the hot metal, he felt suddenly at ease. He had always found tinkering with machinery therapeutic. Unlike some human problems, mechanical ones could be mended, and he was good at mending them.

As he worked, Caine remembered another time when he'd been lying under a car like this. He was sixteen years old, an apprentice mechanic in Steve Moss's garage. Same smell of grease and diesel oil. A wireless playing a Glenn Miller dance tune. What make of car had it been? A Standard, he thought. He had been humming along, lost in his work, when Moss nudged him gently with his boot. 'Hey, Tommy. There's a copper here to see you.'

Caine shuffled out from under, stood up, wiped his hands on a rag. 'What does he want?'

Moss, a kindly, balding man, with a paunch under his greasy smock, looked apologetic. 'I dunno.' Caine knew he did, though, and so did he. He found PC Barry Jarrold in the office, staring at a dogeared calendar for the year 1937 featuring a photo of a sports car. The constable had spidery arms and legs, a grave, withered face with a sparse moustache. Caine always thought he looked too old and weedy to be a policeman: he wore a double row of Great War medal ribbons on his uniform, though.

'I've told you, Tommy,' Jarrold said gruffly. 'You can't go on working here.'

'It's my job, Constable.'

Jarrold's eyes were watery blue. 'You broke both your stepfather's arms with a smithy's hammer, boy. He's all for pressing charges. I've talked to him, though, and he'll drop them on the condition you leave home – go somewhere far away.'

Caine's jaw had tightened. 'And what'll happen to Mum, and my sister? Do you know what he was doing to them?'

Jarrold averted his eyes. 'I know, but in court it won't make a ha'penny's worth of difference. You'll go to borstal for two, three years: you won't be able to look after them there, will you?'

Jarrold laid a lean hand on Caine's shoulder: his eyes were sympathetic. 'You're a good lad, Tommy: they don't come better. But you're an animal when you get riled, and you're as fast as lightning. Your stepfather always was a swine. As far as the law's concerned, though, you attacked *him*. You might have killed him. I know how you feel, son, but the best thing you can do is get yourself in the army. It's all motors now. They need mechanics, and it'll make a man of you – teach you to curb that temper, maybe.'

Caine swallowed to relieve the swelling in his throat. 'They don't take you at sixteen.'

Jarrold winked. 'Lie about your age like I did – in the Great War. Nobody'll check up: it'll be between you and me. Don't worry about your mum and sister. I'll keep my eye on them.'

Caine looked around, searching for a way of escape,

but deep down knew there wasn't any. A week later, he'd turned up at the recruiting office and signed on with the Royal Engineers. That was six, nearly seven years ago. It had been a long road, he thought. He'd seen more than his fair share of suffering and death, lost some good men. But here he was, a captain in the 1st SAS Regiment, with both the DSO and the DCM to his name. He reflected how proud his mum would have been if she'd lived to see it – if he hadn't lost her. He blamed himself: he blamed himself for losing Betty Nolan, too.

6

Wallace and Fiske paced out the bridge. Fiske, in front, his .303 clinched in fleshless arms, halted every few minutes to lean over the parapet and peer at the masonry below. 'What you doing?' Wallace demanded.

Fiske stared at him. He was almost unnaturally thin – his smock hung on his body like a tent – but he was one of those spindly, ropemuscled types who often turned out to be stronger than they looked, Wallace thought. His eyes were brown and cold, his stringlipped mouth without expression.

'Checking for cracks in the stonework,' he said. His voice was sharp, with a contemptuous quality. 'To lay the charges in. Why? What would you do? Hang them over the side and say a prayer? We only get one bash at it, you know.'

He leaned over again: the bed of the ravine lay a good fifty feet down, a snake of ivory sand curving through tufts of waterbuffed boulders and esparto grass. 'We need to put cutting charges on all the spandrels,' he added, 'but the masonry here is too thick for an external charge. Unless we can find cracks to insert our 808 in, we'll have to bore holes, and that takes time. In any case, we'll have to go down on ropes. It's not going to be a stroll in the park.'

Wallace ignored the sneering tone. He guessed Fiske was the sort of bloke who didn't like many people – a loner who had no friends, and didn't care.

'Where'd you learn this demolitions stuff anyway?'

'At the Ordnance Depot. I was with No. 8 Commando too. When Layforce broke up, I was posted back to an Ordnance field unit . . .' He wetted his lips. 'That's when I ended up in the chokey.'

Wallace grinned. 'How long d'you do, then?'

'Six months. Would have been more if I hadn't volunteered for this lark.'

Wallace frowned. 'Just got out of clink myself: only a few days, mind, but that were enough. I'd rather face an 88-mil than six months in the slammer.'

The big man didn't mention the eighteen months' civvie time he'd copped for in Blighty, how the confinement, the shut-in feeling, had almost done for him. Thank Christ he was here in the open, not there, closed in.

Fiske wet his narrow lips again, his eyes leaden. 'So what did they do you for?'

'Belted Paddy Mayne, di'n' I?'

Fiske raised an eyebrow. 'Your OC? I'll bet that made you popular.'

'He was grindin' some poor kid's face to mush at the time. Paddy's all right till he's got two drinks down him, then he makes the Wolfman look like Shirley bleedin' Temple. Anyway, I owed him one.'

'They say he's a tough nut.'

'He ain't *that* tough.'

Fiske made a rasping noise that might have been

a chuckle. 'Belting your OC? No wonder you're still a buckshee private while your pals are sporting pips.'

Wallace stuck out his chin. 'Matter of fact, I bin offered enough tapes to string a parachute, mate. Decorated soldier, I am: MM and bar. Don't want 'em, though, do I? Private's the best rank in the army – at least yer can't get busted, like what 'appened to you. I 'eard you was an officer once.'

'Who told you that?'

'A little birdy. Is it true or ain't it?'

'It's none of your damn' business.'

They worked along the rest of the bridge in silence: on the far side they found a lump of mangled steel lying in the track, a buckled hulk that might have once been a trailer, so rusted through that its sides were thin wafers bent in on themselves. It had a crooked axle, but no wheels. Fiske moved towards it: Wallace's granite brow furrowed. His keen gaze swept the roadedge: there was a lump of oxidized metal peeking out of the gravel no more than four feet away. He grabbed Fiske's bony arm. 'Don't go any closer, mate. Could be a booby trap.'

Fiske shrugged him off. 'Let me be the judge of that.' He took another two paces: there was a sharp click like a breech block snapping shut. Wallace froze, felt the blood drain from his face, waited for the bang that never came. Fiske stood poised in midstep, rifle still clutched in his arms, not daring even to look down at what he might be standing on. '*Don't . . . fuckin' . . . move,*' Wallace whispered.

Sweat beaded the big man's temple: his breath came

in jerks. He saw that Fiske's boot had caught a tripwire flush with the surface, disguised under a thin layer of dust. The wire, almost as fine as cotton thread, had snared against his toe-cap, which had pulled it taut. The pressure, Wallace guessed, had armed an explosive device buried in the verge: that would explain the click they'd heard. The fact that it hadn't gone off yet, though, meant either it was a dud or that it had some sort of delayed-action set-up. In which case, withdrawing quickly would be his own best move. That would mean leaving Fiske in the lurch, though. He willed himself to move towards the thin man: for a moment, his legs wouldn't budge.

'Pressure-release tripwire,' Fiske hissed: his eyes were riveted on the wire attached to his boot. 'If I take my foot away, the wire goes slack, and she blows.'

Wallace nodded with slow and awful comprehension. He shifted the weight of his Bren in his massive arms, felt bird-flutters in his stomach. Fiske was precariously balanced with most of his weight on his front foot: he only had to stumble and they'd both be mincemeat.

The giant swallowed. 'You sure?' he demanded. 'Might be diss.'

'Want me to try it and *see*?'

'No, no, don't move, for Chrissake. Lemme think.'

Fiske swore furiously. 'The only thing to do is to apply equal pressure – can't let the wire go slack, but . . .'

'Yeah. How we gonna exchange the pressure without you movin' yer flamin' foot?'

Fiske had turned so pale his face was almost transparent. Wallace glanced about – there were plenty of loose stones around that might do for a counterweight. The question was, how to make the changeover.

Wallace set his steel jaw. 'I'm gonna put me Bren down. Then I'm gonna pick up one of them boulders and bring it over. It'll be all right, mate. Just stay where you are.'

'Where the hell do you think I'm going?'

Fiske had aged ten years in the last sixty seconds, but at least he wasn't the panicking type, Wallace thought. He laid the Bren down on its bipod, took careful steps towards the nearest scree. There were at least three boulders there he reckoned he could manage. He hefted one of them: it must have weighed five or six hundred pounds – too heavy even for him. A second, smaller, stone, was stuck in place, and wouldn't move. He tried a third boulder: it seemed loose. He stretched clamshell hands around it until they met, squatted and let his thighs take the weight. He shifted it with a groan, came slowly upright in a classic powerlift. He hefted the boulder two or three yards to where Fiske stood. He squatted again, laid the rock as near to Fiske's front foot as he could.

Fiske was holding himself rigid, his eyes still fixed on the wire. 'Slide it up, very slowly,' he said.

Wallace wiped sweat out of his eyes, felt his heart lob. He took a slew of breath, focused all his senses on the boulder – he only had to shove it forward a few inches, he told himself, but if he got it wrong they could both kiss their arses goodbye. The wire was only a fraction above the surface: he shoved the boulder forward as cautiously as he could until it made contact.

'Little bit more,' Fiske said. His voice was strained, but there was no tremor in it.

'All right. All right.'

Wallace wiped his hands on his jerkin, eased the rock forward minutely. 'Tiny bit more,' Fiske breathed. 'That's *it*.'

Wallace jumped to his feet, wrapped a piston-like arm round Fiske's waist, dragged him the few yards to where the Bren lay, scooped it up like a toy, hustled Fiske another twenty yards across the bridge. There was a slap like a leather belt whacking a table. The air shuddered: grit and shrapnel pattered. Something stung Wallace's neck. He fell on top of Fiske, heard the thin man curse. He sat up, clocked the mushroom of dirty grey smoke where the booby trap had been. He saw blood dripping down his arm, touched his neck, felt the groove where a hot steel shard had grazed his skin. It was numb and wet: he inspected the blood on his pansized hand, shook his head in frustration. The blast had been puny as mines went, but if they'd been much closer, they'd both have been frazzled. For a moment Wallace felt dazed. Then he caught sight of Fiske's skeletal face, the cold-fish eyes staring at his wound. '*You bloody nutter*,' he yelled. 'Thought you was s'posed to be an Ordnance wallah. What the hell did you go and do that for?'

The blockhouse was bigger than it looked from below – a stone-built oblong with yards front and rear, joined by a tunnel that passed through the centre of the building. A wooden gate opened into the rear yard: the front yard was filled with rubble and tufts of dry swordgrass. Both were enclosed by stone walls. In a room opening off the front yard, they found the remains of a wood fire, with driedout tubers of desert plants, and the scuff of footmarks.

'Somebody's been here, right enough,' Quinnell commented: he knelt down to feel the ashes. 'Not today, but not so long ago, either. Two men, I'd say.'

Jizzard glanced about uneasily. 'A-rab sheepshaggers. This is where they come to beast their beasts.'

Quinnell stood up, pinned his rifle under one arm, pulled on his earlobe. 'Aye, mebbe, but where's the sheep-turds, then?'

'Whoever it was, they're no' here noo. Let's get oot. This place gives me the creeps.'

The front-yard wall was defended by three stone sangars: on the other side of the tunnel there was a ladder that led up to a flat roof. They found another fortified post up there – a horseshoe-shaped stone emplacement lined with sandbags, sagging and rotten. Jizzard kicked at the nearest bag: it fell apart, spilled sand. 'Solid as the rock of Gibraltar,' he scoffed.

Quinnell took in the view. They weren't that high up – a hundred and fifty feet, maybe – but if you had a machine-gun mounted in this sangar, you'd have perfect enfilade right down the track and across the bridge. It couldn't be more than five hundred yards away. He watched the small figures of Wallace and Fiske moving along it, saw Fiske lean over the side, saw them exchange words. He slipped his waterbottle from his belt, took a swig. Jizzard lit a fag, followed his gaze.

'Wallace and Fiske,' he sneered. 'As fine a pair of clowns as ye'd meet. Ye'd think they were Laurel and Hardy.'

'I wouldn't let the big man hear ye say that,' Quinnell said. 'He'd have ye for dinner.'

'I'd like to see him try.'

Quinnell sniggered. 'Fiske's a gouger right enough. There's many a time I could have throttled him in the slammer.'

Jizzard's eyes needled him. 'Ye'll go through with the job, then, Paddy? You've no' got cold feet?'

Quinnell blinked, pulled again on the lobe of his ear. 'Caine's not a bad fellah. He's a hard man, but he's not a toff. I don't know. It doesn't seem right.'

'*Right?*' Jizzard leaned closer to him. 'You're fond o' playin' the boyscout, Paddy – patrol medic an' all that. Underneath, though, we're the same.' He held up the first two fingers of his right hand, pistol fashion.

'Like hell we are,' Quinnell said. He'd seen through Jizzard's blarney in the glasshouse. He was a bullshit artist first class – most likely a snitch as well. Quinnell guessed that Jizzard was in his element when the odds were stacked in his favour – a savage when terrorizing helpless civilians.

When it came to combat, though, he'd probably be too yellow even to shoot.

Quinnell had done his share of fighting: he'd fought

British peelers, but he'd done it for the honour of the Republic, against the traitors who'd sold out to the British empire for the supposed 'Free State'. Honour and courage were qualities he respected, and Jizzard had neither. He was an uncouth bully whose purpose in life was looking after number one. Quinnell had started out as a hospital orderly: he'd only given up helping to save lives when the Brit bastards had forced him to. He was no ignoramus: he'd read books – James Joyce, D. H. Lawrence, Michael Connolly – he'd studied the history of the British in Ireland, had been loyal to the green flag. Jizzard would have beaten his own grandmother to a pulp for a few pennies, as long as she was tied to a chair, that was. Whatever he, Quinnell, had done, he'd never done it for profit, and he'd never shirked a fight.

'We're not even in the same league,' he said.

'Och, I forgot,' Jizzard snickered. 'Ye did all those bombings and such for the sake of the guid old Starry Plough. Pull the other one, Paddy, it's got wee bells on. If ye were so loyal to the IRA, why the hell did ye join the British army?'

Quinnell fixed him with hawkish stare. 'That's for me to know, and you to keep your Jock nose out of. And don't call me Paddy.'

Jizzard avoided the smouldering eyes, smoked, watched the figures on the bridge. 'Remember Sears-Beach?'

'Another gouger, bent as they come.'

'Aye, he is that. But he's givin' us a chance to ditch the bloody war. It's the only chance we've got.'

57

There was a sudden slapping report from the direction of the bridge. They were alert in an instant, crouching behind the sandbags, weapons cocked. Jizzard peeked over, saw the puff of smoke, saw Fiske and Wallace lying prone on the bridge. 'Those bloody idjits have set a mine off,' he guffawed.

7

Harry Copeland patrolled along the base of the stump until it turned sharply south, where the track passed through a narrow gap, no more than thirty paces across. It was a natural bottleneck with a shallow gully on the left, falling slightly towards a gunpit that was strategically sited to defend the gap. Cope had a shufti at the pit – it was spacious and oval-shaped, with an embrasure for a machine-gun and a rear ramp by which a tank or field-gun could be run inside. Copeland leaned against the embrasure, used his telescopic sights to sweep arcs of fire. Directly to his front lay a rocky plain dotted with skeleton thornscrub, halfa grass, boulders: off to the right, the green line of a wadi followed the foot of the cliffs. It would be dry now but, in the wet season, he guessed, water must run down the wadi into the gorge. He continued his sweep to the left: his eye lingered for a moment on Wallace and Fiske on the bridge.

From a strategic point of view, he thought, the bridge and blockhouse had been sited almost perfectly. Anyone who wanted to cross these hills had no choice but to come through: there was no going round. Men on foot might cross the gorge further down, but they'd still have to pass through this gap, which was defended by the blockhouse and the gunpit. A small force dug in on this side could easily hold off a much larger one.

Not that they were here to defend anything: the SAS was a striking unit: *stealth if possible, force if necessary* was the operational credo. No one expected them to make heroic stands. Copeland liked to create contingency plans, though. In the commandos they'd been trained to *think two ranks up*, and he was always sifting possibilities in a manner untarnished by emotional considerations. Tom Caine was different. He was a very decent chap, but he let feelings interfere with military actions. There would be a clear plan, and Caine would diverge from it – to help someone, to save civilians, to protect women and children. Or he'd have an intuition – a sudden impulse to do something for no reason he could explain. It was exasperating, having to keep Caine focused on the task in hand. Maybe he did sometimes muddle through in ways Cope hadn't expected, but the fact was that almost every time things went wrong, it was because he hadn't listened to Copeland's advice.

Cope had always been bright. At school he'd been top of the class in everything. He often knew more than his teachers did, a quality that had not made him very popular. Some people unfairly called him a *bighead* and a *know-it-all*, but he'd put that down to jealousy. If he'd been born clever, it wasn't his fault. At home, his father used to hold regular quizzes, pitting him against his brothers. If he didn't win he would brood for a week.

Cope had never excelled in team games, not because

he wasn't athletic – he'd been school cross-country champion – but because he always thought he knew better than his team mates. *Your problem, Copeland,* his games master used to say, *is that you want to play every position on the field.* He'd stuck to sports like running and rock-climbing, in which you didn't have to depend on anyone else.

Copeland had always known he would become an officer one day. He didn't think it made him better than men like Wallace. True, Fred could be unruly, and insubordinate, but if you looked beneath the cave-man appearance, he was pretty astute in his own way: a terrific fighter, of course. It was simply that he, Copeland, deserved to be an officer because he was good at planning and seeing how things would turn out: most of the peacetime officers – the regulars – were dunderheads, who hadn't got a clue. That went for most of the general staff, too.

When the war had come along in 1939, Copeland had been a history teacher in a boys' grammar school. Everyone was joining up, and he'd thought that the army needed bright people like him. When he'd walked into the recruiting post, he'd expected to be handed a commission instantly: they would be so bowled over by his abilities, he'd thought, that they'd put him down for the planning staff right away. It hadn't turned out like that. In those early days they'd recruited as officers almost exclusively public schoolboys with plummy accents, whose fathers were stockbrokers or the directors of banks. Copeland hadn't quite fitted the bill.

'What can you do, son?' the recruiting sergeant had asked him.

'I'm a qualified teacher.'

'I mean what can you do that's any *use*? Can you drive a motorcar?'

'Yes, but anyone can do . . .'

'That's it, then. Royal Army Service Corps.'

It wasn't exactly what he'd envisaged, but he had consoled himself with the thought that there was room for improvement. He might not have the right background, but they'd eventually appreciate clever chaps like him.

At the back of his mind, though, he knew that there were times when he hadn't been quite so clever, when he'd let his head be ruled by his heart. Such as the time he'd urged Caine to take on the *Sandhog* scheme, to save his sweetheart, Angela Brunetto. It had been obvious there was something wrong about that mission, but he'd encouraged Caine to accept it anyway – he'd been so deeply attached to Brunetto. With her, it had been the real thing – or so he'd thought. Now they were saying that she'd used him – that she'd been spying for the Axis all along.

If the truth be known, the same thing had happened on *Nighthawk*. He'd actually been en route to OCTU in Palestine, looking forward to his officer training at last, when they'd stopped his vehicle, told him that Caine needed him for a job. They'd only had to mention Caine, and he'd fallen for it hook, line and stinker. It had been a pack of lies from start to finish: the mission seemed straightforward enough on the surface, but was actually as queer as a concrete parachute. Why had he accepted it? Because Tom Caine was his mate. So much for cleverness, he thought.

He heard a low whistle: Caine was waving to him from the edge of the trees. He withdrew from the gun-pit, started moving back to the leaguer. He noticed a mountain in the distance, a flintblue fluted pyramid-shape, towering above the escarpment, twenty miles away, maybe more. It was the highest peak he could see, and it was very distinct: the peak was crowned by two rock chimneys, sharp at the ends and slightly curved, like the tushes of a giant boar. Copeland had an excellent memory for topography: he knew he hadn't seen the peak before, but he thought someone had described it to him not long ago.

8

He found Caine leaning over a map spread out on the bonnet of the jeep. 'Have a dekko,' he told Cope.

The map showed their position: Copeland noticed that the road started winding down into the plain less than half a mile beyond the eastern end of the bridge. Somewhere down there a Totenkopf recce battalion was cruising north-west towards this point. Copeland didn't know much about the Totenkopf: the name meant 'death's head' in German. The Totenkopf Division had originally been formed around Nazi camp-guards. They weren't part of the regular Jerry army, the Wehrmacht, but came under the Waffen SS. Copeland had never heard of SS units being used in North Africa.

'How long do you reckon we've got?' he enquired.

Caine inspected his watch. 'It's 1445 hours. According to Caversham's int. the Krauts won't make it before first light tomorrow. That gives us fifteen hours.'

Copeland frowned. 'We'd better push it, Tom. We don't want to get caught with our pants down by a crack Jerry battalion. There's seven of us. How do you rate our chances of coming through that?'

Caine made a face. 'You worry too much, Harry. Fifteen hours gives us enough time to blow the bridge *and* be home for breakfast. Let's wait and see what Wallace and Fiske have to say.'

Copeland shrugged. He had another gander at the twin-fanged mountain he'd seen earlier, then found it on the map. 'Jebel Halluf,' he muttered. 'That's the one Johnny talked about.'

'What?'

Cope pointed to the distant peak. 'See those twin chimneys, Tom?'

Caine looked at the feature through his binos. 'Yep, quite unusual,' he said.

'You remember when Johnny gave us a debrief on Stirling's capture?'

'Johnny Cooper? Yes, of course.'

Cooper was the SAS 'A' Squadron officer who'd been with David Stirling when he'd got bagged at the end of January. They'd been on a hush-hush mission behind Axis lines in Tunisia, had lain up in a wadi for the night and had woken up to find themselves surrounded by Germans. Cooper, an officer called Mike Sadler and a French sergeant had somehow escaped: they'd made it through to friendly lines. They claimed the honour of being the first Eighth Army soldiers to link up with the Anglo-American force.

'I asked him to show me on the map the exact place where the Huns got Stirling,' Copeland went on. 'He mentioned that jebel as a reference point. Said you could see it from the wadi where they got snatched.'

Caine nodded: Stirling's disappearance seven weeks

earlier had brought on a crisis for the SAS. Until then, nobody had realized how much of a one-man show it had been: Stirling had been the only one who knew what was going on: it had all been in his head. Since he'd gone, they'd had a couple of temporary commanders, both outsiders. Neither had lasted.

Caine yanked the flesh on his chin. 'But Stirling's party didn't come this way, Harry. Must have been on the other side of the hills.'

'Yep. I was just thinking, you know . . . Johnny reckoned the Axis had information that Stirling was here.'

Caine snorted. 'More like his party was knackered after a week on Bennies, and got caught napping. Stirling used to pop those pills like boiled sweets.'

Copeland laughed. 'Maybe. But Johnny's no idiot. He swore there was a tip-off.'

'If there was, it can only have come from inside GHQ. We've always known the Axis have spies in –' He broke off suddenly, remembered that Copeland's sweetheart, Brunetto, had been suspected of spying within GHQ.

Copeland shrugged. 'Anyway, it makes you wonder how safe we are.'

'Yep. That must be why Caversham was so keen to use men whose absence wouldn't be noticed.'

Copeland cracked his knuckles. 'Stirling always used to call GHQ *the layers of fossilized shit*, but in the end he had the same old notions. Remember when he chucked a grenade into a Jerry guardhouse at Berka, then reckoned it was murder?'

Caine cackled. 'Where'd we be without honour, Harry?'

'That's just it, mate. We're up against a team that plays with different rules.'

'That's probably what the Jerries say about us.'

There came the low, flat *booomphhhh* of a detonation from behind the hill. '*What the Dickens* . . . ?' Caine gasped. 'Come on.'

He grabbed his Tommy-gun, jogged towards the bend in the cliffs, cocking the gun as he ran. Cope unslung his SMLE, ran after him. They crossed the gap, followed the gully down to the gunpit, jumped inside. Caine squinted through his binos, saw a billow of bluegrey smoke lying on the air at the far end of the bridge. He realized he couldn't see Wallace or Fiske: he caught his breath, recalled what Cope had said only a minute ago about the possibility of compromise. Could the Krauts have been expecting them? He surveyed arcs left and right, then saw Fiske and Wallace stumping towards them off the bridge, Fiske with an edgy clockwork stride, Wallace with the shambling gait of a bear. They seemed unhurt.

'Not a contact, anyway,' he said, relieved.

'Sounded like a mine.'

They heard boots padding behind them: a moment later Jizzard and Quinnell slipped into the pit, crouched down looking over the parapet. 'Saw it from up there, sah,' Jizzard told Caine. 'The silly sods set a mine off, that's all.'

'That's fine and dandy then,' Caine said. 'Only alerted

any Axis troops within ten miles. You clear the block-house?'

'We did, sir,' Quinnell said. 'We found the remains of a fire and footprints. Two men – might have been Arabs, might not.'

Caine nodded. 'Keep your eyes peeled. Get over to the leaguer, start sorting out the safety-fuse. We'll have a brew, lay the charges after these two report.'

Quinnell and Jizzard pulled out: Caine and Copeland crouched in the pit until Wallace and Fiske were near, then climbed out to meet them. Caine saw that Wallace was bleeding from a wound in the neck.

'What the heck was that?' he demanded

'Tripwire, skipper. I copped a bit of shrapnel, that's all.'

Caine examined his wound. 'Better let Quinnell look at it.'

'How did you come to set a tripwire off?' Copeland enquired.

Wallace glanced at Fiske. 'Accident, *wannit*.' A muscle twitched under his chin.

'The bridge is clear otherwise, sir,' Fiske cut in. 'Not as solid as it looks. Crumbling masonry, missing blocks, cracks where we can lay cutting charges. We'll need to go down on ropes, though.'

'All right. Go back to the leaguer. Wallace, get that wound tended. Fiske, get the climbing ropes out. Harry, you stay here: I want us to put together a sketch map.'

9

Caine and Copeland returned to the leaguer fifteen minutes later to find themselves in the middle of a row. Wallace, with blood still running down his neck, was holding a mass of climbing rope balanced on one of his grappling-hook-sized hands: in the other he held up a length of rope no more than two feet long. More hanks of rope of similar length were scattered like dead snakes around his size fourteen feet. Fiske stood opposite him, looking slightly amused, smoking a pipe: Quinnell and Jizzard were sitting on the ground near the jeeps, smirking. Trubman was leaning over the drop-down table on the W/T jeep about thirty yards away, with his earphones on, apparently oblivious to anything else.

'I wanna know 'oo was responsible for drawin' these ropes,' the big gunner roared. 'Come on. "Oo was it? It weren't me, an' it weren't Trubman, so it must of bin one of you.'

'What's up, Fred?' Caine asked. 'What's the problem with the ropes?'

Wallace turned blackbead eyes on Caine. He threw down the single piece of rope in disgust, riffled through the mass of strands sitting on his other hand, showed Caine severed end after severed end. 'Look at 'em, skipper. All cut. There ain't a single length 'ere over two foot. "Ow the 'ell are we goin' to abseil down the bridge with these?' He hurled the tangle of rope at the ground with both hands.

Caine knelt, examined a few of the ends closely: there was no doubt they'd been cut with a knife.

Wallace pointed a sausage-like finger at Fiske. 'What I wanna know is 'oo drew 'em from the stores.'

Fiske pulled the pipe from thin lips, blew smoke. 'Don't be a cretin, Wallace. We didn't bring the ropes with us. We picked them up with the jeeps after the drop.'

'Yah, ye great nana,' Jizzard sniggered. *"Oo drew 'em from the stores*, indeed.'

Wallace turned his shaggy bull-head on the Scotsman. 'You tellin' me Fraser's crew would of supplied us with dud ropes?'

'Wouldn't put it past those dagos,' Quinnell said. 'It wasn't any of us, was it?'

Wallace clenched his huge fists, held them up like warclubs. 'If I find out 'oo it was, I'll bloody . . .'

'That's enough, Fred,' Caine said. 'It must have been a mistake. We can knot 'em together, can't we?'

'We can, skipper, but it'll be a long job, and it ain't guaranteed.'

'We better get cracking then.'

Fiske, Jizzard and Quinnell began picking up the fallen strands. Caine glanced at Wallace. 'I told you to get that wound fixed,' he said.

Wallace shrugged. 'It ain't much.'

Caine ordered him to sit, told Quinnell to bring his

medical bag. Quinnell carried it over, delved into it for iodine and cotton wool.

He swabbed Wallace's neck: the big man flinched. 'Hey, watchit, will ya?'

'Ye big pussy. It's a fleabite, so it is.'

Quinnell ripped open a field-dressing, applied it to Wallace's rhinocerous-like neck, tied it tightly. Wallace gasped. 'Whatcha tryin' to do, throttle me?'

'Och, I wish someone would.'

Wallace thought fondly of Maurice Pickney, their previous medic, who'd been lost on *Sandhog*. Some had said he was *the other way*, but his reassuring manner had been just right for a field medical orderly. You couldn't doubt his guts, either: he'd been killed covering their retreat.

Quinnell finished tying the dressing. 'You were lucky,' he commented.

Wallace glowered at Fiske, picking up and knotting ropes with the others. 'Not half as lucky as *some*.'

'*Hey, skipper*,' Trubman yelled suddenly, 'get a load of this.'

Caine put down the ropes he was tying, walked over to the W/T jeep. Copeland followed. Trubman was still leaning against the table with his earphones on: his eyes were bright, his face more than usually flushed.

'What is it, Taff?'

'Sounds like a Mayday call.'

Caine put on the headphones, heard a wave of blips stuttering across the airwaves. It was a pattern repeated three times, then a different sequence, also recurring three times, followed by what sounded like a free jumble of dots and dashes. Then came the same two sequences, each repeated three times. The burst stopped abruptly. There was a gap, then it started again. Caine handed the headphones back to Trubman, shook his head. 'Never heard anything like it.'

Trubman listened again: his deepset eyes beneath the lenses dilated with concentration. Caine knew he was an expert telegrapher: in signals training he'd attained the highest marks of his intake for Morse code. He had the uncanny knack of being able to memorize ciphers and decode messages without writing them down. Now, though, he dickered on a signals pad with a stub of pencil.

'It's an emergency distress signal, skipper – Mayday. Mayday. Mayday. STENDEC. STENDEC. STEN-DEC . . . then a series of numbers, then STENDEC. STENDEC. STENDEC. Mayday. Mayday. Mayday again.' He held his watch up, timed the gap. 'Repeated every nine seconds. If I had to put money on it, I'd say it was coming from a Gibson Girl.'

'A what?' Caine said.

Trubman tittered. 'A Gibson Girl's an emergency transmitter, see, shaped like, you know, like a girl's bum?' He made expansive curving gestures with his hands. 'They designed it that way so it's easy to get a grip of. Transmits a Mayday signal at 500 kilohertz, with a range up to two hundred miles. Jerry design originally, but it's been developed by the Yanks. Vacuum tubes controlled by crystals.'

'What's it coming from?'

'Most likely a downed plane, but no way to tell if she's ours or theirs.'

'What about STENDEC – what does that mean?'

Trubman looked sheepish. 'Not any code I know of.'

'Can you triangulate the signal?'

'No need to. I'm pretty certain those numbers are grid co-ordinates.'

'I suppose it would make sense,' Copeland said. 'If you're sending out a Mayday, you want rescue missions to know where you are. All we need to do is transfer the grid numbers to the map.'

'OK. Let's do it,' Caine said.

Trubman listened to the signal again, wrote out the co-ordinates in clear, listened once more to check, then passed the figures to Caine. Caine traced them on the map. '*Christ!* You sure that's right, Taff?'

Trubman whipped off his glasses, rubbed them with a thumb. He replaced them and peered at the figures once more. 'Yep, it's right. Why?'

'It's only six miles away.'

Caine looked at Copeland: Cope frowned, dropped his eyes. Caine saw that Wallace had come across to find out what was going on.

'What's up, skipper?' he enquired.

'Let's get brew on,' Caine said.

Wallace made tea on a Tommy-cooker. Caine sat down against a hassock of grass, laid his Thompson next to him. Cope squatted on a boulder with his sniper weapon on his lap. He lit a cigarette. Trubman sat nearby. Fiske, Jizzard and Quinnell knelt or sat cross-legged around a treetrunk a few yards away. When the tea was boiled Wallace ladled out mugs, sat down on a jerrycan.

Copeland swigged tea, made a face at the giant. 'What the heck did you put in this?'

'Usual dogs' piss. Why? Is there any problem with that?'

'Nah, dogs' piss is my favourite.'

Wallace looked at Caine. 'So what's the big news, then, skipper?'

Caine gulped tea. 'Taff picked up a Mayday signal, probably a downed kite. It's about six miles away.'

Fiske looked up; his eyes lingered on Caine's face. 'If there's aircrew stranded in the desert, sir, I wouldn't want to be in their shoes. Not with that Totenkopf battalion around.' He sounded almost as if he were gloating, Caine thought.

'Aye, poor wee sods,' Jizzard smirked.

'We can't abandon them,' Caine said. 'We could be there and back in ninety minutes.'

'*What?*' Jizzard objected. 'Ah'm no' stickin' ma neck out for a bunch o' Brylcreem Boys . . .'

'No one asked you, Jizzard,' Wallace waded in. He immediately regretted it – SAS tradition had always favoured sounding out the opinions of those whose lives were at stake.

Copeland stamped out his cigarette. 'We're here to do a job, skipper,' he said. 'Even if there *are* fliers down there, who's to say they're ours? We'd be risking an op that could be crucial to Monty's push.'

'No telling what sort of traps might have been laid

either,' Fiske added. 'Judging by what Wallace and I ran into, could be anything. I say it's none of our business.'

Wallace snorted, spilt tea. Caine peered at Fiske, caught a hint of truculent pleasure in his eyes.

He shook his head. 'We should have a shufti, pick up anyone we find. We can still be back by last light.'

'We don't even know they're *alive*,' Cope retorted. 'If the signal's coming from an emergency beacon, they might be dead for all we know.'

'Not possible, sir,' Trubman cut in. He removed his glasses, rubbed them with his scrap of four-by-two. Without them, his eyes looked several sizes too small. He replaced the glasses, scratched his doughy face. 'The Gibson Girl transmitter's handcranked, see. That means there's got to be at least one man alive, or the signal would cut out. One version – I think it's called the SCR-578 – comes with a box-kite aerial: a balloon with a hydrogen generator . . .'

'That's all very interesting, Taff,' Copeland barked, 'but how do we know it's not a decoy? What if it's Jerry trying to lure in Allied troops who want to play the hero?' He gave Caine a sharp look.

'I don't think we ought to take the chance, sir,' Fiske said, looking at Copeland now. 'From what I hear of those Totenkopf boys, they're not big on taking prisoners, so at least if they do find any aircrew, it'll be over quickly.'

Wallace glared at him. 'How would you like it if you was in a tight spot, an' a mate dumped yer to save 'is own skin?'

75

'They're not our mates,' Fiske leered.

Wallace drew himself up to full, formidable height, stuck out his paving-stone chin. 'I'm with the skipper,' he rasped.

Cope cracked his knuckles, his face hard.

'Why not hand it over to Captain Fraser?' Trubman suggested. 'Let him decide. If he gives us the green light, we'll go for it.'

'You got comms with Fraser yet, Taff?' Caine asked.

'Well, no, but . . .'

'It's not Fraser's call anyway, it's mine, and I reckon we can't leave our boys stranded in the Blue.'

'What if we run into Jerry, though, sah?' Jizzard queried. 'What if they're further ahead than you thought?'

'Then you'll get your chance to do some slottin', wontcha?' Wallace beamed. 'Ain't that what you said you was 'ere for?'

Quinnell tittered. 'Sure he's got you there, Jizz. Ever since we got roped into this scheme you've been mouthing off about slotting Jerry, so ye have.'

Jizzard blinked at him. 'An' ye're all for it, are ye, Paddy?'

Quinnell pulled at his earlobe. 'Och, I suppose I am. Like the captain says, it's the right thing to do. And don't call me Paddy.'

'How about sending one jeep?' Cope suggested. 'I'll do the business, while the rest of you lay the charges here.'

Caine shook his head. 'No splitting up. If we go, we all go.'

Fiske bit on his pipe. 'Oh well,' he said. 'Ours not to reason why.'

Caine glanced at Copeland, knew his mate was seeing another mission spiralling out of control, just when he was on the path to promotion. Caine also knew that, deep down, Cope trusted him.

Copeland unslung his sniper's rifle, his wadingbird features poker. 'Well then,' he said. 'If we're going to be back before last light, I suppose we'd better get moving.'

IO

They mounted the jeeps, started along the scalloped track, trailed across the bridge, eyed the pit where the booby trap had been. Wallace and Jizzard patrolled ahead on foot with weapons at the ready, combing the surface for mines: the jeeps crept along behind them, sprawling on their springs, frames creaking. The vehicles were well armed: two of them carried twin Vickers 'K' aircraft machine-guns pintlemounted on the back, and all three had .50 calibre Brownings on the front. Every inch of space was taken up with jerrycans of petrol, water, ration boxes: the wireless jeep had no Vickers, but carried both an M1 stovepipe 'bazooka' rocketlauncher and a two-inch mortar. The men hefted .303 Lee-Enfield rifles, Colt automatics, bayonets, No. 36 grenades: Caine had his Tommy-gun, Trubman an M1 Carbine, Wallace his Bren.

Half a mile from the bridge they came to the top of the pass, looked down across a plain the colour of gunpowder, bounded in the far distance by warped black spurs that seemed to loom out of the baseland in the shapes of dwarves and vultures. Caine swung a deep arc across the valley with his field-glasses. He would have been relieved at the prospect of open horizons, yet the landscape here felt alien – a devil's dumpheap. It was a raddled sea of slate grey: giant cairns and cinder-piles, knobs of gnawed traprock, pinnacles sculpted into teeth, rubblestone escarpments, teetering yardangs like trees petrified in a holocaust. Dustdevils whisk-broomed down there: lightsnares blinked. The sun drifted slowly behind them through bevelled cloud, turning the plain into a centrifuge of shade and sombre light.

'Hey, skipper, see that?' Wallace yodled suddenly. 'Left, ten o'clock.'

Caine switched the glasses, clocked what looked like a silver blob hovering above the rocks, perhaps five miles away. He called Trubman over, handed him the binoculars. 'Ever seen anything like that, Taff?' he enquired.

The signaller took the glasses, peered through them. 'That's it, skipper,' he yelled. 'That's the Gibson Girl. Like I said, it's got a box kite attached – a blimp filled with hydrogen. The tethering cable is also the aerial. It's got a little hydrogen generator that keeps it . . .'

Caine took the glasses back: Trubman blinked. 'That's our downed plane,' he said.

'We'll take a dekko,' Caine said. 'At least we won't have any problem finding it.'

They came down the escarpment at a snail's pace, rattled between pebbledash bluffs, through rock junk-yards where woody plants gripped the stones like claws. What remained of the track was a switchback, so rock-strewn that in places they had to get out and clear a path. Copeland glanced often at his watch, fretting – it was already taking longer than expected. At the bottom they leaguered up close in an old, dry wadi bed, in oblongs of shade under steepscarped walls. Caine jumped down to check the compass bearing, Copeland stood in the back of the jeep, shuftied the plain through his sights. 'Hey, hold your horses,' he hissed. 'There's a dust cloud coming. Go south, skipper, three o'clock.'

Caine lifted his field-glasses, followed Cope's directions, picked up a long smudge of dust above the skyline. It hadn't been there when he'd surveyed the plain from the top of the pass. 'Looks like the Hun arrived early,' he said.

'What?' Wallace boomed. 'They wasn't s'posed to get here till first light.'

For a moment nobody spoke. All eyes were on Caine.

He glanced around him, saw that Jizzard and Quinnell had stiffened in their seats: they were staring in the direction of the dust cloud with taut faces. 'What the hell are we gonnae do now?' Jizzard wailed.

'Shut up, Jizzard,' Copeland snapped.

Caine felt a stab of fear: a melting sensation in his stomach, a prickling at the back of his skull. His heart clumped. He fought to stop any emotion showing on his face, to keep his thinking cool. His first impulse was to do a smart about turn and lead the patrol back up the pass, dynamite the bridge, make a hasty withdrawal to Fraser's lines. That would be the wisest move.

Yet something stopped him. Trubman had said that if the beacon was working, there must be someone alive at the crash-site. The odds were that they were British or Yank. They were only a few minutes away: he couldn't leave them, especially with the Jerries so close. If he did, he'd never be able to forget it. He forced himself to stay where he was, tilted the field-glasses, homed in on the dust cloud again. It was a faint wisp by now, a dark eddy hanging in the haze – hardly visible. If it was a convoy, it had stopped, but he couldn't even say for certain that it *was* a convoy. It could have been a a big dustdevil, a sudden breath of wind. It must be twenty miles away – maybe twenty-five – if it was the enemy, they wouldn't be here for an hour or more, probably not before dark. They might well leaguer up for the night, anyway.

'Come on,' he said: he forced the words out, struggled to keep his voice even. 'Let's go and pick up that crew.'

For an instant, no one moved. Copeland was looking at him with an incredulous grin, as if he'd just made a joke. 'Skipper,' he said quietly, 'we weren't expecting them for another fifteen hours. If we go back now we might just about have time to blow the bridge – even that's pushing it.'

Caine tightened his fists. 'They're not here yet, Harry,' he said.

Fiske watched him from behind the steering wheel of the wireless jeep: apart from a slight pallor around the eyes, his face gave nothing away. Quinnell and Jizzard, though, were gawping at him as if he'd gone batty. 'Oh, *Jesus*,' Jizzard warbled. 'We cannae face a whole battalion of them. I shoulda known it would come to this. I shoulda known never to volunteer.'

'Put a sock in it, Jizzard.' This time it was Quinnell who spoke. 'I'm sick of your whinging, so I am.'

Caine's face snapped shut: 'All right,' he said calmly. 'Start those motors, *now*. Jizzard, I want you on the Vickers; you drive Quinnell. Taff, you're driving – let Fiske take the Browning. Fred, you man the guns, Cope drives. And keep your bloody eyes peeled.'

To Caine's satisfaction, no one succumbed to the temptation to speed: the jeeps spread out in file, twenty yards apart. Wallace, gunner on the lead jeep, covered the forward arc: on the trailing jeep, Jizzard watched the rear. The knobbly tyres spunked boulders, clanked on volcanic shards, ratcheted across dry creek beds and ditches. Caine prayed that they wouldn't land a puncture. He scanned the landscape ahead, navigated the small convoy around tufa reefs, along a flat plate of ribbed lavastone, so weathered at the edges that it appeared to be the sinuous, rawhide flank of a half-buried creature. They wove through an avenue of stone pillars, distorted helixes like immense treeboles, tilted over at a weird slant by the wind; they rounded the elbow of a butte, found themselves on a beach of white chalk pebbles like seashells, scattered among the roots of grass tussocks and clawbone trees. '*Christ*, skipper,' Wallace grunted. 'Just look at *that*.'

At the same moment, Caine caught sight of the aircraft – a dark hulk lying crippled and broken on the undulating plain. He gasped, ordered Copeland to stop, stood up to get a better view.

He knew at once that he'd never seen anything like it.

The aircraft lay no more than two hundred paces away: Caine thought the light must be playing tricks — no aircraft could be that big. She was huge — perhaps a hundred and fifty feet from nose to tail: it was difficult to say exactly how long, because she had broken up into two segments. The tailplane section lay some distance away, its fuselage frayed and torn at the edges where it had fractured off — there was a corresponding ragged edge at the end of the main section.

The aircraft's shape was unfamiliar — she was all planes and angles, as if built of a series of welded flat sheets: more like an armoured car than an aeroplane. The nose was a truncated pyramid: the wings seemed angled back from the fuselage like huge chevrons. The nose appeared undamaged, despite the fact that it had buried itself at least a foot into the earth: the aeroscreens were intact, except for one knocked-out panel from which the blimp was suspended — and there was a cockpit door. That was the only entrance Caine could make out, though: there were no other doors in the fuselage, which meant that she couldn't have been designed to drop paratroops.

He examined the one wing he could see: the wingtip was dug deep into the ground, but must have been a good sixty feet from the main body. The wing supported two massive engine nacelles of a size Caine had never seen before. The whole aircraft was an almost supernatural matt black from nose to tail, as if she had been steeped in ink and smoked with charcoal — the kind of blackness found in the deepest, darkest hole.

'What the bloody hell *is* it?' Copeland wheezed.

'Looks like a giant bat.' Wallace whistled from behind him. 'Maybe some kind of airborne coffin?'

Caine chuckled, glanced at Cope, noticed he was staring at the aircraft with awe. The other jeeps had pulled up alongside: the men took in the sight with open mouths.

'We'll move in, ' Caine told them. 'Keep your eyes skinned. We don't know whose she is – she doesn't seem to have any markings – so be ready.'

As they drew closer, it struck Caine that not only did the aircraft have no recognition symbols, she also had no armaments – no gunturrets, wing cannons or bomb-bays – as far as he could see, anyway. He wondered how many crew a kite like that would need: a B24 bomber had ten, but five of them were gunners, one a bombardier. He had the jeeps pull up only fifty paces from the plane, ordered the drivers to take up tactical positions. 'Be ready to pull out sharpish,' he told them. 'We're off as soon as we pick up those boys.'

'What boys?' Copeland whispered. 'There's no one home, skipper.'

Caine drew his Thompson from its brace, cocked it. 'Maybe gone to ground,' he said. 'Maybe think we're the Hun.'

'Or maybe *they're* the Hun.'

'Anything's possible.'

Caine detailed Copeland and Trubman to accompany him. 'What about me?' Fiske demanded. 'You might need a booby-traps expert.'

Wallace let out a snort. Caine nodded.

They approached the black plane in an untactical gaggle: it was risky, but she exuded an aura of menace that caused them instinctively to bunch. Caine felt a renewed twinge of apprehension: the same dreamlike sensation he'd felt back at the monastery was starting to creep in. Close up, the aircraft looked even more gigantic: the dark fuselage towered above them – perhaps twice the height of the biggest aircraft Caine had ever seen. He found himself wondering what kind of cargo she might carry: she had to *be* a cargo plane, he reasoned: she wasn't a bomber, and she didn't look like any troop transport he'd ever seen.

He abutted his Tommy-gun against his shoulder, touched the plane's skin with an open palm. It was warm, but it wasn't metal, he was certain. It felt coarse, like animal hide, and there was a grain to it, as if it were pitted with invisible cracks, scabs and corrugations. It was, he thought, almost *animal* in texture, like tortoise-shell: as if the whole massive craft was some sort of brooding black turtle that might any moment wake up and devour them.

'It feels like resin,' he heard Truman say. 'Some charcoal mix, maybe, dried rock hard.'

'Why would they build a plane out of resin?' Cope demanded.

Trubman blinked beneath his thick glasses. 'Radar. Radar detects metal, see. If an aircraft was made out of non-metallic material, she would pass through radar defences like a ghost.'

'A ghost,' Caine repeated silently. That was right, he thought – the whole thing gave him the feel of a ghost craft.

Copeland nodded, stared around mystified. 'I don't get it,' he said. 'There's no sign anyone's been here – you noticed, skipper? You'd expect tracks, remains of fires, bits of clothing, maybe rations, shelters, recognition panels. Even if the crew had done a bunk, they'd have left *something*, surely.'

'What if they bailed before she hit the deck?'

'Possible. But then who's cranking the rescue beacon?'

Fiske and Trubman went to inspect the wing. 'Hey, what about this?' Trubman called. Caine and Copeland stalked over to where the signaller was crouching by one of the titanic engine nacelles. Caine was fascinated: it looked like a gigantic black bell: its propellers, now warped and twisted, must originally have been six feet long. He had no idea of the engine's capacity, but since the plane carried four of these huge motors she must generate tremendous power. He peered closely at the nacelle, wondering if he could identify its origin: he found no serial numbers, no maker's nameplate.

'Look here,' Trubman insisted.

Caine and Copeland squatted down beside him, saw that the dark underside of the wing was peppered with rough knobs of hardened red clay, each about six inches long, scored with tiny holes. 'Paperwasps,' Truman announced. He pushed back his glasses. 'Old nests, too.'

Copeland scratched his blond crop. 'How long does it take to build a wasps' nest?'

'That's not all,' Fiske cut in. 'See the earth where the wingtip's buried? It's got grass growing on it – same with the nose section. If the ground is settled enough to sprout, this kite must have been here for donkey's years.'

Caine sucked a breath: it was true, he thought: the aircraft looked as if she might have been here since the dinosaurs, as if she might even have sprung fully formed from the bowels of the earth.

He stood up, remembered why they'd come, remembered the Jerries. He swung round. 'Taffy, you and Fiske check the cockpit. Find out if there's anyone working that Gibson Girl setup. Cope – have a gander at the tail section. I'm going to have a peek inside the main fuselage. Watch out for tripwires, booby traps – if you see anything untoward, for God's sake don't touch it.'

11

Caine watched them shuffle off, levelled his Tommy-gun, approached the jagged end of the cabin, where the tail section had broken off. He paused by the opening, reluctant to enter: his heart raced, perspiration trickled down his forehead. He glanced at the serrated edges of the fuselage, saw that it had been torn like flesh rather than snapped off like steel. When he stepped through the yawning mouth, it felt as if he'd entered a tomb. It was cool and dark – the matt walls seemed to absorb heat and light. The fuselage went on and on, a tunnel built on successive arched frames like a great ribcage, with odd fans of tubing at intervals along it, like sets of organpipes. It was silent, too, as if the walls also soaked up sound. Caine found himself treading deferentially as if he were in church – it had that feeling, like an ancient cathedral, a holy place. There were no seats, no electrics, no wires, no wireless gear, no lockers, no fuel tanks: there were no doors, no windows, no hatches, as if it had been designed to keep something in rather than out.

The dim tunnel wasn't entirely empty, though: a cuboid object was fixed in the centre of the deck, between two of the weird organpipe agglomerations. Caine inched nearer: it was a black box, with the same dull finish as the fuselage itself. He crouched down to examine it: it wasn't big — maybe two feet by eighteen inches — but it had no handles, no lock, no hinges, not even a seamline along which it might open. Caine saw to his surprise, though, that there was single word white-stencilled on its top: STENDEC. He remembered the word — the one repeated in the Mayday signal Trubman had picked up.

The box was the only separate object in the whole fuselage, the only thing that had anything written on it: he felt a sudden urge to know what was inside. He noticed that it was fixed in place by clips at each corner, attached to hooks. He was about to release one of them, when he recalled his last order to the others: *if you see anything untoward, for God's sake don't touch it.*

He retracted his hand: at that moment he sensed movement along the fuselage, smelt something that reminded him of scorched iron. He glanced up, saw a man standing there, staring at him — a man in dark, soiled combat dress, with a waxy face so grained with wrinkles and creases it could have belonged to a corpse. The man carried no weapon, made no move towards him. '*Hello, Tom,*' a whispery voice said. Caine staggered backwards, almost fell over: he stared back into the dull, bloodshot eyes of Maurice Pickney, the RAMC medical orderly killed in action almost six months earlier.

Icewater ran down his spine: he felt sweat drip off his chin: he opened his mouth to speak, but no words came. 'Don't try to talk,' Pickney told him.

Frozen in a crouch, Caine tried to raise himself: his muscles weren't following orders, his whole body was rigid. He attempted to squeeze words out by sheer will-power, achieved only a gargling in the throat.

'Listen, Tom,' Pickney went on. 'The Hun are on their way. You've got to clear out while you still can.'

Pickney moved his wizened head slightly, blinked at the fuselage around him. 'Don't ask what STENDEC is, or where it came from. You don't want to know.' He peered down at Caine, his eyes narrow slots. 'There's a lot going on here, Tom. More than you think. David Stirling, MO4, Sears-Beach, Betty Nolan . . . they're all mixed up with STENDEC in one way or another, even your crew. One more thing, Tom. Don't touch the black box. Don't try to open it. Leave it where it is. You'd be doing the world a favour. Remember, what-ever you do, skipper, *don't open the black box . . .*'

'*Hey, skipper!*' a different voice yelled. 'We found the transmitter . . .'

Caine heard footfalls coming up the deck behind him, found that he could move. He glanced back at Pickney, found the apparition had vanished. He stood up shakily; perspiration poured off him. He turned to find Trubman and Fiske, ogling him curiously.

'You all right, skipper?' the signaller asked. 'You look white as a sheet.'

'I'm OK . . .' Caine stammered, touching his throat. He struggled to find some way of explaining what had just happened. Maurice Pickney was dead. He'd been killed covering their retreat on *Sandhog*. Caine hadn't seen it happen, but he was sure of it all the same: Pick-ney's name had never cropped up in any POW list.

Even if he was alive, he couldn't possibly have been here, in a derelict aircraft in the wilds of Tunisia.

It couldn't have happened, but he'd seen it all the same: that was the frightening part. If he was honest with himself, it wasn't the first time he'd experienced such things. There had been that business in Cairo — the phantom phone calls, the glimpses of Betty Nolan and Eisner. When the quack had refused to pass him fit for active service, he'd scoffed. Now he wasn't so sure. He thought of the Olzon-13, the disorienting agent he and Wallace had ingested: maybe, after all, it had caused some nerve damage. And what had Pickney meant that they were all mixed up with STENDEC? Stirling was in the bag; Sears-Beach had been busted and posted to duty at the detention centre. What had his crew got to do with anything? What about Betty Nolan? What the hell *was* STENDEC anyway?

'What's this?' Fiske said. He was eyeing the black box with interest.

Trubman bent over it, wiped steam from his glasses. 'STENDEC,' he read. 'Hey, skipper — that was in the Mayday code sequence. What the heck *is* this?'

'We'd better get it outside,' Fiske said. He was already crouching, releasing the hooks one by one.

Caine watched him wide-eyed. '*No.*'

It was too late. Fiske had unhasped the clips, and was dragging the black box out of its place. 'Relax, Captain,' he said patronizingly. 'I know what I'm doing.'

There was no explosion, but Caine felt livid. The RAOC man could easily have killed them all. He knew he could order Fiske to dump the box, but he didn't: that would mean admitting that what he thought he had just seen was real. He was just as curious about the box as Fiske was: he wasn't going to stop him on the grounds that he'd been warned off by a dead man.

He snagged a breath, slung his Tommy. 'All right,' he said. 'Give me that thing.'

Fiske flashed him an irritated glance, released the box. Caine picked it up: it was about the weight of a full jerrycan – not featherlight, but lighter than he'd expected. He carried it solemnly towards the fractured opening, with the others following. Outside, they almost ran into Copeland, jaunting back from the tailplane. Cope stared at the black box. 'What's that?' he demanded.

'I don't know, but it's the only thing on the payload.'

Copeland peered at it. 'This great big bird just to carry *that*?'

Caine put it down, Cope crouched to get a better look. 'STENDEC,' he read aloud, squinting at Trubman. 'Wasn't that on the Mayday code?'

'Yep. God knows what it means, though.'

'It must be something important,' Fiske said.

'What're we going to do with it?' Copeland enquired.

'Take it with us,' said Caine. He dekkoed his watch, looked around to see that the jeeps were spaced out in a covering perimeter: Jizzard, Quinnell and Wallace were waiting impatiently behind their steering wheels. The sky had turned leaden: the sun was sinking over the escarpment in a turmoil of angry dark cloud.

'Nothing in the tail section, Harry?'

Copeland shook his head: Caine peered at Trubman. 'What about the cockpit?'

Trubman pressed his glasses back with a stubby finger. 'No sign of anyone, skipper. There were no seats, just rows of instruments – I counted forty different gauges and twenty levers – masses of gear I didn't recognize – a lot of it like those organpipe things in the cabin: pipes and tubes and rigid cables with no joints, as if they came in one piece . . .'

'But what about the Gibson Girl?'

Trubman blinked shyly. 'It wasn't a Gibson Girl, after all, skipper. I got that wrong. There's no cranking handle. Signal must be produced automatically on some kind of loop, battery powered – maybe works like a musical box or a pianola or something, I dunno. See, when I tried to open it . . .'

'*Look at that*,' Copeland hissed. He gestured at the black box with his rifle muzzle.

The box was no longer black: it was turning a rich and glowing fire-red: a scarcely audible rumbling came from inside. Cope touched the top, jerked his hand back at once. '*Shit*,' he gasped. 'It's bloody *hot*.'

Caine saw that Cope's hand had a livid red blister on it. '*Run*,' he bawled. 'Get away, *now*.'

The four men bunked off like greyhounds, threw themselves flat twenty paces away. Caine lay with his chin in the dust, expecting the box to go kerbluey any moment. Minutes passed. Caine chanced a shufti, saw that the orange glow had already faded – the box was returning to its original hue.

'*Jesus wept*,' Copeland swore.

Caine got to his feet, slapped dust off his smock. 'We haven't got time for this,' he grunted. 'The Hun is coming. Let's bugger off.'

'But wait a minute, sir,' Fiske objected. 'Whatever that box is, it's obviously valuable. We can't just leave it. We ought to take it back for the boffins –'

'You blind or what?' Copeland cut him off. 'Didn't you see what just happened? We're not taking the thing – it might go off any second.'

'If it was going to go off, sir, it already would have,' Fiske argued. He stared back at Cope with unreadable eyes. 'It doesn't look like any bomb I've ever seen. Engines get hot, but they don't explode, do they?'

'It doesn't look like any engine *I've* ever seen,' Copeland mimicked him.

'It might be valuable kit, though, Lieutenant,' Trubman suggested tentatively. 'If we don't take it, we'll have stuck our necks out for nothing.'

Caine noticed that Wallace was standing up in the jeep – watching for the Jerry dust cloud, he presumed. It hit him in a rush that he'd made a bad decision in investigating the Mayday signal. Cope had been right all along. He'd risked the mission and put the patrol in danger, with nothing to show for it. The derelict aircraft gave him the creeps. How long she'd been here, where her crew was, he couldn't say. *Don't ask what* STENDEC *is or where it came from. You don't want to know.* Caine shrugged off the words. Pickney hadn't spoken to him: Pickney was dead.

Maybe there never *had* been a crew, he thought – no seats, not even in the cockpit. Maybe she flew herself. Maybe the emergency beacon started up automatically. 'STENDEC' was the only writing they'd found: it revealed nothing about the kite's origins. To Caine, though, the batnosed plane had Axis written all over her. They couldn't take her with them, but they *could* take the black box. Taff was right: it might be valuable. He had to admit, too, that it fascinated him: the odd way the box had behaved only increased his desire to know what was inside.

He soughed a long breath. 'Taff, take the box to my jeep. Be quick about it – we want to make it back up the pass before last light.'

Trubman loaded the box on Caine's jeep: Caine waved aside Wallace's questions. 'Let's get going,' he said.

He was about to jump into the passenger seat when the big man stiffened. 'There, skipper.' He inclined his deepfluted forehead.

Caine looked round, saw a roil of dust rising above the scrub behind the derelict plane. He listened carefully: picked up the low drub of motors. 'I don't *believe* it,' he cursed. He stared wide-eyed at Copeland, already manning the Vickers in the back. 'They're coming from the north.'

'They must have circled round. I'll bet they came to investigate the blimp.'

Wallace tipped the starter: the motor roared. 'Get in, skipper, for Chrissake . . .'

Cope clacked the Vickers' cocking handles, pivoted

the guns towards the aircraft: Wallace turned the jeep on a sixpence. The other jeeps boomeranged towards them, Quinnell and Jizzard at the wheels. 'The Krauts are coming,' Caine yelled. 'I'll take the lead: Quinnell, you're tail-end Charlie. Taffy and Fiske, man the guns. Drive like the clappers.'

They steamed across the stony surface, hugged their previous tracks. It didn't matter how much dust they kicked up, Caine decided. The enemy would soon find their tracks, would know they'd been at the aircraft. The crucial thing was to get up the pass before the Krauts caught them. They rounded the butte, skimmed up scarves of pumice between the arcade of twisted colonnades, shuddered across volcanic clinker, helterskeltered around devil's slagheaps, skirted skewed and squinted cliffs, seared along rock walls dotted with spectral ghost faces, pock-marked with basins of shade. The sun was a smelter of brass above the escarpment, now strangled in sagging clouds, now breaking through to drizzle dark trails across the scree behind.

The jeeps skeetered along the weatherscabbed canyon: sootblack parapets rose on either side, scalpelled into angles, inclines, knotted humps. They followed the cleft to its end, where the steep walls broke into shattered ridges, willowed out into spans of sandscraped scoria and freestanding stones. Beyond these relicts, a barren gravel fan extended as far as the pass: the Matmata peaks rose over the plain like lopshouldered skulls.

Caine's vehicle skidded to a halt: the others drew abreast. Caine leapt from his seat, looked backwards, listened. He saw the dustroil at once, heard engines gurning from within the labyrinth of rock. The enemy was right behind them. He felt a tightening in his guts: the hairs on his neck prickled. It was too late to withdraw up the pass. They still had two hours of light: they'd be easy targets from here.

He hesitated, sucked breath: the classic defence against pursuit was ambush, and this was a good place. He surveyed the area for cover, saw that they could get the jeeps behind the relict screes to his left. 'Hide the wagons behind those stones,' he yelled. 'The buggers'll be here in five minutes.'

12

Everyone is doing time here, thought Robin Sears-Beach, even the staff. Three months back he'd been a major in the Military Police, Deputy Provost Marshal of Cairo. Now he was a paltry subaltern in the Provost Corps at the Military Detention Centre – the arsehole of Empire. He was nothing but a glorified screw.

He'd had ample time to think in the months he'd been here, though, and he'd thought a lot about Caine. He'd thought about Nolan too: sometimes her naked body made unexpected appearances in his dreams. But he'd thought mainly about Caine. Caine flouted the rules, yet no one else seemed to recognize it. He'd had some successes, of course, but they were down to luck and opportunity: he hadn't done anything others couldn't have done given half the chance.

Caine was the blue-eyed boy, of course: a favourite of Stirling and the GOC. Sears-Beach knew his type of old and had always loathed them – the star rugby players at school who'd got away with breaking rules because they were *special*. He'd detested that school ever since he'd been marooned there aged six by a mother whose main interest was having sordid affairs with older versions of exactly those rugged, sports-playing loudmouths he despised. She wasn't particular: some of her boyfriends had been as vulgar as Caine.

His father, who had abandoned her over her infidelities, had rightly called her a *whore* – a word that Sears-Beach still used with a frisson of pleasure. His mother had been a *whore*, a *tart*, a *strumpet* – just like that Nolan bitch. She had never once visited him at school, even though she'd promised, even though he'd sat waiting for her expectantly time after time. Even during holidays she had farmed him out to aunts and uncles, who generally couldn't wait to get rid of him.

Sears-Beach felt that the world hadn't treated him right. He'd trusted people but in the end they'd all let him down: now he trusted no one. He'd been infuriated to learn that Caine had been promoted to captain and now outranked him. He shivered at the thought that he might one day have to salute that upstart and call him *sir*. The worst of it was that he'd almost bagged him last November: shooting Glenn and abducting Maskelyne should have been enough to hang him. Then Stirling and that delinquent Mayne had intervened: it was unlucky that the GOC had taken their side. Montgomery had reported Sears-Beach to his superior, who'd had him demoted, transferred to the Provost Corps and assigned duties here at the detention centre. Well, Stirling was in the bag now, and the SAS wouldn't last five minutes without his old boys' club to protect it. Nolan was out of the picture, of course, and now, thanks to Caversham, he'd acquired the perfect chance to deal with Caine.

Sears-Beach stared out of the office window: a squad of prisoners in full battle kit was being doubled around the square, amid screamed orders and torrents of abuse from provost NCOs. He found the rhythmic crump of their boots jarring. This was the daily torture session: prisoners were made to bash in step round and round the square for hours on end, until they dropped with fatigue. With its brick walls, the place was a heat trap, especially on these hot mornings: it was like doing a route-march through a furnace. Some prisoners begged for it to stop: some had to be carried back to their cells. Although he would never admit it, Sears-Beach disliked this ritual: somewhere deep down, almost lost under time's scar tissue, there was a small spark of sympathy for the prisoners' ordeal. He knew what it was like to be a prisoner: he'd been one all his life.

There was a rap on the door. Sears-Beach pulled down the peak of his service cap, gripped his silver-knobbed stick under his left arm. The door opened: a sergeant in spruce KDs marched in a rakethin prisoner wearing overalls and ammunition boots. The sergeant had the man mark time for a little longer than necessary, just to make a point: Sears-Beach watched the spindly legs jerking, and was reminded of a mechanical toy. The sergeant ordered the man to halt. He saluted smartly.

Sears-Beach returned the salute, dismissed the sergeant. The prisoner stood at stiff attention, his face blank, his mouth tight. There was something almost chilling in those gimlet eyes, Sears-Beach thought, something concealed there, whose true nature you'd never know until it was too late.

'Private Fiske,' he said. 'So good of you to come.'

Fiske eyed him coldly.

'Stand easy.'

Sears-Beach flipped off his cap, sat down at the battered table he used as a desk. He laid cap and stick neatly on the tabletop, opened a slim file, perused its contents: personal histories of Ptes Richard Fiske, Mitchell Jizzard and Dominic Quinnell. They made interesting reading. These were the men he'd selected for what he called the *Caine Job*, and whose names he'd given Caversham. They were perfect for this scheme because they were all ex-commando and all parachute trained.

Jizzard he already knew: before the MPs had bagged him, he'd been a useful informer among the deserters in the Delta. Jizzard had been understandably indignant when he'd been arrested, but he was a hardened criminal whom no time in the glasshouse could reform: Quinnell was a disturbed psychopath whose penchant for violence was hidden under a girlishly soft voice and pretentions to honour.

Fiske was altogether a darker horse, though, an ex-officer in the Ordnance Corps, from a similar background to his own, with a record of fraud and theft. Fiske possessed an almost robotlike lack of emotion, warmth, sympathy or even fear: it was Fiske he was trusting with the *Caine Job*: Jizzard and Quinnell were expendable adjuncts.

Sears-Beach tapped the open file. 'I have here the movement order for you and your two chums,' he said. 'At 1200 hours sharp, you are to leave for the MO4 base in Sinai with a Provost Corps escort. I warn you now not to try to abscond. If you do, you will be shot. Do you understand that?'

'Perfectly.'

Sears-Beach gave him a sliteyed glare. 'Perfectly, *sir.*'

'Perfectly, *sir.*'

'Good. You have already received your orders, Fiske: I just want to make sure we understand each other . . .' He raised an eyebrow, scratched his weak chin. 'This operation is top secret. As far as the staff here is concerned, the three of you have volunteered for a dangerous secret mission behind enemy lines. If you mention your real objective to anyone, the consequences could be very, very unpleasant. Your experience here will be like a kindergarten by comparison.'

'I'm not likely to tell anyone, sir.'

Sears-Beach's eyes gleamed in their mailbox slits. 'When you have achieved your object, you are to split from Caine and his crew, first taking steps to ensure that they are . . . *not in a position* . . . to stop you.'

'I've got it. You can rely on me, sir.'

Sears-Beach was smiling, beaverlike front teeth bared. 'Very good, Fiske. I think you appreciate the situation. Remember, even Jizzard and Quinnell don't need to know the true purpose of your mission, not at first anyway. They need to know only that it involves putting Caine . . . *out of the picture.* You are to RV with an aircraft at a place called Bir Souffra, whose co-ordinates are marked on the map I gave you. You are not to make contact with any friendly troops once you have done your business. That is essential. Do you understand?'

'Of course I do . . . I mean, *yes, sir.*'

Sears-Beach's slabtooth smile flickered. 'Let me repeat,' he said. 'If you are successful in this task, I can personally guarantee that you will be granted a free pardon for your crimes, *and* an honourable discharge.' He sighed as if he had just made a concession costing him an arm and a leg. 'You will *also* privately receive the princely sum of £1,000, to get yourself started in Civvie Street.'

'Thank you, sir.'

Fiske's face remained impassive: Sears-Beach wished for once that he could fathom the man's thoughts. He couldn't trust him an inch, of course, but he reckoned the incentive would be enough to bring him back. After that, his position would be reassessed.

He stood up, replaced his cap, stuck his swaggerstick under his arm. He expanded his chest, straightened his back. 'Well, that's it,' he said. 'I'm giving you the chance of your life here, Fiske. Don't mess it up.'

'No, sir.'

'Do you have any last questions?'

The zinc eyes remained unyielding. 'Just one, sir. What is this operation *really* about?'

Sears-Beach bit his lip, sucked air. 'Just do your bit, Fiske. Whatever else it's about, you do *not* want to know.'

13

Caine carried Wallace's Bren into the lee of a crusted rock bulge, set the weapon down on its bipod. He piled stones around it, built a shallow rampart. When it was done, he squirmed into a firing position. The men were holed up in similar rockpiles under the outcroppings: the jeeps were concealed in the undulations directly behind him. Caine had taken the right-hand cutoff point of the killing ground: Fiske was spraddled behind a Bren on the far left, with Jizzard and Quinnell between him and big Wallace. The gunner crouched in the centre behind a slab of gneiss, the bazooka slatted across his meaty shoulder. Trubman knelt with his arms around the gunner's big torso, like a disconsolate lover. Copeland was proned out in the scree to Caine's left. There hadn't been time to dismount the Vickers or Brownings: Caine reckoned that two Brens, three Lee-Enfields, an M1 Carbine and a bazooka would do the business, as long as they weren't up against Panzer Mk IIIs.

He checked the spring on a magazine, clicked it into place. He tightened his left hand round the stock, braced it to his shoulder, cocked the working parts. He peered down the sights at the curve in the canyon, not more than two hundred yards away. He could hear the whir and jangle of vehicles echoing off the canyon's walls – the motors were pitched too high to be AFVs, he thought. There was no telltale slap and scuttle of tanktracks, either. He swallowed, moistened cracked lips, tweaked the set of the Bren's muzzle. A bead of sweat hit the gun's stock with an audible plop. The snarl of motors was louder: the Hun was seconds away. His body tensed: his scalp prickled. His mind was suddenly as sharp as a razor blade.

A squad of Jerry motorcyclists swept round the curve – six of them, bike-and-sidecar combinations: riders and gunners in fieldgrey, with dustgoggles and Kaiser helmets: a pair of three-ton Gaz lorries pitched behind them trailing swales of dust. Caine touched the curve of the trigger, stalled an impulse to shoot. The motorcycles were in rough file, each with a rider and a spotter-gunner in the sidecar: three of the sidecars carried 30MG Schmeissers. Caine let them come deeper into the killing ground, zeroed in on the leading combination, stroked iron, unleashed a burst *rat-tat-tat-tat-tat*. Tracer rounds torched in bright spliffs, ruptured the gunner's belly, chewed red sutures across the rider's leg and guts. The petrol tank *baroommmfffed*, the air spasmed, the combination blew in a blinding candlebomb, a reek of vapourized oil. The rider flipped off backwards, the gunner howled, the motorcycle hit gravel, came to rest a fiery bag of smoking rubber, scrambled wheelspokes, snarled steel.

The second motorbike swerved, skidded away from the wreck. Caine slipped a grenade from his belt, pinned it, whaled it overarm: he heard it go *babbboooooooom*, felt the tremor, heard grit zap. He saw the combination spew flame, smelt burning oil, saw the rider writhing in the gravel. The gunner was on his feet wrestling with the MG30 on the sidecar. Caine spurted a double tap, slotted him through the helmet, saw him sledge over without a sound.

Fiske's Bren chattered out from the end of the defile: Lee-Enfields grumped, tracers shizzed. Motors squealed, exhausts trumped, gears chomped, dust soughed. A Schmeisser clittered, slugs wazzed, chinged snaps of rock around Caine's head. He ducked, looked up again, saw motorcycle crews leaping into the scree on the other side of the killing ground. Rounds whined and *kapowed*, punked gravel: Krauts crouched and manoeuvred, *chunka-chunked* bursts.

Caine traileyed the leading Gaz wagon, saw her gunner dealing swipes of crimson fire. He shifted his Bren, heard the *whoooooomfffff* of the bazooka, felt the air zip, saw flame rush front and rear, saw the bullseye strike on the radiator grille, saw the bonnet scintillate in a galaxy of steel coils, saw the lorry vault and slump. The cab blew, glass flecks shimmered, blue smoke huffed: a shrieking Jerry fell out, thrashed about in a mantle of fire. Copeland squinched a single shot through his brain.

Totenkopf troopers dropped from the back of the burning wagon, limped, crawled, dragged each other into cover. The second Hun lorry went into reverse: the machine-gunner on her cab covered the runners with wefts of fire as she slewed back round the curve. An

MG 30 started up from screes opposite the ambush party: Jerry sub-machine guns blitzed SAS positions. Caine dodged, popped up, sighted in, hammered fire at the Jerries in the rocks. A smoke grenade burst, then another: wreaths of white dross drifted across Caine's vision like slowly swirling bridal veils.

Caine stopped shooting, breathed acrid smoke. Gunfire petered out, sidecars crackled, smoke whoffed. His body felt numb: a muscle in his shoulder throbbed. He tried to moisten his lips with a raw tongue, spat. He wanted to take a swallow from his waterbottle, but dared not relax. Hun shouts drifted across the battlefield: Caine guessed the enemy were using the smoke to withdraw – the whole canyon mouth was hidden from view. His patrol had won the firefight: he had to pull them out now, before the smoke cleared. He gave Cope the *close on me* signal: Cope passed it down the line. Caine saw Fiske crawl out of his position: Quinnell and Jizzard followed. Wallace, Trubman and Copeland jogged towards him, keeping low.

They had almost reached him when there was an ear-shattering *kaaathuuumppp*. The boys fell flat: a shell scraped air, hit the desert fifty yards away in a 'V'-shaped cascade. The earth rocked: Caine felt the air in his lungs cook. He shuftied up.

'*Jesus*,' Copeland hissed. 'That was a 40 mil. There must be an AFV we haven't seen.'

Caine nodded, a sinking sensation in his gut. They'd lost the element of surprise: they'd be hard pressed to take on an armoured car.

He squinted at Wallace and Trubman. 'Got one up the spout, Fred?'

The big man nodded.

'Get in here. And you, Taff. Hit that wagon before she does for us all.'

Caine edged back from his position: Wallace and Trubman shimmied in. The big gunner hefted the stovepipe, came up in a crouch: Trubman set the sights.

'Mind the backblast, skipper,' he said.

Caine shifted the others out of the blast area, crawled abreast of the bazooka team, heard balloon tyres grind towards them through the smokescreen, heard a gun-turret clank. *Oh shit*, he thought.

Wallace would only have one shot: he'd have to fire the moment the AFV slid into view. If he was too slow, or missed, they'd be sunk. He stiffened, saw the armoured car mooch out of the smoke, much bigger than he'd thought – a bluntnosed leviathan like a great iron barge, all rivets and protrusions on six balloon wheels. He watched her emerge from the smokefog, clenched his teeth, held his breath, awaited the shot, prayed it would be good. He noticed suddenly that the AFV's turret was reversed 360 degrees, the gunbarrel tipped downwards, pointing at the ground. A Jerry was perched at the open hatch: black overalls, headset over tousled blond hair. Caine started: Fritz was waving a white flag.

The armoured car was forty yards off: the commander was in plain sight; the white flag snickered.

Caine took first pressure: he could have shot the chap easily, but he didn't. '*Hold your fire, Fred,*' he croaked.

Wallace didn't move. 'Don't tell me they're gonna *surrender,*' he cackled.

'*It's a trick, skipper,*' Jizzard piped up from behind. 'Let her have it, Wallace.'

'*Shut up,*' Copeland snapped.

Caine followed the AFV's progress through his sights. She inched up until she was no more than twenty-five yards away, scrunched to a stop.

'*Oh Lord,*' Jizzard cawed.

Caine watched the AFV commander jump down from the turret. He faced them straddlelegged, displayed an open left hand, held up the flag with his right. Caine didn't show himself. The officer took a hesitant step forward, hands still raised. When nothing happened he took another, then another. After five steps, he gained confidence, began to walk steadily. Caine let him come within ten yards. 'That's far enough, Fritz,' he growled.

The Jerry's duststained tank overalls had the sleeves rolled up, showing muscular arms. He was no older than Caine, lanky and leanhipped, a pimpled face ghosted with dust, tired eyes, gold fluffspeckles on a stone jaw. Caine saw subaltern's insignia, the twin zigzags of the Waffen SS, and the Totenkopf skull-and-crossbones on his collar. He kept his weapon trained, aware that the enemy couldn't see him. The soldier grinned nervously, showed grainseed teeth.

'Tommy,' he said. 'We want to talk.' His English accent was thick, his voice croupy and dustchoked.

Caine sighed, laid down the Bren's stock, stood up, wiped dust and gunblack off his face. He took in the canyon mouth, the Jerry corpses, the smouldering motorcycle combinations. A sniper could easily potshot him, he knew, but if that happened the Jerry officer would be instant dead meat. He stared at his counterpart. 'Talk if you want, but keep your hands where I can see them. If the turret on that vehicle budges, you've had it, chum.'

The officer eyed the Colt .45 on Caine's belt. He fluttered the flag, let his left hand down. He shot a rueful glance at his dead comrades, the wispy lines of smoke trailing from the wrecked motorcycles. His fingers twitched.

'No more dead,' he said. 'Too many dead already, yes?'

'Ain't they told you there's a war on, mate?' Wallace crooned from behind his hide.

'Leave it, Fred,' Caine said. He eyed the white flag: it looked like somebody's old vest tied to a broomstick. Of course, it would be: no German soldier would go into battle carrying a readymade white flag. He raised an eyebrow at the Jerry. 'Well?'

'I have an offer . . . how do you say in English . . . a *deal*?'

'Oh yes. And what might that be?'

'You have something we want. We would like you to give it to us.'

Mystified, Caine pulled at the whiskered flesh on his chin. 'What is it you think we've got?'

'The blek box. The box you hev taken from the air-craft.'

Caine started. 'What black box?'

'We know you hev it,' the German officer said. His face had turned slightly redder under the pall of dust. 'We followed your treks from the aircraft. Gif us the blek box and we will let you go.'

Caine pulled at his chin thoughtfully. Fiske was right: that box must really be something.

'Why? What is it?' he asked.

The Jerry shrugged. 'I do not know this. I hev my orders, only. My orders are to bring it back.'

Caine hesitated. The Hun's eyes were keen: he was deadly serious. 'What if we don't hand it over?'

'Then we take it.' The Jerry took a breath: his smile wavered. 'To refuse is foolish. You are a small unit. We scout ahead of a whole Totenkopf battalion, which will be here shortly. After that the 164 Panzer Division comes this way. If you do not give us the box you will be crushed.'

Caine fought to keep his face straight. The Hun sub-altern had just given away int. with a grim bearing on the *Nighthawk* op – if it was true, that was. It could be a deliberate bluff. He cursed himself for his impulsive behaviour in investigating the Mayday signal. Now the el-Fayya bridge might never get blown at all, and, if so, it might not be just one battalion hitting Freyberg in the rear, but a whole *division*. That would probably mean curtains for Monty's flanking movement, and maybe a new stalemate in the campaign. He doubted that this Jerry knew that Caine's unit had been ordered to sabotage the bridge, otherwise he wouldn't be interested only in the black box. He must believe that the SAS patrol had also been sent to retrieve it.

Caine sucked air through his nostrils: he had to take down that bridge at any cost, and his decision now might change the course of the Tunisian campaign. A lot depended on how far he could trust this Death's Head wallah.

'How do we know you'll keep your word?' he demanded.

The Jerry let the flag droop, drew himself up straight. 'Because I am an officer and a gentleman.'

Caine suppressed a smirk. 'I need to think about it,' he said.

'I gif you five minutes,' the Jerry said sternly. 'I will go back to my vehicle. Leave the box where we can see it, and go. We will not try to stop you.'

He inclined his head sharply, turned, marched off as if relieved to have survived this far. Caine watched him go, saw the flag snap on its broomhandle.

He ducked back into the cover of the scree, crouched behind the shatterstone jumble. Wallace was still hefting the bazooka in Caine's position, Trubman crouched next to him. 'Keep that AFV in your sights, Fred,' Caine told him. He shuftied Cope lying in the tufa, rifle at the shoulder: he saw Fiske, Quinnell and Jizzard raking him with beaded eyes. 'What do you think, Harry?' he asked.

Copeland's forehead puckered. 'It's a bluff, skipper,' he said. 'Has to be. That black box must be important. My bet is that they daren't blitz us, in case they demolish it. That's the only reason I can think of for waving a white flag when you've got superior firepower. We must have knocked off at least five of 'em. If that was our men, we'd be screaming for revenge, not conflabbing. Yet that chap didn't turn a hair. I reckon he's got no choice.'

Caine nodded: it was an acute observation – why hadn't it occurred to him? He scratched his chin. 'Did you hear what he said? About 164 Panzer Div. coming this way?'

'May be bullshit too.'

'I say dump the bloody box, sah,' Jizzard said, his voice queasy. 'Let's get rid of it and let's get oota here.'

Fiske seared him with steelball eyes. He turned to Caine. 'It would be a mistake to give them the box, Captain. It could be very important. If Mr Copeland is right, they wouldn't dare shell us while we've got it.'

Caine hesitated. He glanced over the outcrops, clocked the Jerry officer leaning against his vehicle, smoking. The AFV hadn't moved, neither had her turret.

He turned back to the expectant faces. 'I'm giving them the black box,' he said.

Fiske's eyelids came down like iron shutters, then snapped open. 'But, sir . . .'

'You sure, Tom?' Copeland said. He ran blackgrimed fingers through his hair. 'You trust that Kraut to keep his word?'

'I don't know,' Caine said, 'but if we do a bunk, they'll come after us. Our priority is to blow that bridge, and we can't do it under fire. It's a risk any way you slice it, but my hunch is that he'll stick to his promise.'

Cope made a choking sound in his throat. For a moment, Caine thought he was going to tell him that he should have got his priorities right before dropping them in this mess.

Fiske licked his lips with the tip of a white tongue: his eyes were as wide and unblinking as a lizard's. 'I don't think that's wise . . .'

'Your bad luck you're not in command, then,' Caine cut him off. 'I've made my decision. Harry, take these three and start the jeeps, bring 'em here. We'll dump the box and drive like the blazes.'

Copeland nodded, tipped his head at the others: they began to crawl back towards the pits where the jeeps were hidden. Caine scrambled abreast of Wallace and Trubman. 'Jeeps are coming,' he said. 'When I give the word, move out – keep that weapon loaded.'

'I reckon you're doin' right, Tom,' Big Wallace grunted. 'We don't need that box. Whatever it is, it's a bleedin' liability.'

'Yeah. We've copped for a lot of those on this trip.'

He heard jeep motors gun. This was going to be a tense manoeuvre, he reflected. He could send two of the jeeps on ahead while the others unloaded the box, but he wasn't sure the Huns would accept that. On the other hand, all three vehicles would be exposed to enemy fire.

His thoughts were cut short by the appearance of the wagons, bouncing over the pebblestone undulations. Cope was driving the leading jeep – the one carrying the black box. Fiske drove the W/T wagon behind him: Quinnell and Jizzard brought up the rear.

Copeland's vehicle scuttered to a stop a few yards from Caine. Wallace and Trubman were already withdrawing from the hide, the big gunner crooking the bazooka in the great hams of his arms, as if it were an infant. Caine watched them climb into the jeeps, took a breath, stood up. He strode over to the small convoy.

'All right,' he said. 'We're going to pull out and stop in full view of the Hun. Quinnell, Jizzard, I want you to fetch the box from my jeep. You set it down halfway between the AFV and us, and withdraw. Got that?'

'Why the bijasus do *we* have to do it?' Jizzard quavered.

'Because I say so,' Caine retorted. 'We'll be covering you.'

He passed his Bren to Wallace, hopped into the seat next to Cope, jerked his Tommy-gun out of the brace. The jeeps moved out of cover, into the plain.

14

Caine stopped the jeeps fifty yards from the German armoured car: the Jerry officer stood upright, studied them. Behind the AFV, in the canyon's maw, Caine could see lorries, motorbikes, a swarm of Totenkopf troopers. They weren't making any move: just knowing he was in their sights made him jittery. He slid from his seat, gripped his trenchsweeper.

A bloodorange sun lay in the peaks, drew a last sill of flash and glitter athwart an ashcoloured sky smudged with long flumes of darkness. The hills were humpbacked goblins laying down reefs of murk on the gilded plain.

Wallace straddled the black box: Caine beckoned Jizzard and Quinnell. They sidled up to the jeep, rifles slung. 'Hand it down, will ye, big man,' Quinnell told Wallace. The gunner clamped racketsized hands each side of the box, heaved. The box didn't move. His mouth garfished: he gasped, let go. 'What the flamin' hell is *this*?' he demanded. He spat on his hands, squatted on his haunches, grabbed the box again, heaved, grunted. It didn't shift.

'Come on, ye great ox,' Quinnell chuckled, blinking. 'And ye call yeself a strong man.'

Wallace let go, fixed Quinnell with a goateyed glare. 'Hey rent-a-gob,' he spat. 'You wanna try?'

Jizzard and Quinnell leaned over the chassis, strained on the box. It didn't budge. 'It won't come,' Quinnell panted. 'It's stuck fast, so it is.'

'It's like it's welded to the jeep or something,' Jizzard spat.

Wallace guffawed. 'Who's the great fairies now?'

Caine elbowed them out of the way, had a go at shifting it for himself: the box was fixed hard – no play, no wobble. He glanced up at Wallace, mystified. 'It's either stuck to the chassis, or it's got heavier.'

'It must be *bloody* heavy,' Wallace guttered. 'I can tote five hundred pounds deadlift easy, but I couldn't shift it a blind inch.'

'How can it have got heavier?' Quinnell said. 'Sure, that's not possible, sir.'

Wallace slid out his bayonet. He was about to probe the base of the box when the blade was suddenly tugged from his fingers. The bayonet hit the box with a clang and stuck there.

All four of them flinched, stared in wonder.

'Mother of God,' Quinnell hissed. 'It's *magnetic*.'

'Stand back!' Caine yelled. 'Hold on to your grenades – if it drags them in they could detonate.'

Wallace jumped down from the jeep: the four of them backed away two or three yards.

Fiske and Trubman were looking on stupefied from the W/T jeep. Copeland moved round to get a better look. 'You mean we can't get it off,' he said in surprise. 'What are we going to tell Fritz?'

Caine cocked a nervous eye towards the German officer: he was watching them curiously. He didn't know what was going on yet, but he knew something was.

'What we gonnae do *now*?' whined Jizzard. 'We'll never get it off.'

Caine scowled. He had no idea what was happening, and he wasn't ready to start explaining it to the Hun. There was no choice: they'd have to hook it, black box and all. He touched Wallace's broad arm. 'You still got the bazooka loaded, Fred?'

'Yep.'

'Get it out – on the sly, mind. Get down behind the front of the jeep. When I give the word, poke a rocket straight through that turret.'

The giant swallowed: his throat tightened. 'Got it, skipper.'

'And Fred, you better hit the spot, mate, or we'll be strawberry jam.'

Jizzard was staring at Caine with mushy eyes. 'But sah, didn't you say they'd follow us . . .'

'You got a better idea?'

'No, sah.'

'Then shut it. We'll have to take our chance. You and Quinnell get back to your jeep. Don't run. The second Wallace lets rip, start up, lay down suppressive fire with the Vickers, motor like the wind towards that pass. If we get split up, RV there. Tell Taff and Fiske to do the same.'

Quinnell and Jizzard stomped off. Wallace took the bazooka from the back of the jeep, used the piled-up kit to mask the action. He squatted behind the chassis, pantherwalked to the front end, crouched alongside the bonnet. He set the sights, hefted the stovepipe to his shoulder. Copeland leapt back into the driver's seat. Caine went round to the passenger's side, stood casually, looking back at the Hun officer. He tried to hold his pulse in check, drew air through drybone nostrils, resisted the temptation to wave. The Kraut had clicked now: he turned and began to shimmy up the AFV's body, the white flag discarded. Caine wondered if he'd spotted Wallace – it was too late to stop it, anyway. He felt sweat seep into his eyes.

The officer was inside the hatch, only his head showing: the turret clattered, the gunbarrel cranked. Caine thought of what Copeland had said – that this might be a bluff – but the 40mm cannon was real enough, and right at that moment he wouldn't have wanted to bet on it. He noticed that the Jerry troops in the canyon had started advancing. The AFV's turret rotated, the gunmuzzle ranged in a low arc. It would be three seconds before the Kraut drew a bead on them.

'Here she comes,' Cope said.

The turret stopped, the gunbarrel tremored: for a horrific instant Caine looked straight into its eye. He was about to hiss '*Fire!*' when the bazooka spewed flame: the jeep's chassis rocked, the ground jerked, gritshards flew: the rocket craunched across their front in a swell of curdling air, bucketed into the AFV just where the turret met the main body. The round *kerbloonked*, the gunbarrel pranged, the turret ballooned out in a gunge of shrapnel and gorehued flame: jags of hot armour plate buzzed, spun, cartwheeled. Caine heard the clack of smallarms from the canyon: bullets razzed past them like fuming bees. Cope had already hit the starter: the motor rumped: they were into a turn before Wallace had plonked the bazooka in the back, vaulted over the side. Copeland swung the vehicle, Wallace planted legs wide, cocked the twin Vickers, pulled metal: twin muzzles speared rimfire, cases clinked, traceries of light leaned into the twilight towards the blazing AFV and the oncoming troops. The other two jeeps were streaking across the plain, laddering the air with coppercoloured dust: Cope accelerated so hard that Wallace had to stop shooting and hang on to the mount. They were soon up abreast of the others, scoring ruts across the matt surface into the last crimson shaftlights of the dying sun.

15

There was a beautiful girl in his headlamps. A split second before he tramped the brakes, it occurred to Driver Jack Davis that he was dreaming. The 3-tonner staggered to a halt, scranched her springs: Davis swore, let out a shoosh of breath, shook his head roughly to rid himself of the apparition. The bint was still there, though, and she was a stunner: shapely figure, blond hair with an enticing peek-a-boo wave over her left eye, nice pins under an evening dress that showed the bulge of proud knockers. She had a cape draped over her shoulders and carried an elegant handbag. She was waving at him.

Davis's lorry was the last in the 'C' Echelon convoy, humping field rations to a dump outside the city. It was 2115 hours on a Cairo night: the moon was a bright cheeseparing, the streets burdened with cobalt shadow. Davis, a cocky 20-year-old from Bedford, with a ratlike face and diapered ears, had already had to work hard to follow the tail lights of the vehicle ahead. Now he'd lost the convoy completely.

He stuck his head out of the window, tilted back his beret. The girl glided closer: Davis saw she had brilliant green eyes, pert nose, full red lips, an entrancing slight unevenness in one of her front teeth. There was something almost sleepy in her eyes – in her whole face – like a little girl lost in the woods, something wistful and far-off: it took his breath away.

'You wanna watch it, miss,' he warbled. 'You'll get yerself run over.'

'You couldn't give me a lift, could you?' she said. 'I think I'm lost.' Her voice was silken, her accent English – a bit plummy. She didn't look a streetwalker: she looked more like Rita Hayworth or one of those bints you saw on the flicks.

Davis scratched his ear, yanked his beret down. 'Blimey, I dunno, miss. I'll catch it if I give anyone a lift. Regulations, see.'

She gave him a melting look, moistened bloodred lips. A raw tingle crept across Davis's belly as if hot fingers were walking there. He shivered.

'Please,' she said. 'I'd be very grateful.'

Her eyes were bottomless: falling into them would be like dropping into a pool of cool water, Davis thought. He wondered *how* grateful she would be.

He shot a worried glance at the road ahead. The street was deserted: chinks of light bloomed dimly despite blackout regs.

'It'll cost yer,' he winked. 'I'll do it for a kiss.'

He got a glimpse of the delectable overlap. 'Only one?' she purred.

He stifled a gasp, nodded at the opposite door. 'All right, darlin'. Hop in.'

He watched the blond head cross in front of the lorry, already lost in a reverie: this was the kind of girl you daydreamed about. He imagined her body naked on a bed under him, saw himself parting her legs, caressing her thighs, saw her panting with pleasure as he did her.

The door cracked: the girl climbed in. Davis dekkoed elegant bare legs, the peaks of shapely breasts under the dress, the scar at the base of the neck that looked like a gunshot wound, but surely couldn't be. She was wearing flatsoled brogues that were out of place with the rest of the attire. She sat down on the long seat, put down her handbag, eyed him through quivering lashes. He caught a whiff of perfume, noticed the almost boyish cut of her hair, the provocative blond curl over her eye.

Fathomless seagreen eyes held him. 'Well?' she asked.

Now she was close, Davis sensed the pull of her body. He gulped hard, as if his throat wouldn't swallow. 'Well what?' he stammered.

Her face dimpled. 'Our bargain. Didn't you want a kiss?'

When she shuffled nearer to him, he felt weakboned. He put his arms round her, snogged her mouth, felt soft lips yield, slid a hand under her dress, stroked the soft reaches of her inner thigh.

'I didn't say you could go there,' she giggled. 'That isn't what we agreed on.'

She didn't close her legs or grab his hand, though, Davis noted. He left it where it was, came up for another kiss, eyes closed. He found her mouth wasn't there: instead, a ring of warm metal jagged the flesh under his jaw. Davis opened his eyes wide, realized that she was pressing a handgun to his throat. She was still smiling the wistful smile. 'Don't do anything silly,' she murmured, 'and you won't get hurt.' She watched him, cateyed. '*Taylor*,' she yodelled.

The door on the driver's side opened: a one-eyed man stood there, a man with a ragged beard, wild hair and a .45 Colt. His face was square, mapped out with creases, and there was an oriental touch in the high cheekbones: wide mouth, long jaw, hook nose, one eye glittering like quartzite, the other hidden under an eye-patch. He was tall, with large, hairy hands. He wore a mixture of military and civilian garb — silk scarf, corduroy trousers, tattered leather jerkin.

'Right, me old China,' he rumbled. 'You ain't got to do nothink but drive and keep yer trap shut. Don't give us no lip and you'll be all right.'

The girl kept the gun lodged against Davis's throat until she and Taylor had swapped places. Close up, the man smelt of whisky and sour tobacco. 'Drive,' he snarled.

Davis felt his heart lump, squeezed the steering wheel with both hands.

''Ere, watchu doin'? This is army property, this is. You must be a pair of 'oodlums.'

Taylor's phlegmy chuckle came again. 'That we are, me old chummy. Why, what was *you* doin'? Thought you was in for a bit of nookies with this lady, did yer? Touch of the old how's yer father?'

'She ain't no lady,' Davis said bitterly.

Taylor's crosshatched face buckled, his good eye

flashed: he bared crooked teeth, jabbed the pistol into Davis's ribs. 'Watch yer mouth, mate. Any more lip like that and they'll be scrapin' yer off the bleedin' road tomorra. Now, put 'er in gear and let's get off. We ain't got all flamin' night, yer know.'

The lorry ramped bluewashed sidestreets, rolled between buttes of tottering tenements where gaslamps flickered: Davis kept silent, followed Taylor's directions. Maddy felt the weight of the pistol in her hand, stared out at the guncotton night, sank into a haze. Nothing was real: she was living in a violent fantasy from which she couldn't wake up. She did not recall her name: she'd told Taylor it was Maddy, but she knew it wasn't. In fact, she didn't remember much before she'd been pulled off the street by his deserter gang – only a fuzzy nightmare of floundering in dark water, of being dragged down, of coming up with lungs bursting, of striking out for the bank. There was another nagging, misty image of a man with Herculean shoulders, stone-coloured eyes and a freckled face, but she had no idea who he was or what he'd meant to her.

Her life with the deserters over the past months had become her world: hijacking vehicles by night in Cairo streets, the battle of wits with Field Security, the near misses, the times they'd had to hide in hovels and basements, running the gauntlet of MP patrols, racing back to their hideout in a stolen vehicle: the feasts, the drinking, the music, the dancing. Sometimes the revels would erupt into wild orgies, but Maddy had remained aloof from the louche promiscuity. She knew that Taylor wanted her desperately, that he considered her almost his property, yet she had never given in to his advances, no matter how violent he had become. For all his roughness, though, Maddy felt a certain loyalty to him: his ferocity had at least kept other men off her back.

Dark hulls of streets fell behind them: the 3-tonner pounded past barbwire thorntrees, driedout palms, through straggling villages redolent of dung and dog-piss, where dark phantoms lurked in huddles in the light of smoky braziers, where fagends winked like alligator eyes, where thin goats and chickens prowled junkheaps, or mooched along the garbage-littered verge. The fineshaved moon was still up, the night flocked with the quicksilver peelings of stars.

''Ere, where you takin' me?' Davis enquired abruptly.

'Shut yer trap,' barked Taylor. 'Keep drivin''

Maddy knew they were only a couple of miles from the RV, where Mitch Jizzard would be waiting. They would transfer the stores to an unmarked lorry, tie the driver in the cab. He'd have descriptions of them, but he wouldn't know who they were. Taylor wasn't Taylor any more than Maddy was Maddy: she didn't know his real name and had never asked. Tracing them in the deserter community of the Delta would be like looking for a sandgrain in the Sahara: there were so many fugitives scattered in towns, villages and hamlets from Cairo to Alex that they called themselves the *lost division*. Now the war had moved far from Egypt to the Tunisian frontier, they'd begun to get organized into smuggling and hijack gangs: there were rumours that their operations were co-ordinated by a new big man at the top. Nobody knew who he was: Maddy doubted that he even existed. The Redcaps occasionally collared a few of them, but to bag them all would have taken a massive manhunt. At this stage of the war no one was going to spare big efforts to mop up people who'd refused to fight.

Maddy had no memory of serving in the forces, but her skill at weapon-handling told her she might have. She also knew songs and dance steps, and had a notion that she might once have been an entertainer. She'd sometimes walked around Cairo streets, rubbed shoulders with off-duty Tommies, seen sights that had given her a thrill of recognition. She'd felt drawn to some of those places, but had stopped going when she'd started to sense that she was being watched. A couple of times she'd had the impression that she'd been photographed from parked cars: then, at the beginning of February, there was the chap in civvies who'd asked her to pose with a newspaper, had taken a snap of her holding it. When she'd told Taylor about it, he'd called her a stupid cow.

The 3-tonner trawled the bluepaddled night: they were on a dirt-track, sawing through cultivated fields, through plots of wasteland with tattered datepalms, rashes of goatgrass, saltbush thickets. They came to an illegible signpost, twisted, bent, riddled with bulletholes.

'This is it,' Taylor croaked. 'Pull off the road, matey.'

They could see the RV from here – a battered Marmon-Harrington lorry parked in the scrub. They were within a hundred yards of it when Taylor said, '*Stop.*'

Davis brought the 3-tonner to a standstill, cut out the motor, peeked at his captor. 'What you goin' . . .'

Taylor shushed him with a muzzleprod in the ribs, surveyed the scene intently.

'Where's the bleedin' fire?' he gurned. 'Mitch always lights a fire . . .'

At that moment, Davis cracked the door, rolled out of the cab, landed on all fours, hared off into the thorns, boots scuffing hardpack earth. Taylor roared, leapt down after him, levelled the Colt at his retreating back.

'*Don't shoot him!*' Maddy screeched.

Taylor let the weapon fall, swivelled to scan the RV, saw no sign of movement. He sifted the night. 'He'll bring the rozzers,' he growled.

Maddy dropped down from the cab, slung her cape and handbag, covered an arc with her revolver. Taylor was stalking towards her when the first gunshots lashed out of the darkness − *bayowww, bayowww, bayo-www*: bullets squiffed air, thwocked space, droned past Maddy's head. Taylor hunkered, fired a volley in the direction of the Marmon-Harrington. Maddy heard the *grump, grump, grump* of his pistol, heard air *hooosh*, saw a balloon tyre rupture, saw the 3-tonner list. She pumped two shots starwards, saw smoke luft, ate sourgas reek. A motor groused, a jeep belted towards them, headlights flared. Maddy was caught in the beams: Taylor clutched her, heaved her down, came back up into a crouch, popgunned a broadside straight into the blinding lights. Maddy heard crumps, heard ragged howls, saw the jeep stall, heard the engine sputter. Taylor was already dashing into the headlights, wild hair flying. *'Come on,'* he crowed.

Maddy bolted after him in hurdler strides, reached the jeep, found him shifting the body of a slim young sergeant off the passenger seat. The NCO had copped a round in the chest: his BD blouse was a bloody pulp. On Maddy's side a woman subaltern with a bush of flaming red hair was draped over the steering wheel, clutching at a throatwound with redslicked fingers, bubbling at the mouth.

Taylor dumped the sergeant, leapt into his seat. *'Get in,'* he stormed. 'Can't drive at night one-eyed.'

Maddy hesitated. 'She's badly hurt,' she said. She scrabbled in her handbag, found a field dressing, ripped it open with her teeth. She pulled the woman out of the jeep, laid her in the dirt, pressed the dressing on her wound. The girl's dovecoloured eyes stared at her blankly: blood trickled from her nostrils.

'Leave her,' Taylor weazled. 'Get in, for fuck's . . .'

'Hey, you there, stop,' a voice cripped. *'Military police.'*

Taylor ranged the Colt, lowballed barbs of fire. He was answered by the *booomfff, booomff, booomff* of .303 rifles. Maddy heard air slashed, ducked, clamped the redhead's hand over the dressing. 'Just keep it there, love. You'll be fine.' The girl's eyes were still fixed on Maddy's face, but there was recognition in them now. Her cracked lips worked. Maddy was about to pull away when the girl grasped her wrist feebly. *'Betty,'* she spluttered. *'Betty Nolan.'*

The words hit Maddy like a punch: she staggered

backwards, wrenched her hand away. *Booommfff, boummfff, boummff.* Rounds whined past her ear, kicked up dirt. 'Come *on*,' Taylor bawled.

Maddy sprang behind the wheel, shifted the gearstick, hit the starter, heard the motor fire. She engaged gear, wrenched the hand throttle: the engine blared, the jeep beetled out into the night, scooted away through a gauntlet of fire.

16

It was full dark when Caine's crew got back to the el-Fayya bridge. Caine called a halt, instructed Copeland and Wallace to check the parapet for recent disturbance, told Trubman and Fiske to set up a trip-flare on a wire stretched across the road: it would give them early warning if Jerry tried to sneak across in the dark. He carried his Thompson fifteen paces back along the track, stood stock still, strained his ears for the rumble of Hun vehicles creeping up the track. He heard nothing but the seashell vacancy of the night. He was satisfied the enemy wasn't following closely: after the ambush, they'd be wary of getting bumped again. If they wanted the black box as desperately as they seemed to, though, they'd be here sooner or later.

He took in the great bowl of darkness beyond the ridge, the threequarter moon riding the reaches of space, skimming the lustre from a million pinwheel stars. Far away, beyond invisible hills, he clocked a lash of dry lightning – a burst of bright filaments like clutching tentacles etched for an instant behind his eyes.

He paced back to the jeeps: the bridge lay basking in moonshine – limestone blocks, spandrels, arches, like the relic of some ancient empire. Vast dark wedges of escarpment closed in from either side. The blockhouse was folded into blacker shadows beyond, skulking between alternating slabs of silvered light. He stepped carefully over Trubman's tripwire, got the thumbs-up from Copeland and Wallace. 'OK, ladies,' he said. 'Let's leaguer up in the old place, get a brew on. After that we'll blow the bridge.'

They recrossed the bridge, drove through the gap guarded by the gunpit, drew the wagons into the tamarix grove beneath the blockhouse. They jumped down, stretched, pissed, smoked cigarettes cupped in palms. The thrill of the contact had receded, leaving only a bonedeep weariness: they were dead on their feet. Caine moved to the edge of the grove, squatted among buckbush and boulders like medicine balls, studied the night. He called Jizzard, ordered him to watch. Back at his jeep, Quinnell and Fiske were standing with big Wallace: the giant was holding the black box over his head like a barbell, his teeth a mouthful of white light. 'See that, skipper,' he rumbled. 'Don't weigh no more'n a feather now. You never see nothin' so rum in yer life.'

He lowered the box, set it at Caine's feet like an offering, slipped out his bayonet, pressed the blade against the top, where the legend 'STENDEC' was stencilled. The blade didn't stick – the magnetic field had gone. Caine knelt down, ran a calloused hand along one side of the box. Like the derelict's fuselage, he'd have sworn it wasn't metal – but if so, how come it had magnetic properties? How could a magnetic field come and go? What about the heat the box had generated after they'd taken it from the aircraft? He thumped it lightly with the side of his fist. Trubman had talked about resin: this might be some oilbased substance like Bakelite, though without its smoothness. He rubbed his hand back and forth vigorously, held his fingers up to his nostrils: you could tell Bakelite from the oily smell, but this stuff seemed odourless. He shook his head. Wallace was right again – it was the oddest thing he'd ever seen. The whole episode – the unmarked aircraft, the nonexistent crew, Pickney's ghost, the black box – had left him with a sense of disquiet, as if he'd crossed some forbidden boundary, transgressed some unwritten law.

Copeland gave him a cigarette: Caine lit it with his Zippo. 'I thought the magnetic field might affect the motor,' Cope said. 'I was waiting for her to conk any second.'

Caine palmed his fag, pouted smoke, scanned the leaguered jeeps, took in Trubman at the tailboard of the W/T wagon, working the No. 19 set. Quinnell and Wallace were still examining the box: Fiske stood looking on from a distance, smoking his pipe. 'The big question,' Caine sniffed, 'is what we're going to do with it.'

Trubman tramped up to him, M1 carbine crooked in an elbow, his face gruelcoloured in the ambient light. 'No comms, skipper,' he announced. 'No response from Captain Fraser.'

Caine swore. He'd been hoping for Fraser's advice on what to do with the box. He hadn't compromised *Nighthawk*, not yet – there was still time to blow the bridge – but at least Fraser might have taken this other responsibility off his hands.

Copeland blew a jet of smoke. 'Dump it, skipper,' he said. 'Whatever it is, it's not what we came for.'

Don't touch the black box. Leave it where it is.

No, he had never heard those words: Maurice Pickney was six feet under. He shivered, realized the night had turned chill. Part of him wanted to jettison the box. On the other hand, if the Hun had sent a column to salvage it, it must be important. There was a third, hazier feeling, he realized: that the black box was special – almost a hallowed object: to abandon it would be sacrilege.

'I say we open it,' Wallace boomed. He held up a hammer he'd retrieved from the toolbox, his face an ogremask. 'I betcha it ain't that tough. Few strokes of Bessie here will do the trick.'

'You're bloody joking,' Copeland stormed. 'You'll get us blown to kingdom come.'

He appealed to Caine. 'We haven't got time for this nonsense, skipper. Let's get on with the job.'

Caine knew he was right: *Whatever you do, skipper, don't touch the black box* . . . Those words again: Caine was tempted to smash the box open just to prove to himself that he couldn't have heard them. Despite his eery feeling that the box was somehow sacred, the evidence that it might be dangerous, he felt an almost overpowering lust to know what was inside. That would be enough, he thought: just a dekko at what it contained, then they'd bury it somewhere.

Fiske moved in with quick lurching strides. 'We should be cautious, sir,' he said sharply. 'Mr Copeland is right. It could kill us all.'

'*Cautious,*' Wallace cackled. 'You got a bleedin' nerve, you 'ave. After what happened on the . . .' He broke off, looked away, wiped his mouth with the back of a coalshovel hand.

Fiske's intervention had tipped Caine over the edge. 'All right, Fred,' he said. 'Let's give it a go.'

Copeland shook his head in exasperation: Wallace boned a meatsaw grin. Caine shouldered his Tommy, picked up the box, noted with surprise that it actually did feel much lighter than when he'd taken it from Fiske at the derelict. 'Come on, Fred,' he said. 'Let's see what makes it tick.'

He laid the box down five yards away. Copeland and Trubman followed, looked on from a couple of paces: Fiske and Quinnell hung back in the treeshadows. Wallace planted puncheon legs either side of the box, raised the hammer, soughed a breath.

'*Stop that now,*' a wirecutter voice snapped. Wallace froze: Caine rounded, clocked Fiske standing behind them with his Colt. 45 levelled squarely at Wallace. His face was pewtergrey, eyes like dark gimlets. 'No one touches the box,' he said. 'Put the hammer down, Wallace.'

Wallace flexed his massive biceps, stood up, bull-horned laughter. 'You're off yer chump, mate. Always thought you was —'

The pistol dropkicked, spasmed flame: a round caterwauled over Wallace's skull, missed it by inches. The big man bobbed, yowed curses. Copeland's rifle was at his shoulder, Caine went for his sidearm: there came a strident clack of cocking handles from the nearest jeep. '*Ah wudnae be hasty,*' a gleeful voice piped out.

Caine saw Jizzard braced behind the twin Vickers in his wagon, not ten paces away, levelling the guns in their direction. Almost simultaneously, Quinnell swept out of Jizzard's line of fire, stood poised with his legs apart, covered them with his .303. The Irishman's jowls were granite.

Caine let his hand drop, felt sweat creep down his spine, felt his throat contract. *They're all mixed up with* STENDEC *in one way or another*, Pickney had said, *even your crew*. Was this what he'd meant?

'What in the name of shit is *this*?' he rasped. 'You going to shoot us all, or what?'

'Just lay your weapons down,' Fiske monotoned. 'Or yes, we'll knock off the lot of you.'

Quinnell traversed the muzzle of his rifle. 'We're not playing April fools here,' he rapped. 'Put your shootin' irons and gewgaws where we can see them. Don't try anything funny.'

Caine caught Copeland's eye, saw his own incredulity mirrored in his mate's dark face. He eyetrailed Jizzard in the jeep: the Scotsman was a whinger and a bully, but Caine had little doubt he was capable of killing in cold blood as long as he had the upper hand. He licked his lips, nodded to Copeland, lifted his Thompson very slowly, pokeydrilled it at arm's length, grounded arms. He laid his Colt, bayonet and grenades beside it, looked up to see his comrades doing the same.

Fiske's lips were taut, his eyes milkblue glaciers. 'Now,'

he said, 'move away from your weapons. I want you to kneel down, hands on your heads.'

'You know this is mutiny,' Copeland said.

'Mutiny's a rebellion against legal authority, so it is,' Quinnel soured. 'Youse have no authority over me.'

Fiske aimed his Colt at Caine's belly. '*Get down*,' he creaked.

Caine knelt on hard earth, clasped hands over his head, saw Copeland, Trubman and Wallace hunker. He felt furious, not just at Fiske, but at himself. They'd all known that *Nighthawk* was dodgy: they'd been expecting something from the start.

'Good, now tie 'em up, Quinnell,' Fiske ordered.

Quinnell slingbraced his Lee-Enfield, brought hanks of cut rope from his haversack: Caine recognized the vandalized climbing rope from earlier, realized that this move must have been planned even before they'd investigated the derelict plane.

Quinnell leaned over Caine, wrenched his arms behind him, tied his wrists: Caine winced – he still bore the scars of Caversham's handcuffs there from three days ago. He felt the rope cut into his flesh, felt the ground painful under his knees. He stared at Fiske. 'Why are you doing this?' he demanded.

The thin man's gravedigger face was an iron mask. 'I've got orders to retrieve the black box,' he said. 'You're in the way.'

The hairs on Caine's neck bristled. *The black box*. That was insane. They hadn't picked up the Mayday signal until after they'd arrived at the bridge, hadn't known of the box's existence until they'd found the STENDEC aircraft. Even the decision to investigate hadn't been a foregone conclusion.

Caine remembered how Fiske's dismissive attitude to the *downed aircrew* had played a part in his determination to go and look for them. He recalled how keen he had been for them to take the box, how he'd argued against handing it over to the Jerries. He must have known about it from the start, must have been aware of the derelict plane, known her location, known that Caine's patrol would pick up the Mayday signal, and – most damning of all – *known* for certain that Caine would make a rescue bid, especially if he argued the opposite way: *I have orders*, he'd said.

'Orders?' Caine grunted. 'Orders from who?'

'From the *powers that be*, the big cheeses. Does it matter? The same arseholes who made this shitty war, the same bastards who'll be left sitting on their wallets when it's all over, after millions of us morons have got scragged.'

'The *legal authorities*,' Quinnell cut in, finishing off Trubman's tie. 'The ones who murdered and starved the Irish for generations.'

'If that's the case,' Copeland challenged him. 'Why are you carrying out their orders?'

Fiske sniffed. 'We're *all* following their orders. They *own* us. All we can do in this life, my friend, is look after number one and let the devil take the hindmost. That's what I'm doing.'

'What about the mission?' Caine said.

'Stuff the mission. Let the Huns shaft Freyberg. It's no skin off my nose.'

Blood drained from Caine's face. He shook his head in disbelief. Fiske's orders hadn't come from GHQ — that was certain: blowing the el-Fayya bridge was crucial to Monty's push. No, someone had used *Nighthawk* as a decoy for a spot of private enterprise: it must have been Caversham and Co. The jigsaw pieces fell into place with a snap — the way they'd been dragooned into the scheme, the deployment of ex-detainees, Caversham's claptrap about *personnel whose absence will go unnoticed*. The gorilla-man had wafted fake photos of Betty Nolan under his nose to forestall his objections. That meant Nolan was dead: probably Angela Brunetto too. He and his crew had been the ideal stooges: reliable, expendable, easily disposable, no one else likely to cause a fuss about it, and — as far as Maskelyne and Glenn were concerned — they *had it coming*. They'd found the ideal way of getting back at Caine and his chums, while pulling off some secret objective of their own.

Quinnell collected the discarded weapons: Fiske lowered his pistol, shifted closer. Jizzard slipped down from the jeep, jounced over to them. He picked up Caine's Tommy-gun with its outsize magazine, weighed it in his hands. 'Always did fancy this trenchsweeper,' he gloated.

'Pity you ain't got the muscle or the guts to use it then,' Wallace sneered.

Jizzard hit him in the teeth with the butt, mashed his lip. Wallace blew tooth fragments, hoiked spats of blood. 'Like I said,' he mouthed. 'You ain't got the guts.'

Jizzard raised the Thompson to lamp him again. '*Stop*,' Fiske yipped. 'Don't play with your dinner, Jizzard. Let's get this over.'

'With pleasure,' Jizzard grinned. He inspected Wallace's bleeding mouth. 'By the way, big man,' he said. 'It was me who cut the ropes.' He mimicked Wallace's gruff tones. '*What I wanna know is 'oo drew 'em from the stores.*'

'Fuck you.'

Jizzard chunked the Tommy-gun's working parts. Caine stared into the muzzle of his own weapon: his heart galloped. After all the ferocious battles against the Axis he'd taken part in, he was going to be shot with his own weapon, by one of his own men. It was almost funny. He closed his eyes, thought of Nolan: he was afraid to die, but he was lost without her anyway.

Nothing happened. Caine opened his eyes, saw Jizzard holding the submachine-gun indecisively. His face was creampale in the starlight: he'd lost his cocksure pose. To his right, Quinnell, too, hesitated, his face shiny with sweat. 'This isn't right,' he burst out, glaring at Fiske. 'I'll not slaughter comrades in cold blood, so I won't.'

Fiske's mouth stayed tight. '*Comrades*?' he scoffed. 'What happened to the *legal authorities* blather, then?' He turned to the Scotsman. 'Kill them, Jizzard.'

Caine saw perspiration drop from Jizzard's slablike chin: he shifted the Thompson, lowered it, backed away. 'Nah,' he spluttered. 'I cannae do it. These lads are our own.'

He threw the weapon down in disgust, wheeled to

face Fiske. 'You're the big effendi,' he said. 'You wannae shoot them, do it yersel'.'

Fiske raised his pistol. Quinnell knocked it aside with his rifle-butt. '*No*,' he bawled. 'We're not murdering our own boys, Fiske, I don't give a flying shit what our orders are.'

Fiske's eyes were cold marbles: he examined his own weapon in silence for a long moment, then, to Caine's surprise, replaced it in its holster. 'All right,' he said. 'Perhaps we don't want their blood on our hands. My orders were to ensure that they were *not in a position* to stop us. I think we can say we've effectively done that.'

'Aye,' Jizzard huffed. 'Let the Krauts decide what to do with them. Our hands are clean.'

Fiske wheeled round jerkily. 'Quinnell,' he ordered. 'Tie their legs. Jizzard, put the black box in your jeep. Put the other wagons out of action – we won't be needing them. Let's get this pathetic excuse for a show on the road.'

17

The farm stood on saltcrusted earth among tilted datepalms, on one of the minor channels of the Delta. They arrived about midnight, breathless after bowling helterskelter along dark backroads: the moon was down, the sky a gown of black silk and purple gauze, sequinned with stars. Maddy stopped the jeep at the gate, hooted: unseen hands dragged open the doors. She drove into a yard of shadows, crossbeamed with bars of window-light. She pulled up, let out a long *ooofff* of relief, flopped over the steering wheel.

Most of the space was hidden in darkness: stucco walls like bad teeth, denuded palm planks, cart hulks, fragments of tractors, perished tyres, oxidized engine blocks, teetering dovecotes limed with guano, a collec-tion of vehicular oddments the deserters kept going on rubber bands and chewing gum – an Itie lorry, a saloon, a pickup, a couple of motorbikes. The walls enclosed the derelict farmhouse – a mudbrick oblong with a concave roof on the point of collapse. Halfdressed men and sloweyed girls drifted out of the shadows, ambled drowzily around them. *Where's the goods? Where's Jizzard?*

'Rozzers musta nabbed 'im,' Taylor whickered. 'Field Security was waitin' for us, see. Must've 'ad a tipoff.'

'Calvin ain't goin' to be happy.'

'Calvin can get stuffed. We on'y got away by the skin of our teeth.'

Maddy slithered out of her seat, leaned heavily against the jeep's hull, waved away questions. She felt drained: her hands were still shaking, her fingers were stiff with the redhead's blood. Taylor hustled her inside the house, through an unkempt room that smelt of piss and hookah tobacco, sat her down on a palliasse in her lamplit sleeping quarters. He stroked her face with his big hands, kissed her neck. Maddy moaned: the thrill of dodging death, of outrunning the hunters, had left her hot. For an instant she was tempted to surrender. She felt grateful to Taylor for rescuing her from the streets, for protecting her. All she knew about him was that he was an orphanage brat who'd joined the army because it was the only job he could get. He was crusty and quick-tempered, but he could also be kind. She knew that he was devoted to her, craved her like a drug. Yet, as always, something stopped her from giving herself to him. She went rigid, pulled away. 'I can't,' she said.

Taylor insinuated his face into hers, ate up the soft eyes, the pillow lips, the faraway, almost *pleading* expression. Resistance was just a game she played, he thought. She knew it drove him wild, made him mad to have her, to screw her until she begged him to stop. He dragged her down on the palliasse, crushed her under him, raked her hair. 'You *like* it,' he growled. 'You *love* it.'

Maddy was aware that there was something in her that derived pleasure from knowing that men lusted

143

after her, just as there was a part of her that desired to be roughly handled. She kept a tight lid on those feelings, though: they weren't for Taylor.

'For Christ's sake, stop,' she said. 'You'll never have me like this.'

She went limp under him, as if all her fight were gone, her face set in a glower of determination that Taylor recognized: she was about to play the old limp-rag ploy. He sighed and let her up. He fetched a bottle of whisky from a cupboard, removed the cap, gulped liquor. Maddy adjusted the oil lamp, caught sight of herself in the cracked mirror hanging on the wall. Someone was lurking there, someone she didn't recognize – a dishevelled girl with bloody hands, bitten nails, ratty hair, soapfilled eyes: someone she might have known long ago, whose name she couldn't recall.

She lit cigarettes, gave one to Taylor, took the whisky bottle from him. She swallowed amber fluid, felt it bite at the back of her tongue, shuddered. She set the bottle on the table, smoked.

Taylor squatted on the palliasse, ogled her with resentment, wet his lips. She smoked the cigarette down, stubbed it in the ashtray, saw the bloodstains on her hands as if she hadn't noticed them before. She examined her fingers curiously, scrubbed at the stains with her broken nails, thought of the dead sergeant, the wounded redhead. The girl had called her Betty Nolan: the name had hit her like a bomb. The woman had recognized her, she was sure of it. If not, why did *Betty*

Nolan sound so right? She tried to remember, found herself straining after fleeing phantoms at the edge of her memory: it was impossible to follow them into the abyss beyond. Tears of frustration pricked up in the corners of her eyes: she held on to the table, broke down in rattling sobs.

Taylor stared at her one-eyed, then laid aside his eyepatch – a distinguishing mark whose removal could change his appearance quickly: both of his eyes were sound. He watched Maddy with an owlish face. ''Ere, what the 'eck's the matter with you, girl? We bin through worse than that.'

'The redhead,' Maddy said. 'She knew me.'

'Don't talk daft. She was delirious.'

'She called me Betty Nolan.'

'*Betty Nolan?* That don't mean a damn' thing.'

Taylor got up with slow deliberation. Maddy faced him: salt slivers tracked her cheeks. She wiped them away with blooded fingers. 'You killed that sergeant. You shouldn't have done it.'

Taylor screwed up his stone-carved face. 'What was I supposed to do, eh? They wasn't playin' pattercake.'

Maddy shivered, wrapped her arms round her shoulders. 'We have rules, Taylor. No killing, *remember.*'

'Maybe the rules 'ave changed.'

'Who says?'

His Adam's apple tightened. 'It come from the top, from *Calvin.* ''Is orders is to knock off anyone as gets in the way.'

'You lying swine.'

Taylor's black eyes swam. He pinched her arms with powerful fingers, shook her. 'No bint calls me a liar.'

Maddy slapped him with an open palm. He recoiled, his mouth blowfished. 'I'll bleedin' kill yer.'

He pushed her shoulders with both hands. Maddy lost her balance, tripped over the palliasse, fell backwards: her head clunked the solid wall. For a moment she lay on the floor, stunned: her senses somersaulted, tiny electric charges pinprickled her body, arclights strobed and spindled, constellations of memory starburst like popping Very flares, dazzling images blew through her head like shards of a shattered mirror: yellowblue desert, sandcoloured armoured cars wheeling, guffs of white smoke, men with gore-red wounds, a machine-gun clattering, shells thumping, veloursheened desert night seen from an aircraft, a parachutist broken on stony ground, a beautiful Senussi girl tossing raven hair, an officer with powerful shoulders and a blunt, freckled face, the crump of a car hitting the dark meniscus of the Nile. *Betty Nolan*, she thought. *Captain Betty Nolan. Honorary Captain Elizabeth Jane Nolan*, GM *and bar. I am charged to record His Majesty's high appreciation . . .* Names and faces elbowed, jostled for room. '*Johann Eisner*,' she murmured,' *Heinrich Rohde, Mary Goddard, Hekmeth Fahmi, David Stirling, John Stocker, Angela Brunetto, Tom Caine.*' She paused, drawn by the last name. A barrier collapsed, a veil dropped: her throat caught, her eyes filled with tears. '*Caine*,' she whispered. '*Sergeant Tom Caine. Lieutenant Tom Caine. Lieutenant Thomas Edward*

Caine, DCM, DSO. *Lieutenant Thomas Edward Caine,* DCM, DSO, 1ˢᵗ *Special Air Service Regiment.*' She opened her eyes, saw Taylor crouching over her with a mournful expression. 'It were an accident, darlin',' he said. 'I didn't mean to push you that 'ard.'

18

He was belly down, wrists and ankles bound tight: his jaw was numb from contact with the earth. Caine felt a deep, visceral hatred for Fiske and the others, and for whoever had put them up to this treachery, but his chief loathing was reserved for himself. The worst aspect of it was that, not for the first time, the bastards had anticipated him. The only thought he'd had when the last echoes of the jeep's motor had dopplered out in the night, though, was that Fiske had gone off with the Nobel 808. That meant *Nighthawk* had failed before it started: even if they got free, they no longer had the means to carry it out.

Big Wallace grunted, strained at his bonds. '*Cocksuckers*,' he guttered. 'If I ever get my hands on them fuckin' rats, I'll wring their scrawny necks, I'll . . . *Christ*, these bleedin' ropes are tight.'

'Don't waste your energy, mate.' Copeland's scoff came out of the darkness. 'You won't break 'em by brute strength.'

'Why, what *you* goin' to do, yer majesty?' Wallace grouched. 'Work it out by arithmetic? Or mebbe you want to lie here like a pound of rottin' haddock, till them Death's Head blighters stick a bayonet up yer arse.'

'I reckon mine are loose, boys,' Trubman gasped from Wallace's right. 'I got small hands, see.'

'Better get on with it then,' Cope cackled bitterly. 'It's a long walk back to Fraser's lines.'

'Belt up a minute,' Wallace shushed him. 'I heard sommat.'

Caine lifted his head, cocked his ears. The night was crisp and silent, the sky a leadgrey dome with pigtails of stars looped in shadowed recesses, lapped across by the gossamer trails of the Milky Way. Nobody spoke. Caine heard the scuff of movement, the chink of disturbed stones: someone was moving towards their position furtively in the darkness, he was sure of it – creeping up on them in fits and starts. His jaw tightened: his fingers itched for a weapon. His first notion was that Fiske's crew had come back, his second that it was Arabs intent on looting. His blood pounded, neckhairs twinged: he'd never felt so vulnerable. He tried to turn over, made a futile attempt to scrabble to his feet, heard more footsounds, wondered if it could be an animal. No, but not Arabs either: they went barefoot, silent as spirits. He tilted his head back, heard the scufflings clearly, saw smokeshadows coalesce into closer densities of darkness: not an animal, but men – a pair of them. His heart whomped, his muscles tensed, his breath stabbed. An aching anticipation filled him: he waited for the click of a bolt that never came.

'Cap'n Caine?' a hollow voice rasped. 'That you?'

Even before the men had separated from the anonymity of the darkness, he knew who it was: Cutler–Mike

Cutler, Lancejack, ex-Scots Borderers, a limber youth who'd been in his 'A' Squadron troop in the Western Desert. An instant later Cutler stood unsteadily over them in the milklight, tall, emaciated, lankhaired, bearded and filthy, his BD in tatters, his eyes craters in a bleachedout face. With him was another SAS soldier Caine recognized, Trooper Shorty Grimshaw, a stumpy man with shotputter's shoulders and a sedgebush beard. Grimshaw, too, was ragged, pale and twitchy: neither of them carried kit or weapons other than bayonets, Caine noticed. What really amazed him, though, was that they were here at all. They'd both been listed as captured with David Stirling's party back in January.

'What the blazes are you doing here?' Caine growled at them. 'I thought you were nabbed with Stirling.'

'Not quite . . .' Cutler began.

'What you waiting for, the bleedin' *Armistice*?' Wallace roared. 'Cut us free, you bloody great bloops.'

Caine was amazed to find that the damage to the jeeps was slight. The deserters had disconnected the camshaft arms, ripped out sparkplug connections: it seemed that their hearts hadn't been in it. He inspected the motors, ran his hands from part to part, built up a mental picture of the damage: both motors were reparable, he thought. He glanced up to see Trubman's bulk hunched over the No. 19 set on the rear ramp. The signaller's eyes were invisible behind lenses that held dim miniatures of the moon. 'They did a good job on the wireless, skipper,' he said morosely.

'Can you fix it, Taff?'

'I dunno. These sets are very sensitive, see, and —'

'Just do your best, mate,' Caine cut him off.

It was painstaking work, even with the assistance of the whole crew. Often, Caine forced himself to stop, took half a dozen breaths, reminded himself that you couldn't rush a job like this. What was needed was clear thinking: a methodical approach. His fingers worked deftly, connecting camshaft arms, reconstructing torn cable, reconnecting tubes. When the motors finally flared into life, there was a subdued round of cheers.

Wallace tooled Cutler and Grimshaw up with grenades and spare weapons: Grimshaw got Fiske's ditched Bren gun. The giant was about to hand Cutler a .303, when he hesitated, considered the weapon as if he were having second thoughts 'You sure you remember how to use a rifle, Corp?' he said teasingly. Cutler snatched the .303 from his big paw, slid out the magazine, clicked the bolt, checked the breach, snapped the mag back on. He held up the Lee-Enfield with one hand, clamped the other hand over his balls, recited:

'This is my rifle,
This is my gun,
This one's for fighting
And this one's for fun.'

Wallace hawed with laughter, clapped the youth on the shoulder, tipped his shaggy head to one side. 'You sure you ain't forgot 'ow to use yer *gun*, an' all?'

The SAS men slumped down under the trees. Caine lit

a cigarette, pondered a question that had been bothering him: why hadn't Caversham tasked him to retrieve the black box *and* blow the bridge? Either he hadn't wanted him and his mates blabbing about the box once they got back, or he'd done some deal to scrag the four of them out of pure spite. Or maybe Caversham himself had been on the level, and Fiske was working for someone else. At least, thanks to unexpected qualms of conscience from Jizzard and Quinnell, they were still alive.

Copeland treated Caine's ropeburns with salve from the medical kit, doled out Benzedrine tablets to the crew. Wallace broke out a flagon of Wood's *Rocketfuel* brandy, boiled water on a Tommy-cooker. He handed out mugs of tea, thick with sugar, Carnation milk, generous lashings of Wood's. The big man racked up a grin, a starlit glimpse of chipped incisors, lips swollen the size of frankfurters. 'This'll perk you up, lads,' he told Grimshaw and Cutler, who were sprawling close together in the darkness. 'Don't knock it all back at once, mind. The shock to yer insides'll make yer puke.'

'That's an everyday hazard with your tea, mate,' Copeland smirked.

Caine wiped motor-oil off his hands with a rag. Wallace thrust a mug in his direction, towering over him like a dark chess piece, eyeballs bleached in the cream-cake light. Caine took the mug, gulped at the mixture, felt the rocketfuel scour his palate, coughed. 'That's damn' *good*,' he declared hoarsely. '*Blimey*, I needed that.' He lifted the mug, saluted the newcomers. 'You saved our necks, lads. We owe you.'

'Shame you didn't get here a bit more sharpish, though, *innit*?' Wallace humphed. 'Before Fiske got away with the demolition kit.'

Cutler took a swipe of tea, swilled it round, swallowed. He gasped, examined the milky liquid with startled eyes. He was one of the youngest men in the regiment, Caine recalled – last time they'd met he'd looked about sixteen. Now, though, he had to search Cutler's features hard to find the relics of that youth, concealed under the ingrained dirt, the ragged beard, the sunravaged flesh. 'We heard our booby trap go off hours ago,' Cutler said. His voice was boyish, frayed at the edges. 'That's why we came to the bridge.'

'*Your* booby trap,' Wallace howled. 'Gimme that tea back now. You fuckin' *arseholes*. It was you as rigged up that pressure-release wire?' You nearly did for me, you . . . you . . .' He pointed dumbly to the wound on his neck, realized for the first time that the dressing had gone.

'Lay off the agony, Fred,' Grimshaw cackled. 'You're still 'ere, aintcha? Our last bit of 808 that was.'

'There was a twenty-second delay,' Cutler cut in. 'It wasn't meant to kill anyone. Just a warning for us.'

'We was up on the escarpment when it blew,' Grimshaw explained. 'Saw you trottin' off, like. Mike thought 'e recognized yer – couldn't miss Big Fred there, anyway.'

He burst into a paroxysm of coughing, slopped tea, steadied his mug with his left hand. He must have been about five years older than Cutler, Caine reckoned, squat with bandy legs, beerkeg chest, boarish head, split lips beneath the shaggy beard, eyes like marbles bulging from sagging eyepits. He didn't look much like a cavalryman, but Caine recalled he was Yeomanry: he'd worked as a coal delivery-boy before the war.

'We thought we'd missed the boat,' Cutler went on. 'Then we heard a hell of a firefight going on down in the valley. We thought you might have been slaughtered, the lot of you, but after dark, we heard your jeeps coming back. We knew you'd leaguered up here: we were coming in then, but there was a gunshot. A bit later a jeep took off – we didn't know what to make of it.'

'That was Fiske,' Wallace spat, 'and his two pet worms.'

'Who's Fiske? Never heard of a Fiske in "A" Squadron.'

Caine shook his head. 'He's not "A" Squadron, Mike. Not even SAS. It's a long story. Anyway, there was a bit of a barney. Fiske and two other lads buggered off with the explosives.'

Cutler eyed him incredulously. 'A barney about what?'

'It were that bleedin' black box, *wannit?*' Wallace boomed.

Cutler and Grimshaw froze; ghosted eyes pinned Caine.

'*Black box*,' Cutler repeated. 'Don't tell me you were sent after it, too?'

'What do you mean, *too?*' Copeland demanded.

'That were *our* objective, weren't it?' Grimshaw chortled. 'I mean, the boss's – Stirlin''s – that was why he come on the scheme. I mean, you don't need a half-colonel for a demolition job, do you?'

An icy finger walked Caine's spine: his napehair tingled. He took a shufti at Copeland: his mate's face was grave. All Caine knew about Stirling's mission back in January was that the patrol had entered Tunisia not long after Tripoli had fallen, with six jeeps and fourteen men. They'd made a bold rush through the coastal bottleneck known as the Gabes Gap, planning to hit the Sousse railway the same night. They'd lain up by day in a wadi, been spotted, boxed and bagged by the Hun. According to Johnny Cooper, only he, Mike Sadler and the Frenchman, Taxis, had got away. Cooper obviously hadn't realized that Cutler and Grimshaw had also escaped. 'Wait a minute,' he said. 'You're telling me that Stirling wasn't planning to blow the railway?'

'Nope, I'm not saying that, sir. The railway job was a sort of cover. Mr Stirling had special orders on top of that: to locate a derelict aircraft, and to salvage a black box. Only we never got that far.'

There was a loaded silence while Caine wrestled with the revelation. Stirling had come for the black box – the box that the Jerries had tried to bargain for, the box that Fiske and the others had mutinied to acquire, the box that had caused all the grief. He fumbled for words: Copeland beat him to it. 'I talked to Cooper,' he said suspiciously. 'How come *he* never mentioned a black box?'

'You mean Johnny got back?' Cutler asked in a wondering voice. 'How the heck did he manage it?'

'He and Sadler and a Frenchman . . . Taxis, I think his name was . . .'

'*Freddie?*' Grimshaw gasped. 'He made it too?'

'Yep. They reached French lines at . . . I forget where it was. They made contact with the First Army, anyway. After a while they were flown back to Cairo.'

'Good lads,' Grimshaw said.

'Yes, but why didn't Johnny tell me about the black box?'

'Wouldn't have, would he?' Cutler retorted. 'Strictly speaking, I shouldn't have let the cat out of the bag either. After what you said about Fiske doing a bunk, though, I thought you needed to know.'

'Damn' right,' Caine said.

Copeland wasn't to be appeased. 'How come you weren't bagged with Stirling?'

'Steady on, Harry,' said Caine.

'No, it's all right,' Grimshaw said. 'We made a break for it, sir, hid out in the hills. Musta tabbed forty miles, right across these hills. We used that twin-peak – the one with two chimneys, Jebel Halluf – as a reference point.'

'*Halluf?*' Copeland said. 'I spotted it this afternoon. Johnny Cooper described it to me.'

'Anyway, we finally found the blockhouse here. Didn't seem to be frequented, so we used it as a base.'

'That explains the sign Quinnell and Jizzard clocked,' Caine commented.

'But Stirling was captured seven weeks ago,' Copeland cut in. 'How did you survive for seven weeks?'

Cutler sighed. 'Hares, birds, grasshoppers, berries, nettles, you name it, sir. We liberated some compo rations – that kept us going for a while. Begged stuff off A-rabs. It wasn't exactly a picnic.'

Caine was going to ask why they hadn't headed for a French outpost like Cooper and the others, when Cope butted in again. 'No one back in Egypt could credit Stirling's capture. Everyone thought he was invincible.'

'Maybe started to believe it hisself,' Wallace commented. 'Got sloppy.'

Cutler sipped tea, sniffed thoughtfully. 'I tell you what, sir, it was dead fishy. Take that laying-up place in the wadi, for instance. I'd swear Mr Stirling didn't pick it at random – I think he was looking for it . . .'

'Yeah,' Grimshaw nodded. 'It was like he knew where to go.'

Caine pulled on his chinstubble. 'A pre-arranged RV? He'd agreed to meet someone, maybe? A local guide?'

'Maybe,' Cutler shrugged. 'Only he never said so. Then there was the Hun unit that nabbed us – skyblue uniforms we'd never seen before. You've seen these hills, sir – there's a million wadis like the one we were in. Yet they homed in on us like bugs on a stinkpile – like they were *expecting* to find us there.'

'It felt like a trap,' Grimshaw nodded.

Caine considered it, wondered if it could be true. Only this morning, Copeland had said that Johnny Cooper had claimed the same thing. Grimshaw and Cutler looked worn out, but their minds seemed sharp enough. He told them about the STENDEC Mayday signal, the derelict aircraft, the box's bizarre qualities, the Death's Head unit sent to retrieve it, how Fiske and the others had cleared out. 'We came here to do a job

157

on the bridge,' he concluded. 'Fiske and his pals were marching to a different tune. Christ knows who put 'em up to it. Now they've run out with our demolition charges *as well as* the box: we're about a million miles up the creek without a paddle.'

Caine cleaned his mug grimly with a handful of sand, returned it to his knapsack. 'Whoever ordered Fiske to get that box has put the mockers on the whole campaign,' he said. 'Not only were they ready to condone mutiny, they were also prepared to let the Krauts encircle Freyberg. There's one thing for certain: that box must be something special – or, at least, *somebody* thinks so.'

For a moment nobody spoke: it was Cutler who broke the silence. 'Don't you reckon we should get after those chaps right away, sir? They can't have more than a couple of hours on us, and there's no way they can go but the old highroad. Maybe we can't call in support, but we could head 'em off. You'll get your demolition charges back as well as the box.'

'It makes sense,' Cope agreed.

Caine dekkoed his watch: another three hours till first light. If he knew anything about the Krauts, they'd show up right on the dot. He lit another fag, took long pulls: it felt like the last cigarette of a condemned man.

He glanced around at the shadowed faces, more animated now the Benzedrine had set in. He could feel the drug coursing through his body like a piledriver, shearing away fatigue, buffing his mind clean. He was tempted to agree with Cutler: the knowledge that Stirling himself had been after the black box made it even more intriguing, even more mysterious. It had to be the key to something big, and Caine felt an almost ravenous yearning to know what it was. On the other hand, once he'd committed himself to going after Fiske, Freyberg's flank would be wide open.

He stamped out the fag, spat into the sand, squared stiff shoulders. He looked straight at Cope, saw blue moonglow in his eyes. 'Even if we do get the explosives back, it'll be too late,' he said. 'The Krauts will have taken the bridge. Game over.'

'You ain't thinkin' of *holdin' it*?' Grimshaw shivered. "Scuse me, sir, but maybe you ain't noticed, there's only six of us 'ere. No 'eavy weapons, no air support.'

'We're SAS, though, ain't we? ' Wallace crooned.

'Does that make us bulletproof?' Cope said. 'The Jerries outnumber us a hundred to one, Fred. Blowing the bridge is one thing: making a stand against odds like that is another.'

'Yeah,' Grimshaw cut in. 'It's blinkin' suicide, that's what it is.'

They were right, Caine thought – a six-man crew against a motorized recce battalion – let alone an armoured division – would be a kamikaze action. The sick thing was that he was to blame for this: if he'd stuck to orders instead of gallivanting off after some phantom signal, the bridge would be down, the black box would still be where it belonged, and they'd be on their way back to Fraser's lines. *And then what? A life without Betty Nolan? Is that something I really look forward to?*

Whoever was behind this, they had scuppered him all

right, but he wasn't yet finished. His duty was clear. It was to defend Freyberg's rear so the Kiwis could penetrate the Tebaga Gap – so Monty's push could succeed. To hell with the black box: his first concern was the fate of the Eighth Army. Whatever happened, he was not going down in history as the officer whose negligence had knackered the Tunisian offensive. He couldn't live with that.

'The skipper's right,' Big Wallace rumbled. 'We can't go after the box *and* hold the bridge. Anyway, if we clear off now they'll say we was ratshit.' He stuck out his kerbstone chin. 'There ain't no yeller stripe down *my* back.'

'Yellow and stupid are two different things,' Cutler wheezed. 'Isn't that what Stirling always reckoned? SAS don't take on big battalions. SAS don't fight dingdongs. SAS aren't cannon fodder. Maybe it'd be all right if we'd got an icebucket's chance in hellfire of lasting more than five seconds, but we haven't.'

'That's not *entirely* true,' Copeland cut in musingly, as if analysing a proposition in a scientific debate. 'This place is an outstanding defensive position. The Hun can't go round: the only way they can approach is across that bridge.'

'It'll be bloody *Thermo-polly* next,' Wallace confided confidently. Cope beamed at him as if he were the class's star pupil. 'Thermopylae is a good example of what I mean: how a small force can fight off a much stronger enemy by compelling him to fight on a narrow front, where his strength is no advantage.'

'How many were they at Thermo – whatever?' Cutler grunted. 'I'll bet it was more than six.'

'Hah,' Wallace chuckled, 'they wasn't SAS, though, was they?'

'Exactly,' Caine grinned. 'Harry's right, too. We'd only have to hold off the troops or vehicles the Hun can get on the bridge at any one time.'

'Yep,' Copeland agreed, his voice excited now. 'As long as we're dug in we'll have a chance. Site the bazooka, the mortar, and the heavy machine-guns at the blockhouse. We'll have enfilade fire right down the bridge. The Krauts won't have anywhere to hide.'

'We've got two Brownings, and a Vickers "K",' Caine said. 'We can mount 'em on the defences, covered by the rocket launcher and mortar . . .'

'There's that gunpit by the gap, too,' Wallace added. 'A twenty-five pounder'd be just the job . . .'

'*Hey!*' Cutler's voice lashed. 'You're off yer rocker, mate. We ain't *got* a twenty-five pounder, *remember*?'

At that moment a flare *spooshed*, signed a high parabola over the blockhouse stump, plopped open in a green lattice, shed a soft hail of emerald stars. The SAS men stared. 'What the *Dickens* . . . ?' Caine exploded.

'My tripwire,' Trubman blinked. 'I think we're in business, boys.'

19

They moved out in double file, with Copeland and Caine on point, Bren-gunners Wallace and Grimshaw at the rear. Caine was proud of the way the men slipped instantly into tactical mode, after what they'd endured that day. They passed through the gap: Caine led them off the track to the right, gave the sign for arrowhead. They fanned out silently into formation, with the Brens on the flanks, moving slowly through the scrub, across the stonecobbled ground, listening for nightsounds, all senses trimmed. The pale masonry of the bridge came into Caine's view: a file of humped shapes was slinking towards them in the silklight, not fifty yards away.

Caine stiffened, his eyes went wide: his pulse leap-frogged. For an instant he groped in a timeless dimension, every action was an agonizing slowness, distant and abstract, as if this were happening to someone else. The Totenkopf patrol was creeping forward – four, five, six of them – trawling the ground with the care of men superbly disciplined, perfectly trained in tactical night movement. Caine caught moonlit details of faces, weapons, equipment, saw Hun bodies tense as they clocked the SAS patrol, saw weapons come up.

He tried to shout, found his words choked, as if his mouth were full of molasses. He saw Cope go down on one knee, saw his SMLE poke out from his shoulder, saw flame-red firegas bulb out from the muzzle, heard a *keeerackkk* that bludgeoned his senses. Caine held his Tommy-gun low, tweaked iron, blitzed a burst at the Totenkopf boys. He felt the weapon buck, felt the stock vibrate, felt the earth toss, smelt the burnt brass of ejected cases. He eased the trigger, registered the *rap-rap-rap-rap* of Brenfire right and left, heard the gnash of rifles, heard deep echoes like angry red threats rumble off rock walls.

He peered through smoke coils, saw Squareheads duck and hunker, heard Goth voices jabber. Weapons flashed: rounds whammied past him, sang with aching notes, plucked at the night with rippling echoes: airblast slapped at his eardrums, bonged in his head. Cutler ran out from his left, bellowed incoherently, rifle in one hand, a Mills bomb in the other: Caine saw him bowl the grenade overarm, saw Hun tracer swarm, saw Cutler beanbag over, heard him yell, '*I'm hit. I'm hit.*'

Caine gritted his teeth, picked a Kraut, fired from the hip with both eyes open, spewed long squalls of electric hail across the no-man's land *gumpa, gumpa, gumpa, gump*. The gun felt welded to his hands: it was like brandishing a long scythe of light. His ears were too dead to hear the Jerry's scream, but a part of him *felt* it, *felt* the snubnose bullets whamp, *felt* the shapeless lead pigs rupture organs, crepitate bone. He was just thinking, *Got the bastard*, when Cutler's grenade clamshelled with a wallop that snatched the air from his nostrils. Flame horned up, dirt and pebbles bow-waved, smoke-riffs blew.

Caine stopped shooting: Brens pumped, rifles cracked, a raft of green tracer groped through the smoke in slow threads. A Jerry slumped, another jack-knifed sideways: Copeland drilled .303 rimfire through his skull. A German almost the size of Wallace came lumping towards them screeching 'Totenkopf, Totenkopf,' a spudmasher in each mitt. He raised his hands to lob the bombs: Caine hit him with a five-round crumpler that sheared the flesh off his right thigh. The big Jerry toppled, crashed: the grenades bashawed in a double blast that hacked his body to bits: thundering after-blasts echoed off the scarp walls.

Caine felt the shockwave, felt his lungs squeezed. He swivelled off a last spurt, yodelled, *'That's enough, lads.'*

Silence fell: smoke vorticed, fusilgas reeked, nightbirds broke into squawking protest above. Caine swallowed, licked numbed lips. His weapon felt light in his hands and he realized the mag must be almost empty: he couldn't believe he'd fired the best part of fifty rounds. The contact had lasted a minute in all. He swapped mags with steady hands, swept a shufti around him: some of the boys were reloading, others watched the ground. Caine signalled advance. As the patrol inched forward Cutler stood up, clutching his left shoulder. His hand and arm were slick with blood where a Hun bullet had lacerated the hard muscle: the wound was cushy, though – the round hadn't struck bone. Caine gave him a field dressing, told him to go back to the leaguer and wait for them there.

Five of the Jerries were dead: maimed bodies with waxwork faces and vacant eyes, filmed with dirt. Close up, some of the wounds were gut-curdling: Caine saw a trooper whose neck had been broken and almost severed: his head lolled back at an acute angle: blood still pumped from a mess of gouged arteries. Another Jerry corpse had yolky matter seeping from a skull crushed like an eggshell.

It was miraculous how lightly his patrol had got off, he thought – almost uncanny. Both patrols had been taken by surprise, both had had the same split-second chance to react: Caine didn't believe that his SAS were faster or better shots. Then he realized that the Hun's formation – Indian file – had made him more vulnerable. The Death's Head leader should have formed his men into arrowhead as they left the bridge. He wondered why they'd advanced so quickly after the flare had gone up: his own reaction would have been to go to ground and wait for what came. In pressing on, the Jerry patrol leader had taken a gamble that hadn't come off.

Wallace called him over to look at the sixth Jerry – a sergeant. He was still alive, writhing with lurching spasms, his demented rambling punctuated by shrieks that gave Caine the willies. He scrooched down next to the sergeant, a stalk-necked youth with a hollow-templed head, face black and puckered with tiny cuts, eyes shiny and deranged. Caine took in the Waffen SS insignia on his collar, the Jolly Roger design on his field cap, wondered if this was the patrol commander. He was mortally wounded. His guts had been clawed out: his entrails squirmed like red snakes. The German stared at him, blinking, trying to focus. '*Help*,' he gasped.

Caine shook his head sadly, knowing there was nothing he could do: even water would make the gut-wound worse. 'Poor sod,' Wallace growled. 'Shall I finish him, skipper? It'd be a mercy.'

Caine paused, nodded, avoided the German's eye.

The big man drew his Purdey sawnoff, knelt beside the sergeant's head. The Jerry's eyelids fluttered at him: there was a frozen, sad smile on his face. *'They'll get you,'* he croaked. *'They will be here soon.'*

'Maybe they will, mate,' Wallace intoned gravely, 'but that ain't your concern now. You did your best. I don't care what you are – Death's Head, ex-screw, ex-jailbird or whatever – you're a brave soldier. I ain't much of a one for churchifying, but God bless.'

He pulled both triggers: the double report slammed Caine so hard he almost fell over: his smock was spattered with gore. He moved away without looking back at the dead man. 'Collect the weapons,' he told the patrol. 'Grenades, ammunition, everything. Do it fast: if that bloke was right, we'll soon be fighting for our lives.'

20

Caine left the Totenkopf dead on the field, but not out of disrespect: any Jerry follow-up party might be tempted to retrieve the bodies, giving the SAS a tactical advantage. It was a mean ploy – in other circumstances he would have let the enemy lift their dead under a white flag – but they were in a tight fix, and couldn't afford to miss a trick. He remembered grimly what Copeland had said only that afternoon, about honour, and playing by the rules.

Caine detached Grimshaw at the old gunpit on the gap, with the Bren and a Very pistol, and orders to watch for further enemy movement. His own feeling was that they'd encountered a probing recce patrol. He guessed that the main body of Krauts was gathering at the bottom of the escarpment and wouldn't advance until just before first light.

They moved back to the leaguer, found Cutler leaning on a jeep, whitefaced and woozy. He'd cleaned and dressed his wound as best he could, but he'd lost blood, and his whole left arm had gone to sleep: the elbow joint was stiff, and he could only just move the fingers. 'That's me out for rifle shooting,' he told Caine apologetically. 'I might manage a Bren.'

'You can man the mortar,' Caine said. 'You only need one hand for that.'

They moved the jeeps up the steep track into the blockhouse courtyard, dismounted the heavy machine-guns. Cutler led them through the tunnel to the three sangars on the wall overlooking the approach. Caine detailed Wallace to occupy the middle sangar with the bazooka, and to shift the remaining rockets there. He assigned the two-inch mortar to Cutler and told him to set it up in the same place. He and Copeland took the side sangars, mounted heavy machine-guns on tripods, set up the Vickers 'K' at one, a .50 Browning at the other. 'What about the spare Browning?' Copeland asked.

Caine glanced up at the dark walls of the blockhouse behind them. 'Didn't Quinnell say there was a sand-bagged position up there?'

While the others set about improving the defences, Caine sent Trubman to have another gander at the wireless set – getting comms with Fraser might be life and death now. Then he and Copeland climbed the lad-der to the roof, inspected the post.

'It'll do,' Caine said. 'Only thing is, it stands out like a sore thumb. It'll be the first place they'll hit.'

He gave Copeland a smoke: they stood quietly for a few moments, gazed down at the yard, watched shadows scurrying back and forth with ammo boxes and weapons, heard low voices, the clink of an entrench-ing tool. There was a view of the bridge from here, mother-of-pearl in the milklight. Cope smoked silently, studied the scene. 'Ought to lay some mines down there, Tom,' he said. 'Round the bridgehead.'

Caine nodded. 'Have to get water, too. We'll lay the mines, pick up Grimshaw, fill the jerrycans in the gorge.'

There was a breath of wind, carrying with it odours like old resin and baked shale. Beyond the rise at the far end of the bridge, beyond the shoreless void of blackness, lay the far hillpeaks, dark chiselled chines and blunt chimneys, with a pale frame of vanilla thickening slowly along the edges. 'Soon be light,' Copeland said. He threw away his fag, met Caine's eyes for a long second. 'This is going to be a sticky one, mate.'

Caine nodded again, felt a sudden overwhelming surge of emotion: fear, gratitude, sadness, guilt, love, a longing for Betty Nolan, nostalgia for a life that could never be again.

'Thanks, Harry . . . I –'

'No speeches, mate. We'll get through it all right.' He wrinkled his face, stuck his chin out, Fred Wallace fashion. '*We're bleedin' SAS, ain't we?*'

Trubman was still tinkering with the wireless at the tailboard of the signals jeep: he glanced up as Copeland and Caine approached, scratched his eyes under his glasses, as if he'd just woken from a dream. 'Any luck, Taff?' Caine enquired.

'Haven't got comms yet, skipper. I'll need to set up the Windam aerials for that. It's a dicey job, see, these sets are fragile as anythink, like I always say, and –'

'No *comms*?' Caine cut him off. 'You mean you've got the damn' thing *working*?'

Trubman gave him a dazed look. 'Didn't I tell you? Got it going a while back. I'm just doin' the fine tunin', see . . .'

Copeland grinned massively: Caine clapped the stumpy signaller on the back. 'You're the best, mate. Now we've got a chance.'

Trubman turned crab-coloured. 'Well, I . . . working is one thing, see, comms is another . . .'

'Keep at it,' Caine said. 'All we need is Fraser's Bubbles and Frogs, and a flight of bombers, and Bob's your Aunt Fanny.'

There were a dozen No. 2 mines: Caine, Copeland and Wallace loaded them into the other jeep, together with four empty jerrycans. Caine left Copeland to set up the .50 on the roof, reminded him that either he or Cutler should be stood to at all times. Cope nodded. 'Don't hang about, skipper. It's going to get lonely up here.'

Cutler helped Copeland hoist the parts of the .50 calibre up to the roof as best he could: the feeling was already coming back to his arm: Cope assembled the gun, then went back for the ammo boxes, which Cutler couldn't manage. When the Browning was standing on its tripod in the sangar, loaded and made safe, he climbed down into the courtyard, checked that the other Browning and the Vickers were in place, crouched in the support weapons emplacement with Cutler, shuftied the ground below. The ashen band on the skyline had become a butterwedge, the drapes of the night fraying along the edges in tattered dark filaments. Segments of the hills on both sides of the blockhouse were coming slowly into focus, angles and contours emerging from ironblue shadow like a slowly waking presence. It was silent: the final chapter of night when the whole world seemed to be waiting. They could make out the dark stains of the Totenkopf dead to their front, an asymmetrical configuration of bodies, lying on purple ground scattered with thornscrub and grass tussocks. Directly beyond the corpses, they could see the pale outline of the bridgehead, where Caine and Wallace were minelaying, a few paces from the jeep. About two hundred yards to their right, where the escarpment dropped sheer into the gorge, thicker trees hid from view the drywash that cut through the slope, ran along its base for a short distance, debouched into the ravine. 'That's the weak point in our perimeter,' Copeland observed. He pointed to the copse. 'The enemy could cross the gorge on foot and mass for an assault under the cover of those trees.'

Cutler nodded. 'Yep, maybe they're that good. But they'd still have to cross open ground between there and here.'

Cope surveyed the terrain immediately to their left: the old highroad passed through the gap between the blockhouse knoll and the northern scarp: no one could get through that without being spotted. 'The only way they can get behind us is by climbing the escarpment,' he commented.

'Forget it, sir,' Cutler said. 'Me and Shorty reccied that cliff – it's unclimbable, and it goes on for ever.'

Copeland gave a grunt. 'Not much more we can do then.'

Cutler nodded. He admired Copeland's careful attention to detail – that was one of the things, he thought, that made a good soldier. He liked to think he had the same thoroughness himself: it was one reason why he was already a lancejack at nineteen, when many of his comrades who'd seen longer service were still Tommies. Mike Cutler came from a town in Dorset, where his father had a small business building fences. His dad had been too young to serve in the Great War, but his uncle, Herbert, had been in the Royal Hampshires, and had been killed at Gallipoli. Mike had three elder sisters and a younger brother, who'd suffered from polio as an infant, and wasn't able to attend school. Mike, who'd been good at his lessons, had repeated them every night for his benefit. He'd left school at fourteen, taken a job working at the local railway station for thirty-five bob a week. It wasn't much even then, but times were hard and jobs were scarce. At sixteen he'd become apprenticed as a wool grader: it was skilled work, and well paid when you were qualified, but Cutler had never settled to it. When the war came, he'd been one of the first at the recruiting office and had signed on with the Devons and Dorsets. He'd done well in basic training: his stamina and determination had made up for his spindly physique: his boyish good humour and frankness had charmed even the hardest-nosed drill sergeants. No. 8 Commando had snapped him up, and when Layforce had been disbanded, he'd volunteered for the SAS – a unit never intended to fight defensive actions. Yet here he was, preparing to hold a bridge against overwhelming odds. He'd argued against it, but since Caine had decided this way, he was resigned to it: it seemed impossible, but he kept reminding himself of what his instructor at the depot had been fond of reciting: *give me six good men and I can do anything you like.*

Copeland was drowzy, but he was starving too: they hadn't eaten since before the foray to the derelict aircraft. That seemed a lifetime ago: they'd fought two actions since then. Some scoff, a brew and a few Bennies would keep the demons at bay, he thought. If they didn't get some grub down their necks, they might not get another chance. 'I'll get a brew on,' he told Cutler. 'Keep your eyes on the bridge.'

'Right-oh, sir.'

Cope opened compo tins with his clasp knife, lit two Tommy-cookers, heated bully-beef stew in a mess tin, boiled tea. When it was ready, he called Trubman in from the back yard. The signaller's broad face was animated. 'You get through, Taffy?' Copeland asked.

'I got the Windam aerials up,' Trubman said, taking a mess tin of stew and a mug of tea. 'That's a hard job, see, specially on ground like that, and I had to do it by myself . . .'

'Yeah, I know, but did you get comms?'

Trubman spooned stew. 'Comms is a twoway business, see . . .' He spoke rapidly through his mouthful of stew. 'I got on to the guard net, but they didn't answer my signals check. I sent out an SOS call with our call sign and location over and over: it went out all right, but no one rogered it.'

Copeland frowned, put down his mess tin, wiped his mouth with the back of his hand. 'So we have no way of knowing if the message was heard.'

Trubman nodded vigorously, his mouth too full to speak.

21

Before they approached the bridgehead, Wallace, Caine and Grimshaw drove along the foot of the blockhouse cliff to the point where the rock wall turned sharply left towards the gorge, where the drywash cut down steeply from above, reaching the cleft further along, in a thicket of grass clumps and trees. 'That's where Mike and me have been gettin' water,' Grimshaw said, pointing. 'You dig into the wadi bed, and it's about a foot down.'

'Good,' Caine said. 'Mines first, then water.'

Before they pulled out, Grimshaw showed them a second gunpit dug in just where the cliff turned south: it was the twin of the gunpit on the gap, big enough to take a field-gun or a tank, with a ramp at the rear. 'Not well sited, though,' Caine commented. 'If you get caught in there, there's no way out.'

At the bridge, Caine didn't post a watch: all three of them worked together to lay the anti-tank mines – big steel saucers with a pressure plate on top that wouldn't go off at less than a minimum weight. At least that was the theory. They worked quickly, dug out shallow scoops with hands and entrenching tools, armed the mines, placed them, covered them over with gravel and soft sand. They arranged them in a rough semi-circle around the bridgehead, far enough apart to prevent sympathetic detonation.

Caine had spent a lot of his time in the Sappers with mines, but the experience had only endorsed his view that they were the most inhuman weapon ever invented. He'd seen what they could do – the vision of Moshe Naiman dying with his leg torn off on the *Runefish* op was still fresh in his mind. So was the time at Tobruk when they'd lifted five hundred Axis mines and transferred them to an Allied minefield. His RE troop had lost two men on that scheme – one wrong move and *kerblooey*. That had been the most nerve-racking night of his life.

The sky was a shade lighter by the time they'd buried them all: they jogged back to the jeep, wiped dirt off their hands. Before jumping into the back, Grimshaw stood silently for a moment, listening to the night.

'What's up, Shorty?' Caine whispered. 'You spot something?'

Grimshaw scratched his hog's nose. 'Didn't *see* nothin', sir . . . but . . .'

'But what?'

'Just a *feelin'*, you know – like there's someone about.'

'You gettin' the jitters or what?' Wallace demanded.

'Maybe. Sometimes I know what's gonna happen before it does – like there's a voice talking to me or sommat. You know what I mean?'

Caine thought of the apparition of Pickney he'd seen on the STENDEC aircraft. He shivered.

'Next thing is water,' he said.

Caine drove, Grimshaw directed them two hundred yards along the edge of the gorge, to where the dry-wash fell into the ravine over a steep scree of jumbled boulders. The wadi was edged with swordgrass, tangled stands of dwarf oak, palmetto and prickly pear, masking a bed of soft sand. Caine halted the jeep, cut the engine, listened to silence. An owl hooted suddenly, broke cover in a flutter of wings, tacked past them so close that Caine ducked. 'Just an owl, mate,' Wallace chortled.

'Owls is bad luck,' Grimshaw said.

They unloaded jerrycans, mess tins, entrenching tools. 'We'd better all go,' Caine said. 'Keep your eyes trimmed.'

They dug down into the sand, making separate hollows, piling up little heaps of spoil. They found water calf-deep: Caine sampled it – it was earthy-tasting and warm. They set to, scooping the liquid up with mess tins, pausing every now and then to listen: birds cranked up a dawn chorus in shrill sequences. Caine filled one jerrycan, carried it to the jeep. He had arrived back, and was just starting on the other, when he heard a dull metallic clink, so faint that for a moment he thought he'd imagined it.

Wallace and Grimshaw stared towards the end of the wadi: the sandy bed gave way there to the cataract of boulders on the edge of the ravine. Wallace laid down his mess tin quietly, drew his sawnoff. Grimshaw let the Bren lie, unholstered his Colt. Caine picked up his trenchsweeper, glad he'd left it cocked. He hefted the weapon in both hands, eased off the safety, moved cautiously towards the stonepile: Grimshaw lagged a little behind. A Jerry in a coalscuttle helmet popped up like a jack-in-the-box, glugged fire from a Schmeisser sub-machine gun. Rounds thrashed, hit Grimshaw as he turned, snagged his arse like a hacksaw.

Caine blasted slugs from the hip, heard them chump, saw Jerry's face cleft into a mash of teeth, red pulp, white bone. The Hun tottered: a stick-grenade sailed over, *karrummppped* in a spasm of white light: air heaved, smoke stabbed, iron chinks vortexed. Caine went spinning, hit the deck, tasted sour cordite, felt the air knocked out of him. He got up, spat dust, heard bells clang in his ears. His left arm was cottonwool, diced by shrapnel furrows: the sleeve of his smock smouldered. He slapped out fire, saw fieldgrey shadows mass at the scree, more than there could possibly be, knew he was seeing double or triple. He slipped his pistol, squeezed steel, slammed rounds, heard the *blammmmppppp* of Fred's buckshot.

He scooped his Tommy, saw Grimshaw roll in purple dust, saw chunks of his arse hacked out. Wallace tossed a smoke-tin: Caine heard it plop, saw smoke huff in coiling riffles. He *rat-tatted* rounds into the smoke. '*Get Shorty out,*' he bellowed.

An MG41 chattered from the other side of the gorge: tracer rounds blipped out of the smoke, lashed sand, spiffled bushes. Wallace grabbed the Bren, slung it, heaved Grimshaw across his shoulders, padded into the trees. Caine zigzagged behind, bliffed off singles, double taps. Tracer chirruped: a thornbush exploded. Caine clocked shapes reaving through smoke billows, pulled a grenade, chucked it underarm, ran out through the foliage.

Wallace gunned the motor. Caine jumped in, saw Grimshaw lolling behind him in a blood-puddle. Machine-gun fire creased air: another bush went up in a hoosh of flame. Wallace hit the hand-throttle: the jeep shot forward. Caine forced his Tommy into the mount, traversed the muzzle, drew steel, sprayed lead, felt the gun jam. He swore, tried to clear the stoppage, found his left hand too feeble. Wallace wheeled the jeep one-eighty, shoved the throttle up. The wagon threshed gravel, welted dust. 'The berm,' Wallace grated. 'We can fix him up there.'

Caine's head hammered: his ears fizzled. It took him a blink to remember the gunpit. It would be a bad move, he thought. They might get trapped there. Once the Huns were in position it'd be hard to break out. If they didn't, though, Grimshaw might bleed to death.

'Go for it,' he yelled. He pulled his Colt, swung round, saw Grimshaw writhe. 'Hold on, Shorty, mate. Stay with us.'

Tracer guzzled air. Jerries charged out of the trees, thrummed fire from rifles, SMGs. Caine honked rounds back: the jeep jiggled, spoiled his aim. The hammer clicked: he scrabbled for a fresh clip, dekkoed forward, clocked the blockhouse, wondered where the hell Harry was.

Cope heard the sprazzle of shots, dropped his

mug, lurched for the Vickers. Cutler went for the mortar: Trubman ran up the ladder to the Browning on the roof.

Staring down the sights, though, Copeland hesitated: he could see the jeep standing by the trees at the end of the watercourse, but he wasn't sure of Caine's position. Smoke spindrifted: he clocked the muzzleflash of the MG41 from across the gorge. A grenade thumped: bushes flambeaued. He saw Wallace emerge from the trees, carrying a body in a fireman's lift, saw Caine behind, splurting fire. *It's Grimshaw. He's been hit.* He saw Wallace lay the casualty in the back, saw him swing into the driving seat, saw Caine jump in. The jeep reeled away: Jerries darted out of cover. He swung the barrel, snapped the sights, yelled, *'Two o'clock. Five hundred yards. Enemy outside treecover. Fire.'*

He heisted steel, cued an arabesque of bright cables, jacked rounds at the low ground. Cope pulled and eased, saw Jerries jitterbug. He peered over the sights, saw the jeep accelerate along the foot of the scarp, saw Kraut fire spindle.

Cutler still hadn't fired the mortar. Copeland guessed he was guaging range, waiting for a gap, not wanting to drop a packet on Caine. Either that or his wound was slowing him. The MG41 *rickyticked* from across the ravine. *'Taffy,'* Copeland bawled. 'For Christ's sake, knock out that gun.'

'*Gotcha.*'

The Browning blunderbussed splines of flame: Copeland shuftied the sangar to his right, saw Cutler hunched over the mortar. 'What the heck's up with you?'

'Dropped the round in, sir. Nothing happened.'

'You armed it?'

'You have to *arm* these?'

'Yes, you great dollop.'

A round chunked the wall close to him, spun off with a crippled-bee buzz. There was a sniper down there. The mortar plumped: a bomb droned, smoketrailed, blatted apart in an asterisk of scarlet and brown four hundred yards away. '*Raise elevation one degree,*' Copeland bawled. He sighted on running Fritzes, crackled a long burst, saw them duck and swerve. Cutler popped two bombs in quick succession: Copeland watched them screwtail, heard them hum, saw them trolley up reverse cones of debris, saw Huns gouged into splits of flesh, dismembered limbs, vapourized gore.

The Browning tattooed an unbroken thread, so long that Copeland thought Trubman's finger must be stuck. It stopped abruptly: Cope heard a bellow of glee. '*Hit it, see that boys? Knocked the sod out, didn't I.*'

They heard Cope's Vickers start up just as they reached the berm: a second later mortar rounds crepitated, the ground mulekicked, broils of flame splashed up among the Krauts. Caine saw enemy knocked down, saw survivors stumble back in disorder. The echoes played out, gave way to the metallic chuckle of the Browning.

'About bloody time,' Wallace gurned.

The berm had been fortified with cement: the ramp

181

was deep enough to cover the jeep. They hoisted Grimshaw out, laid him face down on the dustriddled floor. He wailed: the numbness in his wounds was melting into desperate pain. Wallace removed his webbing: Caine slit open bloodsoaked rags with a bayonet, winced at the gory mash: the bullet had munched through his right buttock, exited through the left. The flesh was shredded, almost sheared off, leaving a flap of mauled meat: the exit wound was a cleft of crimson black. Grimshaw howled: 'It's all right, Shorty,' Caine told him. 'You'll have to give up sitting on your arse, that's all.'

Wallace passed him a syrette of morphia. Caine considered it: he shook his head. 'I dunno,' he said. 'He's lost a lot of blood. Morphia might do him in. We'll just cover the wounds with shell-dressings.'

Wallace nodded, groped for his dressings, came up with a couple, handed them over. Caine dropped them, swore at himself. His head pendulumed, his ears zipped: there was a tightness in his chest. He gaped at the blood on his arm, remembered with a start that he'd been wounded. For a moment, the world receded down a long tunnel: he reeled backwards, felt Wallace's goliath hands steady him. 'I'll see to Shorty, mate. You look after yourself.'

Grimshaw was breathing easier, but he still wasn't sure where he was. Sometimes, he was lying in the middle of the high street at home. He'd just crashed the coal lorry into a baker's van: he'd staggered out of the cab and fallen down. *What will Mr Smith say? You were drunk, Grimshaw, drunk at that time of the day. Disgraceful.*

No, sir, I wasn't, sir. I was just mindin' me own business, sir, and that tosser Sid Atkins cuts across me in the baker's van.

He'd known it was going to happen: he hadn't even wanted to take the lorry out that day: he'd thought of saying he was sick but his mum hadn't let him. He often knew what was going to happen: never anything you could cash in on, like which horse was going to win the races. Sometimes it would only be a bad feeling: sometimes particular things would pop out of the blue, like the time he knew his brother Bob was going to be knocked down by a horsecart. It was usually bad things like that, and in the end he'd stopped saying it out loud, because people didn't like it and it got him into fights.

They said he was a fighter. Well, you spend your life humping sacks with coaldust in your eyes and up your nose, no girl will look at you, and the other lads pull your pisser, there's no wonder you have to stick one on 'em now and again, especially after a couple of pints on a Friday night down the Bull and Hound.

His dad, Alfie, was a fighter too, or had been in his day. He'd been in the trenches in the Great War with the Somerset Light Infantry. He used to tell Shorty about his time on the Somme: how, when you got over the top you hardly knew if you were awake or dreaming, dead or alive, and all you could think of was getting the Huns and killing the bastards. Alfie had stopped a salvo of machine-gun bullets during an attack, and had lost a leg. He'd been a cripple for the rest of his life, doing odd jobs to support his family.

Shorty hadn't fancied the infantry. He'd joined the

Yeomanry to start off with: when he'd found himself crewing an AFV in the Western Desert, part of 10th Armoured, though, he'd had a bad feeling about it – a very bad feeling. Rightly, too, because his squadron had been virtually wiped out at Bir Hakeim. Thank God, he'd been out of it by then, serving in the ME Commando. Then that mob had folded and he'd become SAS. Now here he was, lying in the high street by the coal-lorry, just where he'd started.

He opened his eyes, blinked, licked split lips, felt a raging thirst. Big Fred loomed over him, proffering a waterbottle that you'd have thought came from a doll's house in his enormous hand. The big man looked wild with his gypsy hair, his bristling cliff of a jaw, his broken teeth, his pokerball eyes, but there was something comforting about him. He was invulnerable, like the gentle giant in the fairytale. Grimshaw muttered: Wallace leaned closer to hear it. '*Told yer*,' Grimshaw croaked. '*Told yer owls was bad luck.*'

Caine had dressed his arm: he felt steadier. He'd been peppered lightly with grenade fragments, but the main force of the blast had passed over him – a few paces back and he could have been ratshit. There was no damage to nerves or bone. His arm was stiff, but he could still move his fingers.

He mounted a Bren on an embrasure in the berm. For a while the enemy had stopped shooting: now they'd opened up with intermittent fire. Rounds hustled dirt, pitched out of the air with lazy *plips*. The Totenkopf boys were in cover: they hadn't gone away.

Caine couldn't help admiring them: they'd crossed a fifty-foot ravine, scaled the nearside so quietly that he and his mates hadn't rumbled it till the last minute. They were well trained and they had guts: sooner or later they were going to launch an assault – three men in the blockhouse weren't going to stop them. While he and Fred were pinned down here, the defence was halved. Then there was Shorty – he needed better medical support than they could give him.

'We have to buzz off out of here,' he told Wallace.

The big man stowed his canteen. 'That's gonna be a piece of cake, innit? Last time I looked, the only way out is across Jerry's front. We'll be askin for it.' He paused, gestured to the escarpment that rose steeply above them. ''Course, we might wanna consider luggin' Shorty up a sheer cliff in full view of the Hun.'

Caine bent to peer through the embrasure overlooking the northern approach: the gap was only two hundred yards away, along the foot of the blockhouse butte. Once they got through it, they'd be out of danger. Wallace was right, though: to get there they'd have to run the gauntlet of enemy fire.

He considered a skirmishing breakout, making use of the sparse cover, realized they could hardly do that carrying Grimshaw. Leave him here? No, then there'd be no chance of getting him out till the action was over: by that time he might be dead. Come to think of it, they might *all* be dead by then.

'We'll make a dash for it in the wagon,' he said. 'It won't take more than a minute.'

Wallace's forehead creased: his eyes were wary. 'A minute's a long time when a hundred Krauts are throwin' shit at you.'

'Harry'll give us covering fire.'

'You sure he can see us from up there? How will he know when to start?'

Caine shuftied up the cliff to their left: the berm might be just visible to someone standing on the blockhouse roof. He thought for a moment. 'We'll fire a blue flare,' he said. 'Cope will know what it means.'

22

The firefight had petered out: Copeland told Cutler to stand fast and keep his eyes open. He left the sangar, ran through the tunnel, climbed the ladder to the roof. He wanted to find out what had happened to Caine since the jeep had gone out of sight – the roof would be the best observation point, but dicey if there were Hun snipers in place. It was still cold: dawn was a blood-red rag on the distant hills, a spread of forked tongues blistering the darkness: strobes of fingergold spindled from behind plumes of cloud, split them into woolpack flotillas, argosies of cumulus in great candyfloss whorls. The battlefield below was a weft of gold and silver, crisscrossed with thorntree shadows in elastic doglegs: the escarpments on both sides were lizardskin with glistering brilliants, pocked with cavities of purple shadow. Copeland smelt wormwood, tasted scorched dust.

He crawled across the roof to the emplacement, found Trubman huddled against sandbags smoking a cigarette. The .50 Browning stood on its tripod loaded with a fresh belt and made safe: Cope noticed that Taff had gathered all the spent cartridge cases into a neat pile. The signaller was slackfaced: the eyes behind his lenses were black pips.

'Nice shooting, Taff,' he said.

Rosepink blotches bloomed on Trubman's cheeks: a smile frayed his mouth. 'They always said I couldn't shoot for toffee, see. Been saying I wasn't the right stuff all my life.'

'You got your Skill at Arms test, didn't you?'

'Yep, but they still said it.'

A slug tickered stonework, flew off with an electric *whaaaazzz*. Cope ducked: Trubman didn't flinch. He seemed to have passed through some sort of barrier, Copeland thought: or maybe he was just plain exhausted.

He squeezed himself in next to the signalman, lit a cigarette.

'You're as good as any of 'em, Taff: better than most. Got the MM twice, didn't you?'

Trubman smoked morosely, eyes distant. 'It was my father, see. I'm from Merthyr Tidfil – slagheap capital of the world: dah was a miner, like his dah before him. Would have liked me to go down the pit, but reckoned I wasn't up to it. *Never amount to anything, you won't, boy*, he used to say. *No good at sports. Can't play rugby. Couldn't knock the skin off a rice pudding.* Even when I enlisted he said I should have gone for the Fusiliers. *Royal Signals*, he said. *That's for nellies, that is.*'

Copeland punched his arm. 'And here you are with the nellies. Does he reckon they hand out medals on a plate with chips?'

'He'll never know, will he? Died in a pit collapse two years back, see.'

Stray rounds plinked the parapet, huzzed off in sparkling glimmers.

'Jerry's spotted us,' Cope said.

'Yep,' Trubman replied, his voice croupy. 'You got any more of them stay-awake pills? Either that or I'll have to peg my eyes open with matches, see.'

Cope gave him two Bennies, took two himself: they shared a canteen of water to wash them down. 'Don't stand too close,' Trubman said. 'This stuff makes your breath stink like rotten fish.'

'Did you spot Tom and the others?'

Trubman removed his glasses, cleaned them on his sleeve. He squinted at Cope, his dim brown eyes gauging him like feelers. 'They're holed up in the berm at the foot of the cliff. You can see them from here if you stand up, but I wouldn't want to stick my nob over that parapet.'

'I'll take your word for it.'

Caine removed the Bren from the embrasure, cocked his Tommy-gun. Wallace tossed a piastre to decide who would drive. Caine knew he'd be hampered by his wounded arm, but that applied equally to his shooting ability. In any case, Wallace won the toss. 'Just give her all you've got,' Caine said.

They laid Grimshaw face down in the jeep bed: Wallace had reversed the wagon into the ramp: no manoeuvring was needed to get her out. He checked tyres and fuel: Wallace adjusted the seat, jumped in with a creak of springs. Caine clambered into the gunner's place next to him, attached the Bren to the forward mount with Wallace's help: he reckoned he could handle it well enough, but he'd have to shoot across the driver's front. He made sure the mag was full, that he had his wallet of spares. A shot fishtailed over them with a decelerating drone. Caine loaded the Very pistol with a blue flare. He was aware that firing it would alert the enemy, but that had to be weighed against securing covering fire.

He took a deep breath: he felt like he did before a parachute drop – painfully alert, as if he'd just stuck his head in an ice-bucket. His mind was hollow, unfocussed on anything but the way ahead – everything was blank but the course of that one-minute dash under fire. A minute seemed nothing, but Caine knew that Wallace was right: once the bullets were flying, it would be forever. He broke out in goosebumps: his guts churned. He glanced at Wallace, saw his scalloped forehead shiny with sweat. They locked eyes for a second. '*Ready*.'

Wallace nodded, his great jaws set. Caine hooked iron: the flaregun popped. Wallace toed the starter, engaged gear, whamped the throttle. The jeep wheeled out of the berm: Wallace yanked the wheel sharp right, changed gear, shoved the throttle to top: the motor chirred, treads crunched gravel, the wagon bucked, lurched, skidded across stony ground. Caine had the sensation that they were moving in slowtime, that everything had gone quiet: he was hardly even aware of the shivering Jerry broadside from the gorge, the bullets that screeched over them. His world was only Wallace's Quasimodo shoulders hunched over the wheel, the pancake hands gripping it as though he wanted to wrench it off, his forehead furrowed, his Neanderthal face rocklike with concentration. Caine swivelled the Bren, hoiked the trigger, heard the *blatta-blatta-blatt*, saw lances of explosive gas lick out across the bonnet. The noise was deafening: he heard nothing else – not until the high metallic stridor of the Vickers and Browning began shrilling out from the blockhouse above. Even then, he only half registered the sound: the jeep seemed to be floating on an air-cushion through turbulent cloud.

Copeland was back in his own sangar when the flare budded above him, laddered into blue threads.

He stiffened. 'That's them,' he yelled. 'They're breaking out.'

Trubland dropped fire from the roof. Cope saw the jeep come into view, speeding along the concave part of the rock face below them. He clocked whoffs of smoke from Jerries holed up along the gorge, heard the rattle of musketry, the *ricka-ticka-tick* of machine-gun fire. He fed the Vickers another pan, cocked the works, hammered long sprawls of ball, tracer, armour-piercing, flayed the slategrey air with lashes of quivering light. Then he saw something that took his breath away. A six-wheeler Jerry AFV was trundling across the bridge, a giant angular bug with a gun-mounted turret and half a dozen Totenkopf troopers hanging on to her skin. Copeland stopped shooting, waited for the AFV to hit the mine necklace the boys had laid: he didn't know its exact position, but he knew they'd planned to cover the bridgehead. He watched as the armoured car ramped off the bridge and sailed forward.

Nothing happened: there was no detonation. At the same time, Cope spotted two more armoured cars, also carrying troops, approaching the bridge from the far end.

The first AFV was crawling directly towards the gap: troops dropped off her back, deployed among sparse cover. '*Cutler*,' Copeland bawled. 'See to that wagon.' Cutler was already picking up the bazooka. Cope saw him heave it to his shoulder, switched back to the scene before him: the AFV's cannon trumped.

The shell hit paydirt fifteen paces from the jeep; a dreadbolt wallop rocked the surface, raked up a mousse of vermilion fire. Caine felt the gutpunch, felt the jeep turn turtle, smacked into the deck, passed out in a snowstorm of dazzling white. He awoke lying on his left side, opened his eyes, felt his mouth coated with petrol, felt his face puffed like a balloon, eyes heavy as fishweights: his left arm burned, his lungs felt seared. He clocked Wallace, only a yard away, trying to raise himself on arms gone to jelly. Grimshaw was a couple of paces behind: the shock had brought him round: he was worming for the nearest boulder, pistol gripped tight in bloodcaked hands. The jeep lay on its side, wheels spinning: the air was a peasoup, alive with the whine of hurtling rounds. Hot lead chipped stones, punched through the jeep's hull with metallic snaps.

Caine saw the Jerry AFV mosey towards them, machine-gun ribbing fire. A fan of Jerries advanced behind her, slipping from rock to rock. Machine-guns yammered out from the blockhouse. Caine saw a Jerry's head squelch crimson, saw another's chest mauled with rings of black flesh.

Wallace was on his feet: he took two strides to the jeep, grabbed the discarded Bren, braced it: Caine saw the splurt of fire, saw Wallace knocked off his feet by a slug that skewered his calf, saw him crash with the Bren still rattling, saw mercury splits leap into the sky. Caine's Tommy was lying in the dust: he reached for it, climbed blearily to his feet. He saw Kaiser helmets bob across his front at fifty paces, belted out bursts at them one-handed: the shots went low. He made for Wallace, saw the armoured car's turret rotate towards him. An anti-tank rocket squealed over his head, hit the AFV with a tympanic *barrrooooommmffff*, in a jagged swastika of light. Her turret was sliced off like an eggtop: whitehot steel hunks flew. A big Hun in a peaked cap trotted out of the miasma with fixed bayonet, showing pavingslab teeth. Caine dropped him with a double tap that blew his mouth away. There was a crunching blow in his right side, as though an engine block had fallen on him: he staggered, hiccupped air: the world went cateyed.

23

He surfaced a second time to the slap of detonation from the bridge, guessed that one of the No. 2 mines had gone up. He opened his eyes, saw a lacquered sky, whiskbroom cirrus, cottonfluff pads. Another bazooka rocket torpedoed over him: he watched its smoketrail shred the blueness, heard its rhonchoid scrape, heard the distant *ka-thump* as it cherrybombed in.

He rolled over on to his side, found that he was lying in a brown mush of blood and sand. Pain hit him in savage waves: his left arm felt like it had been plunged in vitriol. He groaned, looked down to find a fillet of red meat hanging off his abdomen, just above the pelvic bone. A mass of flies swarmed on it: he held his good hand over the wound, brushed flies away. His senses strobed: his mind swung towards darkness. He took a dozen sharp breaths to keep his wits together.

The ground looked different: limestone nodules had become jewels as big as carbuncles: the earth swarmed with carthorse-sized ants. He tried to focus on the bridgehead: saw it infinitely far off. A pall of smog hung over it: Axis vehicles there were on fire. He moved his head slightly, clocked the nearer AFV, a giant broken cockroach belching gulps of rancid gas. The shattered bodies of her Totenkopf crew lay around her like a necklace, some of them smouldering. German dead were scattered across the field as if slashed down by a great scythe. Jerries had taken cover in shallow scrapes behind trees and rocks: they were still shooting. Rounds clipped stones, spittlebugged dirt. Curries of fire curled out from the blockhouse above him, keeping Fritz in place. It was clear that the Totenkopf attack had lost momentum.

Wallace was humped in the dirt by the overturned jeep, swearing obscenely: his left leg was a mess of gore and blackened cloth. He lifted his puddingstone head, met Caine's eyes. His face was puce-coloured, his pupils needlepoints. Caine looked for Grimshaw, spotted his head pop up behind a swordgrass clump. Blood slopped inside his smock: a vice tightened on his guts. It felt as if a horse had kicked him there, like the horse that had killed his father: what an irony that both he and his dad should suffer the same fate. Rounds beetle-buzzed, hit stones, tore off in disconsolate soprano wails.

He knew he had to force himself to move. It would be too easy to give in, to fade away and never come back. He fished for his Tommy, drew it to him by the sling, dragged it towards Wallace at a crawl. He struggled to keep his mind clear. Slugs pranged through the jeep's chassis. It took forever to cross inches of ground: by the time he and Wallace were head to head, the giant was trying to raise himself again: he'd taken a round in his right calf: it had skimmed bone, missed the artery. He was still losing blood, but Caine didn't think it was as bad as it looked. He reached in his pocket for a field dressing, remembered he'd used the last one on himself. Wallace blinked at him, strobed pinpoint eyes.

'Hold on, mate,' Caine choked. 'We'll get out of this.'

Wallace wiped blood off his lips with shaky knuckles. 'That's a good one, that is, Tom.' His voice was a hollow rasp. 'There ain't no way out.'

Caine knew he was right. None of them was going to make it without the help of Copeland and the other two up in the blockhouse. It would take at least two men to pull them out: that meant reducing covering fire by two thirds — and that was the only thing holding the Boche back. Even if Cope risked it, he'd have no more than an even chance of survival. The problem was that he almost certainly *would* risk it, and that would jeopardize everything.

A round whopped past his ear. Caine realized the bullet had come from behind, glanced back to see Grimshaw doling out fire in single shots, his Colt pistol lodged against a stone. He was bawling like a madman. *'I'll 'ave yer, yer bastards. Come on. What's wrong with yer, bleedin' Nazi wankers? Ya* . . . Death's Head? *I've shit 'em.'*

Caine grinned. 'That's the way Shorty. Fight to the last bullet.'

'I say we rush 'em,' Wallace croaked.

Caine felt a titter gurgle in his throat. 'You can't even stand up.'

'Who says I can't? If we lie here much longer, mate, Harry's gonna come and get us, and then *he'll* be scragged an' all. I ain't waitin' to be butchered like a pig in a poke.'

196

For a moment, Caine thought he must be hallucinating: maybe he was dead already, maybe he hadn't survived the jeep-crash. But no, the pain was too vicious, too real for that. He cursed, tried to moisten his lips with a sandpaper tongue. What Wallace had just said sounded crazy, but Caine saw reason in it. If they stayed here, Copeland would make an attempt to get them: if enemy fire kept up they would both be hit again. Fred was right – better go out now, on their feet, in a blaze of glory. The only thing was, he wasn't certain that *he* could get on his feet, let alone Wallace. He drew his Tommy-gun in, gripped the butt under his shoulder, felt for the grooves on the forward stock. He was comforted by the feel of the weapon: it had been part of him for so long. He saw Wallace fumble for his Purdey, saw him lift the sawnoff in his knobby hand with a moan. 'How we gonna do this?'

'I'll count to three. On three, we get up and give it to 'em. That's it.'

Caine wasn't afraid. The pain was agonizing: any escape from it had to be welcome. He'd suffered enough – they all had. When he'd lost Nolan, something in him had died, anyway. He'd taken on *Nighthawk* knowing that it stank like rotten fish – he'd only agreed on the slimmest chance that he might get Nolan back. *It's a lie, just like it always is. The whole fucking war's a lie – Fiske was bloody well right about that. No one gives a toss about Thomas Caine or his men. Fuck the brass – Alexander, Monty, Freyberg – the lot of them. They're all out for number one, out for the nobs. They can stuff their bloody medals. Nolan's dead. Who cares about life without her? I've done what I had to. I made my stand.*

He nudged Wallace. 'You ready, then?'

The big man blinked: blood trickled from his nostrils. 'See you on the other side, mate.'

Caine sluiced a rattling breath. '*Trooper Grimshaw,*' he yelped. '*Covering fire.*'

'*Very good, sir.*' The voice was so faint that Caine couldn't tell if he'd imagined it. He and Wallace locked eyes, looked away. 'One,' Caine counted, 'Two . . . Thr–'

He didn't finish the count: his jaw seized up and something went *snap* in his head. He became aware of a figure walking nonchalantly out of enemy lines directly towards them – not a Jerry, though: a Tommy with a withered, skeletal face, spitting-cobra eyes, in a soup-bowl helmet, carrying a rusted Bren. Caine gasped in shock: the soldier was Cpl Maurice Pickney, RAMC, deceased. He seemed almost to be floating above the ground, his legs moving, his feet not quite connecting. Suddenly, Caine was aware of the same burnt steel smell, the same spine-chilling voice he'd heard back in the derelict aircraft. *Don't do it, Tom. Don't move. Help is coming.*

The ghostly Pickney drifted nearer: he seemed to pass right between them. Caine felt a waft of cold air, shivered. 'Did you see that?'

The big man stared at him, confused. 'What? Why did you stop?'

Caine didn't look behind: he heard the ghostly voice trailing off into the distance. *Shouldn't have taken the black box, Tom. I warned you what would happen. You brought all this on yourself by taking the black box.*

The words were replaced by the contralto tipple of a Bren: Caine heard a tracked vehicle's rattle, glanced over his shoulder just as a Bren-gun carrier bumped around the bend in the rock wall. She was an ungainly vehicle like an iron boat, with a gunmuzzle protruding through a slit in her forward turret, splattering spurts of gunfire in skipping threads. Caine gripped his weapon hard in disbelief. The rattletrap shot directly towards them, rising and falling as if she were breasting choppy waters: for an instant Caine thought she would roll right over them. At the last second, though, she swerved, slavered to a halt broadside on. A carrot-top head appeared over the side: foxy eyes, a doorstep chin, a face only just recognizable under stubble, filth and soot. 'Your transport is here, gentlemen,' Mitch Jizzard declared.

24

When the orderly told Major John Stocker that a Captain Elizabeth Nolan was waiting in the interview room, the DSO's only reaction was to remove the pipe from his mouth. He betrayed no more surprise than a curl of the lower lip. 'Did you see any ID?' he enquired.

'She didn't have none, sir. No paybook, noffink.'

'What's she like?'

'Corkin' blonde, sir. Nice legs, knockers like . . .'

'That's quite adequate, Corporal. Show her in.'

Stocker, a stoutish, balding man with a forehead like a cupola and thickframed glasses, laid his pipe in an ashtray, glanced round the room. It hadn't changed much since Nolan had last seen it, he reflected – cluttered with overstuffed bookcases, academic ornaments – all the drooping furniture he'd salvaged from his room at Cairo University, where he'd once been a professor. In his creased and ill-fitting battledress, he looked more like a boffin than a soldier, but many had found that it was a mistake to underestimate him. He had a mind like Occam's razor: he was capable of a ruthlessness that had been known to make senior officers quail.

Stocker wasn't as surprised by Nolan's visit as he might have been. Until a couple of weeks earlier he'd believed her dead – killed in the car crash that Tom

Caine had survived. When his men had picked up Jizzard, though – the night Bill Pike and Celia Blaney had been shot – the Scotsman had been ready to sing. He'd told Stocker he'd been due to RV that night with a man called Taylor, and a blond girl known as Maddy: whether those were their real names, he had no idea.

Maddy had been Betty Nolan's cover name on the *Runefish* op. It might have been coincidence, but Stocker had had a hunch. He'd quizzed Jizzard about the girl, found out that the deserter gang had picked her up the previous November: she'd been involved in some sort of accident, and *wasnae playin' with the full deck*, as Jizzard put it. Stocker had been intrigued: Jizzard's description of Maddy not only matched the Nolan he knew, it also tallied with the picture of the female hijacker Driver Davis had given. Stocker knew it was rare for the deserters to use women: most deserter girls were civilians, the majority Egyptian or foreign prostitutes who'd found an easy ticket among the gangs.

'Aye, but this lassie was different,' Jizzard explained. 'She was mustard wi' smallarms. Fired left-handed. Ye wouldnae believe how handy she was.'

That had been the clincher. The only female military personnel trained in smallarms were special-ops agents: Nolan had done the Grant-Taylor battle course, had passed with flying colours. And she was left-handed. Stocker had been certain it was Nolan even before Celia Blaney's testimony had put the icing on the cake. 'I thought I was dreaming at first, sir,' she'd told him from her hospital bed. 'Either that or I was dead and she was an angel – there she was among flying bullets, dressed up to the nines. She applied a field-dressing to my wound while they were still shooting, and I knew she had to be real.'

Stocker had decided to sit on the information for a while. From what Jizzard had told him, he guessed Nolan was suffering from some sort of disorientation: she was too loyal and dedicated to have joined up with a mob of traitors otherwise. If she recovered, though, she could still be a useful agent. With a twinge of conscience he remembered the bungled op in which she'd been used as bait for the spy Eisner the year before.

'Captain Nolan, sir,' the orderly said.

When she'd parted with Taylor that morning, Nolan hadn't been entirely clear about what she was doing, or why she was doing it. It had been hard enough to persuade him that it was safe to wander around the city centre, especially after what had happened last time, when a chap claiming to be a journalist had photographed her holding a newspaper. Nolan was aware how winning she could be, though: on the *Runefish* op she'd influenced Rommel's strategy by convincing the Abwehr that the false documents she was carrying were real. Compared with that, Taylor was a pushover.

Cairo lay under the ashlar skies of February: cavernous streets and squares faded into greyness under towering icebergs of cloud. The vendors were still out with their trays of oddments: the occasional group of off-duty Allied soldiers in battledress sauntered past. Since the Eighth Army had moved to Tunisia, though, the city had lost the hectic excitement of pre-Alamein days.

Before steeling herself to confront Stocker, Nolan walked down the Nile corniche, watching feluccas breasting bleak, pewter-coloured waters. The memory of those waters made her shiver.

She retained only broken images of the night she and Caine had plunged into them in an out-of-control taxi, driven, she thought, by Eisner himself. She hardly dared whisper Caine's name now: the thought of him was like a festering wound. She had no idea if he were dead: he might easily have drowned that night. Even if he was alive, though, she felt she was no longer worthy of him. She'd debased herself by getting mixed up with Taylor and his crew. She might not have been in full control of her faculties, but it had happened, and there was no going back on it. And despite Taylor's violence, she had to admit she felt a certain affection for him: he had none of Caine's honour, but he was honest in his own roughshod way, and there was no denying that he'd taken care of her. Nolan wasn't a flag-waver: she didn't care much about institutions. She cared about people, about the individuals who mattered to her.

She was the daughter of an alcoholic home counties GP; the eldest of five children. When her parents had split up, dividing the kids between them, Betty had chosen to stay with her father: she'd dedicated her whole early life to looking after him and her younger brothers. He'd never abused her, but she'd had to suffer the drunken rages, the erratic behaviour, the brushes with the police, the self-recrimination, that went with his drinking. She'd managed it all, and survived, because she knew deep down that her father and brothers depended on her. It was during those years that she'd become accomplished at appearing to comply with the expectations of others, while preserving her own integrity. This, and her deep ability to empathize, had made her a superb actress.

Nolan loved music and dancing, children and animals. She was capable of utter dedication, but reserved a merciless hatred for those whom she felt had wronged her: she made no distinction between officers and other ranks. She could mix with bar-girls and royalty with equal ease. She was a skilled performer and could fit into a role without losing sight of herself: she wasn't highly educated, but her mind was sharp – she was articulate, quick to grasp ideas and had a photographic memory. She knew that men found her attractive, yet she wasn't conceited about her looks: in wartime Cairo any girl with one good eye and a pair of legs could have as many admirers as she pleased. She knew she was capable of manipulating men, but she used that ability only when there was no other option. Since her memory had returned, she'd become aware that she owed loyalty to her former comrades, but she also felt some commitment to Taylor and the deserters who'd helped her. Now she was intent on reporting to Field Security, knowing that she'd have to find some compromise way of serving them both.

Field Security HQ was located in an inconspicuous

three-storey town house in Medan Sharif. For a long time she hovered on a street corner, trying to work out what she really wanted. Until recently, she'd felt at home with the deserter gang: Taylor's latest escapade, though – when he'd shot the two FS operatives – had shaken her. The most horrifying thing was that, in retrospect, she'd realized she knew the wounded redhead. It was Stocker's assistant, Celia Blaney, a placid, warm-hearted girl. She hoped to God that Blaney had pulled through.

In the two weeks since that incident, the MPs had clamped down on deserter gangs: they'd even raided the farm one night. Luckily, she and Taylor had moved to a safe house in the Delta by then, but it had been a close shave. Taylor had no doubt how they'd located the place. *Jizzard. That Jock bastard sold us out.*

A Redcap patrol-jeep cruised past: two NCOs with black armbands and scarlet cap-covers gawked at her. Nolan lowered her eyes. She'd deliberately worn a light jacket over a blouse and a sober grey skirt, but it hadn't deterred the wolf whistles from Tommies on the corniche. If she was still here when the patrol returned, they'd almost certainly question her. She had nearly given up at that point. After all, she was a deserter: she'd taken part in armed hijack operations against her own side. That was treason: they could have her shot for that. Would they believe she'd lost her memory? They might. But they would also expect her to give up Taylor, and, whatever pressure they put her under, she wasn't prepared to do it. She owed him too much. If he found out she'd handed herself in, of course, he'd consider it betrayal anyway. That couldn't be helped: her conscience was too strong. Or was that just another excuse? Was it simply that, underneath it all, she was there to find out what had happened to Tom Caine?

Stocker looked up to meet the familiar *little-girl-lost* expression that he'd always considered Nolan's most dangerous weapon. She was a mite worn around the eyes, perhaps, but otherwise as he remembered her — wavy blond hair, parted on the right, with the lush sweep over the left eye, the melting set of the lips, the cute overlap of the front teeth: the athletic curves that even the jacket and sensible skirt couldn't hide.

'Hello, Major,' she said.

Stocker frowned: he hadn't had time to decide how to play this, but made an instant decision to treat her with cold aloofness: he gave no sign of recognition. 'Sit down,' he said.

Nolan sat primly in the upright chair facing the desk. Stocker peered at her through his spectacles, watched her fingers held perfectly still in her lap. *Cool*, he thought. *Calm and collected.* Then he reminded himself that he was dealing with a woman capable of controlling her outward appearance. He whipped off his glasses, began polishing the lenses with a piece of four-by-two.

'So the prodigal returns,' he commented. 'Perhaps you'd like to explain why you have been absent without leave for the past four months?'

Nolan's jadecoloured eyes moistened: Stocker was sure that she wanted to ask him about Caine.

He wasn't going to play along – not yet.

'Just answer the question.'

His voice was a whiplash, but Nolan didn't flinch. 'I was in a car accident,' she said slowly, 'but of course, you knew that.'

'Certainly I knew,' Stocker said airily. 'I was with you and Caine at Shepheard's just before it happened. Like everyone else, though, I assumed you were dead. Since you obviously are not, I'd like to know why you have never reported back to duty.'

'After the crash, all I remember is wandering through the streets, soaked to the skin, with no idea who I was or where I was going. I suppose the MPs might have picked me up, but they didn't. Instead I was found by a gang of deserters. They took me in, looked after me. Since I couldn't even remember my name or where I belonged, I stayed with them: I had nowhere else to go, you see – not as far as I was aware, anyway.'

Stocker snorted. 'You lost your memory? You expect me to believe that?'

He felt himself pulled into Nolan's eyes – the deep reefs of seawashed green. 'What other explanation do you want?' she said. 'What possible reason would I have for not coming back, if I were in control of all my faculties?'

'You abandoned your post, which means that you are a deserter too. You have been involved in armed hijackings, *including* an incident in which one of my sergeants was killed and my female assistant badly injured.'

Nolan flushed. 'Celia?' Her voice was a trickle, but

Stocker heard genuine anxiety in it. 'Is she going to be all right?'

'She's out of danger, if that's what you mean, but it's no thanks to you and your murderous friend. It was a nasty wound: she'd lost a lot of blood. She still hasn't recovered.'

'I didn't shoot her, Major. Nor did I shoot the sergeant.'

Stocker tilted his head to one side, examined her face gravely. 'Even if you didn't, you certainly *did* hijack a lorry by . . . er . . . *seducing* . . . the driver. You stole a military jeep. Even if your shots missed, you're still guilty.'

Nolan wiped her eyes with the corner of a handkerchief. 'I wasn't myself,' she said. 'I told you . . . I lost my memory.'

'Very convenient. Also a rather difficult defence in a court-martial, when the defendant is a skilled actress.'

Nolan sat up straighter, put the handkerchief away, took a breath. 'I was recruited by G(R) eighteen months ago, Major,' she said stiffly. 'I was trained at Ramlat David: parachuting, wireless transmitting, the works. Since then I've risked my life over and over. I spent eight days locked in a Cairo basement in handcuffs so that you could bag Johann Eisner. I volunteered to drop in behind Axis lines in Libya to warn . . . to warn . . . the *Sandhog* mission . . . that they had a traitor in their midst.'

Stocker noted that Nolan had deliberately avoided saying Caine's name: his smile remained bloodless. 'There's no doubt that you've done some extraordinary things, but that's ancient history. In war, people some-times go off the rails.'

'Does hijacking supply lorries and bumping off Brit-ish troops sound like the sort of thing I'd do if I had the choice? I'd . . . *forgotten* . . . I was a serving officer. My memory only started to come back a couple of weeks ago. You must have seen shellshock victims suf-fering from disorientation before?'

'Perhaps.'

There was silence for a moment. Nolan straigh-tened her shoulders. 'If that's it, then, I'm ready to face a court-martial. I can tell you now, though, I'm not giving up names. Whatever those people are, they saved me.'

Stocker couldn't hold back a flush of admiration. This was a woman whose capacity for self-sacrifice seemed endless – a woman you wanted on your side.

He steepled his fingers. 'Let's just suppose I accept your claim that you were not fully compos mentis. Would I be correct, then, in assuming that you remain loyal to His Majesty?'

'Yes.'

'So if I were to ask you to return to your life with the deserter gang, this time working for us, you'd have no conflict of loyalties.'

Nolan's eyes widened: her eyebrows arched. She couldn't believe what she was hearing: she didn't know quite what sort of reception she'd been expect-ing, but certainly not this. 'I've just told you, Major, that I –'

'– That you won't betray Taylor and the rest of the worthless scum?' Stocker asked wryly. 'No need. I know all about them already . . .'

He knew about *Taylor*? It made sense if he knew about her: informants' tongues had been wagging: *Jizzard*.

Stocker stood up abruptly, as if seeking a relief from the tension. He picked up his pipe, stuck it in his mouth, took it out again. He turned to a large-scale map of the Delta on the wall behind him, tapped it with the stem of his pipe.

'I'm after bigger fish than Taylor,' he said. 'Are you aware that deserter groups are now attacking fuel dumps, M/T parks – even airfields? Did you know that they are targeting Allied personnel? Did you know that they are thought to have abducted more than fifty young women over the past few weeks?'

He turned sharply on his heel, fixed her with an intimidating glare. 'There are rumours that there's a new big man in charge, a man who's trying to stop gang rivalries and create a single organization, that these changes are emanating from him. Does the name *Calvin* mean anything to you?'

There was a pause as he and Nolan eyed each other. Stocker watched her hands fidgeting, saw a tiny muscle twitch beneath her ear. She looked down. 'I've heard the name, that's all,' she said. 'I've never met him – I don't know where he's based, or even if he really exists. I don't know about sabotage attacks, but I *do* know there's a new attitude. Killing Allied troops used to be taboo: not any more.' Stocker clasped his hands behind his back, nodded with satisfaction: it was beginning to fall into place. 'That's a start, anyway. What about the kidnapping of women?'

Nolan hesitated, cleared her throat. 'There are women living with the deserters,' she began. 'A few are AWOLs, most are Egyptian or Arab street-girls. I've heard rumours about kidnappings, though. Once, I saw ten or twelve women in the back of a 3-tonner who didn't look like the usual types. I was told they were *in transit*, but nobody knew where to. Someone said they were being sent to Calvin. I can't say if that's true, but I know these women didn't settle among the deserters. They just vanished.'

Stocker felt excitement gnawing at him: Nolan had provided the link he'd been hoping for: a possible connection between girl-trafficking and the new big boss. The Egyptian stepfather of the Nazi spy Johann Eisner, Idriss, was up to his neck in white-slaving: it might be coincidence, or it might not.

He sat down at his desk again, relaxed for the first time. 'Does anyone know you came here?' he enquired.

Nolan shook her head.

'Do they know that you've recovered your memory?'

'No.'

'Then here's your task. Go back to the deserters. Live as you did before, but find out if those kidnapped girls are really going to this Calvin. Find out where he's based and who he is.'

'That's not going to be easy.'

'I never said it would be easy: if an actress like you can't do it, who can?'

'What if I refuse?'

'That *is* easy. You'll be court-martialled for treason or murder, or both. I can't guarantee that a plea of temporary insanity will be accepted.'

'What's to stop me agreeing then just vanishing into thin air?'

Stocker looked like a thoughtful ferret. 'I'll be watching you – and I'll be sending backup. Someone who'll be able to fit in easily among the deserters: you'll be able to keep contact with me through her.'

'*Her?* Who?'

'When you see her, you'll know.'

There was silence for a moment while Nolan considered it: she nodded almost imperceptibly, letting the blond wave fall over a moist green eye. Stocker hardly considered himself a ladies' man, but he had to admit to himself that she looked incredibly attractive.

'I want to ask you one thing, Major,' she said croupily, 'and I'd appreciate an honest answer.'

Stocker heaved his chair back awkwardly. *Here it comes*, he thought.

'Where's Tom Caine?'

Stocker took a breath: his eyes beneath the glasses were hard pins. 'He didn't survive the crash. Caine's body was never found.'

25

Not long before midnight, the jeep copped a puncture on her front offside wheel. Quinnell brought her to a halt under a limestone cliff, ghostly in the moonlight: stunted camelthorn scrabbled out of the schist, and a fan of fine sand flowed from a wadi cut through the rock on their left. Fiske glowered at him, dark eyes baleful with shadows. 'Now what?' he demanded.

'Now we fix it,' Quinnell scoffed. 'Unless you want to ride the rest of the way on a flat.'

'Not wi' this thing on the back,' Jizzard said. For the past two hours he'd been crouched in the rear, trying vainly to avoid contact with the black box. The tremulous note in his voice was genuine terror, Quinnell thought.

'All right, but pull off the road,' Fiske said. 'Drive up this wadi on the left.'

Quinnell started the engine and put her into gear: she bumped up the shaly creek-bed, trailing a long shadow from the waning moon: a nightowl scooped low over them with a whop of wings.

Jizzard ducked. 'Bloody things,' he hissed.

Soon, the wadi opened out into a wide ampthitheatre – a floor of brash pebble, palmetto scrub and halfa clumps, blackstone walls chiselled into canyons and corridors, devilled with dark alcoves and skirts of sand.

'This will do,' Fiske said.

Quinnell halted: Jizzard jumped out at once as if he couldn't wait to get away from the black box. Quinnell got out the tool kit, started assembling the jack.

While Jizzard and Quinnell changed the tyre, Fiske looked on, smoking his pipe.

Jizzard went off to pee: Quinnell tightened the nuts with a spanner. 'Make sure they're good,' Fiske told him. 'I don't want a wheel coming off at the wrong moment.'

Quinnell leaned back on his haunches, tried to stop himself blowing up. Since they'd jumped Caine and the others, Fiske had given more orders than the GOC, in that dry-as-leather officer's drawl that made Quinnell's flesh creep. He'd had doubts about this job all along, and now, only a few hours on, he regretted what they'd done to Caine and his crew. All right, he was an Irishman and had no loyalty to the king and all those other bloodsuckers, but this wasn't about the king. This was about your comrades, your *mates*. The king didn't come into it: you didn't let your mates down. And if the truth be known, Fiske was more of a snob than Caine was, anyway.

Quinnell wiped sweat off his forehead. He was just about to rise when there was a yell from the shadows. 'Hey, look at *this*.'

Fiske took a shufti in the direction of Jizzard's voice: Quinnell stood, jerked his .303 from the brace, followed Fiske into the night.

They found Jizzard staring at a small graveyard of military vehicles and equipment – piles of artillery shells, a brace of jeeps with missing wheels, a punctured water-bowzer, two broken and rusted 3-tonners and what looked like a perfectly intact armoured Bren-gun carrier with a field-gun yoked behind.

As they came up, Jizzard blinked at them in the star-light. 'Take a wee look at this,' he gasped. 'Most of this stuff's diss, but the Bren-carrier looks all reet, and that gun's sound as a bell.'

'So what?' Fiske sneered. 'More junk.'

Quinnell ignored him and examined the field piece: it was a long-barrelled six-pounder anti-tank gun on a carriage, with small wheels and an armoured shield. He stepped on the yoked arms and scrambled into the back of the carrier: there were six-pounder shells stowed there, and a couple of jerrycans strapped to the hull: he opened one and found it full of petrol. The interior was covered in dust, but, as far as he could make out, the engine seemed undamaged. He found a field-telephone set, with a long cable, neatly coiled in the rear: there was even an ammunition box packed with No. 36 Mills grenades.

He peered over the side at the others. 'She's sound enough, so she is. Didn't you use to drive one of these things, Mitch?'

The Scotsman poked at his stubbled jaw. 'Used to be in a carrier platoon. Wee bit rusty, mebbe, but, aye, I've driven one. Ye *nudge* the steerin' and the drive wheel warps the track, slews her left or right. Wee bit more and the track locks, and she swings around.'

'Hey, what's this nonsense?' Fiske growled. 'Get out

of there, Quinnell. These things only do thirty miles an hour – we've got the jeep.'

Quinnell clambered down silently. A working carrier, with a six-pounder gun, plenty of ammunition *and* a field telephone: they would be a boon to anyone trying to hold the El-Fayya bridge – it would make all the difference. He thought of Caine's crew, wondered if they were still trussed up, or whether they'd managed to get free. Of one thing he was certain, Caine wasn't the kind of man who'd abandon his task willingly. The kind of man, he, Quinnell, ought to be: the kind he could yet be, if he returned with this artillery-piece. Even at thirty miles an hour they could make the gorge by first light. It wouldn't remove the stain of betrayal, of course, but it would rid him of that terrible burden of guilt. Quinnell knew suddenly and without a shadow of a doubt that he had to go back. Fate had given him a second chance: the means to restore his honour. But he was going to need Jizzard's help.

He stole a measured glance at Fiske: the thin man had left his rifle in the jeep: he was wearing a Colt .45 in an unbuttoned holster. Quinnell took in the shielded dark eyes, the twitching slender fingers. 'Ye can keep the jeep, Fiske,' he said. 'I'm takin' the gun back to Caine.'

Fiske let out an astonished guffaw. 'You're insane. The Jerries will have you for breakfast.'

'Mebbe, mebbe not. But the most insane thing I ever did was listen to you.'

'You think Caine is going to welcome you back with open arms? He'll never forgive us for what we did.'

'That he won't. But maybe I'll be able to forgive myself.'

Fiske bit his lip: his fingers played for a moment on his pistol-butt: Quinnell was ready for him. His rifle was in his hands and there was a *sproocckkk* of working parts as he rammed a bullet into the breech. 'Try it and I'll kill ye. I mean it, Fiske. I'm havin' no more of your shit. It's done. I'm going back.'

Fiske raised his bony hands contemptuously. 'This is sheer craziness.' He glanced sideways at Jizzard, who was frozen to the spot: he stared wide-eyed at them both. The Bren was still slung on his back.

'Come on, Mitch,' Fiske said. 'You're not going to put up with this lunatic, are you?'

Jizzard scratched his stubble, shuftied Quinnell. 'Why don't we just take the carrier? Leave this turd and his bloody black box to rot, and hoof it?'

'And get picked up by the Kiwis and shot as deserters? Die of thirst in the desert? Not me, mate. We owe Caine and the lads, and I'm goin' to pay my debt. Now's your chance to do the same. I know ye've got it in ye, Mitch: under the blarney there's a brave man waiting to come out.'

Jizzard drew his palm across chapped lips. 'We could die there,' he stammered.

'Aye, we could. But one thing's for sure: no one will forget what we did.'

'Don't listen to him, Jizzard,' Fiske interrupted him. 'Be smart. You weren't cut out to play the hero.'

Jizzard raised his chin. 'Who sez?'

'I *know* you. You've spent your whole life squirming out of situations like this. Why change old habits now?'

'*Squirmin*' . . . ?' For a second Jizzard was so tongue-tied he couldn't speak. He felt a flush of almost feverish rage: deep down he'd always known that he was a stoolie, a bully, a coward. He'd pushed people about because he'd been scared. He was scared now: shit-scared of that black box, of what would happen to him when they got it back – if they got it back. *I know ye've got it in ye*, Quinnell had said. He didn't know if the Irishman had meant it. He'd spent his whole life ratting on others, even on Taylor and the deserter gang. *I know ye've got it in ye*. Even if it killed him, he suddenly and desperately wanted that to be true.

He spat on the ground, sent Fiske a look of disgust, stepped towards the carrier, climbed over into the front compartment. He laid the Bren against the mount behind the extended hull-turret, brushed dust off the vertical steering wheel. He jabbed the starter: the engine wheezed, spluttered. He jabbed again: the engine roared and died. He frowned, hit it a third time: there was a guttural roar from the rear section: the motor grumbled, the air was suddenly full of fumes. He let out a yell of triumph. 'We're in business.'

He lifted his head over the side in time to see Fiske and Quinnell grappling furiously: Fiske had grabbed the stock of Quinnell's .303 and was trying to pry it from him. Quinnell was powerful, but Fiske's limbs were steel cables: finally, the thin man rammed the

Irishman against the side of the carrier, let go of the rifle, turned and hared off into the night. Jizzard drew his pistol, aimed after the mechanically loping figure. 'Sure, let him go,' Quinnell grunted. 'We'll see no more of him.'

26

A clawhammer was doing a job on his insides: Caine opened his eyes, found Quinnell staring at him. The pain was brimstone: he closed his eyes, opened them again.

'Thought we'd lost ye there, sir, so I did.' Quinnell's voice seemed to echo around the walls.

Caine was lying on a stretcher in one of the block-house rooms: a makeshift aid post. He recalled snatches of the journey back: Jizzard's face over the side of the Bren-gun carrier; Quinnell pressing a shell dressing into his side: smells of cordite, dirt, burning gasoline.

'What the hell . . . ?' he wheezed. His words were barely audible even to himself.

'Don't try to talk, sir. You may be in shock. Just wiggle your hands and feet a wee bit, will ye?'

'Shock? Bloody right I am. Last I heard, you deserted.'

'Just wiggle your hands and feet, now, sir.'

Caine felt himself doing it, sensed tension in his extremities.

'That's all right. No spinal injuries there. Hard to tell with gunshot wounds. By the look of it, the round hit soft tissue between the ribcage and pelvis. In and out, no bother.'

Caine groaned: Quinnell loomed over him with a

morphia syrette. He tried to pull away: his responses were sluggish. He hardly felt the jab.

'Should be OK, now,' Quinnell said. 'I didn't want to give ye morphia till ye came round. Ye feel a wee bit cold?'

Caine clutched the Irishman's wrist: his fingers closed around it with a pressure that surprised him. 'What are you doing here, Quinnell? You and those other turds left us in the lurch . . .'

Quinnell didn't try to pull away. 'Aye, so we did, sir, but we had a change of heart. Just lie back. The morphia'll start working in a minute.'

Caine didn't ease his grip: he suddenly realized how vulnerable he was. Quinnell might have given him a fatal dose. Then it hit him that the deserters – the *mutineers* – Jizzard and Quinnell, had just pulled him off the field under enemy fire. His head spun. *What the Dickens is going on here?*

Quinnell extricated his wrist, laid the syrette in a mess tin, wiped his hands on a rag. 'If ye'll just lay back and let the potion do its job, sir, I'll tell ye the good news.'

'Wallace and Grimshaw . . . ?'

'Och, they're all right. The big fellah's already up and about. Sure it'd take an elephant to squash him. The other fella, now – Grimshaw, is it? He's over there.'

He gestured: Caine turned his head, saw Grimshaw laid face down on another stretcher. He seemed to be asleep.

'Copped a bad one in the backside, but he'll pull through.'

Caine swallowed, tasted blood. He tried to shake off the heaviness, to sort out the confusion.

'Fiske?' he murmured.

Quinnell chuckled. 'Not *him*, sir. That wanker's off up the Blue with the wondrous black box. Good luck to him. Never did like Fiske, nor that box, whatever it might be. Now, Jerry's poised for another go, and you'll need all the help ye can get.'

Caine couldn't remember clearly what had happened after the jeep had turned over, wasn't certain how much of it he'd dreamed. *Did I really make a suicide pact with Wallace? No, that's insane. I must have imagined it. I thought I saw Maurice Pickney on the battlefield. That's not possible either. There was a salvo of rockets from the bazooka. The Jerry attack lost momentum.*

'Yer man Cutler played a blinder, so he did,' Quinnell said. 'Blasted the AFVs on the bridge with the bazooka, detonated a minefield, blocked the approach. The foot-sloggers melted away – what was left of them, poor sods.'

Caine tried to get up, felt his arms tremble. 'They'll soon have them shifted. You said they're ready for another go.'

'Aye, they are, sir, but ye see, we evened the odds a bit. We brought back a present from our wee jaunt.'

'What are you talking about?'

'We came across a vehicle dump – all British stuff. Hun must've captured it and left it there to collect later. Some was diss, but there was a working Bren-gun carrier, and . . .' His face lit up with triumph, 'a six-pounder field-gun.'

For a second Caine didn't believe it. He tried to stammer something, but Quinnell steamed on.

'That was when we decided to come back. Couldn't let that stuff go to waste, not when it would give you a chance. So we towed the thing back, shells an' all. 'Course, Fiske wasn't happy about it, but there was two of us and we had the jump on him. He was all taken up with that black box. We let him go, turned round. Mebbe it was the stupidest thing I've ever done, but here we are.'

Caine watched him incredulously. 'And Jizzard *agreed* to this?'

Quinnell smirked. 'In a manner of speaking, sir. Sure, he had a crisis of doubt halfway back. In the end, though, he gritted his teeth and went through with it. Even drove the Bren-gun carrier into the eye of the Hun attack to pull you out. I always had Jizzard down as a jibber if ever there was one. It's queer the way a feller will turn when the chips are down.'

Caine grunted: the pain in his side was already beginning to taper off. He closed his eyes, felt himself drifting to sleep: he snapped them open. 'Give me some Bennies. Preferably a lot.'

'Ye don't want to be taking Bennies on top of morphia. Ye'll end up in cloud-cuckooland.'

'Better that than lying here. The next attack's going to need every one of us, six-pounder or –'

He was cut off by the pop of a mortar from the yard outside.

27

Harry Copeland was lobbing mortar-bombs, keeping the elevation low. He watched them raunch in slow parabolas, saw them rupture around the gunpit in fingerpokes of smoke. *The Hun might think this is the prelude to a counterattack. They don't know we have the six-pounder yet. Let's keep it that way.* Cutler, Wallace and Jizzard would soon be at the pit towing the gun behind the carrier. If all went well, they'd haul it into place under the cover of smoke: a nice surprise for Fritz when he advanced.

Copeland had been astonished to see Quinnell and Jizzard back at the blockhouse that morning: he'd been too engrossed in the firefight to do anything but call them a couple of insubordinate fuckers. He hadn't mentioned anything about punishments or courts-martial – the fact that they'd brought the Bren-carrier, the field-gun and the field telephone convinced him that they must really have had a change of heart. If they wanted to help, he'd told them, they could unhitch the gun, dump the phone set, get the carrier round to the base of the spur and liberate Caine and the others. Quinnell had leapt at the chance. Jizzard had turned white: he'd needed some serious encouragement.

Copeland watched the smoke puffs spread like tentacles across the gap between the escarpments. He stopped hurling bombs. There was a yip of smallarms fire from the direction of the bridge. *Jerry knows something's going on, but he doesn't know what.*

The door behind him creaked: Cope turned to see Tom Caine swaying towards him, still clad in his blood-soaked smock: he was carrying his Tommy-gun in one hand and his webbing in another. He knelt unsteadily next to Cope, ashfaced, his eyes redthreaded, glassy with amphetamine glow.

'How you doing, Tom? You shouldn't be wandering about.'

'Not the first time I've been wounded, mate.' Caine's words came out slightly slurred. He laid his weapon on the ground, slung the big web pouches across his shoulders. 'Hurt like hell at first, but can't feel it now. Quinnell fixed me up. Can you believe those blighters, walking back into the firing line cool as cucumbers after trussing us up?'

'I know: they came bearing gifts, too . . .' Cope nodded at the field telephone still in its haversack: Trubman had rigged it up with batteries: Wallace and Jizzard were playing out the cable that would connect it with the gunpit.

Caine raised his eyebrows: Quinnell had told him about the field-gun, but hadn't mentioned the phone. He followed the cable with his eyes, saw that it fell over the precipice, snaking down into the lake of smoke that lapped against the buttress wall across the gap. 'What's going on down there?'

Copeland looked smug. 'Wallace and Jizzard are shifting the six-pounder into the gunpit . . .'

'Wallace and *Jizzard*?'

'Apart from Fred, Jizzard's the only gunner we've got. I told Fred to keep his mouth shut and settle any scores later. Cutler went with them to help set up the field telephone and bring the carrier back. When it's all shipshape, we'll be able to direct our artillery from up here.'

Caine snorted; *artillery* sounded grandiose for a single six-pounder. He had to admit it, though: the gun gave them a fighting chance.

He scanned the battlefield, realized he hadn't seen it from up here in daylight: it was high noon, the sky loaded with seafroth in helixes and crescents, punctured by lightspots like peacock-tail eyes. The plain was stark, bisected by the hard dirt track – a barren reach of gravel and rubblescree, catclaw thorns, peppergrass clumps. Caine took in the windlines of fieldgrey corpses, the overturned jeep below, the pyres of black smoke from the Jerry AFVs – one was just a couple of hundred yards off, two or three more on the bridge. It was true then – Cutler had blocked the bridge with his skilful use of the bazooka. He deserved a medal for that.

Caine groped in a pouch, found his field-glasses, surveyed the edge of the gorge: Kraut soldiers were dodging between cover there, but they hadn't removed the obstacle yet: every time they showed signs of concentration, Trubman kept their heads down with a machine-gun blast from the roof. Copeland had the bazooka near at hand, ready to whack any AFV that threatened to bulldoze the smoking wrecks out of the way.

'What do you reckon they'll do?' Caine asked.

Copeland shrugged. 'Their best bet would be to wait till sunset, but I don't reckon they have the time – not if they want to catch Freyberg from the rear. I think we'll see a rolling infantry assault, maybe in company strength, supported by armoured cars.'

Caine rubbed his chin. 'You reckon we can hold them?'

Copeland's Adam's apple bobbed. 'Ammunition's low, Tom. We've got enough for one more attack, but after that we've had it.'

'If only we knew what's going on with Freyberg. Once the Kiwis are through Tebaga, we can withdraw. Taff get comms yet?'

Copeland shook his head. 'He's been trying his best, but no luck so far.'

There was a sudden burst of fire from Trubman on the roof: *chunka chunka chunka chunk*.

Caine looked up. 'Hey, Taff, go easy on the ammo, mate.'

'I tell you, skipper,' the Welshman's voice descended, 'Fritz is getting ready to attack.' He'd hardly finished the sentence when Caine heard the tubercular chirrup of mortar-bombs a fraction of a second before they struck the plain with a low descant of *barooooommms*. The ground wobbled, smoke mushroomed, shrapnel shards went *teeeeeeeeee*. Copeland and Caine covered their heads: Caine was the first to look up: he saw ragged smokepads blossom across the battlefield, saw them coalesce into waves and vortices edged with violet and brown crud.

'*Smokescreen*,' he yelled. 'They're on their way.'

28

It took them half an hour to manhandle the field-gun into the pit: Wallace glowered at Jizzard in silence. His calf muscle stung like poison: it felt as though he'd got an iron manacle tightened around it. The dressing was drenched in blood, but at least the bleeding had stopped.

His lips were still sore from the whack Jizzard had given him: he wouldn't forget an old score – not even if Jizzard had been driving the carrier that had whisked them out of the killing zone, not even if he'd brought back this wonderful gun. Wallace couldn't fathom why they'd come back: he half suspected more hanky-panky: he was watching Jizzard like a hawk.

Cutler attached the field telephone: Jizzard and Wallace unloaded the twenty-one 57mm shells from the carrier, stacked them by the gun in neat piles. Cutler twirled the phone handle, spoke into the receiver, laid it back in its cradle. 'You're all set up. Be good.'

He went off to the carrier: Wallace heard her engine treadle. The noise receded: they lit cigarettes, ogled piles of shells. Wallace stubbed out his fag, spat in the sand. 'Twenty-one ain't goin' to get us far. Pity yer couldn't 'ave found a few more.'

Jizzard screwed up his parboiled face, stomped his fagend. He gave Wallace a bulge-eyed look.

'Stow it, Wallace. I laid my arse on the line to come back here for the likes of you.'

'Oh yeah? Well, the likes of *me* could o' bloody done without the likes of *you*, you ratfaced piece of shit . . .'

Before he'd even realized what he was doing, Wallace had thrown his massive bulk on the Scotsman, knocked him off his haunches, closed his pansized hands round the thick neck. He might have done real damage, but just then a probing sniper-round hit the parapet and yowled off with an adenoidal sigh: it passed so close to Wallace's ear he felt its wind, buried itself in a sandbag with a low *phut*.

Wallace let go of Jizzard, shuffled backwards. For a second, the Scotsman lay glued to the spot, shaking like a grass-stalk, his face sapped of colour, his eyes millstone-sized.

'You're flamin' scared to death, ain't yer?' Wallace said.

Jizzard's face collapsed. He shifted back, slumped against the sandbagged wall, wiped spittle off his mouth with an unsteady hand. His eyes glimmered, his lips trembled: a muscle twitched under his jaw. Wallace guessed he was on the verge of breaking down.

'Ye've never been scared in ye life, have ye, big man? Born brave you was . . .'

'Don't talk soft, mate. Anyone tells you he ain't scared is lyin'. You know what they say: in any dingdong half the men is scared stiff, and the other half is terrified.'

It was a weak attempt at a joke, but Jizzard didn't take the bait. 'I know I'm no gonny make it.'

Wallace felt a flush: cold fingers touched his spine. Despite himself, despite everything, he felt a twinge of pity. Jizzard had lost all pretence: the cocksureness had all drained out of him. He'd forced himself into the situation he'd avoided all his life, and now there was nothing left of him but the reality of his own fear.

'Every bugger's shit-scared,' Wallace said. 'Only some shows it more than others. Some runs away, but some fights.'

Jizzard raised himself into a crouch. 'Not me. I'm off.'

'No you ain't, mate. You and me are the only ones as can fire this gun: I need you here.'

'I'm no stayin', I tell ye, I'm –'

He was cut off by a chorus of sharp smacks: Kraut mortars firing in series. Wallace heard the missiles snatch air, heard the feral moan as they fell, heard them hit deck in staggered plumps. Neither of them moved. Jizzard's eyes bugged: Wallace popped sweat. He crawled to the machine-gun emplacement, peered over, clocked a stain of smoke spreading across the plain in roils. 'They're comin',' he spat.

The telephone trilled. Wallace reached for the receiver, heard Caine's voice, clear but remote.

'Jerry's advancing in force. Two AFVs supporting company-strength assault. One of them's heading straight towards the gap.'

'We'll have her, skipper.'

'Good. We'll keep the footsloggers off you from up here.'

Wallace put the phone down: Jizzard cowered against sandbags. 'Fritz is here,' the big man told him. 'Now you've got two choices. You can either pick up one of them flamin' shells and ram it into the flamin' breech, or you can stay where you are and wait till the Krauts come over the flamin' top. Only make up yer mind quick 'cos we ain't got all flamin' day.'

Wallace set the Bren on its bipod on top of sandbags in the emplacement: he laid the haversack of magazines next to it, with the wallet of spare parts. Then he crouched against the six-pounder's guntrail, drew out his sawnoff, made sure he had cartridges up both spouts. He slid it back into its home-made holster, pulled out his Colt .45, checked that it was ready to fire. He took a breath, opened the field-gun's breech. Strands of smoke drifted over the pit: mortar bombs burst around them with vacant pops like paper bags. A swell of noise surged: Squareheads jabbered, rifles clacked, sub-machine pistols zipped, volleys furrowed air in angry bow-waves: slugs yawed off stones with doppler skreaks; rockchips pitched, dirtpowder blew.

Jizzard dipped down at Wallace's elbow, a slim 57mm shell gripped in trembling hands. Wallace cocked a grim eye at it. 'That armour-piercin'?'

Jizzard nodded, swung the shell into the bore. Wallace slammed the breech, let his big paw linger on the firing handle. He peered through the sights. The smoke was clearing: he could see most of the way across the plain – fieldgrey bodies with Kaiser helmets were skirmishing towards the gap in sections and platoons, advancing with methodical purpose, dropping, crawling, firing, popping up, running, zigzagging in all directions. Wallace concentrated on the armoured car leading the attack: another six-wheeler with a turret-mounted cannon. She was about four hundred yards off, and her gun was tilted up towards the blockhouse: as Wallace watched, she fired a stab of ochre flame. He heard the *croooommmppp*, felt the vibration. His fingers itched on the firing handle. '*Now*,' he said to himself. '*Now*.'

He didn't fire, though. Instead, he let the vehicle trundle forward. *I can't afford to muck this one up. The AFV crew hasn't clocked the gun, yet. Once I fire, they'll know it's here. There won't be a second chance.*

He traversed the gunbarrel slightly, depressed the elevation a touch. He felt the firing handle under his fingers: the only thing that was real now. Battlesounds faded: he didn't hear the screams or bulletwails. Every tendon in his body drew bowstring taut, every sense engaged: it was the old feeling he'd known as an artilleryman – that sense of power, as if you were about to do something momentous, to make a big noise that no one would forget. His eyes were riveted on the AFV's turret as it moved back towards him: a red light flashed behind his eyes. *Fire*. He tugged the handle: the shell triphammered, the gun rocked on its carriage: the barrel spewed flame. Wallace heard the shell scrape air like an untuned violin, saw it steamtrail, skim the turret, saw the magma eruption as the round thunked the surface thirty yards on.

His heart sank: sweat ran down his face. *Fuckin' missed.* '*Fuckin' hell*,' Jizzard said.

Wallace whamped the breech open, let the smoking shellcase tumble. 'Lamp one in there. *Now.*'

Jizzard was white-gilled: his eyes popped: he moved like a man in a dream. He grabbed a shell, slid it into the bore. Wallace clunked the breech, narrowly missed Jizzard's fingers. He took a deep breath, held it, got the AFV in his sights, watched her dome traverse, knew they'd been spotted. *This is it: last chance.* The turret was a fraction out of line when Wallace pulled iron. The gun *whoooooompped*, the barrel pitched, the shell droned, pierced the AFV's turret. Wallace felt the impact, saw the wagon teeter, saw downdraughts of flame whoosh from her insides. He clocked a charred Hun wriggle out of the burning cocoon just as there was another blitz of fire and a surf of smoke: the AFV went up like a haystack: the Hun flew aloft on blazing shards.

Caine saw the AFV disintegrate, blinked in the dazzling tinfoil glare. He watched Hun footmen scatter, saw them go to ground, saw them roll, fire, pop up, trot forward in duck-and-drake pairs. He lined up the Vickers, hoicked iron, blatted a firespurt, saw a Jerry scoop air with an open hand, saw another go down like a wet sack. Cutler whocked off a mortar bomb from the middle sangar: Caine heard its undertone hiss, saw it strike earth, turf up brown chiffon smudges, saw Germans tenpinned. In the third sangar, on Cutler's right, Copeland stopped firing the machine-gun, started loosing aimed shots with his sniper's rifle. Trubman, still on the roof, ranged his Browning at the bridge, etched squalls of fire across the haze.

The Totenkopf were a tide of fieldgrey advancing on a ragged front, coming on under a curve of tracer rounds that floated over their heads, spatted along the blockhouse wall like stinging flies. The Jerries sloped forward in loose formation, dropping, rolling, welting fire, never presenting a target for more than a few seconds.

Caine stuck his head up: slugs whistled and crooned, hived off sharp bats of stone around him. He focussed on the Jerries nearest the gunpit, clocked a squad creeping forward with stick-grenades. The six-pounder lofted fire: a high-explosive shell scammered, light burned, a fireball ballooned up in a shuddering maelstrom: flying iron took off a grenadier's legs, sent others squirming. Caine followed through with the machine-gun, gusted lead, *blattablattablattablat*, saw his tracer camber in, saw his rounds sabre the enemy down.

He heard a cannoncrack from his right: a shell ploughed a hot furrow right-angled across his arc of fire. It hit the rock wall behind the gunpit in a burst of white-hot slivers and oilrag smoke. He had almost forgotten the second AFV, riding shotgun on the Hun's right flank. She was now traversing left not far from the foot of the cliff: she'd spotted the field-gun and was homing in to take it out. 'Knock out that armour,' Caine brayed.

Cutler laid the mortar tube aside, crouched on one knee. Quinnell picked up the rocket-launcher with both hands, kneewalked over to Cutler, set the weapon on his shoulder. 'OK,' Cutler winced. 'Load her up.'

There was one rocket left. 'Which one do you want?' Quinnell joked.

'Gimme the lucky one.'

Quinnell armed the rocket, lifted it gently, knelt down behind Cutler, eased the bomb into the tube, heard it click home. He edged himself out of the back-blast path, threw his arms round Cutler's torso to steady him. 'No good,' Cutler objected. 'I'm going to have to stick my neck out for this one.'

'Ah, shame, and here's me thinking you needed a cuddle.'

'There'll be plenty of time for shenanigans later.'

Cutler leaned out over the sandbags, angled the bazooka's snout low, lined up the sights against the AFV's balloon wheels. It was always hard to hit a moving target, even a big one, even at close range: Cutler knew he'd only have one go. He swung the tube, aimed ahead of the armoured car's hull, drew a tight breath, took the pressure. Just as he squeezed iron, he felt a stabbing pain: a Jerry round snapped through his right hand, drilled into the base of his left thumb, wazzed off and scored a furrow across Quinnell's cap-comforter. The shriek of the bazooka drowned Cutler's yell: the backblast *whooomped*, the rocket pinched air, slewed across the AFV's deck with the scranch of steel on steel, exploded ten yards away with a concussion that knocked two Jerry soldiers off their feet.

More enemy rounds chewed stone, lashed sandbags: Cutler dropped the bazooka, staggered back, sat down heavily, stared at the burnt and bloody wrecks of his hands. '*Shit. Shit. Shit.*'

Quinnell scrabbled at his cap-comforter, shuftied it,

saw that the round had missed him by a hair's breadth: his heart banged. He forced himself to peek over the parapet, saw the six-wheeler careering through dust, saw her drum another shell at the gunpit, heard it reave air, heard it blat apart. For a second he wondered if he should drop a mortar bomb on her. *No, she's too close.* He was about to go to Cutler's aid when a Bren-gun carrier rattled around the butte, reeled into the AFV's path. He shook his head in amazement. *Am I seeing this?* Caine, Copeland and Trubman were still shooting: Jizzard and Wallace hadn't left the gunpit. *Who the bleeding heck is that?*

Shorty Grimshaw was hanging on to the wheel, throttling the carrier straight at the armoured car. When he'd crawled out of Quinnell's makeshift aid-post in the blockhouse minutes before, unnoticed by the others, his only idea had been to get back into the fight. He'd lost a lot of blood: he was lucky to have lasted this long. For a while he'd lain on the stretcher, half comatose. When he'd come round, heard the *rickticktick* of machine-guns, heard the whine of mortars, he'd ached to be back in the thick of it. He was ratshit, but Quinnell had dosed him with morphia, and his arse felt like dead flesh. If he'd just crawled out into the yard and opened up, Caine would have made him go back, and he wasn't going to die in bed. Not with a fight going on.

He'd lurched through the tunnel, steadied himself against the wall, found the Bren-carrier unattended. *Can I drive her? Is the Pope a Catholic? I can do anything. I'm SAS, my son. How does that poem go, the one they're always recitin' to* us in training? 'If you can force your heart, and nerve and sinew, to serve their turn long after they are gone, and carry on when there is nothing in you, except the will, that says to you, "Hold on" . . .'

He'd forgotten the rest, but it didn't matter: he was holding on, like the poem said. As he'd dragged himself into the carrier, he'd noticed that somebody had set up a daisy-chain of grenades in the back – seven or eight No. 36s attached to a string. Grunting with effort, twisting his shoulders, he'd reached for the string, looped it round his wrist. All he'd have to do was yank it and the grenades would be armed.

He hadn't clocked the Hun AFV until he'd swerved round the end of the rock face: she was haring straight at him, and he suddenly knew what he had to do. *Alfie charging Jerry machine-gun nests on the Somme, bayonet fixed: Go for 'em. Kill the bastards.*

His head swam, his senses strobed: *I'm behind the wheel of a Bren-gun carrier.* A pulse of terror swept through him. *What* am *I doing? This is fucking insane.* He was oscillating through awareness, one moment hearing the roars and shrieks, the cradlesong of rifle-shots, the palpitation of ordnance, the expletive shrill of machine-guns: the next he was floating through silence. He saw the AFV's turret swing *slow, oh so fucking slow*, saw the gun-bore fix on him like an evil eye. *Kiss my arse, Kraut bastard.* He gave the carrier full head, saw the blurt of smoke as the Jerry cannon ramped, heard the shell chigger. *Missed me. Couldn't hit a whale in a fucking duckpond.*

She was a hundred yards away and closing: the carrier's tracks clappered, the engine honed: Grimshaw choked, felt blood gush from his mouth. He took in the AFV with her iron plates and angles, felt his strength wilt, clutched the wheel with rigid fingers. *If you can fill the unforgiving minute, with sixty seconds' worth of distance run, then yours is the earth, and everything that's in it, and what is more, you'll be* SAS, *my son.*

The AFV loomed above him like a battle-cruiser. Grimshaw let go the wheel, yanked the daisy-chain. *Gotcher,* he crowed.

29

Wallace and Jizzard loaded, fired, covered their ears, felt the barrel jump, pitched shells, dropped geysers of flame and shrapnel among the advancing Hun. An AFV shell mushed into the rock wall behind them with a *baaarowwwwmmmm*: they ate raw cordite, snuffled hot dust. Wallace took a dekko through the sights just in time to see the Bren-carrier carambole into the Hun ironside: his jaw dropped. He heard metal chomp, saw the carrier detonate, saw the outrageous fishtail of light, saw whorling lava swallow up both wagons with a *vroooooooosshshshh* that seemed dim and distant to his shelldeafened ears. '*Bleedin' hell*,' he said.

Totenkopf infantry pepperpotted nearer: rounds devoured air, twanged off the gunshield. *Should of brought my friggin' tinlid.* He snatched a shell from Jizzard, rammed it up the breech, jobbed a porkchop finger at the Bren. 'Get behind that, mate. They're getting' too close.' *What're they playin' at up there? What happened to the coverin' fire?*

Wallace banged the breech shut, peeked through the sights. Jizzard monkeywalked to the Bren: he was pale, his eyes as wide as a weasel's. He blew his cheeks, chewed his tongue, braced the weapon, yocked the handle. He saw two Squareheads sweeping at the pit from an oblique angle, ahead of the Totenkopf point platoon: a porky trooper with a Schmeisser, a lanky one with a rifle, bayonet fixed. They worked with practised ease: one crisscrossed, the other fell prone, yomped rounds. Jizzard saw Porky drop, saw Lanky leap up: he wrenched iron, plumped a burst with both eyes wide. The Bren bucked, firegas popped, ballfire splittered. Jizzard saw Lanky's fieldgrey tunic split, glimpsed the pattern of gules he'd painted across it, saw the Jerry timber. He saw Porky's coalscuttle bob up five yards away, ripped rounds through it. His finger seemed to be stuck on the trigger for an eternity before the helmet went still.

Krauts screamed towards him from all sides – scores of fieldgrey ghosts, too many to count. The Bren kept stomping rounds, firing as if by its own volition, switching left and right without his guidance. He wasn't aiming: the weapon was choosing his targets. He felt his finger tense and release as if the gun were compelling it, saw tracer whip out red razorwires, saw Jerries lashed down, saw limbs cleaved, saw faces demolished: it was as if he was watching it all from outside.

The field-gun *whommfffed*, brought him back to earth: he realized he'd been shooting for only a few minutes. He felt shellrush, felt the round skew past on a vapourtrail. He didn't have time to look where it landed, though: three Squareheads were hurtling out of the roil, not ten yards distant, crowing like roosters. Jizzard clocked bayonets, saw faces, black with dirt and powder, distorted into deathwatch grins. These Krauts had given up skirmishing, were launching a frontal charge. More

Jerries moved behind them through the dusteddies — shadowmen, cloaked with haze. *Where's the covering fire? Where's the bloody* covering *fire?*

He jabbed the trigger furiously, spunted rounds, saw a Jerry crash and burn. He squeezed again: the breech-block chumped. Jizzard cursed: he'd forgotten to count rounds. *It's Caine's bloody job to keep the bloody Hun off the pit.* The Totenkopf were still coming, reaming off rounds in spasms: bullets buzzed, leapt off the parapet.

A .30 ricochet hopscotched off the gunbarrel, passed between Wallace's jaw and windpipe, threw him off his feet. *I'm hit. I'm fucking hit.*

Jizzard traileyed him, saw him sprawled on his back between the guntrails like a great washed-up walrus, grasping his neck with shovelhead hands: blood pulsed between his fingers. His dark birdeyes were glassy, his mangled jaw worked, but no words came out. Jizzard's pulse tripped. *Get up, man. For Chrissakes, get up.*

He was furious with Wallace, furious with the Krauts, furious with Caine. Jerries darted nearer: Jizzard clocked Kaiser hats, squinteyes, rictus teeth, rifle muzzles, bayonet-glint. He reached for a fresh mag, changed his mind, drew his Colt .45. He saw Squareheads on the parapet, felt a hammerblow in the chest, stumbled back, wheezed bile. He felt no pain, only anger. *I'll fix ye, ye Nazi swine.* He whoffed rounds at the first Kraut, felt the Colt jerk, heard flesh punched, saw a redblack eruption on a fieldgrey chest.

Another Jerry dropped into the pit, growled like a dog: a squat soldier with mad eyes, bad teeth, and a two-day stubble, hefting a Schmeisser. Jizzard gave him two bullets, point blank, hit him in the chops, mashed his underjaw, severed his tongue, drilled a .45 calibre cavity through the roof of his mouth. The Jerry thrashed: Jizzard backed away, hit the wall, saw blood tricking from his own chest, gagged for air. Wallace was still down. *Get up for Jesus' sake. I'm sorry I cracked ye one: don't dump me now.*

Wallace blinked, drank in sootsmudged sky, felt a searing pain in his jaw, saw his hands blood-drenched, heard the rasp of his own breath. He turned his head, clocked Jizzard against the far wall, clocked the writhing Kraut, whiffed blood, tasted scorched meat. Two more Germans leapfrogged into the pit: Jizzard fired at them, missed. A broadhipped Kraut with sergeant's insignia and mildewed teeth stuck a bayonet into Jizzard's midriff: Wallace heard the squelch of guts, heard Jizzard squall, saw him drool blood, saw him slide down the wall. The sergeant bent over to pull out the bayonet: the other Jerry shot Jizzard in the groin.

Wallace rose, grunting, reaming blood: he drew his Purdey sawnoff, levelled it, hooked twin triggers, pumped both barrels, heard the double *whoooooomppppphhhh*, watched buckshot snag both Krauts side-on: he saw the Jerries jerk, saw cloth fried, saw tissue blasted, saw arterial gunge squiff, glimpsed white ribcage under peeled-off skin. He dropped the sawnoff, shipped his Colt, dragged himself forward, held his neck with one hand, gulped down bloody gloop. He beaded more

Huns on the parapet, heard the air quaver, heard a machine-gun snarl, felt the earth rumble, felt his senses burn. He let his weapon fall, let the world shrug, slipped down a long black valley into stardecked night.

30

Cutler's hands felt like they'd been put through a meat-grinder. His right palm had a hole through it: his left thumb was hanging off: both hands were pumping blood. Quinnell wrapped them in field-dressings. 'Thumb needs stitches, but you'll be all right.'

Rounds *thunka-thunked* off the wall: Cutler and Quinnell dipped: unseen Huns bawled orders below.

'Can't bloody shoot back,' Cutler moaned.

Quinnell was still thinking about the collision he'd witnessed: someone had sacrificed himself deliberately. The door of his aid-post was open: it didn't take much nous to work out that Grimshaw had hoofed it: it could only have been him in the Bren-carrier. *That's my grenade daisy-chain up the spout. Took me hours to set that up. I was saving it for the last ditch, too.*

He told Cutler what he'd seen. 'Must have gone bonkers,' he said.

Cutler's face was grey. 'Shorty's a bloody hero. That AFV could have done for us. It would've been all right if I hadn't muffed the shot.'

'You couldn't help it. You were hit. '

'Shut up, Paddy. Give me a wet.'

Quinnell leaned over, gave Cutler a gulp from his canteen. 'Take it easy,' he said. His own throat was parched, his lips split and sore: there was half an inch of paste on his tongue. *There were jerrycans lying around the jeep when we pulled out Caine, Wallace and Grimshaw. I was too windy to stop and pick them up.*

Vagrant rounds clattered: Quinnell corked the water-bottle, heard Copeland's steady rhythm of aimed shots from his right. The pattern of bursts from Caine on his left, and Trubman, above, had dwindled: *they must be short of ammo.* He heard the *ratatat* of a Bren from the distant gunpit, heard the six-pounder *gumf,* heard the shell pancake: *Wallace and Jizzard are still fighting.*

Quinnell crouched against sandbags: his smock was splattered with Cutler's blood. He dug in his webbing, came up with a bandolier: two clips, five .303 rounds each. *That's all there is.* His hands were shaking. *Look what happened to Cutler. There's no way I'm going to stick my head over the top.* He forced himself to pick up his Lee-Enfield, released the magazine, gripped it in his left hand, set his teeth, fed in clips with rigid determination. Cutler watched him through painshot eyes. His gaze fell on the two-inch mortar. He nodded at it. 'I reckon I could still fire that.'

'There's only two bombs left.'

He clicked the magazine home, lugged the cocking handle, coiled the sling round his elbow, murmured a Hail Mary, steeled himself. *Come on, you Paddy wanker. Get going.* As he turned away, Cutler raised himself to his knees, made a bid for the mortar. Quinnell didn't hear the falling shots that carved off one side of Cutler's head: he saw the face expand, billow like a rubber mask, saw a skull unrivet, saw a cheek ripped out, saw jaws unhinge, saw an eye pop like a soapbubble, felt himself splashed with brainmatter, felt an intense burning pain in the knee. *I'm shot.* Quinnell folded: his head millwheeled: he fought to stay alive.

In the next sangar, Copeland had been grazed by a bullet that had flipped off the wall, travelled along his left arm, scored a groove in his bicep. He bellowed in shock, pressed himself against the sandbag wall. It took him only a second to work out that the volley had come from high up. *The Krauts have got on to the ridge above the blockhouse.* He craned his neck to shufti over the side, was met by a barrage that tattered sandbag tops: he ducked, but not before he'd clocked pokes of fire from the ridge, maybe two hundred feet up. The Totenkopf boys had done what he'd thought impossible – they'd scaled the sheer cliff of the gorge, put a squad on the slab above. It was only smallarms fire: when they got a mortar up there, it'd be like spearing fish in a tidepool. *Our position's done for. There's no option but to pull the defence. Even then, we've got about as much chance as a snowflake in a furnace.* Copeland felt deep regret for Angela Brunetto, the moody, sensuous, incredible Italian girl he would probably never see again. He knew she'd been in love with him, knew she couldn't possibly have been the spy they said she was. He wondered if she was alive, wished he had had the chance to kiss her goodbye.

Blood blubbed from his left arm: it felt as if he'd been branded. He willed the pain away, cursed himself for underestimating the enemy. He'd told himself that the blockhouse was the perfect position, and he'd been wrong. It had been a mistake to try and defend it: SAS troops weren't meant for defensive actions.

Cope swallowed, flexed his bloody left hand to make sure he could still use it, saw redgored fingers ripple. He wiped the palm on his smock, grabbed the forward stock of his SMLE, shouldered the butt, scraped a round into the chamber. *This has to be the fastest shooting I've ever done.* He took five quick breaths, drew his upper torso clear of the sandbagged wall, snapped his eye to the telescopic sights, zeroed in on dark blobs on the ridge above, snatched steel, boosted fire, worked the handle like lightning, fired again, again, again, again and again. He didn't wait to see if he'd hit anyone: he bobbed down, laid his weapon across his forearms, snaked out of the sangar working elbows and knees.

Slugs dropped from the blue with a tuningfork hum, pranged metal, twisted steel. The Browning was shot out of Trubman's hands: he went down with it on top of him, got the redhot barrel across his wrist, smelt seared flesh, screeched with pain. He shoved the gun away with a fist, lay frozen in a foetal curl: bullets rained down like hailstones, sawed through the sandbags, cut them to pieces, showered him with sand. He had never felt so petrified: he couldn't move. *That's enough. That's enough. I'm nothing to do with this. I'm a signalman. I shouldn't be here. Stop it now.* A bullet mosquitoed past his ear: a bolt of cold terror shook him wide awake. *Never amount to anything, you won't, boy. No good at sports. Can't play rugby. Couldn't knock the skin off a rice pudding. Royal Signals, that's for nellies, that is.* The enemy was above him: if he tried to crawl to the ladder, they'd spot him from up there, and they'd kill him. A round screwlined past his ear, galvanized his body into action. His heart jolted, he drew in sand-dust, ate cordite stink: he willed his hands to move, felt the wristburn sting, whimpered. *I'm a twice-decorated soldier. Bravery, dah. His Majesty's High Appreciation. I'm* SAS. *Special Air Service Regiment.*

He forced himself up on hands and knees, wheeled his body, monkey-ran out of the sangar headfirst. Enemy fire shaved air, notched masonry: his limbs worked with what seemed like impossible speed: for a moment it felt so ridiculous that he gurgled with madcap laughter. He saw the shaftends of the ladder in front of him, knew it was the moment of truth. He grasped one shaft with his sound hand, swung his body off the roof, felt hot iron snap his left elbow. He almost fell, managed to steady himself with the other hand, felt himself sliding helterskelter down the ladder, felt woodburn, felt splinters lacerate his right palm, hit the yard beneath, went down like a ton of lead.

Copeland paused at the middle sangar, shuftied inside, saw a scene so sick he almost puked. Cutler's corpse lay propped against the wall: his head was like a weird melted-wax sculpture, one side intact, the other a red pulp of shirred bone, charred steak: an eye like a crushed grape dangled on a string of nerve. *Explosive bullet.* Cutler's chin was missing: bits of his shattered jaw poked out, relics of teeth protruded like dogfangs from the mess. Brain matter dripped down his shoulders, pooled under his legs: the sangar smelt like a firegutted abbattoir: the floor was smeared with blood: the walls were spattered with fried skinparings in burgundy streaks.

Quinnell sat opposite Cutler: his eyes were glazed white clockballs in a face purple with arterial blood, speckled with globs of tissue-like congealed glue. His kneecap was one big exit-wound – sheared sinew, shanked meat, stripmined bone. Cope guessed the bullet had scraped his shin, chiselled nerve-ends, chamfered flesh. He shivered. *Quinnell's alive. The pain must be hellish.*

Enemy weapons squittered: bullets flew past with ribald shrieks.

'Come on, Quinnell,' Copeland croaked. 'You've got to get out of it, *now.*'

Quinnell opened his eyes: his pupils bulged. Yellowgrey saliva oozed from his mouth. 'Can't do it, sir.'

Copeland hustled furiously into the sangar, kneeslid on gore, handskated on bloodslick. He hung his rifle over a shoulder, gripped Quinnell's arm, pulled him hard. Quinnell let out a shocking scream: Copeland swore, kept heaving. Hun rounds guffawed: Copeland bit his lip, tried not to imagine the agony Quinnell must be in. He flexed whipcord muscles, dragged the screaming Irishman clear of the sangar, lumped a breath, came up into a crouch, snaked an arm between Quinnell's legs, boosted him across his shoulder in a fireman's lift.

In the end-sangar, Caine watched Grimshaw's kamikaze crash with disbelief. He didn't have time to think about it: the Totenkopf point-platoon was mooching dangerously near the gunpit. The morphia was wearing off: he felt queasy. He had a splitting headache, his lips were parched, his wounds smarted like fire. He'd been confident at the beginning, but the Krauts were moving in steadily, drawing the net tighter and tighter: his ammunition would soon be out. He slapped a fresh pan on the Vickers, slammed down the top cover, lined up the muzzle just in front of the leading Huns. He boosted a spread, saw a Jerry go bowbacked, saw another saw air. He wellied off more short bursts of three and four rounds, aimed at bodies, tried to make every bullet count.

Rounds thrashed behind him, banged out wall-chunks, flamed up sandbag hemp. *What the devil . . .* He dekkoed over his shoulder: it took him a sec to spot the Huns up on the ridge: then he flushed cold. *The bloody bastards have got up there after all.* It hit him that none of the SAS boys was shooting back: Trubman's Browning was dumb. *Where the heck are Cutler, Quinnell and Cope?* Sweat stung his eyes: his heart clumped. For a horrific second he thought he was on his own: they'd all been scragged. Then he heard Copeland's trusty bunduk crank with incredible speed: *bomfff-chack bomfff-chack bomfff-chack bomfff-chack bomfff-chack*: five rounds. A second later Copeland came leopardcrawling frantically out of the sangar as if his arse were alight.

Volleys from the ridge went quiet. Caine gripped the Vickers' tripod with his right hand, shifted the gun a couple of yards to the opposite wall, squatted behind it. He elevated the barrel, saw Copeland dive into Cutler's position, heard the pitch and crack of Jerry's reprise, heard the eddy of echoes, the backslam of ricochets. He braced the gun, saw Copeland lug Quinnell out of the sangar, saw him heist the shrieking Irishman across his shoulders, saw him stagger straight for Caine's position. *He'll never make it. He's a sitting duck.* Caine's guts fluttered: he pulled a breath, hauled iron, brimmed fire, felt muzzlekick, heard spent cases chink, saw tracer darn a helix of rockchip splashes along the ridge. He didn't ease off until Copeland collapsed into his sangar, pitched Quinnell forward at his feet. Caine clocked the gash on Cope's arm, saw Quinnell's blown-out knee. The Irishman wasn't bawling any more: his eyes were closed.

'Where's Cutler?' Caine asked.

'Bought one, mate.'

'Trubman?'

'Dunno.'

'How the heck did the Huns get up there?'

Copeland shook his head. 'We've had it, Tom.'

Caine heard a Bren pattercake from downside, heard the six-pounder go *kapppowwww*, remembered the gunpit, realized with horror that he'd just given the Jerries a chance to overrun it. He yanked the Vickers back to its original position: Copeland struggled to help. Caine lowered the muzzle, angled the sights, dekkoed the pit. It was shrouded in dust and smoke. He saw Huns jogging through the murk. The Bren-fire stopped: he listened in vain for the bang of the field-gun, heard only distant yells, dull smallarms slaps.

'They're in,' he grunted. 'They've overrun the pit.'

He grabbed the field telephone, turned the handle. There was no answer. He spun it again, heard silence.

Copeland crawled alongside. 'Nothing we can do, Tom. We've got to leg it.'

Fizzers from the ridge started up again, spunked and crossfired, divotted shrapnel flotsam, creaked up parachutes of stonebats and dust.

Caine was already reloading the machine-gun. 'Get Quinnell into the tunnel, Harry,' he said. 'This is the last belt. I owe 'em that.'

'Tom —'

'Beat it, Harry. That's an order.'

'No, *sir*. Not without you.'

Caine spat grit, snapped the cocking handle, declined the barrel, drew a line as near to the pitedge as he could without dropping fire inside. Copeland unslung his weapon, stuck it over the parapet, chambered a round. *'Say when.'*

'Fire.'

The Vickers steamdrilled, vented orange, blustered fire. Caine hammered twenty rounds in a single sequence, saw smokeveiled bodies stumble, saw a Kraut writhe on the parapet, breathed fire on him till he went still. Two Jerries wove uncertainly: Copeland's rifle whammed so close to Caine it stung his ears: one of the Jerries staggered, tried to right himself: Cope blew off his chin. A bunch of Totenkopf figures scurried away from the pit: Cope picked the tailender, spiked him through the back, saw his guts spew out front. Caine blitzed the rest with his last twenty shells, saw Jerries dance and jiggle, jounce and flip: a sole survivor headed for cover, dragging a maimed leg. Caine squeezed the trigger: the Vickers stopped firing with an obstinate final chunk.

Trubman was out for a few seconds: when he came round the pain in his elbow was so bad he almost passed out again. His wrist was burning, his right palm stung: his elbow felt as if it had been squeezed through a mangle set with broken glass. He guessed that the bullet had hit the joint: he'd seen a wound like that before: the phrase *ulnar nerve palsy* sprang into his head. He was lying under the ladder at the base of the blockhouse wall, out of sight of the Jerries on the ridge. That, at least, was good: he could still hear shooting out front.

He sat up, felt for the field-dressing in his top pocket, couldn't find it. Instead, he snatched off his cap-comforter, padded it under his elbow, folded the useless arm across his chest. He daren't look at the wound: he felt warm blood soak his fingers through the cap.

He became aware that he was sitting in a pool of gore, knew he must be losing blood. The wound had to be dressed. He gazed around the yard, saw it out of focus, realized he'd lost his glasses. He couldn't remember if he'd had them on when he'd made his dash from the sangar: he felt a sudden wave of helplessness. Then, to his relief, he clocked them lying in the dust a couple of feet away. He stretched to pick them up: the frames were twisted and one of the lenses was cracked, but they would do.

He put them on, saw the wireless jeep parked by the wall, noticed that the yard gates were open. It struck him that something was missing: the Bren-carrier had gone. He'd been so focussed on the firefight he hadn't been aware of her exit. The Jerries could have come up behind him and he wouldn't have heard a damn' thing. He turned his attention back to the jeep. The drop-down wireless shelf was open: the No. 19 set was still on, with the headphones and Morse key attached, just as he'd left it. The Windam aeriels he'd set up with such effort were still standing: the wire antenna drooped between them like old washing-line.

There was a spare medical kit in the front of the jeep. He had to get it, but with his wounded elbow he couldn't crawl. His head girandoled: the yard cart-wheeled about him. He closed his eyes. *It's all right, sitting here. It's peaceful. Why move? I can just sit here and go to sleep.* He was drifting away, floating slowly undersea. He heard a series of five staccato cracks from a .303 on the other side. It brought him back. *Five shots. Copeland's* SMLE. He forced his eyes open, knew he had to shift: if he didn't he'd bleed to death.

He lurched to his feet, jellylegged it towards the jeep. He made it to the W/T shelf, sprawled across it, mewled through his teeth, leaned on his right arm. He was about to launch himself to the front of the jeep when he heard a rasp of static: the *tee-ta-tee-ta-tee* dicker of Morse from far away. For a moment he thought it was a hallucination: but no – it was coming from the head-phones. *I've got comms. Someone's trying to contact me.* His good hand was trapped under him, holding his cap-comforter to his injured elbow. He tried to grab the headset with the other hand, howled as a new pulse of agony crackled. He ground his teeth, flexed his fingers, felt them wriggle, felt his senses pirouette, let out a long *aaaaaaiiiiii*, felt the headset in his hand, held it shakily to one ear.

At first there was only mush: then a stream of Morse code blipped suddenly out at him through the headphone – the steady hand of a master, lucid as crystal. Trubman gasped: the message was coming in *clear* – in unciphered Morse. The airswell of dahs and dits spoke to him in the familiar syllables of a mother tongue: he grasped its meaning instantly: *Charlie Delta Bravo, this is Charlie Delta Alpha. Nothing heard from you. Your position unknown. Message from Sunray. Our objective achieved. Situation now mobile. Your presence in field no longer required. Withdraw immediately. Repeat. Withdraw immediately. Return to base. Echo Foxtrot Zulu dispatched to cover you. Sunray's message ends. Roger this message, over.*

Trubman couldn't believe he'd heard right. He contracted his hand to take the Morse key, knew he couldn't do it: the message would have to go unacknowledged. There was a pause: the message was repeated. He smiled blissfully, felt tears of gratitude in his eyes: it was all over. *Charlie Delta Bravo* was his own callsign: *Charlie Delta Alpha* was Fraser's SAS HQ: *Sunray* was Fraser. *Our objective achieved* meant that Freyberg's New Zealand division had taken the Tebaga Gap: *situation mobile* meant the Kiwis were now heading for Gabes, outflanking the Axis on the Mareth Line. *They've done it.* Caine's patrol hadn't blown the el-Fayya bridge, but that didn't matter: they'd held off the Totenkopf battalion long enough to prevent them harrassing Freyberg's rear. Even if the Totenkopf battalion broke through now, they'd never catch up with Freyberg before he reached Gabes. The best news of all was *Echo Foxtrot Zulu dispatched to cover your withdrawal. Echo Foxtrot Zulu* was a flight of Blenheim bombers of the Desert Air Force: the Brylcreem Boys were on their way.

Trubman let the headset fall, tried to raise himself. He heard a ruckle of machine-gun fire from the front position – *the Vickers* – three extended bursts *tack-tack-tack-tack-tack* . . . The shooting stopped: Trubman heard the distinctive *clang* of working parts closing on an empty chamber. For a moment silence hooshed. The smile was wiped off his face: it hit him suddenly that *Echo Foxtrot Zero* might be here too late.

Caine and Copeland dragged Quinnell to the tunnel, set him down against the wall. He looked bad: his eyes were flipped over so far that only the whites showed. Caine inspected his mutilated knee, saw bone-ends like jagged sawteeth. He guessed that the round had hit his ankle, travelled along the shinbone, blown out through the kneecap: there wasn't much blood, though.

Quinnell was still carrying his medical pack: Caine fished in it for a syrette of morphia, gave him the shot above the knee. He took out two field-dressings, ripped one open with his teeth, pressed the pad on the main wound, knotted the ends. He tore open the other, tied it tight around Quinnell's shin. It took him about five minutes, and by that time the morphia was starting to work. He could see the Irishman's pupils again: his breathing was heavy, his lips set in an idiotic smile.

The wound in Caine's side stung like hell: his arm felt as if it had been barbecued. He was also starting to get Benzedrine burnout: he retrieved Bennies from Quinnell's medical bag, popped four, washed them down with a gobful of water from his canteen.

Copeland crouched against the wall, tried to bandage his left bicep. Caine went to help him.

'Looks like a soft-tissue job,' he said.

Cope spat sideways. 'You should have seen Cutler. He was . . .' He winced: the butchershop scene was distant, as if it had happened a week ago. 'Must have been an explosive bullet . . .'

Caine thought about Grimshaw, recalled the image of the Bren-carrier ramming the German AFV. 'What the flaming heck did Shorty think he was up to?'

'Must have been popped up.'

'Either that or he was a brave bastard. Must be dead, anyway.'

'I'm not going out there to look for bits of him.'

Hun rounds went *goompah*: stone chips shellacked across the entrance. They ducked, forgot they were protected by the blockstone walls. 'They'll soon be down,' Copeland said. 'We need to get out, skipper.'

Caine finished tying the dressing. 'I'm not going without Fred and Taff.'

'Taff? You volunteering to go up for a dekko?'

'*I'm hit, boys,*' a voice croaked.

They gandered sideways, saw Trubman crab it in through the opposite end of the tunnel, his pudding face like death warmed up, his smock goresoaked, clutching his left elbow, his arm limp across his chest. Caine saw his eyeballs roll, jumped up, grabbed him before he collapsed. He helped him over, sat him down against the wall next to Quinnell.

'Where'd you cop it, mate? Elbow?'

'I gotta tell you, skipper . . .'

'Don't talk. Let's have a dekko.'

Caine knelt, lifted Trubman's arm, heard him yawp.

'You need morphia.'

'No, I gotta tell you . . .'

'It can wait.'

He was about to snatch another syrette from the bag when the Welshman stuck out a pudgy hand: Caine clocked the rabid scarlet burn on his wrist. '*Shit*,' he said.

'Never mind that, skipper. Message from Tac-HQ. Freyberg's through Tebaga. We're to hook it. RAF Blenheims are on the way.'

For a second Caine thought Trubman was delirious: he glanced at Cope, saw disbelief in his eyes.

'It's true, Tom,' Trubman pleaded. 'Came in clear, with all the access codes.'

Caine nodded, spat. 'How long before the kites get here? They give you an ETA?'

'Nope. They don't know our position. I couldn't work the Morse key even to roger the message. I reckon they'll fly in along the highroad: they'll know we're here somewhere.'

Caine frowned. 'Could be any time between five minutes and an hour. We can't wait for 'em. We have to go.'

He made a quick decision: they'd put Quinnell and Trubman in the jeep, lam it down into the lee of the butte, out of Nazi sight. Then he would take a shufti at the gunpit. 'The wagon still in order?' he asked.

'Looks OK. Bren-carrier's gone, though.'

'Yep. Grimshaw wrapped it round a Kraut AFV.'

'He bought one?'

'No one could have come through that. Dunno about the two in the pit, but I'm not sloping off without a gander.'

'You mean broach the gunpit?' Copeland cut in. 'That's crazy, Tom. There's a shitload of Squareheads down there, remember?'

'Didn't we just grease their backsides?'

'So they scarpered. That doesn't mean Wallace and Jizzard are still standing. Anyway, the Krauts'll be back soon as they realize we've stopped shooting. Probably already are.'

'What if Wallace and Jizzard *are* alive? You want to leave them to those cocksuckers?'

Cope swallowed hard, fingered his injured arm. 'Listen, mate. When those Jerries on the ridge get here, they'll drop fire right down on the pit.'

'No they won't,' Quinnell's voice rasped. 'Not if I've anything to do with it.'

Caine and Copeland turned to stare at the Irishman. His face was still green, but his eyes were bright. His lips had lost their dreamy pout: he looked grim and alert.

'You're badly wounded, mate,' Copeland said. 'You don't know what you're talking about.'

Quinnell smiled painfully. 'I never thought I'd be happy to hear a Brit officer call me *mate*. But I am. You pulled me out of that sangar under fire. You risked your life. That was a brave thing to do, and I thank ye for it. Now I'm going to return the favour. No bloody Kraut'll get past that tunnel end while I'm still breathing.'

Copeland held Quinnell's gaze for a second, wondering if he was still compos mentis. 'You're wounded,' he said again. 'You're in no state to cover us.'

'I'm wounded in the leg, not the arms. I can still shoot.'

Copeland glanced at Caine: Caine returned the look. On the one hand he was tempted to agree: Quinnell was partly responsible for their predicament. He'd deserted, and it seemed fitting that he should make amends for it. On the other hand, he'd come back of his own free will, fought bravely: he and Jizzard had saved their bacon when they were in trouble. Caine couldn't dump Fred: the big gunner was his friend. Quinnell wasn't, but he *was* a comrade, and to sell one comrade's life for another wasn't right.

'We're getting you out, Quinnell,' he said.

Quinnell chuckled. 'I'm not going anywhere. The only way ye'll get me out of here is by shooting me in the head. I'm done for anyway. The moment I turned back with that carrier, I knew I'd have to pay my dues. So here I am. This is me.'

The words brought a sudden flush of sympathy to Caine's cheeks. He stared at Quinnell, realized he was deadly serious. 'What are you going to shoot with?' he said. 'You've lost your weapon. Anyway, you'd need a machine-gun for that job.'

Quinnell's eyes fell on the Tommy-gun slung over Caine's shoulder.

'I've always fancied that weapon of yours,' he said. 'Reckon one of they big magazines'd do it?'

Caine sighed. His Tommy had been his talisman in so many battles: it was an old friend, and he felt he could never part with it. It occurred to him suddenly, though, how mean-minded that was: Quinnell was offering everything, and Caine was ready to begrudge him what was no more than a piece of hardware. He unslung the weapon, checked the 100-round magazine was full, clicked it back in place. He cocked the working parts, weighed the gun for a moment as if he were having second thoughts. Then he thrust it into Quinnell's hands. 'Pulls to the right on a long burst,' he said. 'Don't fire too many at once: the working parts get hot.'

Copeland stood up, hustled Trubman to his feet. 'We'll come back for you if we can,' he told Quinnell.

'Make sure ye do that, now.'

'In case you don't make it,' Caine said. 'Any last message?'

'Long live the Republic,' Quinnell said.

32

Shooting from the ridge had stopped: the Germans must be climbing down to the blockhouse, Caine thought. He scanned the high ground from the back yard, couldn't see the enemy. *Good: we've got a chance to shove off without being potshotted.* The jeep looked untouched: Caine jumped into the driving seat, started the engine. There was a spare .303 in the seatbrace: he hefted it out, checked the mag. The weapon felt unwieldy compared with his Tommy-gun, but it was better than nothing. He hopped out, signalled to Copeland, still hovering in the tunnel with Trubman. He jammed the brass-edged butt of the Lee-Enfield into his shoulder, hissed at the pain from his arm, crouched over the bonnet, beckoned to Cope, covered him while he supported the signaller across the yard and helped him into the back of the jeep. 'The Windam aerials,' Trubman wailed. 'We might need 'em.'

'Dump them,' Caine roared. 'Detach them, Harry.'

They bumped down the track: Caine heard sporadic fire coming from beyond the gunpit, guessed the Jerry platoons had dug in and were building up for another rush. He couldn't hear the patterpat of the Bren-gun: the six-pounder remained ominously silent.

He halted the jeep in the tamarix grove. He and Copeland leapt out, helped Trubman down. They crouched among the tangled trees and big stones, chugged water from canteens. Caine satisfied himself that the place provided solid cover: it was shielded by the rock wall from both the blockhouse above and the Hun units beyond the gap. He noticed that Trubman had found his M1 carbine in the jeep.

'What you doing with that weapon?' he demanded.

'Same as what you're doing with yours, skipper.'

'I'm going to recce the gunpit.'

'I'm coming with you.'

Caine let out a gasp of exasperation. 'You're out of action, Taff.'

'And you're not? You copped it worse than me, but I don't notice you excusing yourself.'

'Privilege of command. Anyway, I need you here to make sure the Huns don't nab the jeep.'

'That's Quinnell's job. That's why he stayed up there.'

Copeland was scanning the skies for aircraft: he looked worried. 'Where the heck are the kites? There must be three Jerry platoons out there. As soon as we stick our noses out, they'll snaffle us.'

'Why not do it in the jeep?' Trubman suggested. 'Just drive up fast with all guns blazing.'

'There's a better way,' Caine said. He pointed to the base of the escarpment on the other side of the gap, about fifty yards distant. 'There's a gully on that side. It's only about two feet deep, but it'll do. We can crawl down as far as the gunpit.'

Copeland nodded warily. 'We've still got to get across the gap, skipper. We'll be picked off.'

'We'll cover each other and take our chances,' Caine said. He cleared his .303, ejected a round, caught it with his left hand. He removed the magazine, thumbed the round back in, searched his pouches for ammunition. He came up with only a couple of rounds, regarded them sadly. 'Got any ammunition, Harry?'

Copeland didn't need to check. 'One full mag of .303 for the SMLE and one of .45 for the pistol. That's it.'

'You, Taff?'

'Thirty M1 rounds, and a full magazine in my Colt.'

'Give me the M1. It'll be more use in the gunpit than a .303 with ten rounds.'

Trubman scratched his eye under the cracked lens. 'I'll need it myself, skipper. It's light enough to be fired one-handed, see.'

Caine felt irritated: technically, Trubman had just refused two direct orders. Not that he'd ever stood on ceremony, but the signaller's new resolute manner was disconcerting. 'I told you you're staying here,' he snapped. 'With your arm in that state you'll never manage to crawl down the gully.'

'I'm not sitting this one out, skipper. We've been through plenty of shit together: I'm not deserting you now.' The signaller sounded as determined as Quinnell had: Caine knew it was an expression of deep personal loyalty rather than of insubordination: he was moved almost to tears.

He turned away, dekkoed Copeland, watched him

jack a sniper-round into the chamber of his weapon. 'I don't suppose it's any use my ordering you to stay, either, is it, Harry?'

Cope's ice-coloured eyes were strained: he shook his head grimly. 'Not on your nelly, Tom. But let's make a dash for the gully together: fire and movement will only alert the Krauts, and one of us is bound to cop it.'

'OK.'

They checked their weapons: Trubman considered his M1 carbine gravely, frowned at it, handed it reluctantly to Caine. 'You're right,' he said. 'I'll never fire it one-handed. I'll stick to the Colt.'

Copeland found the Very pistol and flares: they would need them when the RAF arrived – if they ever did. Copeland and Trubman swallowed Benzedrine tabs: Caine found a crushed packet of Victories in his pocket. There were only two flattened fags left: he slung the M1, lit one with his Zippo, passed it round.

He took the last long drag, closed his eyes, held the smoke in his lungs, felt the nicotine fire up in his drug-laden blood. Was he doing the right thing? He'd already lost most of the patrol: he couldn't deny that it was his decision to investigate the STENDEC aircraft that had dropped them in it. If they'd just blown the bridge and run, they'd be back with Fraser's force by now. Fiske wouldn't have had any reason to mutiny and desert. *That bloody black box. Maurice Pickney warned me not to touch it. No he didn't: Pickney's dead.*

But wasn't he making the same mistake again? *We've been ordered to withdraw: it doesn't matter that the Totenkopf are across the ravine – it's too late for them to stop Freyberg. It'd be so easy to just hop into the jeep, pile back down the road and let the bombers deal with the Krauts.* There was no more than an even chance that Wallace and Jizzard were alive, but if Caine dumped them, he'd have it on his conscience for ever.

He let the smoke dribble from his nostrils, stamped the fagbutt under his boot, paused for a moment, conjured up a vivid image of Betty Nolan. *She was the one thing I had to live for, and they knew it. That was how they got me into this. I'll never find anyone like her again. If I get through it, though, I'll wrap that fucking black box round Fiske's head. I'll see to it that Caversham and the others rot in hell.*

Copeland touched his hand. 'Ready, mate?'

Caine put an arm round both their shoulders: he wanted to say something, to say sorry, to say thanks, but he couldn't. 'Let's go for it, then,' he said.

They sprinted across the track in a cluster, so fast that the Jerries didn't have time to sight up on them. It wasn't until they were safely in the gully that rounds started scissoring over their heads, scuffing sand, starbursting stones. The shooting was languid, Caine realized: they'd been clocked all right, but the Squareheads weren't wasting any ammo. They squirmed like maggots along the sandy bed, Caine leading, Trubman in the middle, crawling lopsidedly on his good hand, Copeland bringing up the rear. They covered the distance to the bend in jerks, pausing for breath every ten yards. By the time Caine judged he was abreast of the gunpit, he was in agony from his wounds. He snorted breaths, saw that Trubman was dragging behind.

He took a dekko over the side. The gunpit was still shrouded in dust, but there was no movement: Hun bodies lay in dark huddles around its edge. Further on there was a wider swathe of Jerry dead, where he and Cope had mowed down the retreating horde. To his right he could see the smoking wreck of the armoured car that the gunteam had bagged, with more corpses scattered around it. Beyond that lay the jeep, still on its side, and, at the foot of the cliffs, the AFV Grimshaw had taken out, with what was left of the Bren-carrier smouldering half under its melted wheels.

He could make out no activity on the bridge: the Totenkopf platoons had gone to ground about four hundred yards away behind boulders, trees and grasstufts. There was an occasional puff of rifle smoke from their lines, the irregular rap of a machine-gun, but it was obvious they were making no effort to concentrate fire. *What the hell are they waiting for? Why don't they attack the gunpit?* Caine wondered if they were playing it safe, waiting till their mates occupied the blockhouse on the stump above.

Trubman crept up to him panting, with Copeland close behind. 'There's something odd here, skipper, ' Cope wheezed. 'Why haven't they renewed the assault?'

'They've taken too many casualties?' Caine suggested. 'Waiting for reinforcements, maybe?'

'Or maybe,' Trubman said, 'they want prisoners.'

Caine narrowed his eyes, caught Copeland's keen

gaze. 'Taff might be right,' Cope said. 'They could be waiting for us to spring the trap.'

Caine considered it, realized it was a possibility, decided he was going in whatever the risk.

'Anyway,' he said, 'it gives us a fighting chance.'

He peeked over the side again: the gunpit was no more than ten yards away – they'd be there in seconds. 'You ready?' he asked.

Copeland clasped his weapon across his chest: Trubman drew his Colt .45. They nodded.

'*Go.*'

They made the run in line, spread five yards apart: Caine blasted off a couple of .30 rounds as they raced over the stony ground. Answering bullets scrooped air, slashed around their feet. They'd almost made the pit when Trubman stumbled: Caine grabbed his good arm, dragged him over the parapet. They both landed on their feet inside: Copeland dropped down beside them.

They stared openmouthed at the carnage: the field-gun pocked and bullet-scarred, her shield smeared with blood and draped with flaps of raw tissue, the Bren lying on its side in a winedark pool. Three Huns with their guts spilled, flesh filleted, white bones gaping, were slouched out like blowfish among fricasseed skin and gristle that was spread everywhere: more dead Germans hung over the parapet, arms dangling, bleeding from mouths and nostrils. Fred Wallace was on his back between the guntrails, a downed colossus, stewpan mitt clutching his bloody throat: the legwound he'd taken earlier had opened up – his smock was stiff with gore. Jizzard was sitting against the side of the pit five yards away, arms wrapped round his body, blinking and drooling blood.

Copeland crouched over Wallace. '*Jesus wept*,' he said.

Caine picked up the Bren: the stock was wet with gore. He retrieved the haversack of spare mags, found a full one. He set the gun on the parapet, cleared it, racked a fresh mag in place.

'Reckon you can fire a Bren?' he asked Trubman.

The signaller flexed the fingers of his left hand. 'I've got enough strength there to to hold the stock steady. It's not going to be Bisley standard, but I reckon I can do it.'

'If you can't, use your pistol. If any Kraut gets within fifty yards, blast him.'

Trubman holstered his pistol, moved to the gun without another word.

'Fred's alive,' Copeland said. 'He's still breathing, but he's lost blood.'

Caine suppressed a surge of relief: there was no time for congratulations. He still had Quinnell's medical pack: he knelt by the big gunner, listened to his frayed breaths, took in the neck wound. It didn't look critical, he thought. He gave Copeland a field-dressing and a morphia syrette. 'You see to him,' he said. 'I'll check Jizzard.'

He squatted by the Scotsman: Jizzard blinked at him with inflamed eyes. 'You'll be all right,' Caine said. 'We'll get you out.' Jizzard went on blinking: Caine couldn't tell if he'd recognized him, or was even aware of his presence. He lifted the Scotsman's arms gently, saw that he

270

had a gunshot wound in the upper chest, a bayonet gash in the guts: the crotch of his overalls was black and bloody. Caine marvelled that he was still alive, let alone conscious. He drew his bayonet, cut open the trousers at the crotch to examine the wound: saw the red curry of minced tissue that had once been Jizzard's testicles. There was surprisingly little blood: he'd been hit at point-blank range: the flesh had been cauterized by the hard contact shot. Caine shuddered, dug a pack of gauze out of the medical bag, wadded pads into the wound, bound the area with a dressing. He was turning his attention to the bayonet wound when Jizzard groaned. 'I can't *feel* anything.'

'You're numb from shock. It'll wear off, though. I'm going to dose you with morphia.'

'Don't bother, sah. I'm not going to make it. Look after the big man. You let us down, ye know, sah. Ye stopped covering us. The Hun got through.'

Caine's throat constricted. 'We got bumped from the ridge. Had to switch fire.'

'In any case, I reckon I still owe you an apology. For doing what we did. Och, I didnae even wannae come back here. It was Fiske that did it. Saying I was yellow.'

'No one can call you yellow after this.'

A feeble smile played on Jizzard's lips. 'There won't be any *after this*, sah.' His hand sought Caine's: Caine held it firmly, felt it tremble. 'I wannae make it up to you, sah. Ye still wannae catch Fiske?'

'If we get out of this, of course.'

'I've got a map with his RV marked on it. The place he's taking the black box. I sneaked a look at his map, and marked it on mine. Just in case. It's in mah map pocket: help yourself, sah.'

Caine made a move to retrieve the map, but Jizzard clung to his hand. 'There's something else I have to tell ye.'

'Don't waste your strength.'

'No, ye'll want to know this, sah, believe me. You lost your girl, didn't ye? In a crash in the Nile.'

Caine flinched: why the heck was Jizzard bringing up Nolan now?

'When was it, sah? The date, I mean?'

'What are you talking about?'

'What date was it?'

'The day after *Torch*: 6 November 1942.'

'Let me tell ye aboot a lassie named Maddy.'

'*Maddy?*' Jizzard was rambling, Caine thought. When he'd first met Nolan she'd been using the cover name Maddy Rose.

'Och, Maddy wasnae her real name. It was when I was with the deserters. Some of the boys found her wandering the streets in Cairo one night, soaked to the skin. She hadnae a clue where she was: didnae even know her own name. Blond lassie, she was: green eyes you could ha' drowned in. Knew how to shoot, too. Fired a pistol left-handed . . .'

A finger clawed at Caine's spine: he felt his face flush, felt his grip tighten on Jizzard's hand. *A blond called Maddy. Green eyes you could drown in. Fired a pistol left-handed. Maddy. Maddy Rose. It can't be. It's another trick.*

'What are you getting at, Jizzard?'

Jizzard made a gurgling noise. 'I recall the night the lads found Maddy wandering the streets of Cairo, soaked to the skin. I recall it well. The day after *Torch*, it was, sah. 6 November 1942.'

Caine's jaw dropped. He felt as if Jizzard had just punched him in the gut. *Maddy Rose – Betty Nolan. Living with the deserters . . . didn't know where she was . . . didn't even know her own name.* He remembered Caversham's voice: *All I can do is offer . . . tentative explanations . . . that she suffered some sort of disorientation, and is no longer aware of her identity.* Had the monkey-man been right first time? Could it be true? *The deserters.* He couldn't bring himself to believe it.

'It must be . . . must be a coincidence.'

'She was still living with them a few weeks ago . . .'

'Where? Where was . . .' Caine broke off.

Jizzard's eyes had fogged up: he choked suddenly, coughed bloodspats. 'Don't let go of my hand, sah. I'm frightened . . .'

'You're not going anywhere. Hold on. *Jizzard.* Don't go away. Hold on. *Jizzard.*' He clutched the hand that had just become precious to him: his last link to Betty Nolan. He was still holding it when Copeland's voice said. 'He's had it, Tom.'

Jizzard's head drooped: brown sludge slavered from his mouth. Caine let go of his hand: the throb of gunshots brought him abruptly to his senses. He recognized the faraway, deepthroated *grumpa-grumpa-grump* of his own Tommy-gun. 'That's Quinnell,' he said. 'The Huns are in the blockhouse.'

'Let's get Fred out,' Copeland said.

Caine felt in Jizzard's patch-pocket, found the map marking Fiske's RV: it was dogeared and bloodstained. He stuck it in the map pocket of his trousers, spider-walked over to Copeland, saw that Wallace's eyelids were trembling. 'Lift him up,' he said.

Copeland slid both arms under the giant's armpits from behind. Caine bent to help.

'Hey . . . Tom.' Wallace grimaced suddenly: his voice was weak, clogged with blood and phlegm. 'What kept you?'

'Never mind that,' Caine said. 'Let's get you . . .'

A new broadside welted the parapet with a savage crackle, shed sparks, ground flint. The Bren burped, blattered out a trail of bright flechettes – *tacka-tacka-tacka-tack*. Trubman screamed from the pain in his elbow, but he didn't let go of the stock. 'They're moving, skipper,' he panted. He strung out another burst, paused. 'They were waiting for the boys upstairs after all.'

Caine's pulse jammered. For a split second he was torn between the idea of defending the position and getting Wallace out before the enemy poled up: it couldn't be done, though, he realized. It would mean leaving the badly wounded Trubman to cover their withdrawal. There were the Krauts on the stump, too. How long could Quinnell hold them off?

He skipped over to the parapet beside the signaller. 'Help Cope with Fred,' he said. 'I'll keep the Hun away.'

Trubman opened his mouth to argue: a mortar bomb hueyed in, zapped the pitedge in a blinding corona, shockwaved a scourge of blue-white flame and hot steel into the pit. Trubman shrieked and spiralled away: Caine spun sideways in slow motion, hit the pitside, smelt butchermeat, saw Trubman beached on his belly with flaps of flesh torn loose from his back.

The gunpit was awash with smoke and fumes: Caine blinked, realized his eyelids had been burnt off: his mouth was sour with cordite, his face raw from the blast: its main force had somehow missed him, though, clobbered Trubman instead. Then he saw that Wallace had also been hit; his treetrunk legs were gouged and cratered with fresh wounds: Copeland was on knees and elbows behind the giant – he'd been furthest from the blast, and looked unhurt. Caine guessed he'd been in the process of hoisting Wallace to his feet and had been shielded by his barndoor body.

He shook his head roughly: a crushing volume of enemy fire was pouring down on the pit: he thought he could hear in it the rasp of voices like the chatter of demons. The Hun would be on them in minutes.

He dragged himself over to Trubman, amazed that his limbs still worked. The signaller was conscious, babbling unintelligibly. Caine's heart slumped: he knew they'd never evacuate both Trubman and Wallace. It was too late. There was no way out: they were finished. He grinned madly: after all he'd endured, his war was over, just when he'd found out that Nolan was alive, just when he'd rediscovered something to live for. 'Hold on, Taff,' he said. He felt for the medical haversack: it was gone.

He backcrawled to the guntrails, where Copeland

was desperately trying to pull Wallace up. The big man was awake and roaring. *'Leave me alone, you bloody great twat. Get out of it, you bleedin' moron. Don't you know when to cut and run.'*

Caine nodded to Cope to let go of him, cradled the great shaggy head in his arms. 'We can't leave you, mate,' he said. He felt tears stinging the raw flesh of his cheeks. 'Not after all we've been through.'

Wallace's eyes popped like dark stars beneath the knobbly forehead. 'You're a bigger bloody fool than I thought you was, Caine. You think they can do for Big Fred so easy, you great pansy? I'll come through it: they won't stop me. I heard what Jizzard said. Nolan's alive. Go and get her, mate. You can't help us. Fuck off out of it, before I get up and kick yer soggy arse.'

Caine didn't let go of the bloodsmeared head: Copeland touched his arm. 'He's right, Tom,' he said. 'We can't get him out: it's either leave him, or face the music.'

For a moment they locked eyes. Cope didn't look away. 'Your call, skipper,' he said.

Rounds were buzzing closer: Caine faced the most agonizing decision of his life. He'd always promised he would bring back his wounded mates if it were humanly possible. But this time it wasn't. And this time it was Fred Wallace. And if he stayed, fought to the last round or surrendered – what about Betty Nolan?

'We'll never get out, Harry. Not with all that fire coming down.'

Copeland wasn't listening: his eyes were far away. 'What's that?'

Caine heard it, too: the boom of aero-engines, a basso-profundo resonance that seemed to chafe the sky, quite distinct over the smallarms fire. For a moment they stared at each other, frozen-eyed: the aircraft noise sounded distant: it was increasing steadily, though.

Wallace had also heard it. 'Get out now, lads.' There was a new desperation in his voice. 'The kites'll cover you. Go, skipper, for Christ's sake, or it'll be too late.'

Caine nodded. 'Can you fire a flare-gun, mate?'

'Me? I can do anything. I'm SAS, my son.'

Copeland loaded a flare into the Very pistol, pressed it into Wallace's giant palm. 'Don't shoot yourself, you big dollop.'

'Get out of here.'

Caine braced his Tommy-gun, paused. 'Fred, I –'

'Don't say it, Tom . . . Just get the hell out.'

They hauled over the pitside, rushed for the gully: a blue flare whooshed and popped above the gunpit behind them. At almost the same moment, a pair of Blenheim bombers swept in triumphantly over the blockhouse in a strafing configuration, engines snarling thunder, light flashing quicksilver on their plexiglass noses, bellyslung gunturrets spitting hellfire. Caine threw himself into cover, heard the whistle of bombs, felt the devastating quake of ordnance, so near it seemed almost on top of him.

33

A girl was screaming in Italian: *Cazzi. Stronsi. Lasciatemi stare.* Nolan heard the scrape of furniture, a slap, a man yelling. '*The bitch bit me.*' She recognized the high-pitched voice of Dick Willets, one of Taylor's gang, then the bass tone of Taylor himself. 'Stick her in the shed. Let her cool off there.'

Nolan's watch told her it was a quarter past seven. It was Saturday evening, already dark, but a bit early for a rumpus, she thought. She was lying on a mattress on the floor of the cubicle-like room, trying to catch up on her rest. In the week since she'd talked to Stocker, she'd been almost sleepless, brooding over Tom Caine, trying not to think about him, only thinking about him more. At the same time she'd had to work hard to prevent Taylor and the others from sensing any change: that was doubly difficult now she'd regained her memory, now that she had become a spy in their midst. She was acutely aware that she'd told Taylor her real name – or at least that Celia Blaney had called her Betty Nolan. Taylor had dismissed it at the time, but he wasn't stupid. He only had to do a little checking up to discover that Captain Elizabeth Nolan of G(R) had been reported lost in a car accident in the Nile the same night that Maddy had appeared.

She'd poured her energy into finding out about Calvin, eavesdropping on conversations, asking discreet questions, picking up hints. When necessary, she'd used her charms to wheedle out information, but she knew she was walking a tightrope: appearing to be too interested would have been suspicious. It had taken all her dramatic skills to bring off the act without a slip.

She'd talked to a Polish deserter who'd admitted kidnapping two Egyptian schoolgirls and delivering them to a place in Alexandria: he couldn't or wouldn't tell her its location, and she hadn't pressed it. A Cypriot girl living with another deserter gang had confided in her that one of her girlfriends had vanished after being given the chilling message *Calvin wants to see you*. The woman was certain that her friend been taken to Alexandria. Others had hinted that Calvin was a Bluebeard figure with an insatiable appetite for women: that he'd have girls delivered to his castle, where he would torture and butcher them. She didn't believe the tales, but no one she'd spoken to, not even Taylor, seemed to know anything definite about Calvin's identity: some said he was a cashiered British officer: others had him down as Greek, Turkish – even Albanian.

One thing was certain: the attitude of the deserter gangs had become more robust in recent days. It was said that Calvin was making a bid to take over the whole show, to organize the gangs on a businesslike basis, to run them as a mafia, controlling smuggling, gambling, prostitution, drugs. There'd been some talk of turf wars between deserter groups: rumours of attacks on military bases, mainly for weapons. Taylor's group had started running a protection racket in the Miski, shaking down Egyptian shopkeepers under threat of burning them out.

Nolan heard footsteps, heard a door bang. She waited a few moments, then threw a man's trenchcoat over her pyjamas, belted it loosely, opened the door, walked out into the derelict room Taylor had facetiously christened the *ops centre*. Their safe-house was an old Fellaheen homestead in an almost deserted Delta village, with boarded-up windows, crumbling mud walls, and a ruined yard out back.

She found Taylor and Willets lounging in wicker chairs in the lamplight, smoking, drinking snorts of whisky from chipped mugs. A brown bottle stood on the plywood sheet mounted on piled bricks that passed as a table. Taylor looked rough: he was wearing his superfluous eyepatch. Willets, an overweight former Catering Corps cook, had a head like a picklejar and an aggrieved expression. Swarthy and unshaven, he was dressed as an Egyptian in tattered shirt and trousers, broken shoes, a shapeless fez.

They glanced at her as she entered. '*Cor*,' Willets gasped. 'You were right, mate. Talk about dead ringer. Got a twin sister, darlin'?'

Nolan yawned, swept the golden quiff out of her eyes. 'What's going on?' she asked. 'Who was that screaming just now?'

She picked up the bottle, unscrewed the cap, sniffed it, made a sour face. It was cheap Palestinian hooch: the only whisky available these days. She leaned over Taylor, took the cigarette from his mouth, puffed it coolly, blew a stream of smoke. She ran a hand through her tangled curls, arched her head back so that her coat fell away slighly from her shoulders, revealing the smallest cleavage. Willets stared: his fatlipped mouth formed a small 'o' before she readjusted the coat.

'The cow bit me, didn't she?' He displayed a fat, grubby hand, showed her five neat bite-marks in the palm.

Nolan put the fag back between Taylor's lips. 'Who?'

Taylor removed the cigarette from his mouth. 'Your twin sister. Either that or your doppelganger.'

'I haven't got a twin sister.'

'No, 'course you ain't. An' this bint's an Itie. Spittin' image 'o you, though. Just as feisty an' all.'

Nolan nodded, kept her face blank, disguised her interest. There weren't many Italians at large in Cairo now. Most male Italian residents of military age had been interned by the British back in 1940: a lot of the women had been placed under house arrest.

'Where is she now?'

'Locked in the shed. Any longer an' she'd 'ave 'ad Willets's flamin' arm off.' He chuckled.

'It ain't funny. I'll have to put iodine on it. Never know what you might catch.'

'So what's the story?' Nolan insisted.

'We was doin' the rounds in the Miski, leanin' on Gyppo shopkeepers, when we come across this blond bit. Only holding up a grocer's with a pistol, wasn't she?'

'For a minute I could of sworn it was you,' Taylor cut in. 'I said, 'allo, what the 'ell is Maddy doin' here?''

'Anyway, the Gyppo cuts up rusty,' Willets went on. 'Tries to slice her with a cleaver. Lucky for her we 'appened to be passin'. We gave the old bugger sommat to think about and pulled her out. Was she grateful? Was she heck. Scratched and fought like a cat all the way out. Good job the flamin' Redcaps didn't catch us.'

'Pistol wasn't even loaded,' Taylor chortled. 'Amateur job.' He brought out a handgun from the pocket of his leather jerkin: an old Beretta revolver. Nolan examined it, gave it back to him.

'Ain't been fired in years,' he said. 'Firin' pin's broke. She reckoned it'd belonged to her father – MPs didn't find it when they interned 'im, she said.'

'We took her off to the Bulaq house, asked her a few questions. She kept tryin' to escape, so we had to tie her up. She reckoned she was brought up in Cairo, went to the Italian school, worked as a secretary for a cotton company. Name of Camilla, Camilla Pellozzi . . . sommat like that. Father owned a garage. He and her brothers got rounded up before the war, and she and her mum was forbidden to go out. Said it was like bein' in clink: she couldn't stand it, so one day she takes her dad's gun and does a bunk. Said she'd been livin' rough. Only took to robbin' 'cos she got hungry.

'So all the time I'm askin' 'er these questions, I'm thinkin' she could almost be your twin – I mean, all right, she's a bit more wiry, maybe, eyes a different colour, and she's got a different look on her face – like someone just farted – but in a certain light, she could have been you.'

'Except she's an Itie,' Willets added.

Nolan giggled, tried to suppress the excitement she was starting to feel. Italian women were a rarity in Cairo: she only knew one, and, by coincidence, that woman bore an uncanny resemblance to herself. But why would that woman be robbing a shop at gunpoint?

'So what are you going to do with her?' she asked casually.

'I know what I'd like to do with her,' Willets wheezed. 'I'd like to . . .'

'Shut it,' Taylor snapped. 'None of that talk in front of a lady.'

He scratched his flopping tuft of hair. 'We could 'ardly turn 'er in, could we? I suppose we could of dumped 'er, but she might have snitched on us. Then I thought, why not take 'er with us? After all, she's on the run just like we are, and 'avin a bird that's almost Maddy's double might be handy. When I put it to her, though, she threw a bleedin' wobbler. We 'ad to drag her here, an' she was still fightin' when we arrived. Tell you what, though: she's got some spirit: she'd be good with us if she'd just come round, but she won't see reason.'

'She will,' Willets grinned.

'Maybe she will. But I don't want you layin' a finger on her, mate. If I find out any bloke's messed about with 'er there'll be hell to pay.'

He looked at Nolan. 'Maybe you could 'ave a word with her, love. Help 'er see sense.'

Nolan hesitated. 'I don't know. It's not my business, is it?'

'Go on. She won't feel threatened by another woman.'

'All right then. But let me talk to her on my own. Girl to girl, no blokes breathing down my neck.'

'You're on. But watch it – she's as full of moves as a monkey.'

Two scrawny dogs barked when Nolan entered the yard carrying a torch: they recognized her and soon sat down. The moon was waning and gibbous, the night warm, scattered with stars. The outhouse was small: it had once been occupied by goats and Nolan knew it was still full of their droppings. Its crude wooden plank door didn't fit properly: it was held in place by a wooden bar. She paused to make certain that Taylor and Willets were out of earshot before she slid the bolt back. She pulled the door open, shone her torch inside. Huddled in a corner among the goat turds, her face bruised and tearstreaked, sat Angela Brunetto.

I'll be sending backup. Someone who'll be able to fit in easily among the deserters. You'll be able to keep contact with me through her. Nolan had wondered who it might be: she'd never guessed it would be the Italian woman who'd saved their lives on the *Runefish* mission, who'd prevented her own husband, Michele, from assaulting Nolan, who'd killed that same husband with a knife in defence of Harry Copeland, the man she loved.

Nolan didn't know much about Brunetto's life: she was originally from Milan: she hated Mussolini. Her father had been killed fighting the Germans in the

Great War, and she'd never forgiven them. Aged seventeen, she'd been sent to live with an uncle who had a business in Tripoli, but she had been so wild and unruly that he'd threatened to send her home. It was then that she'd met Michele, an Italian soldier and a communist, who'd later deserted and taken her with him. Brunetto had very clear ideas about personal loyalty: she'd never been unfaithful to her husband until she'd found him playing around with other girls. Then, she'd set her sights on Harry Copeland, gone after him like a torpedo, and had been ready to risk her life for him. She appeared excitable sometimes, but she was as cold as ice when the chips were down. She didn't have the diffident greyness that made the ideal agent, perhaps, but she was resourceful, independent and tough. Nolan was delighted to see her.

Brunetto rose to her feet, blinked in the torchlight: she was wearing black FANY one-piece overalls that made her almost invisible in the shadows, but for the pale, angular face and feral blond hair.

Nolan shone the beam obliquely on herself. 'Good evening, *Camilla*,' she said.

Brunetto's eyes widened: Nolan put a finger to her lips, beckoned her out of the shed. She led her across the yard, through one of the gaps where the mud walls had collapsed. They stood outside in the moonlight under part of a wall that was still standing. 'If anyone comes, the dogs will bark,' Nolan said.

They wrapped their arms around each other, held on tightly for a long time. 'I thought you were dead,' the

Italian girl whispered. 'That night with Caine. In the river. Then Stocker, he tell me you are alive, hiding with deserters . . . just like me in Libya, no?'

'Not exactly,' Nolan said. 'I didn't know who I was when they picked me up. Tom was . . . he didn't make it.'

Brunetto flushed. She broke away, squeezed both Nolan's hands. 'I'm so sorry.'

Nolan dropped her eyes. 'What about Harry?'

'That *cretino* Stocker. I say yes I do this, and he tell everyone I am a dirty little Itie spy all along, as . . . how you say . . . *cover*. He don't even *tell* me this until after. Now my Harry believe it is all *falso*, you know, him and me.'

'No he won't. He'll never give up on you.'

Nolan fished for a packet of cigarettes in the trench-coat pocket, lit fags for both of them.

Brunetto drew in smoke.

Nolan peered at her face in the moonlight, inspected the bruising on her cheek.

'I'm sorry they knocked you about.'

'I have to fight to make it look true.' She shrugged. 'But they are *stronsi*, no? How you stand them? The fat one, he is *brutto*, but the other, with the bad eye, he is handsome, maybe? He is your *friend*, now?'

Nolan shivered despite the heavy coat. 'He'd like to be. He can be violent, but he adores me. He has his moments, but he's not –'

'Not Thomas?' Brunetto smiled. 'You never give up on *him*, no?'

'They'll be here in a minute. What are we going to tell them?'

'That Camilla agree to stay, because she cannot go back to her family. You tell them also that I am not *puta*, that I am, how you say . . . a *hard bitch* . . . and if any man touch me I cut his throat. You know I do it, too.'

Nolan nodded grimly, remembered how Brunetto had once shot her husband, Michele, in the foot, crippling him for life – a life that she herself had terminated when she'd buried his own knife in his gullet. She'd do it all right.

Brunetto finished her cigarette, stubbed it out against the wall.

'Now tell me quick about this Calvin,' she said.

'I don't know much,' Nolan said. 'Only rumours. Stocker's right about him taking control of deserter gangs: girls *are* being abducted, and the gangs *are* carrying out operations against military targets.'

'*Sì. Sì.* But who is he? Where he live?'

'No one knows. The rumours seem to point to Alex as his base, maybe in a villa of some kind.'

'That is no good for Stocker: he want name, address *and* telephone number.'

'How are we going to get hold of those?'

'You get invited home by Calvin. Is the only way to find out.'

34

I'll have to tell him, Johann Eisner thought. *Calvin will have to know.* He paced the floor, cursed, paused for another gander at the four-by-six photograph that lay on his desk. He peered out of the window across the harbour, saw the mirrored waters of the Mediterranean, saw drifts of seagulls on straffing runs, saw the bright hulls of Allied vessels riding at anchor under a hazeless sky. Among the ships, he knew, lay Admiral Godefroy's renegade French fleet, which Winston Churchill had as yet adamantly refused to release. Eisner's house stood on the Alexandria waterfront, a stone's throw from King Farouk's rambling seaside palace at Ras el-Tin.

The photograph showed a beautiful blond girl with an enticing kiss-curl, wearing a calf-length skirt, a white blouse and a light jacket. She was smiling, revealing the cute overlap of her front teeth, holding up a copy of the *Egyptian Gazette* to the camera. The headline was clearly legible. *Tripoli Falls to the Allies.* The paper was dated 23 January 1943.

It's no good. Calvin will have to be told.

The photograph had arrived that morning in a manila envelope, accompanied by a letter embossed with the royal seal. It was signed by Mohammad Hassan, the king's butler, whom Eisner knew was also chief of the palace intelligence service. He'd sometimes made use of Mohammad Hassan's organization – a surprisingly efficient spy network of mainly Nubian and Berberine waiters, barmen, maids and other domestics, who had access to almost every establishment in the country.

The documents had been delivered by a blueskinned Berberine with grave eyes and long fingers, in a spotless white gallabiyah and skullcap. He had stood very still while Eisner studied the image: Eisner had had to hold on to the edge of the desk, waiting for the rage and shock to subside.

'It must be a fake,' he'd grunted finally.

'I can assure you it is not, *effendi*.'

'Then where did you get it?'

'That, I can't say.'

Eisner had examined the image minutely with a magnifying glass, but found no sign of tampering. No, he had to face it: it was *her*, the Nolan bitch, standing there as brazen as ever, holding a newspaper that indicated she'd been alive and kicking three months after she was supposed to be dead.

It's not possible. She died that night. She drowned in the Nile. I know Caine escaped, but not Nolan. There was no record, not the slightest rumour.

He tasted bile, felt dry fury welling up once more. He touched the scar on his throat – the scar from the wound *she'd* given him with a knife. Nolan was as slippery as a tart's crack: she'd eluded him on every single occasion, from that first time she'd stumbled on him in the ladies room at Madame Badia's nightclub, to the time he'd broken into her flat in al-Hadiqa Street, when her stand-in, Susan Arquette, had accidentally been killed. He'd had her cornered that time in his step-father's villa: she'd even been handcuffed. Yet she'd escaped, thanks to the knife – given her by that traitor-ous whore Hekmeth Fahmi, whom he'd once regarded as a sister. *And the last time, on the Nile Corniche. I planned it so meticulously: I risked everything by going back. To get her and Caine in one fell swoop. It was all going perfectly until she recognized me. She tried to snatch my weapon. I lost control. The car shot through the barrier, plunged into the Nile.*

How he himself had survived the crash he couldn't say. He'd come round after the impact to find himself floundering in dark water some way downstream, car-ried by one of the Nile's maverick currents. He'd been lucky. Some boatmen had pulled him out: he'd still been wearing his *fellah*'s clothes, and he'd managed to bluff his way without attracting the attention of the police

He'd been chagrined to find out later that Caine had been rescued, of course, but for five months now he'd been convinced that Nolan's bones lay at the bottom of the Nile. All this time he'd thought her dead, yet here she was again, popping up like an infernal jack-in-the-box.

His first concern, after the initial rage had faded, was for his own security. Nolan didn't know he was alive, and he wondered if she'd still be able to recognize him. He dressed Egyptian-style now, and was known to the world as Sayfaddin Lutfi. Only members of the palace inner circle knew him as Hussain Idriss, supplier of the king's pleasures – in the form of an endless stream of nubile girls.

The fact that Nolan might be able to identify him as the man who'd murdered Mary Goddard at Madame Badia's didn't matter to him any longer: that man had not been himself, just a shadowy presence that haunted him. He hadn't really been responsible for sodomizing and murdering the cabaret-girl Sim-Sim, either, or Susan Arquette, or the others. He'd simply been *away* for a moment and found them dead when he came back. No, there was something else about Nolan that itched like a sore on his back, something that he'd never be able to admit to anyone. Her dreamy, unselfconscious *presence* – it was almost fey – made him feel helpless and impotent. Yet despite that or, more likely, because of it, somewhere in the dim recesses of his mind, he *wanted* her. The very knowledge of her existence would eat at him until eventually he would be obliged to take her, to have her for himself.

He didn't know where she was, of course. At first he'd concluded that she must be in Cairo: the photograph had certainly been taken in a Cairo street. But how was she living? Where? Why hadn't his sources picked up any intelligence about her? The only explanation was that the British were keeping her under wraps. But that didn't add up either. If so, why would they allow her to wander around the streets, or to pose for such a photograph?

It was the Berberine messenger who'd provided the

solution. 'The woman is known to be living among deserters,' he'd said. 'We have no idea which group or where.' Eisner had been puzzled at first, then the only possible explanation occurred to him: Betty Nolan had lost it completely – she no longer knew who she was.

35

There was an underground tunnel connecting Eisner's house with the sprawl of basements Calvin inhabited, under the ruins of the old Baylun palazzo. There was another secret passage from there to King Farouk's magnificent Ottoman citadel on the waterfront at Ras el-Tin. They were so close that you could walk between all three places in thirty minutes, yet it was an hour and a half, and two stiff drinks, before Eisner arrived at Calvin's abode. There were no guards here, no obvious security, but Eisner knew Calvin could summon a platoon-sized mob of thugs at the snap of his fingers. He hurried down the decrepit pasages, lingered nervously outside the heavy iron door.

Calvin was one of the few men who could reduce Eisner to a stuttering wreck. The wholly German stepson of an Egyptian Muslim, brought up in Egypt, he spoke Arabic as fluently as he spoke German, English, French, Italian and several other languages. He was unique: he'd been more useful to the Abwehr than any other agent in Egypt, he told himself. The problem was that he'd never really been a German patriot, never been truly committed to the Nazi cause. He'd been able to pull the wool over the eyes of his Abwehr instructors, but not Calvin. Calvin knew.

The war suited Eisner: he wanted it to go on and on. In a sense he'd been relieved that the Axis hadn't captured Egypt: it looked unlikely now that it ever would. In fact, things weren't going well for Hitler anywhere. First Alamein, then the Anglo-American landings in the Maghreb, the defection of the Vichy French in Tunisia, and, just last month, the most devastating event of all – the defeat of Axis forces at Stalingrad, and the capture of 90,000 soldiers. True, they seemed to be holding off the Allies in Tunisia, but it was only a matter of time before they were kicked out.

The war in Egypt would continue, though: at least, Eisner hoped so. That was Calvin's mission. To create a fifth column of Allied deserters, who would strike from within, at both military and economic targets. The beauty of it was that the deserters wouldn't even know they were working for the enemy: they would be convinced that their operations were being carried out in the glorious name of private enterprise. It was Calvin who had planned this scheme, who'd suggested using Eisner's family business – trading in women – as a way of sponsoring the project, as well as moving in on smuggling, drugs, gun-running and prostitution. Despite having been bedridden for months, Calvin had also been instrumental in devising the STENDEC operation, a complex Abwehr plan to destroy Allied command in Egypt.

Eisner lifted his hand to knock on the door, hesitated. He was still chary of telling Calvin that Nolan was alive. Calvin had his own reasons for being satisfied that Eisner had finished her off: he'd even complimented him on it – a rare honour. Eisner suspected that Nolan had had something to do with the state Calvin was in – the crippled, scarcely human shell that lurked in these basements. Calvin had always thought him incompetent: he would be consumed with vitriol when he discovered that Eisner's claim was empty – that he hadn't succeeded in killing Nolan after all. He raised his hand again: before he could knock he heard a sibilant whisper. *'Come in, friend Sayfaddin.'* Eisner opened the door.

The cellar stood in shadow, apart from the corona of light around a single oil lamp. The walls were covered with faded hangings, the room dominated by an ancient four-poster bed, draped with mosquito nets. The place smelt of mildew and wet rot. On one side there was a wireless cubicle, partitioned by curtains, and on the other a desk, bookshelves and a dilapidated leather armchair. The armchair was occupied by a Buddha figure in dark clothes, visible only in outline.

Calvin usually kept his face hooded, but Eisner had glimpsed it once and had been appalled. The features were so hideously disfigured it might have been a mask – a composite of scars, burns and skingrafts, brittle jawhinges, relict scabs of nose and ears, a mouth like a sphincter, eyepits concealed behind round lenses of dark glass. Calvin's right leg was a stump: he had shrapnel in his trunk and knees, and his right arm had been amputated at the shoulder. His remaining arm tapered down to abnormally long fingers, like thin spiderlegs.

Eisner knew that it was these fingers that had given rise to Calvin's nickname, the *Black Widow:* his real name was Heinrich Rohde.

Rohde watched Eisner strut into the room. Despite his mutilated body, his senses were acute – more acute than ever: he was perfectly aware that Eisner had hesitated for a long time before coming in: that meant he had bad news to impart.

Rohde had been in Egypt for only a few months, yet he'd already begun to whip the deserter bands into shape, had already set in motion the STENDEC op. His recovery had been nothing short of miraculous. On that last job in Libya his hand had been almost slashed off: his throat had been cut from ear to ear. He'd been exposed to an explosion so powerful that it would certainly have killed him had he not been shielded by the bodies of his men. He'd been careless, though. He should have suspected that Caine's team had set charges secretly among the Olzon-13 cylinders. Thanks to the SAS, the entire supply had been destroyed. Not that it would have made any difference to the Allied offensive. The SAS mission had, in the end, been part of a deception plan aimed at giving the Panzer Army the impression that the advance would start later than it did. The British had made a fool of him: all that had kept him going during his months in traction was the desire for revenge. He'd dreamed up STENDEC while lying in his hospital room: if it succeeded, it would be the ultimate payback.

Eisner was standing nervously in front of him,

clutching what looked like a photograph. Rohde let him squirm. Eisner was no fool: his special skills and attributes gave him unique value. Yet he had a fatal flaw. Rohde had suspected it for a long time, but now, living under the same roof, so to speak, he had proof. He knew about the girls who'd vanished in transit to the palace, the breathing holes in the boot of Eisner's car, the grottoes where he played his horse-and-jockey games, the shallow graves in the desert. Rohde had served in Heydrich's Einsatzkommando in Russia: he'd done his share of butchery. Eisner's penchant for sodomizing and murdering girls, though, was an addiction he couldn't control. Rohde guessed that, on a conscious level, he was hardly even aware that he was doing it.

He wondered what had perturbed Eisner – if he, too, had had news of STENDEC. It was unlikely: Rohde had never revealed the full details of the STENDEC scheme to him, knowing that the man, though a professed German, was actually Egyptian at heart: he would be horrified by what the contents of the black box implied.

'*What's that you're holding?*' he enquired abruptly.

No matter how often Eisner heard Rohde's voice, he never ceased to find it chilling. Rohde spoke German with a breathless lisp that to Eisner sounded effeminate, as if Rohde himself wasn't there – as if some queen possessed his husk of a body.

He took a shaky breath. 'It's a photograph, delivered by a messenger from the palace this morning. There's no doubt it's genuine. It shows the Nolan girl. It was taken the day Tripoli fell – 23 January 1943. That means she was alive three months after the crash. She survived.'

'*Give it to me.*'

Eisner handed him the photo: there was a long pause. Eisner popped sweat, waited for the explosion. Calvin's hollow rasp of laughter made him jump. It wasn't what he'd been expecting: it sent a shockwave down his back.

'So, all this time you've been telling me that Nolan was at the bottom of the Nile, when she's actually alive.'

Eisner rubbed sweat off his forehead with a handkerchief: it angered him that Rohde could make him feel this vulnerable.

'How could I know? There wasn't even a hint. The current intelligence is that she's living with deserters.'

'Women like Nolan don't desert.'

'No, that's true. She's had some kind of breakdown, I think.'

Rohde didn't answer. The shadows, and his hooded, expressionless face, masked the fact that he was fighting back absolute fury – a rage so acute that for a moment he was tempted to slip out his weapon and shoot Eisner in the guts. *He'd let her get away. Again. He would pay for that.*

Nolan had been responsible for Rohde's fall from grace with Rommel. It was Nolan, not Caine, who'd been the chief architect of the Olzon-13 debacle: her sudden arrival had changed everything. Caine and his big gorilla friend had been happily ripping each other apart before she'd turned up. Rohde desperately wanted her dead, but he'd learned patience lying in those hospital beds. It would come: that was certain, and this time he wouldn't have to leave it to Eisner.

He let the anger drain out of him. What mattered now was STENDEC. If it succeeded, STENDEC would do for them all.

'If Nolan is with the deserters, we will find her. Until then, forget about her: STENDEC is more important.'

If Rohde's tone was intended to put Eisner at ease, it had the opposite effect. The Abwehr man was as vindictive as they came, and this dismissive attitude was unnerving. Eisner was quite aware that his blunder would come back to haunt him, just when he least expected it.

He pocketed his handkerchief. 'Why, is there a hitch with STENDEC? I thought it was all going according to plan.'

'Yesterday I received a disturbing report from my source in Panzer Army command in Tunisia: a battalion of the Totenkopfverbande has been tasked to retrieve the black box.'

'*What?*' Thoughts of Nolan vanished abruptly from Eisner's mind.

'I didn't know the Totenkopf Division was even deployed in North Africa.'

'It isn't. This is just one unit – a motorized battalion. Officially, it's scouting ahead of 164 Panzer, east of the Matmata Hills. I don't believe this is a coincidence. My latest report confirms that the battalion's recon company caught up with a small British commando group just short of the el-Fayya pass. They were in possession of the black box.'

'You mean Caversham's squad?'

'I'm assuming so. There was a contact: the British escaped. The Totenkopf gave chase, but something unexpected happened. The Tommies made a defensive stand at el-Fayya bridge.'

'Against an entire Totenkopf company?'

'Yes, and they held it for a night and a day. That looks to me like a classic holding operation: keeping the enemy at bay while they sent the black box on ahead. We must salute them, my friend. They risked their lives in order to make sure *our* black box is transported behind *their* lines.'

Rohde grated a chortle. Eisner shook his head in apparent confusion. He smiled inwardly: now Rohde was praising British courage in defeating German soldiers, who were going all out to impede an operation *against* the British. It was going from the sublime to the ridiculous. He knew that the Abwehr had set up the STENDEC op with infinite care and great expense. How incredibly irritating for them that the black box should be intercepted by their own side.

'I don't understand. Why would the Totenkopf interfere with an Abwehr operation?'

'I can only speculate. Their orders come from SS command, of course. Himmler and his cronies have been trying to discredit the Abwehr for years. There've been arrests, even allegations of treason. Now things are turning sour on every front, they may be trying to put the blame on us. If STENDEC succeeds, it will be a major coup. It will reinstate us in the eyes of the OKW. Their objective may be to prevent that.'

'So what can we do about it?'

'Nothing. We can only hope that whoever has the black box now is good enough to elude the Totenkopf. We can also pray that they don't open it. At least, not before they get it inside GHQ.'

36

SS-*Sturmscharführer* Gert Lohman had confiscated the Tommy-gun that No. 2 Platoon had found in the block-house tunnel. The rifleman who'd picked it up had been reluctant to hand it over. 'A souvenir, that is, sir. That Brit potted three of us with it before we got him. I reckon he was already wounded: stayed behind to hold us off.'

You had to give it to the Brits, Lohman thought: they were stubborn in defence. There'd been only a handful of them, yet they'd inflicted more than seventy casualties on the recon company, *and* taken out all five of the armoured cars they'd had in support. Their position had been favourable, of course, and they'd had a bit of help from the Desert Air Force, but still, you had to admit it – they were good.

Lohman's No. 1 Platoon had been held in reserve during the assault – rightly so, in his judgement, because they'd suffered a battering in the ambush at the foot of the pass and had had an entire night patrol wiped out. They'd moved up after the battle, traversing the killing zone on foot: in those five hundred yards Lohman had come across some of the worst carnage he'd ever seen: headless bodies, limbless torsos, men with their guts spilling, men grovelling in gore, begging to be put out of their misery. The place was dotted with wrecked armour: the whole place reeked of sulphur and burnt meat.

Bloodshed didn't unnerve Lohman. A 32-year-old warrant officer of the Totenkopf Division, he'd been with them since the time they'd cleared the Warsaw Ghetto, since the days when all his comrades had been blond-haired, blue-eyed Nordics like himself. In those days the Waffen SS had been an elite: it was only their high casualty rate that had obliged them to accept any riff-raff – even Slavs. People they'd originally been told were subhumans were now wearing the Death's Head badge.

Lohman had been a camp-guard before the war: he'd learned early that authority was force. He didn't think of himself as a dishonourable man, but he had no namby-pamby ideas about chivalry. The aim of war was to kill the enemy in any way possible: he'd been with the Div. in 1940 when they'd machine-gunned almost a hundred men of the English Norfolk Regiment, *after* they'd surrendered. Orders were orders: war was war.

Lohman had taken command of 1 Platoon when his officer, SS-Obersturmführer Franz Mueller, had copped it in the ambush. He wasn't exactly heartbroken over Mueller's demise. The man had been a conceited little prig who, in Lohman's opinion, would sooner or later have dropped them in the crap. He'd insisted on riding with the motorcycle detachment rather than hanging back with the riflemen: he hadn't listened when Lohman had warned him about the possibility of ambush. He'd been one of the first to get blitzed.

Then there'd been that ridiculous business of *negotiating*

for the black box, instigated by the commander of the armoured-car unit. Lohman knew there were strict orders not to damage the box but, after all – *seven men in jeeps* – they could easily have bagged it without having to wave a white flag. It had all gone cockeyed anyway: the AFV commander had got scragged, and the Brits had hopped it.

Lohman's men had gone over the gunpit and the blockhouse with a fine toothcomb: they'd found a field-gun, smallarms, three heavy machine-guns, a mortar and a rocket-launcher, but no trace of the black box. Now, they were assembling in the blockhouse yard, smoking and slurping water. Lohman squatted by his wireless operator, wondering what message to send Company HQ. 1 Platoon had been tasked to find the black box, and he was loath to report a failure. If the box wasn't here, it must have been moved – but when? They'd found two dead Brits in the blockhouse, one dead and two wounded in the gunpit. Another had been blown to smithereens when he'd rammed the sfz60 with a Bren-gun carrier. Two had been seen bunking it just before the RAF bombers had come in. That made eight, but Lohman knew for certain there'd only been seven after the ambush. At that point, they must have left at least one man at the bridge. At the ambush site, too, he'd seen three jeeps. One was still lying on her side on the field: two were missing. It was possible they'd dispatched the black box by jeep before the contact at the bridge was even initiated. It could easily be behind enemy lines by now, in which case the game was up.

Lohman hoped so. He didn't know what the black box was, only that it was trouble: he didn't want to waste any more time on a wild-goose chase. He had a feeling that the whole strategic situation had gone batshit. Forward elements of B Company, who were supposed to secure the bridge, had reported that 164 Panzer Division had turned back: the el-Fayya position they'd fought so hard for was going to be abandoned. Lohman didn't know exactly what this meant, but he had a damn' good idea: the enemy must have broken through.

He watched a solemn procession of stretcher-bearers trooping in with the two wounded Brits. He'd already seen them at the gunpit: one was a plump type with a face like a fish, the other a seven-foot giant with shaggy black hair, grizzled features, an overhanging cliff of a forehead, limbs like crane-gantries. He looked like an ogre out of a nightmare: Lohman remembered drawing a bead on him after the ambush, thinking that he couldn't miss such a target.

He told the wireless operator to wait for him, got up, ordered the corporal in charge of the stretcher party to halt. He unstrapped his helmet, tipped it back, peered at the two POWs on the stretchers. He had wanted to interrogate them back at the gunpit, but neither had been fully conscious, and the corporal had been busy patching them up. He noted that their eyes were open now: the plump one had been laid face down: his back was covered in bandages that were seeping gore. The big man stared vacantly at the sky.

Lohman glanced at the corporal-orderly, a slightly built, milk-skinned farm-boy who'd probably been recruited straight out of school.

'Given them any morphia?' he asked.

'Not yet.'

'They say anything?'

The corporal grinned. 'The big one said *Fuck off, Fritz.* That's all I understood, anyway. I don't speak English, do you?'

'A little. Find anything on them?'

The corporal hesitated. He took a short-barrelled firearm out of his belt, handed it to Lohman. The *Sturmscharführer* made a *tsk tsk* sound. It was a British-made shotgun — a twelve-bore, with its barrels sawn short. 'Is it his?' he demanded, nodding at the giant.

'Must be. Found it right next to him.'

'This is an illegal weapon. You could get in trouble for having this.'

He weighed the shotgun in his hands, eyed the orderly questioningly.

'Take it,' the corporal said. 'I was going to hand it in, anyway.'

'Any ammunition?'

The corporal dipped in a pouch, brought out a couple of twelve-bore cartridges, gave them to Lohman. He waved the stretcher party on into the tunnel. Lohman watched them until they disappeared, paused for a moment, then followed in their footsteps. He found them in the makeshift aid-post in one of the blockhouse rooms. The stretchers were on the floor:

the corporal-orderly was preparing to give the giant a morphia shot.

'Wait,' Lohman told him. He crouched next to the prisoner. The man glared at him: his eyes were black nails deepset in shadowed pits.

'Name, rank and number?' Lohman said in passable English.

'Wallace,' the man coughed. 'Frederick. Private. 811610.'

'What's your unit?'

'I ain't tellin' you that.'

Lohman smiled frostily, held up the sawnoff. 'You were found carrying a banned weapon. I could have you executed.'

'Never saw it before in me life.'

Lohman chuckled. The giant's face was pale behind thick bristle: his lips were bruised and swollen, his neck swathed in field-dressings. His trousers had been cut away: his legs were wrapped in bandages from thigh to ankle. 'Shrapnel wounds,' the corporal told him, 'but he had a gunshot wound in the calf, already dressed. Quite nasty.'

'Which leg?'

'Left.'

Lohman stuck the shotgun in his webbing, slid out his bayonet, slit away the bandages from Wallace's left calf, exposed the wound.

'What are you doing, *Sturmscharführer*?' the corporal protested. 'I can't let you . . .'

'Shut up.'

He put the bayonet away, drew the shotgun. 'That looks a little painful,' he said to Wallace. He examined the sawnoff end for a moment, then thrust it powerfully into the wound.

'*Fuck you, fucking Kraut bastard*,' Wallace screamed.

The corporal grabbed Lohman's arm. 'Sir, this is not . . .'

The *Sturmscharführer* shrugged him off. '*Don't interfere. How many of our lads do you think he's flayed alive with this vicious little toy, eh? There are no haloes here.*'

The corporal bit his lip. 'We don't have to behave like animals.'

Lohman ignored him, noted with satisfaction that the big man's wound had reopened: it was bleeding profusely. He raised the shotgun. 'I want to know where is the blek box. Tell me, and I will stop.'

'Fuck you . . . . *Aaaaaiiiihhhh.*'

Lohman kept up the pressure longer this time. 'Where is the blek box?'

'Don't know nothin' about no black box.'

'I saw you with the blek box after the ambush. Where is it now?'

'Go take a flying . . . *Aaaaaaaaaiiiihhhh.*'

Lohman thrust the weapon into Wallace's wound three or four more times, each time with increasing frustration. The big man twisted in agony, clenched his massive fists, but only expletives escaped him. The corporal stood in a corner, glowering.

The *Sturmscharführer* stood up, sighed. 'You are a big, stupid man,' he scoffed. He broke the shotgun, blew sand out of the chamber, took the two cartridges from his pouch, fed them in, snapped the weapon shut.

'I used to shoot a twelve-bore like this on my uncle's farm in Breslau when I was a boy,' he said. 'Except that it had proper barrels. A cartridge fired from this gun will do great damage, I think.'

He leaned over Wallace, pressed the twin muzzles firmly against the shaggy morass of hair at his temple. 'Tell me where the blek box is, or I kill you.'

'Sir,' the medical orderly pleaded. 'This isn't right . . .'

Lohman's blue eyes were flame and ice. '*I'll do it*,' he snapped.

Wallace spat bloody saliva, flashed Lohman a look of contempt. 'I ain't tellin' you nothink, mate. So do as yer bleedin' like.'

He looked away, stared at the ceiling.

Lohman felt furious: he was a hairbreadth from squeezing the triggers, when a new voice breathed, '*Stop. I'll tell you.*'

Lohman glanced over at the other soldier, the plump, fish-headed one: it was he who had spoken. He was still on his stomach, his trout-shaped face crushed against the stretcher. Lohman realized he'd made a mistake in picking on the big man: he should have tried the fat one first.

'What's your name, soldier?' he said.

'Trubman. Edward. Corporal 833674.'

Lohman turned his eyes back to Wallace: he pressed the shotgun muzzles harder against the craggy temple.

'Tell me now or I kill him.'

'Don't tell 'im nothin', Taff,' Wallace croaked. 'Keep yer mouth shut.'

'It doesn't matter, Fred. They've had it. Monty's out-flanked the Mareth Line.'

Lohman pricked up his ears: this news was just what he'd expected. He still had a job to do, though.

'You bloody fool,' Wallace groaned.

Lohman tickled the twin triggers. 'Last chance. Where is the blek box?'

'One of our lads . . . stole it.' Trubman's jaw worked desperately. He was in agony from the wounds in his arm and back. He was finding it difficult to breathe, even more difficult to speak.

'*Stole it?* You expect me to *believe* this?'

'It's true. He was a deserter. Took off in a jeep last night . . . about . . . eight o'clock.'

'Then why did you not pursue him?'

'We had to defend the bridge, see.'

Lohman thought about it: *deserter* sounded bizarre and improbable, but he couldn't immediately see any motive for a lie. If the box had really been moved, whether it was by a deserter or otherwise seemed unimportant.

'I counted eight of you here,' he said. 'Why only seven at the ambush?'

Trubman gulped air urgently: snot dribbled from his nostrils.

'We picked up two men last night . . . they'd been hiding out here . . .'

Lohman absorbed the information with interest: at

least the numbers tallied. Eight Brits had defended the position: one had gone off with the black box.

'Where did he go, this man?'

'I don't know.'

'And the other two? The ones who ran away from the pit. They went after him?'

Trubman moaned: his eyes flickered. Lohman realized that he was about to pass out. He doubted that he'd get any more. There were only two possibilities: either the box had been hidden here, or it had gone: it seemed more likely that it had gone. If it had been moved the previous night, the chances of finding it were slim. On the other hand, there was only one way out: the old highway across the Matmata Hills.

He lowered the shotgun, stood up straight, nodded at the corporal. 'You can give them the morphia now.'

At the door he paused, wheeled round, tipped his tinlid forward. 'By the way,' he said, 'the fight you put up here was really something. Pity you will hev to sit out the war in a prison camp.'

He clicked his heels, saluted lightly, turned to go.

37

Jasper Maskelyne and Miles Caversham dined on bully-beef stew in the refectory at St Anthony's, then took a jeep and drove five miles across the desert to temporary landing ground LG101. They were followed by a 3-tonner carrying a ground crew with petrol-tin flares and an Aldis lamp. The airstrip was shielded by overlapping ridges visible only as denser areas of darkness: a gilded moon like a clipped sovereign formed a hub for unspanned nebulas of stars. The evening wind was cool: the MO4 men had put on duffel coats and cap-comforters. They placed the Aldis lamp at the end of the runway: the ground crew laid out flare-tins every five yards.

'Not a good idea to light them till we hear the aircraft, sir,' Maskelyne said. 'Just in case.'

'In case what? The Axis haven't had a kite over Egypt for months.'

'It always pays to be on the safe side.'

They left the flares unlit, and went to sit in the jeep. Maskelyne produced a hip-flask of cognac, offered it to Caversham.

The colonel took a swig, handed it back, consulted his watch.

'She's due in about 2100 hours,' Maskelyne told him.

'Good. Let's hope she's carrying the black box. It's been long enough.'

Maskelyne swigged Cognac: Caversham contemplated the night.

He saw himself as a man who knew what the war was really about: it was about preserving the establishment; that is, the way of life of the wealthy, the landed and the well bred: the kind of people who ran military intelligence. The rest were just minions. Caversham despised men like Caine – nobodies who were ready to risk their lives for their country, quite ignorant of the fact that their country was in reality a small elite who didn't care how many of them were sacrificed, as long as they remained supreme. Not that he would ever dream of sharing such a view: the illusion of democracy and the authority of the people had to be maintained.

The scion of a brewery empire, with an estate in Wiltshire, Caversham belonged among the elite by birthright. He'd served in the Royal Engineers so long ago that he hardly remembered it. He was a surveyor and mapmaker by trade, but also a brilliant linguist, whose fluent German had landed him a posting with the British mission in Berlin in the late 1930s. There, he'd got to know some of his counterparts in the Abwehr: Prussian aristocrats with backgrounds similar to his own, who had no sympathy with Hitler or the Nazis. Despite the war, he'd maintained contact with one or two of them secretly. That was how the *Nighthawk* scheme had come about.

'You think it's going smoothly, then, sir?' Maskelyne asked.

The colonel nodded. It had been only three days since Caine's team had taken off from this same airstrip, in the Bristol Bombay that had dropped them in Tunisia. Caversham knew the drop had gone reasonably well: the RAF special operations dispatcher had reported to him personally. There'd been a delay that had made it necessary to jump in daylight, and a small problem with a Messerschmitt, but Caine's stick had landed on target: the reception committee from Fraser's composite SAS squadron had been waiting for them on the DZ, with equipment and jeeps.

They'd heard nothing since, but that didn't bother him. He knew his chickens. Caine, being Caine, wouldn't have failed to respond to a Mayday call, any more than a signaller as good as Trubman would have failed to pick it up. That big oaf Wallace would follow Caine into the jaws of hell. Copeland would have argued, but in the end would have backed them up.

As for Fiske, Sears-Beach had assured him that the man was as cold as a razorblade, and twice as bright. He'd make sure that Caine and his men weren't . . . as Sears-Beach had put it . . . *in a position* . . . to hamper the operation.

Maskelyne screwed the top back on the flask, slipped it into his pocket. He twirled his fingers, produced a cigarette, offered it to Caversham, who shook his head.

Maskelyne put the cigarette in his mouth, rubbed his hands together, opened them to reveal his Ronson lighter. He lit the cigarette pensively. 'The only problem I can see is Fraser. He'll know that Caine and company were in the field.'

'He won't know we recruited them. When Caine and his men fail to return, he'll just assume they were captured or killed.'

'Yes, sir, but he's bound to report it to SAS HQ. They'll find out we were behind it, and ask what authority we had to hive off their men, and, in particular, an officer on sick leave, and others who were off the active list.'

Caversham bared chiselled teeth. 'They won't find out it was us. If they accuse us of anything, we'll just deny it. Remember, there are no records: no roll call, no movement orders, no written plans.'

Maskelyne's skull-head wobbled nervously. 'They'll blame me. They'll say Glenn and I were out for revenge.'

'Forget it, Jasper. None of this is personal: in war one has to make harsh decisions. We needed Caine and his crew to get the black box. Thereafter, they became expendable. I don't deny that they behaved appallingly towards you, nor do I deny that I would be distressed if they returned safely and spilled the beans, or claimed *Nighthawk* as an SAS coup. However, that's not relevant. Keep your mind on the black box: it contains secrets that could give us victory. That's what counts.'

Maskelyne seemed unconvinced. He was one of the British army's most accomplished deception artists — the man who'd moved the port at Alexandria by sleight of hand, and deceived the Axis into bombing some-where else. He knew better than anyone that, in war, things were rarely what they seemed. Maskelyne hailed from no such exalted background as Caversham: his father had been a bank-clerk in Wimbledon, and he'd started his career doing magic shows for children. It had been a long grind up to the pinnacle of fame as the Great Maskelyne. He was astute enough to sense that Caversham looked down on him: he was aware that he was nothing more than a useful tool.

'How can you be sure the black box really contains what you think it does?' he enquired.

Caversham pursed his fat lips smugly. 'That's classi-fied.'

Maskelyne looked as if he'd been slapped in the face. The colonel pulled his coat around him defensively. *Well, let him. He's unforgivably nosy and extremely acute. Knows far too much already.* Caversham couldn't risk telling Maskelyne the real story, but neither could he fob him off with a cover-tale: the ex-magician was sharp enough to see straight through it. *It's not that I really have anything to hide. My motives were pure. I've been given a rare chance to bring off a triumph that will help ensure Allied victory. If the price I've paid was Caine, and a few SAS men and ex-prisoners, it's a small price. All right, if the truth be known, I also sacri-ficed David Stirling. He wasn't a nobody: he was one of us. But he had to be got rid of. If he'd had his way MO4 would no longer exist.*

In early January he'd been contacted by one of his for-mer Abwehr associates, a Prussian junker codenamed

Groot. He'd known *Groot* personally before the war – a secret anti-Nazi conspirator from the group British intelligence called the Schwarze Kapelle. Caversham hadn't seen him for years, but they had a complicated series of recognition codes and safeguards to ensure that neither had been compromised.

Groot had passed him some intelligence that had made him sit up. It concerned a prototype German aircraft of a completely new class – a *silent aircraft*, *Groot* called it – that had been lost on a test flight in Tunisia. The aircraft had been carrying a very special cargo: a black box containing an experimental electronic counter-measures device called STENDEC. Developed by German scientists at Peenemünde, the device could produce an effect that deceived enemy radars into indicating that a huge airfleet was on the move. It could also be used in ships, giving radar images of non-existent battlefleets. The silent-aircraft prototype was designed to elude enemy radar shields, making the STENDEC equipment mobile and undetectable.

Caversham had known at once that STENDEC was the kind of invention that could win the war. It could deceive the enemy into thinking that an invasion was coming in one place, when in reality it was coming somewhere completely different. He didn't know much about radar, but it sounded plausible, and *Groot* was a solid source. He assumed that *Groot* had brought the information to him because they were old friends, and because *Groot* knew and trusted his superior talents. At this stage, he could have shared the int. with the DMI.

Instead he'd kept it under his hat. If there was any kudos to be gained in this affair, he wanted it to be his.

There was only one catch, *Groot* explained. If the Allies got the STENDEC device, the Abwehr would be blamed and demoted. They had to have an intelligence coup of their own that, even if not of the same calibre, would at least show Axis command that they were doing their job. Caversham had thought long and hard about it, and had come up with David Stirling.

Stirling's SAS had been highly successful in disrupting Axis lines of communication, and had put the wind up the Panzer Army. With that success behind him, and a bit of wheeling and dealing with old school chums, Stirling had wormed his way into the confidence of Winston Churchill. Not only had he proposed to make the SAS a brigade with himself as the brigadier, he'd also suggested amalgamating all the special ops outfits, including MO4, under SAS command. The thought that MO4 might be disbanded had appalled Caversham. Stirling was gentry all right, but he, a seasoned player of the game, didn't relish the idea of serving under an upstart who'd been considered an incorrigible delinquent only eighteen months ago. If Caversham wanted to do something to secure MO4's existence, he first had to get Stirling out of the way. *Groot*'s request for a tit-for-tat coup provided him with a perfect chance.

It hadn't been difficult to rope Stirling into the scheme, or to feed *Groot* the location of a certain RV in Tunisia, where the Boche would be waiting for him. Some of his men had unexpectedly escaped, of course:

even Stirling had got away initially but thankfully been recaptured.

Thereafter, *Groot* had released details of the location of the STENDEC aircraft and the black box. All Caversham had needed was a crew of special service troops who could retrieve it without being missed: Maskelyne had asked for expendable commando-trained volunteers from the detention centre. Provost Corps officer Robin Sears-Beach had come up with the idea of using Tom Caine.

Caine didn't matter, but Stirling did. Caversham had sold out one of his own for the black box: he wasn't proud of it, but sometimes, in war, you had to make harsh decisions.

Maskelyne touched his arm. 'She's coming in,' he said.

The ground crew lit the flares: a path of fire blazed up, peeling back the darkness, casting the airfield in a bronze glow. Caversham and Maskelyne saw shadow figures scurrying off the runway. The sound of the aero-engines grew louder: a moment later they watched the medium bomber touch down, taxi forward with her twin propellers churning. By the time the Blenheim had come to a standstill, the flares were almost out. Caversham felt excited. Any minute now he would be taking possession of the black box, the object he'd expended so much time and trouble to obtain. This would be the high point of his career.

They hurried towards the aircraft carrying torches, arrived in time to see the pilot climbing down from the side door. He was clad in a fleece-lined flying jacket and helmet.

'Where is it, Willington?' Caversham demanded. 'Where's the black box?'

Willington was a very young, very spindly RAF pilot officer with a stiff moustache and a laconic manner. He stuck a pipe in his mouth, reconsidered it and brought it out again. 'Sorry, sir,' he said. 'We didn't get it. Chaps didn't turn up. Never put the panels out.'

Caversham bit his lip. 'You were given orders to return to the RV at the same time every night for as long as it takes.'

'With due respect, sir, if we run into a flight of Messerschmitt 109s or something, our goose is well and truly roasted. Navigation's a nightmare, too: either there aren't any landmarks, or there are too many, all the same.'

'I didn't say this job would be easy. Now, get that thing refuelled and get back into the field. Don't come back without the black box.'

38

Fiske missed the RAF Blenheim at Bir Souffra by minutes: he arrived in time to see the aircraft flitting away
between bars of a smoke-grey and magenta sky, a fly-
sized dot on the vast horizon of sunset. He drummed
the steering wheel with his fists in fury at the incompetence of the RAF. He halted the jeep under the palm
trees, jumped out, lay for a long moment stretched in
the sand. Then he sat up, looked at his watch. It was six
fifty in the evening. He'd been told that the aircraft
would return to the RV at the same time every day until
he arrived. That meant that he was stuck here for
another twenty-four hours.

He knew he'd taken longer than he should have done
to reach the outpost: he hadn't reckoned on the Allied
units following Freyberg's push. He'd come across no
traffic on the old highroad, but once into the plain, it
had been like Piccadilly Circus: Allied convoys in almost
constant movement. He'd had to pick his way, laying up
when necessary. He might have been able to brass his
way out if challenged, but he hadn't wanted to take the
chance.

He'd been flummoxed by the defection of Quinnell
and Jizzard: he couldn't understand what had got into
them. What on earth had they hoped to gain by going

back? They were probably dead by now: perhaps Quinnell believed that his return was an act of contrition that would bring him rewards in the afterlife. Fiske scoffed. *All actions are transactions. It's a big market out there, even the war. The most advanced industrial nations in the world, throwing tons of hardware at each other, day after day, feeding the vultures safe in their nests – the arms-manufacturers, the big companies. They're the ones who profit from the suffering of men like me. Well, I'm not stupid. Not like the Thomas Caines of this world. I want nothing to do with it.*

Fiske had grown up in Portsmouth, the only child of a naval officer. In Civvie Street he'd worked in a hotel until they'd found him pocketing the petty-cash. Luckily, they'd never reported it to the police, so when he came to apply for a commission, he'd had no criminal record. He'd wanted to be an officer in the Pay Corps, but instead they'd given him the Ordnance Corps, where, as a store supervisor, he'd worked a lucrative black-market scheme. He'd done well on the demolitions course, though, and found himself in demand by the commandos. He'd joined them only to escape from the inevitable consequences of his pilfering: once in Egypt he'd managed to get back into the RAOC. They'd caught him embezzling unit funds, and this time he'd ended up in the detention centre. Until Sears-Beach had come up with this transaction – the one that had got him . . . here.

He did a careful recce of the outpost. Its main feature was a tangled forest of date-palms and underbrush, six or seven hundred yards square. The trees had obviously once been tended, but not for years: they'd been left to grow wild, probably after the inhabitants moved out. That someone had lived here was evident: there were remains of mud walls, roofless huts melted by rain and sandstorms, squares of sparse soil that might previously have been cultivated. There was a wellshaft full of sand inside a fractured mud enclosure. Fiske saw sun-scoured bones, hide fragments, goat-turds like buckshot, but he was sure no one had used the place in a long time.

The outpost lay in a shallow basin, stretching as far as some lizardback ridges, about half a mile away to the east. In the west he could see a wall of knucklebone hills. The sun had already gone down behind them, leaving a blush of chrome-yellow against a black silhouette of soft peaks: cigar-shaped rolls of darkness floated above the outline, across remnant patches of blue, ranged by strands of cirrus, like bleached ribbones. Between the outpost and the hills, on the hard shoulder of the desert, he made out the white-painted boulders that marked temporary Landing Ground LG120 – a mile-long strip from which the stones had been cleared. That was the real reason he was here. Tomorrow, he'd lay out the purple recognition-panels: he wouldn't miss the boat a second time.

He walked back to the jeep, decided to camouflage her in the overgrown palm thickets. *She'll be damn' hard to spot there, even from the air.* He pulled his .303 from the brace, checked the black box, debated whether to leave it where it was or unload it. It wasn't going anywhere, he thought, but he decided he'd feel better if he kept it where he could see it. He slung his weapon, placed a wary hand on the box: it didn't do anything unexpected: he picked it up, carried it over to the enclosure round the disused well. It wasn't much of an enclosure, really: more than half of the wall had collapsed, but it gave him some cover from view.

He put the box down, leaned his rifle against the wall, went back to the jeep for rations, water and kit. He stood by the wagon for a moment, studying the tin boxes of Nobel 808 explosive in the back. He didn't know why he hadn't dumped it: maybe he'd thought it might come in useful if he was followed. Thinking about it again, it struck him that it could happen. It was obvious that the Totenkopf troops they'd encountered had had orders to retrieve the black box. Jizzard and Quinnell might have got back in time to release Caine and the others: it was possible that a mechanic of Caine's skill could repair the jeeps. They might even be able to patch up the wireless, contact Allied units. A shudder of paranoia ran through him. If he'd made it on time there'd have been no problem, but now he was stuck for another day, someone – Jerries or his own side – might catch up with him. *Tomorrow, early, I'll set up the Vickers in a defensive position, just in case. I'll bury fused charges of 808 in a perimeter. If anyone tries to take me, they'll get a shock.*

Dark was falling rapidly. He ferried weapons, water and explosives to the well-circle, spread a poncho, pulled a couple of tins from his haversack. He read the printed labels with his torch: *Chicken soup (self-heating)* and *Cocoa (self-heating)*. He'd been saving these for a special occasion: now was the time. He pulled the tab on the soup, heard a fizz, smelt a waxy odour that almost put him off. He opened the can, poured the soup into a mug and tasted it. It was cold.

He ate it anyway, lit a cigarette, stared round in the darkness. There were rustlings in the trees: the sound of dry palm fronds chafing. It didn't bother him to be alone. *Jizzard and Quinnell, good riddance.* On the other hand, it did worry him that Sears-Beach and the others might not keep their side of the bargain. They'd been ruthless in dumping Caine, after all. Why should they be expected to spare him, once the job was done? The only leverage he had was the black box. He considered burying it here, hijacking the aircraft back to Cairo, then demanding his reward before revealing its location. If he knew what was inside, it would help.

He switched on his torch, pointed the beam at the black box. It was fascinating, he had to admit. It had required that strange black aircraft to carry it: special units on both sides had been sent to bring it back. Whatever it contained had to be something big. *Why not have a peek inside?* He had time on his hands and no witnesses: nobody would ever know, and . . . it suddenly occurred to him that he'd found his solution. He could take whatever was in the box, conceal it in his kit. Once back in Egypt, he would hide it somewhere: when Caversham found out the box was empty, he'd offer to reveal its whereabouts on payment of his due.

First he had to open it, and that might not be easy. It

had some weird properties: it appeared seamless, as if it had been made all in one piece. It might even be primed with a booby trap that could be disarmed only by someone who knew what they were doing. Of course, he'd been trained in neutralizing booby traps.

Fiske stubbed out his cigarette, took out his clasp knife. He knelt by the box, began probing its surface carefully with his fingers. He spent a long time feeling every part of it. It had a curious matt feel, but the surface seemed perfectly uniform in all other respects. Finally, he touched the STENDEC letters stencilled on top. Or were they stencilled? Was there a slight protuberance there? Fiske brought up his knife, pressed the first letter lightly with the blade. A deepthroated vibration started: the surface began to shiver. The sound built up steadily until it reached an unbearable high-pitched sibilant scream. Fiske bawled, dropped the knife, covered his ears. The box glowed fire-red, seethed, crackled: the top sprang open suddenly with a shriek, glass shattered, wetness sprayed his face, a high-voltage shock cracked his body like a whip, stood his hair on end, clamped his jaw, paralysed his muscles, knocked him flying into the dust.

39

Second-Lieutenant Celia Blaney was so well known for her beacon of fire-coloured hair that her Field Security comrades referred to her as *Red*. She was one of those girls from county families who abounded in Cairo, yet she was anything but stuck up. Modest, sensitive and astute, she'd been training as a lawyer when war broke out. She'd been on the danger list for a while with the gunshot wound Taylor had given her. Now, though, she was back in Stocker's office at Medan Sharif, standing in front of the DSO's desk with a foolscap page in her hand.

Stocker looked worried: he was so engrossed in reading a dispatch that he didn't seem to have noticed her presence. She cleared her throat delicately.

Stocker glanced up, took in the jungle of red curls, the pert nose, the rose-and-white features, the steady cobalt-coloured eyes. She looked a little paler, he thought, a little slimmer: the battledress suit that had previously clung to her shape admirably now appeared slightly too big.

Stocker smiled distractedly. 'What is it, Celia?'

'Dead letter drop from Brunetto. I thought you might want to read it, sir.'

Stocker sighed, nodded. It was two weeks since he'd sent Brunetto to liaise with Nolan, and in that time he'd heard nothing. He'd started to think that she'd been compromised.

He removed his glasses, started cleaning them with a rag. 'Why don't you sit down?' he said. 'Give me a synopsis.'

Blaney sat elegantly in one of the overstuffed arm-chairs, took a breath. 'Brunetto's living with Nolan as part of the Taylor group. She's been out with them on a couple of stunts – a lorry-hijack, a warehouse robbery – she believes she's been accepted – says her *Camilla Pallozzi* cover's intact . . .'

'Good. Anything else?' The DSO seemed impatient.

'She and Nolan have documented several deserter sabotage operations over the last fortnight. A firebomb attack on an M/T depot in Heliopolis, an explosion at a railway station . . .'

'We can look at those later. Anything about Calvin?'

Blaney ran her eyes down the page. 'Yes, sir. She says that they've also discovered more cases of girls being shipped to Calvin's base. The address is a heavily guarded secret, but she's certain that girls were taken to Alexandria.'

'That narrows it down then,' Stocker sniffed. 'I think we knew that already.'

'There's something else, sir. Calvin has set up a wire-less network among the deserters. Nolan made a lucky contact with an operator – an ex-Royal Navy chap. He told her that the network home-base is Alex. The chap insisted he knew Calvin's personal callsign – *Cheshire Cat*.'

'*Cheshire Cat?*' Stocker chuckled. 'That's a good one. The cat that disappears, leaving behind only its smile.'

'She seems quite sure,' Blaney insisted.

'All right, check with "Y" Service. Find out if they're aware of the *Cheshire Cat* callsign, and if so, where the transmitter is located.'

'Very good, sir.'

'If you can get a message to Brunetto, tell her that what we really need is to put Nolan inside Calvin's base. I don't care how she does it, but we must find out where he is.'

Blaney stood up. 'Will that be all, sir?'

Stocker frowned, glanced at the dispatch on his desk.

'Perhaps you should have a look at this. It's top secret, but I know I can trust you.'

'What is it, sir?'

'Message from the DMI – one of the oddest I've ever had.' He paused. 'You remember Colonel Stirling?'

'The SAS commander? Yes: he was captured back in January.'

Stocker brought out his pipe, chewed the stem, laid it on his desk. 'I've always thought there was something fishy about his capture. In fact, the whole operation was peculiar. He was supposed to go to Tunisia to meet an officer from Combined Operations. Instead of taking a plane, though, which would have been the obvious way to do it, he drove right across the desert, and passed through Axis lines.'

Blaney looked interested. 'What reason did he give for that, sir?'

Stocker picked up his pipe. 'He said that he was leading a sabotage mission against a stretch of railway in

Tunisia. The question is, why would one require a lieutenant-colonel for that? Anyway, read this, see what you make of it. He handed the dispatch to her.

Blaney took the document, read:

Dispatch

From: DMI
To: Maj. Stocker
Int. Corps
Field Security HQ
Cairo

Maj. Stocker

Capture of Lt.-Col. A. D. Stirling 24/1/43

Intelligence from a highly reliable but confidential source suggests there have been secret communications between one of our special operations divisions, MO4, and Abteilung I, Abwehrdienst, Berlin. We do not know the exact nature of these communications as the Abwehr code remains unread, but our source believes they concern the capture of Lt-Col, A. D. Stirling in Tunisia on 24 January 1943. In particular, our source suggests that Stirling's mission was not, as stated, the sabotage of a railway line in Tunisia. Our source believes that Lt-Col. Stirling was given an RV point in Tunisia, which was then deliberately revealed to the enemy, resulting in his capture. Confidential reports from escaped members of Lt-Col. Stirling's patrol tend to confirm that sabotage of the railway

line was not the primary objective of their mission, and
strongly suggest, though do not absolutely confirm, the idea that
their RV might have been known previously to the enemy. If
it is the case that the commander of the SAS regiment was
deliberately compromised by a division of our intelligence, this
is obviously highly serious.

Since counter-intelligence falls under the auspices of Field
Security, you are instructed to launch a discreet investigation
into the work of MO4.

Col. P. M. Brookman
Office of the DMI

Blaney finished reading: she stared at Stocker wide-eyed. 'Shopped by our own people? Surely not, Major?'

Stocker took the document back. 'I don't know. Strange things happen in war.' He snorted a breath. 'MO4's commanded by a half-colonel – Caversham, I think it is. After you've completed the Nolan task, I want you to check up on him and his principal staff officers. Then perhaps you'd better pay a discreet visit to MO4's base. See and not be seen, you know what I mean?'

Blaney nodded enthusiastically. 'Where is it , sir?'

Stocker gave a toothy smile. 'In Sinai. St Anthony's monastery. Apparently they share it with the monks.'

40

The jeep ran out of fuel as they came down the escarpment. Caine was amazed that she had taken them this
far: Fiske had gone off with most of the spare petrol.
He reckoned they had an hour before first light. There
was nothing for it but to stuff everything they needed
into haversacks and continue on foot. It wasn't much:
ponchos and sleeping bags, torches, binos, compass, a
canteen of water each, some ship's biscuits, a handful
of rounds apiece. Cope had his SMLE and his Colt:
Caine was still carrying the M1.

'Let's get off the track, get a brew on,' Caine said.

They left the jeep standing in the road, tabbed off
slowly into the darkness until they came to a wadi leading off to the right: they followed it for a hundred yards
or so, found some stunted camelthorn, broke off the
brittle branches for firewood. Copeland used a handful
of dry grass to light the fire: he poured water from his
canteen into a mess tin, laid it on an Arab-style hearth
of three stones. Caine sat with the carbine nestled in his
arms, staring into the flames, rocking to and fro: the fire
seemed to be alive, a third entity that had sprung into
being between them. He stroked the carbine, remembered that it belonged to Trubman: they'd left him and
Wallace to the Hun.

'We should have waited,' he said. 'If we'd hung on till the moment the aircraft came in, we could have got them out.'

Copeland added tea-leaves to the water, stirred it with a twig.

'You got a gasper, mate? I could do with a smoke.'

Caine shook his head. 'We dumped them, Harry. We deserted our best mates.'

Cope sighed: he found sugar in his haversack, shook it into the tea. He sat back on his haunches, cracked his knuckles, stroked his arm: it felt as if it had been pierced with redhot knitting needles. 'It was the right decision, Tom,' he said at last. 'Even if we'd got them out, which I don't reckon we could have done, they needed emergency treatment. They'd never have lasted the drive, and even if they had, we'd have had to leave them here.'

Caine looked up. 'You reckon they're dead, then?'

'Krauts are pretty good at tending enemy wounded. Jury's out on this Totenkopf lot, of course.'

Caine continued rocking, glowering into the fire. *You have to pay for everything. I finally found out Nolan's alive, and I've paid for it by leaving my mates in the lurch. I sold out Wallace and Trubman for the chance of seeing Nolan again. What about Quinnell and Jizzard? They deserted, and paid for it by sacrificing themselves. I'm responsible for their deaths. I'm responsible for Grimshaw and Cutler, too. You have to pay for everything. That's the price of being in command.*

'I'm going to miss the big dollop,' he said.

'Remember that time he found two cheetah cubs in a cave in Jebel Akhdar?'

Caine smiled fondly. ''Course I do. Over the moon, he was. You'd have thought his birthday'd come early.'

'He brought them to the leaguer in his haversack, with their heads poking out. They made squealing noises all the way and the other lads complained it wasn't tactical. Fred said it meant they liked him.'

'He fed them on Carnation milk. Happy as a sand-boy.'

'When he got to the leaguer, Paddy said he had to take 'em back. No one could remember where the cave was, so he had to turn 'em loose in the Jebel. Reckoned wolves and hyenas would get 'em. Poor old Fred. Came back in tears.'

Copeland sniffed suddenly, looked away, saw the tea was boiling. He took the mess tin off the fire, laid it on the ground to cool. 'How're *you* doing?' he asked.

'You mean, apart from deserting my chums, and losing almost my entire patrol?'

'No, I meant how bad is your wound?'

'I expect I'll live. Hurts like hell, though. How about yours?'

'Arm's stiff as a plank. Could do with some anti-septic dope.'

'Get it out, then.'

Cope spread his scarf on the ground, took a brown envelope from his haversack, shook pills out on to the scarf.

'This is the last of it. Two sulphonomide and two Bennies apiece.'

'Save the Bennies. We might be glad of them later.'

Copeland nodded, put the Bennies away, handed Caine his share of the sulphonomide. He fished out the ship's biscuits, gave Caine two, took the remaining two himself. He picked up the mess tin, blew on it, passed it to Caine.

'Nah, after you, mate.'

'No, you need it, Tom.'

Caine took the mess tin. He swallowed the sulphonomide, took a swig of tea, dipped a biscuit in it, took a bite. 'Damn me, that's good,' he said.

He drank half of the tea, passed it back. Cope finished eating and drinking in silence.

He wiped his mouth with his good arm. 'That's it then,' he said. 'Rations finished.'

He threw away the dregs, scoured the mess tin with sand. 'So. What do you want to do?'

Caine hesitated, brought Jizzard's map out of the patch-pocket of his trousers. 'I'm going after Fiske. I know where he's heading.'

Copeland took the map, examined it by the light of his torch. 'That RV's ten miles away. We're knackered. We'll never make it in this state.'

'I'm going,' said Caine wearily. 'I'm going after that bastard even if I peg out doing it. You don't have to come, Harry. I'm not ordering you to.'

'Christ, Tom. As if the drama at the bridge wasn't enough. You're the most obstinate bugger I've ever had the misfortune to serve with.'

Caine felt tears bud in the corner of his eyes. 'I probably am,' he said, 'but I owe it to the lads, Harry. I'm not letting that bloody traitor get away.'

Copeland slotted the mess tin into his equipment. He took another shufti at the map. '*Bir Souffra*,' he said. 'That's where Fiske's going. Why there? Ah, did you see this, skipper? There's a temporary landing ground, LG120. He must be getting picked up by plane.'

'I'd put money on Caversham or Maskelyne. Those sods are up to the hilt in this. They set us up, Harry. We both knew it from the start, but we still walked into it.'

Caine took back the map, folded it carefully: instead of returning it to the patch-pocket, he inserted it into the space concealed in the lining of his overalls.

Copeland watched him with alert eyes. 'How did they persuade you, then?'

Caine twitched, pulled at his chin. 'It was Nolan. They had photos of her alive, taken months after the crash. They promised to help me find her if I accepted the job.'

'Now you know she's with the deserters, why risk it? It'd be better to make for our own lines.'

'Who knows where our lines are? By the time we've found them, it'll be too late.'

'You reckon the black box is that important?'

Caine tugged at his chin again. 'You know when we were at the derelict? I didn't tell anyone, but I had a sort of . . . well . . . it was like a dream, except I was awake. I saw Maurice Pickney.'

Copeland raised an eyebrow. 'Pickney's dead, Tom.'

'Yes, 'course he is, but there he was, talking to me just like I'm talking to you. He told me not to take the black box, said there'd be a disaster if we opened it.'

Copeland cracked his knuckles. 'You still took it. You even tried to open it.'

'I don't believe in ghosts, Harry. I wasn't going to leave it behind just because of some hallucination.'

'Perhaps that's what it was – a hallucination. You were exposed to Olzon-13, weren't you? Remember the craziness that stuff caused among the Senussi? It could be the lingering after-effects.'

Caine repressed the desire to tell him that he'd also seen Pickney on the battlefield, or about the persistent visions of Nolan and Eisner he'd had in Cairo: Cope would start to think he really *was* round the twist.

'Whatever it was, I can't help thinking that there was a message in it, even if it came from somewhere inside, you know, like an intuition? That's one of the reasons I'm making for Fiske's RV, Harry. But I'm going it alone this time. I'm not dragging you into any more shit.'

Copeland shook his head, amazed at the sheer cussedness of it. Then he remembered how Caine had taken on the *Sandhog* mission, mainly because he, Copeland, had wanted to rescue Angela Brunetto. He felt a surge of grief when it struck him that Brunetto was no longer there. He spat into the sand. 'Don't talk daft, mate. If we get through it, though, I reckon you'll owe me a couple of beers.'

They moved down the escarpment at dawn with the sun flaring up behind them in reefs of coral and carnation rose. They followed the road through screes and huddlestone outcroppings, looking down across a plain where quilts of caramel fanned out in ripples, where the new sun wove a tapestry of purple blisters and shimmering bright pools like polished glass. At the base of the slope, they came across the tyre-tracks of many vehicles, softskinned and armoured, all heading south–north towards the Tebaga Gap. They cast out in separate arcs looking for signs of a jeep going west towards Fiske's RV.

'Hey,' Caine called. 'Look at this.'

He showed Copeland the tramlines of a Willys Bantam, heavily laden, travelling west. The tracks were fresh.

'How do you know it's him?' Copeland demanded. 'Could be anyone.'

'No.' Caine crouched down, showed him damp patches in the sand between the tracks. 'Water leak, Harry. Remember I fixed the condenser on that jeep. Looks like I didn't do a very good job.'

'That can't be the only jeep in Tunisia with a leaky condenser.'

'It's Fiske all right. The tracks are slap on our bearing. Come on.'

He set off along the tracks fast, with Copeland tagging along after him.

Within two hours they were shattered. Yet they continued to dog the jeep tracks through windscoured atolls, dragging their feet across lodes of jetblack clinkers that lay in strange configurations like the parts of fossil beasts, through thorngroves where the sand had built up around driedout roots in pillowed ruffs. They tottered through fields of grass tussocks littered with

338

the hard pellets of goat droppings, where flakes of sunwhitened bone lay on the surface, where fragments of goat-hide and twists of decayed rope were scattered round three-stone fireplaces that had once marked shepherds' camps.

Caine kept his prismatic in his hand, made sure the jeep tracks were still on course: they seemed to be curving towards a far-off wall of razorback ridges, veiled at the base by dust flurries and quivering tentacles of haze.

They'd covered about seven miles when they saw smoke ahead, rising in loose coils from the scree. They carried on for another ten minutes: the jeep tracks warped away from the smoke, then back towards it. They halted: Caine dekkoed through his field-glasses. The smoke was coming from a coppice of big tamarix: the kind of place marked on the maps as a *hattia*. He made out dark figures there, Bedouin shacks, goats browsing in shadow.

'Arabs,' he said. 'No sign of the jeep. You think maybe they'd give us food and water?'

'How do we know we can trust them?

'We're armed, mate. Let's just do it.'

Before they got within a hundred paces of the camp, a dog began to bark. Copeland brought up his rifle.

'Leave it, Harry. We don't want to appear hostile.'

As they approached, a grey dog skeetered out at them, baying. It planted its feet firmly as if to make a stance, backed away when they didn't stop. They found two Arabs standing by the fire. They looked like father and son – one older, one younger, both small men with sandfox faces and pointed beards, dressed in desert-stained long shirts and ragged headcloths. Neither of them was armed, but Caine saw an old bolt-action rifle hanging from the beam of a shack nearby.

There were three shacks, crudely pieced together from deadfall and dried grass, roofed with mats of woven goathair, standing in the umbrella shade of the huge tamarix. An earthenware waterjar stood outside one of the shacks: Caine noticed a leather well-bucket and a coiled rope hanging from another. He ran a parched tongue over split lips.

Caine didn't speak Arabic, but he'd picked up a few words and phrases from Layla, the Senussi girl he'd known in Libya. He touched Copeland's arm, stopped ten paces from the men. '*Salaam alaykum*,' he said.

'*Wa alaykum as-salaam.*'

There was a moment's silence: the Arabs stepped towards them, shook hands over and over again. Caine knew this was the Arab way: the desert people used the greeting ritual to size newcomers up. The grey dog sniffed at their feet, sidled off and sat down in the shade.

'*Almani?*' one of the Arabs asked. '*Italiani?*'

'*No. No.*' Caine shook his head rapidly. 'British. *Inglizi.*'

The men smiled, showed white teeth.

Caine made a gesture towards his mouth with closed fingers.

'*Eat. Drink.*' He patted his stomach. 'We're hungry.'

The older man nodded: his face was cracked into

clefts and crevices: one of his eyes was a slit through which only a speck of white showed. He beckoned to them, drew them into the shade of the trees, called out something. A moment later a young girl trotted out of one of the shacks, carrying a roll of woven matting. She was barefoot and wore a dress of brilliant primary colours: her face was nutbrown and almond shaped, with eyes like shiny black coals. Her hands were doll's hands, and she had a wealth of braided black hair. She must have been thirteen or fourteen: a perfect younger version of his Senussi friend.

The girl spread out the mat under the trees. The old man pointed at it. '*Itfaddalu*,' he said.

They dumped their haversacks, removed their webbing, sat down on the rug. They kept their weapons close. The old Arab sat crosslegged in the sand opposite, watched them with his good eye: the girl brought leather cushions, placed them behind their backs. The younger man fetched water in a wooden bowl encrusted with rinds of porridge and dried milk: he passed it to Caine with both hands.

'Take it easy,' Copeland told him. 'Don't drink too much at once.'

Caine swallowed water: it was clean and deliciously cool: he passed the bowl to Cope. The girl boiled tea squatting at the fire, poured it into an enamel teapot, brought it over on a battered tray with small glasses, placed the tray before the old man. He spoke to her again, and a minute later she came back with a woolly black sack. The Arab rummaged in it, brought out a box containing chunks of sugar. He popped sugar into the teapot, fished out a bent spoon covered in green mould. He spat on the spoon, rubbed it with sand, stirred the tea. He poured it into two of the glasses, handed them to Caine and Copeland in turn. Caine sipped tea: it was hot, strong, stiff with sugar. 'By golly, that's wonderful,' he said.

The girl came back again with a tray of dates, set it down before them. '*Okulu*,' the old man said, indicating his mouth with clenched fingers.

The dates were hard and dry, but sweet. They set to work on them ravenously. The old man refilled their glasses, then refilled them again.

Caine finished the tea, declined another glass, sat back against the cushion. 'I could get used to this,' he said. A wave of drowsiness washed through him. He closed his eyes.

'Don't go to sleep, Tom,' Copeland warned him.

Caine opened his eyes, stared up at the thick boughs of the tamarix above, wondered how long the tree had been here: hundreds of years, probably. Life was incredible, he thought. *Life. Betty Nolan is alive. I've got to get through this. Got to see her again. First I've got to deal with Fiske.*

He sat up, faced the old Arab. 'Has a man in a jeep been here?' he asked. He braced an imaginary steering-wheel, made a farting sound through pursed lips. He pointed at his smock.

'English soldier? Dressed like this?'

The Arab blinked his good eye, looked mystified. He shouted to the younger man, who jogged over: they

342

had what sounded like a heated discussion for a few minutes. Finally, the older one turned to Caine: he pointed to the space beyond the camp. '*Hinaak*,' he said. '*Ma jaa hinna.*' He patted the ground, shook his head emphatically.

'I think he means the jeep passed by,' Copeland said.

Caine pulled at his smock. 'A man dressed like this?' Both Arabs nodded. '*Aywa. Aywa.*'

Caine pointed at his watch. 'What time was it?'

Again the men looked puzzled. 'They don't use watches,' Cope said. 'They don't know the time.'

Caine pointed at the sun, made a rising-falling gesture with his hand. The young man seemed to grasp his meaning. '*Amis*,' he said. He directed both hands towards the western horizon. '*Amis fil-asur.*'

'Evening time,' Copeland said. 'Before sunset, maybe.'

Caine remembered that the word *amis* meant yesterday. 'Yesterday afternoon,' he concluded. 'He's not more than half a day ahead of us.'

'We'd better get cracking.'

'We can't. Not yet.' Caine nodded in the direction of the shacks: the girl was walking carefully towards them carrying what looked like an enamel washing bowl, two feet wide.

'I think lunch is served,' Caine said. 'It'd be churlish to leave without sampling the fare.'

Copeland grinned.

The girl set the bowl down in the sand by the mat: the old man crouched on one knee, summoned them with a bony hand. The food was a savoury stew of meat, gravy, lumps of fat: the old man called the younger Arab, dug out an oval loaf from his sack, divided it into four thick hunks. He handed one to each of them.

'*Okulu*,' he ordered. '*Bismillahi*.'

Caine paused for a moment, watched how the Arabs broke off pieces of bread, dipped them in the stew with their right hands, groped with their fingers for fat and meat.

'Hand job, then,' Copeland commented.

'Come on. Dig in.'

Afterwards, the girl came round with a metal jug and poured water over their hands. They sat back. 'Makes the world look a different place,' Caine declared.

'We have to move on, though, skipper. I reckon LG120's only another two miles.'

For once, though, he didn't sound convinced: he was lolling against his cushion, eyelids heavy.

Caine winked at him. 'Let's give it a minute or two to digest.'

He lay back against the cushion. His side wound was still sending occasional hotwires through him, his face felt razorscraped, his arm was throbbing. He was completely shagged out, yet the meal had given him a sudden glow of well-being. It was peaceful lying here in the shade with these simple folk, with a full stomach, listening to the languid hum of flies, the soothing sound of goats snaffling in the trees. It seemed as far away from el-Fayya bridge as heaven from hell.

He closed his eyes. In a moment he was asleep.

Someone was shaking him: it must have been Copeland, but he couldn't be sure. It was very dark. He
wondered how long he'd been there. 'Come on, Tom,' a
voice growled.

He followed the shadowy figure through the tamarix. On the other side of the copse, the inkblack night
was split by strings of blue lightning: for a split second
it illuminated the derelict STENDEC aircraft, loom-
ing out of the sand like the fractured carcase of an
enormous pterodactyl. *What the hell is* she *doing here?* Her
black wings heaved: her fuselage groaned like punctured bellows: he saw cat's eyes wink at him, heard the
tremor of thunder. The derelict was huge, much bigger
than he remembered: entering her fuselage was like
crawling through a gangrenous wound into a whale's
belly. The cabin was a vaulted ribcage hung with diseased organs, festooned with green fungus, seeping
fluid like coagulating pus. The windpipe extrusions had
come alive, glowed with slimy phosphorescence,
squirmed and thrashed like spilled viscera. Skullheads
gaped at him out of dark recesses. He heard the grating
of voices, grinding laughter, muffled screams. Oily-
skinned snakes coiled away from him, turned into
impossibly long human fingers, like spider's legs. In
places he had to push through cobwebs as limp and
cloying as wet silk. He was about to ask his guide where
they were going when the figure turned on him. It
wasn't Harry Copeland: it was Maurice Pickney. He was
standing by the black box: the word STENDEC was
burning on top in letters of blue fire.

Pickney's eyes were smouldering diamonds in a corpse's face: his mouth was a vacant, toothless buttonhole. 'You were warned not to take the black box.'

A rill of fear fingered Caine's spine. 'What's in it?' he stammered.

Suddenly, Pickney was standing right next to him, whispering in his ear:

'He left bleached bones in the desert,
Wrestled with centaur and satyr,
Defied the demon hosts,
Put out the Holy Fire.'

Caine recoiled. 'What? What does that mean?'

'Don't touch the black box. Don't go near it.'

41

A dog barked. Caine awoke, found that he was still lying on the mat under the tamarix tree. It was late afternoon, and Copeland was gone. He heard shouts, sat up with a start, saw that two German lorries and a light car had halted two hundred paces out of the *hattia*: more than a dozen men in fieldgrey uniforms and Kaiser tinlids were moving in on the Arab camp. The grey dog hurtled towards them yapping: a Jerry with a long face and a lopsided camel's jaw shot it in the belly. The dog whimpered, lay still in the sand.

Caine snatched his carbine. '*Get out of it, Harry*,' he bellowed.

He fell flat, dug the carbine into his shoulder, rocked a round into the chamber, beelined the cameljawed Kraut. The soldier spotted him, halted, bawled something in German. Caine ignored it, pulled iron, knobbed a .30 calibre needle smack in the Jerry's midriff. A puzzled expression came over the man's face. He looked down, noticed blood on his uniform, sank slowly to his knees.

Shouts went up left and right: Jerries were advancing from both sides: bullets zinged, hooked sandspouts, hit the tree behind Caine with a *pluck pluck*. Caine braced the carbine. A forest of fieldgrey legs sprouted around him: a size-twelve jackboot punted his weapon out of his hands, a rifle-butt smacked him between the temple and the bridge of the nose. For a second he was stunned: hands yanked him to his feet, relieved him of his pistol and bayonet, dug into his pockets, came out with his compass, his clasp knife – even his precious Zippo lighter. There was blood in his eyes: he tried to wipe it away, found himself staring at a torpedo-shaped Jerry with a square head, full lips, sunreddened cheeks and hard luminous eyes. He was older than the others: his face had the battle-scathed look of a veteran. He wore the SS collar-tab, and the rank insignia of a warrant officer first-class. He was holding a Walther pistol inches away from Caine's face.

'I am SS *Sturmscharführer* Lohman,' he said, 'and you are a prisoner of the Waffen-SS. Raise your hands.'

Caine raised his right hand, made an aborted effort to lift his left.

Lohman noticed the bloodstains on the torn arm of Caine's smock. 'All right,' he said. He snapped orders: someone tied Caine's hands behind him: another wiped the blood off his face.

Lohman holstered his pistol, unbuckled his helmet, removed it. Caine saw that his hair was straw blond, almost exactly like Copeland's. He wondered where Cope was, guessed he'd gone off to relieve himself before the Hun had arrived. He hoped he'd heard the warning shout and got away. He looked round for a sign of the Arabs, saw Totenkopf troopers forcing the two men and the girl out of the shacks at gunpoint: one of the Krauts was carrying the old rifle Caine had seen earlier.

Caine heard a howl of agony, saw it came from the cameljawed Jerry he'd shot in the guts: a group of Totenkopf was trying to lift him on to a stretcher: he was screeching, writhing, trying to fight them off. Caine felt a twinge of sympathy: there was nothing worse than a gut wound.

One of the stretcher-bearers shouted to Lohman. As he turned towards them, Caine saw something astonishing. Slung on the *Sturmscharführer*'s back was a Tommy-gun: not just any Tommy-gun, but *his* Tommy-gun, with its fat magazine and bayonet lug. He flushed, remembered he'd last seen it in Quinnell's hands. *Lohman must have been at the blockhouse. He must know if Quinnell, Wallace and Trubman are alive.*

Lohman pivoted round to face Caine. 'That soldier you shot was asking you to surrender,' he said. 'Now he is dying. We can do nothing for him. It is a bad way to die.'

Caine didn't move or speak.

'What is your name?' Lohman demanded.

'Captain Thomas Caine.'

'Your unit?'

'I can't answer that.'

'No, of course not. I do not care. I want only the blek box. Where is it?'

For a moment Caine was surprised: then he realized he shouldn't be. *They didn't come all this way just to pick up a couple of stray Tommies. They must have a good reason to deploy a unit behind enemy lines when their whole army's in retreat.* The black box. *That's what they wanted all along.*

'I don't know anything about a black box,' he said.

Lohman sighed. 'Captain, you came here after a . . . *deserter* . . . who took the blek box yesterday morning.'

This time, Caine had to struggle to keep the astonishment off his face. *He knows about Fiske? One of the lads talked. That means at least one of them's alive.*

'You hev come for the blek box,' Lohman declared. 'There were two of you. You were easy to follow. There is only one road, no? We find your vehicle. We find your treks. Now we find you. Where is your comrade, I do not care. I want to know where is going the man with the blek box?'

Caine remembered that he still had Jizzard's map stowed inside his overalls. They hadn't found it.

'I don't know,' he said.

There was a chorus of shouts from the direction of the Hun lorries. A trooper jumped down from one of them, bawled and gesticulated at Lohman. The *Sturmscharführer* shouted back: when he twirled round again, Caine saw smudges of anger in the hard blue eyes.

'The man you shot hes died,' he said. 'He hes died in very great pain. Now my men say you must pay.'

Caine stared at the ground. *You always pay for everything*, he thought.

Lohman beckoned to the soldiers guarding the three Arabs: the troopers dragged them over, paraded them in front him. The old man's dead eye gleamed whitely: he and the younger one stood up straight, stared Lohman out. The girl was trembling, but doing her best to control herself. At Lohman's order, the Death's Head

350

troopers tied their hands behind their backs, made them kneel.

'We hev not time for nonsense,' Lohman said. 'You will tell me where is the blek box, Captain, or I shall shoot these people.'

He drew his pistol.

'Last chance, Captain.'

Caine glanced at the Arabs. For a second he locked eyes with the girl: her face was bewildered and confused. Caine felt a flush of pity. He'd brought humiliation to her and her people, who had no part in the war, whose only crime was to offer him hospitality.

Lohman grunted. He took a step closer to the younger man, held the Walther against his temple. Caine was just opening his mouth to protest when Lohman pumped a round into the man's skull at point-blank range. The Arab's eyes went out like lights: blood dropped from his nostrils: his body keeled over. The girl shrieked, set up an eery high-pitched keening, raked her head hysterically from side to side. The old man's good eye blazed: he bull-bellowed, struggled to his feet. Jerries wrestled him down: one kicked him in the stomach, another cuffed his head.

Caine felt as if he'd been punched in the gut: the air drained from his lungs. His throat went tight. '*You . . . you . . .*' were the only words he could get out.

Lohman wheeled round on him. 'Not *me*,' he said. 'This is *your* doing. The girl will be next.'

He pointed the pistol at the girl. Her eyes almost burst from their sockets. She thrashed, retched, spat, cursed, tried to get up. Krauts grabbed her slim shoulders, snatched at her hair, wrenched her down, stretched her head back. She squealed, frothed at the mouth, snapped at their hands with her teeth. Lohman leaned closer to her, laid the muzzle of the pistol under her jaw. She went quiet: her body quivered.

Lohman turned his head to Caine, raised a blond eyebrow.

Blood beat a harsh tattoo in Caine's ears. An innocent civilian had just paid the price of his silence: one more death added to the long list of dead souls he was responsible for. Now another, a young girl. *What am I doing here? Bringing suffering to the harmless. I don't care what's in the black box. It's not worth it. The whole world's not worth this child's life.* He felt deeply ashamed: not only had he brought death to this family, he was also helpless to defend them.

Lohman focused on the girl: his lips trembled slightly.

'Don't,' Caine yelled. 'Don't kill her. I'll tell you where the black box is. Just give me your word that you won't do any more harm to these people.'

Lohman stared at him, his palefire eyes curious.

'You hev my word. Now, where is the blek box?'

'You'll find it at Bir Souffra,' Caine said in a rush. 'Inside my overalls, there's a map.'

Lohman lifted his pistol from the girl's throat, spoke to the soldiers in German. A couple of them frisked Caine, tore off his smock, tugged at the buttons of his overalls. Hands wormed over his chest, found the map, ripped it from its hiding place. One of them handed it to the *Sturmscharführer*.

He put away his pistol, examined the map, nodded with satisfaction. He glanced at the dead Arab, shook his head. 'A pity you didn't speak earlier. You could have saved him.'

He folded the map, placed it inside his tunic, strutted away.

The girl was sobbing: the old man was mumbling to himself. Caine heard Lohman snap orders: Jerries hustled the Arabs to their feet, marched them back towards their shacks. Caine eyed them anxiously, wondering if Lohman would keep his promise. He looked away, knowing that, whatever happened, he couldn't stop it. He wished to hell he knew where Cope was. He forced himself to concentrate: Lohman's next move would be Bir Souffra – LG 120. Maybe he'd find the black box there, maybe he wouldn't. Would he let Caine go now? More likely he'd take him along as insurance. Lohman had left two troopers to watch him: he tried to weigh up his chances of making a break.

He was distracted by the sound of shovels hitting earth, looked up to see Jerries digging pits about midway between the tamarix grove and the wagons. It was a burial party, he realized: the pits were graves. He watched the Germans with riveted eyes. There were six men in the party: they were working in pairs, two men to a grave. A shiver ran through him. *Three* graves. One for the Jerry he'd shot. One for the dead Arab. Whose was the third grave? Lohman wasn't taking him along for insurance after all.

Caine rose shakily to his feet, felt hands clamp his shoulders. '*I have to piss,*' he bawled. He made a hissing noise. The Krauts kicked his legs, slapped him down. The pain in his side flared up: his left arm burned. He remembered his last meal – the stew the Arabs had brought them. If they hadn't eaten it, they might not have fallen asleep. He was going to pay for that meal with his life. He made a second attempt to get up: a Jerry booted him in the kidneys, another cracked his head with a rifle-butt.

Caine didn't know how long he'd sprawled there dazed, but when he sat up, he saw that the burial-party was already filling in the first two graves. Lohman was standing in front of him, surveying the boughs of the tamarix tree. The *Sturmscharführer* gazed around as if looking for something: his eyes alighted on the well-rope coiled on the frame of one of the shacks. He pointed to it, instructed a soldier to bring it over. He had the man tie a slip-knot in the rope, sling it over the lowest bough of the tree. The soldier succeeded on the second attempt. When the loop came down, Lohman draped it over Caine's head, called four or five more Totenkopf men over to brace the rope.

Caine felt the loop tighten round his neck, tried to struggle. The two guards held his arms fast.

Lohman examined him with polished flint eyes. 'You are a brave man, Captain Caine. Your defence at el-Fayya was admirable. On the other hand, you shot one of my men when he asked you to surrender. This is not so good. I dislike hanging a fellow soldier, but . . .'

Caine clamped his lips shut. He wasn't going to demand a court-martial, plead for his life. He was guilty: he'd known deep down that the cameljawed Jerry had been calling on him to surrender. He'd shot him anyway, just like Lohman had shot the Arab. There was no difference in the end.

Lohman barked a low order to the men on the end of the rope.

The loop constricted, cut into the flesh of Caine's neck, burnt his skin, choked off his breath. He felt helpless, paralysed with fear, felt pressure on the blood vessels in the cavity beneath his jaw, felt his spine stretch as his feet were lifted off the ground, felt his blood pound in his ears, felt his head loll like a dead weight. His throat was bonded with flame: his lungs were burning. His eyes blacked out, his senses dimmed. Over the drum of his heartbeat he heard the hammer of iron on iron, the familiar sound of his father shaping metal in the forge, the reassuring rhythm of his childhood. Since his father had died, he'd only heard that sound when he was in mortal danger This was it, then. He'd be with his dad, and his mother now – and with all the lads he'd had to bury up the Blue. *Goodbye, Betty*, he said.

It wasn't the forge, though, it was a cool place – a church, maybe. It was quiet: he made no sound on the floor. He was moving silently up an aisle between great pillars like the trunks of living trees. Was it a forest? It was shady: light spread in brindles through the foliage.

He could smell the trees, could see the leaves and branches, but there were arched windows among them, as if the forest were inside the church, or the church were part of the forest, or the church and the forest were one.

He was moving towards a stained-glass window, a mandala of light and colour. He saw that the glass mosaic formed the image of a man in a monk's robe: a saint with a gold halo, and a long white beard divided in two. The saint seemed to be floating in the air above pale water and dark rocks. He was surrounded by monsters: hairy-limbed apes with hyena-like heads, spiny seahorse demons with cockatrice skulls and bat's wings, creatures with scaly fish bodies, leering red mouths and forked tails. The monsters were quivering around the saint: they seemed to be trying to tear him apart. Caine's gaze was drawn to the saint's face, in the centre of the tableau: despite the demons clamouring around him, he wore a countenance of utter serenity.

Caine was transfixed. He knew he'd seen this image before: had viewed the whole scene somewhere else. Then he remembered. It was in the room where he'd met Caversham, in St Anthony's monastery. He'd glimpsed it over Caversham's shoulder – a painting on the wall. *That was what? . . . four, five days ago? . . . seems like a lifetime.* It had grabbed his attention momentarily because he'd felt some sympathy with the subject, harassed by devils. Caine had felt himself in the same position. What had Caversham said about it? It was called the *Temptation* – no, the *Torment* – *of St Anthony*. He was a hermit who lived in the Sinai two thousand years ago. He had struggled with demons and monsters. They'd named a cluster of plagues after him – St Anthony's Fire. He'd left his bleached bones in the desert.

Left bleached bones in the desert. It was the last phrase that stood out: it was familiar. He'd heard that somewhere else recently. Who'd said it? Harry Copeland? No, not Cope. It was Maurice Pickney. The ghost of Pickney he'd seen in his dream. He'd asked him what was in the black box, and he'd recited a verse.

> He left bleached bones in the desert,
> Wrestled with centaur and satyr,
> Defied the demon hosts,
> Put out the Holy Fire.

Of course: the Pickney apparition had been talking about St Anthony. The saint had left his bleached bones in the desert. He'd defied demons, tangled with monsters, given his name to a cluster of plagues collectively known as St Anthony's Fire.

Were Holy Fire and St Anthony's Fire one and the same? Pickney's ghost had recited that verse when he'd asked what was in the black box. What had Holy Fire got to do with it? He tried to recall what Pickney had said when Caine first encountered him in the derelict aircraft? *Don't touch the black box. Don't try to open it. Leave it where it is. You'd be doing the world a favour . . . whatever you do, skipper, don't open the black box . . .*

He'd warned Caine not to open the black box, because

357

there was something terrible inside. Something that might ravage the world. Not an ordinary weapon. Something small enough to be carried in a box: the smallest thing you could think of: plague, disease, bacteria, bacilli, germs: St Anthony's Fire, *Holy Fire*. Once let loose they could could wipe out an entire army, devastate a whole population.

Holy Fire. That was what the black box contained.

Then the lights went out. The image on the stained-glass window faded. Caine was in limbo, in a ghostly no-man's land between worlds. He groped forward: there was a featureless wall in front of him, with a single black door set in it. There was no other exit. *That's it, then.* He moved to the door, opened it, fell out into a starless universe.

42

He hit the earth with a thump, inhaled a choking breath. His eyelids flickered: he saw Harry Copeland moving towards him with his SMLE in one hand, his bayonet in the other. Cope knelt down by his head, sheathed the blade, laid his rifle aside, started groping at something tied round his neck. '*Jesus wept*,' he said.

Caine remembered the noose, lifted his hand, felt the shape of the taut rope. He tried to speak, made only a gurgle in his throat.

'Don't talk,' Cope said. He pulled the rest of the rope off.

Caine coughed, touched his neck, felt the flesh sting. He sat up, took in the huge tamarix tree, the mats they'd slept on, the Arab shacks, the dead dog, the freshly dug graves with the third one still unfilled. He wasn't dead and buried, then? There was no sign of Lohman or the Totenkopf men – perhaps they'd decided to come back and bury him later?

'You were dangling about three minutes, I reckon.' Copeland whistled through his teeth. 'Thought you'd had it, mate.'

Caine remembered the black door he'd stepped through: it had seemed pretty final to him, too. 'I was dead,' he croaked huskily. 'I was really fucking dead.' His throat ached when he spoke. 'What happened to you?'

'I went for a piss. Heard motors, Kraut voices, then you shouted at me to get out. I took cover, couldn't see what was going on.' He gave Caine a mouthful of water from his canteen.

'Soon as I heard motors gunning, I came in. Found you hanging from this bloody tree: the rope end was tied round the trunk. Cut you down.'

Caine coughed. 'Jerries pushed off, then?'

'Yep. What were they after?'

'The black box. I gave them the map. They shot one of the Arabs, threatened to kill the girl . . .'

In a rush Caine recalled his vision – the apparition of Pickney, *Holy Fire*. He grabbed Copeland's wrist, dragged himself to his feet. 'Harry, I know what's in the black box. If they open it there's going to be hell to pay.'

Copeland watched him with worried eyes. 'You all right, Tom? Better take it easy, mate.'

'No, we've got to get to the box before the Krauts do. There'll be a catastrophe.'

'Tom . . . you must be a bit giddy . . .'

Caine shrugged off Cope's helping hands. 'You ever heard of Holy Fire, Harry?'

Copeland considered it a moment, frowned. 'Holy Fire is what they used to call some types of plague in the Middle Ages.' His eyes were wary. He picked up his rifle, brushed dust off the stock. 'Also known as St Anthony's Fire. Why?'

'That's what's in the black box. Holy Fire, or some modern version of it. Whoever opens it is going to release a plague. It'll spread like wildfire, kill everyone, Axis and Allies alike.'

Cope's jaw dropped: he looked as if Caine had just punched him. 'You mean like germ warfare?'

'Think of it – the mother of all booby traps. A weapon that can kill more people than the biggest bomb ever made, and you can carry it in a box.'

Copeland took a deep breath. 'Germ warfare's as old as the hills, Tom. They reckon the ancient Babylonians used to lob diseased bodies at their enemies. The Mongols would catapult infected corpses over the walls of enemy towns. Krauts tried using anthrax in the Great War . . . it's against the Geneva Convention, though.'

'What did you say about the Axis playing by different rules?'

Copeland cracked his knuckles. 'OK, I'm not saying it's impossible. What I don't get is . . . how do you know?'

Caine considered it for a moment. 'Remember I told you I had this . . . dream . . . of Maurice Pickney . . . ?'

'Oh yeah – the chap who's been in the ground nigh on half a year. You've been through a lot, mate. I wouldn't blame you if –'

'I know it sounds crazy. I told you I thought there was a message for me, and this is it. I know dreams are only in your head, Harry: I'm not nuts. It might be the after-effects of Olzon-13, it might be shellshock, it might be battle fatigue, or just a bolt out of the blue. Thing is, I'm certain it's true. We've got to stop them opening the black box.'

'Who, the Jerries?'

'Fiske, the Jerries ... anybody.' A new thought occurred to him. 'What if it's already on its way to Egypt? What if they open it there? It'd be like the Black Death all over again.'

Cope gazed around uncertainly.

'Trust me, Harry.'

'We'd better head for Allied lines, warn them.'

'Too far. The RV's only a couple of miles away. We'll be there in under an hour.'

'How are we going to take on that lot? Must be two dozen of 'em. You haven't even got your weapon.'

Caine recalled that he'd seen Lohman hefting his Thompson: that *hadn't* been a dream. 'No,' he said, 'but I know who has.'

They found the old Arab and the girl still tied up in one of the shacks, cut them loose, made signs at them to leave quickly. They stared at the two SAS men coldly: Caine wouldn't have blamed them if they'd wanted to throttle him. He'd brought the Germans here, caused the death of one of their family. He wanted to apologize, but it wouldn't have meant much to them, and he didn't have the language to do it anyway. They filled their waterbottles from the earthenware pot, gulped down what was left, swallowed their last Bennies. Caine no longer had his compass, but the Hun vehicle tracks weren't hard to follow.

They staggered painfully after them towards the distant brokenbacked hills, pink-rimmed now from the light of the lowering sun. The plain was a carpet of laddered patterns – stepfaults and soft clay ridges, long beaches peppered with sculpted rocks on pedestals, like huge petrified artichokes. They trogged across atolls of flat sand, climbed convex inclines, crossed shallow arroyos of fine-veined clay, where olive-coloured thornscrub bloomed, and swordgrass grew in clumps.

It was slow going: Caine's body was wracked with pain. His neck chafed: he felt as if he'd aged fifty years. He was glad of the Bennies, though.

They'd been walking about half an hour when they spotted a wagon lying in the bed of a wadi. Cope identified her through his binos as a German light car. They approached her cautiously, creeping from rock to rock. She was deserted: the sandy floor around her was greasy with oil, disturbed by footmarks. Caine examined the car for booby traps. 'Don't suppose they bothered,' he told Copeland. 'Weren't expecting pursuit.'

Cope searched his face. 'Couldn't you . . . you know . . .'

'Fix her up?' Caine shrugged wearily. 'I can't work miracles, Harry.'

He had a gander under her chassis, found what he'd been expecting: a fractured camshaft. 'No way to repair it short of a field-workshop.'

He got to his feet, found Copeland grinning at him. 'What'd you just say about miracles?'

'What the . . .'

Cope held up Caine's Tommy-gun, complete with

the bloated 100-round magazine he'd left for Quinnell. 'It was in the back. And that's not all Santa left.' He showed Caine Fred Wallace's sawnoff Purdey.

Caine took the shotgun, broke it, found two cartridges in the breech. He shut it, smiled at it sadly: Fred Wallace had saved his life with this weapon more than once. That made him think about what Lohman had said. 'The Jerries knew about Fiske,' he said. 'That means at least one of our lads must be alive . . .'

'Save it, mate.' Cope held out Caine's Tommy. 'We haven't got time.'

Caine stuffed the shotgun into his haversack, took the Thompson. He angled it to one side, removed the magazine, checked it: the mag was about half full. 'Quinnell must have bought one before he ran out of ammo,' he said. He worked the bolt three or four times, left it cocked, thumbed the safety. He fitted the mag back in place, made sure there was no play.

'Come on, let's . . .'

The flat *thwwwommmpppp* of a detonation came from behind the nearest ridges. The bang was muffled by the rock walls, but Caine knew by experience it was a demolition charge – a big one.

He locked eyes with Copeland. 'That's Fiske.'

'Now we know what happened to our Nobel 808.'

They heard the sprazzle of sub-machine carbines, the pop and thump of rifles: a heavy machine-gun jiggered out in slowtime spurts.

'Vickers "K",' Cope said. 'The blighter's holding out.'

Caine nodded. 'Then we can still bag that box.'

They moved towards stone outcroppings, wove into a defile where water had carved its way through strata of chocolate and vanilla, like creamcake layers. They climbed carefully up the cluttered scoria at the far end, snaked through the last few yards of scree to the sky-line. They found themselves looking over a concave valley the colour of tobacco, sloping down to the Bir Souffra *hattia* – an outpost of desiccated palms, drab underbrush, the ruins of mud huts and irrigated plots. Beyond it, low sunlight was hanging on the razored peaks of the distant spurs, picking out bronze walls like knotted gristle.

A *drub-drub-drub* of Vickers-fire came from the out-post: Jerry rounds yipped. Caine took a shufti through Copeland's glasses, saw that the gunfire was emanating from behind a dilapidated mud wall, fortified with boulders: Fiske had taken some trouble to dig in, he thought. Shifting the binos, he clocked a dozen or more fieldgrey figures crawling towards the outpost across sawgrass, scrub and barren gravel. There wasn't much cover for the attackers, but the defensive fire was too feeble to keep them off for long: in any case, Caine could see from the stobbed-up dust that the shots were falling low, as if the gunner had messed up his sight-setting. He shook his head. Fiske was commando-trained: he should have known better than that.

He scoped the palm-groves looking for the jeep, but couldn't find her: Fiske must have cammed her up well. On the far side of the outpost, he noticed the airfield marked on the map as LG120 – a strip of hardcore desert cleared of stones, delineated by white-painted boulders: he made out the purple gash of ground-recognition panels laid out on the strip.

'There's a plane coming in,' he said. 'If Fiske gets on that, the black box will be in Cairo or Constantine before you can say *Jack Robinson*.'

Copeland gave him a doubtful glance. 'He's going to have a job on, with all those Jerries on his back.'

Caine followed Cope's line of sight back to the Totenkopf attackers: a few of them were on their feet now, skirmishing towards Fiske's position. There was a shuddering *bawoooommmmpph*: the ground in front of them heaved up in a swelling firebubble, spikehorned streamers of flame and flying grit: two Jerries cart-wheeled, flew somersaults through lilac nebulas of smoke and dust.

'See that,' Cope said. 'Fiske's covered his perimeter with fused charges. Knows his business after all.'

'He can't keep it up, though.'

'What we need to do is draw them off, get round behind him.'

Copeland tipped his head, indicating the ground immediately below. Caine lowered the glasses, squinted raweyed, clocked what Cope had seen. The Huns' Gaz lorries were leaguered amid low rockpiles and sand-drifts not thirty paces from the foot of their ridge: a pair of mottleskinned 3-tonners with canvas backs, balloon tyres, long-snouted prows. Caine clocked a Totenkopf man on stag there, a brawnbacked trooper in full battlekit and coalscuttle, carrying a Gewehr rifle, with two stick grenades in his webbing. Caine gave him the onceover through the glasses, recognized the wide nose and blunt mouth: one of the boys who'd relieved him of his belongings back at the Arab camp. The Jerry wasn't paying much attention to his surroundings: he was straining to see what was happening further on.

Copeland studied the lorries. 'If we hit the wagons, it'll make 'em sit up. It's a long hike back.'

'Good one, Harry. We'll blow them, wait till we see the Krauts coming, then scoot round Fiske's flank.'

'We'll need a big bang. Reckon that chap might give us his spudmashers . . . if we ask politely, that is.'

They crawled back from the skyline, clambered down the scoria to the floor of the defile. Copeland slid out his bayonet: Caine shook his head, pointed to his Tommy-gun. They moved with agonizing slowness: Caine's wounds had made him clumsy. They'd crept to within ten yards of the sentry when his foot scuffed a stone. Caine froze: the Jerry whirled, rifle at the shoulder. Before he'd completed the spin, Caine was up, his Thompson locked in low-hip position: he blowtorched .45 calibre slugs, felt them slam the Jerry's chest, saw red squills bud. The Jerry fell over on his back: his limbs spasmed: he coughed blood. Copeland sprinted over to him, pistol drawn, ready to drill another round into his head. The Jerry vomited gore, tremored, lay still. Copeland detached the two stick-grenades from his belt: Caine rifled through the dead-man's pouches and pockets. Copeland primed one of the grenades. 'Come on, Tom. No time for stripping corpses.'

Caine came up grinning, holding his precious Zippo lighter, still in its protective condom. 'My good-luck charm,' he said.

He slung his Tommy, took the second grenade, primed it: they slipped over to the wagons.

'Under the bonnets,' said Caine.

He chose the first truck, let Copeland move to the second before he felt for the release catch, lifted the bonnet, stood it on its prop. He pulled the pin on the stick-bomb, planted it on top of the engine-block, closed the bonnet. He dekkoed Cope, exchanged thumbs-up. They ran for the nearest sandpile, threw themselves down, pressed their faces against the sand. '*Five-six-seven,*' Cope counted.

They felt the earth deepdump, felt a kettledrum boom in their ears, felt deadweight on their chests: they heard sheetiron rupture, heard the craunch of engine parts torn to pieces with the ease of cardboard, heard glass cubes crepitate, heard shrapnel squib. They tasted carbongas, heard the wagons backslam on broken wheels, heard canvas whoosh and crackle like a bonfire. They peeked over the dune to see iron frames blazing, lofting claws of flame, whoffs of inkblack smoke.

Copeland crouched ready to move. Caine had to drag himself up: he felt shattered, his neck stung, his joints ached, his head was full of pain and fire. A stunt like this would have been hard at peak fitness, let alone in his condition. He told himself it was the last round: the next few minutes would be make or break. He got to his feet, braced his Thompson, took in the blazing lorries, felt oily heat on his face. He made a sign to Copeland: they backed away from the burning vehicles, took up positions behind low outcrops, five yards apart. It wasn't tactical enough, Caine knew, but if they were going to do this, they were going to do it side by side.

Lohman's platoon had crawled to within a hundred yards of the Bir Souffra outpost. Defensive fire had dwindled, then stopped: Lohman's battle-sense told him the gunner had been hit. Or perhaps he'd been wounded before they'd started: from the beginning the fire had seemed laboured: the shots had continually fallen low. The only casualties he'd taken had been the two men injured by those damn' hidden charges. That had been a clever touch for a one-man defence, but he doubted there would be any more.

It was now or never. Lohman had seen the purple recognition panels laid out on the landing ground: an aircraft was expected, and he guessed she'd be here before sunset. He didn't want to have to take her on, or to come up on the radar of the Desert Air Force: he wanted to get the black box and get out sharp. He didn't relish the idea of being stranded behind enemy lines with no aircover. That reminded him of another reason they had to overrun the enemy position.

They'd located fresh jeep tracks threading this way: they could do with that vehicle to replace the damaged light car they'd lost on the way from the Arab camp.

Lohman sucked a breath, stuck his head up: nothing happened. He gave the order *advance to contact*. The Totenkopf men rose like shadows out of their niggard cover, charged the outpost in a long roll, spanging off rounds as they ran. They came in through the ragged palms, encircled the machine-gun position: Lohman was the first through a gap in the wall. He saw that he was in a broken enclosure around a disused wellshaft, now filled with sand. The Vickers was still standing on its tripod with a pan attached: it was surrounded by a litter of ammunition boxes, spent cases, charge igniters, safety-fuse. The black box lay on the opposite side of the circle: Lohman saw that it was open, and that a khaki-clad body was slumped next to it, face down.

He signalled to a couple of his men: the three of them approached warily. Lohman was relieved to have found the black box at last, but concerned that it had been opened: he crouched, peered into it, saw that the interior was almost entirely taken up with a maze of tubing: fans like multiple sets of tiny organ pipes, intricately connected and seeming to grow out of each other like the roots of a plant: the tubing looked like a smaller version of the strange protrusions he'd seen inside the fuselage of the derelict aircraft. Inset in this organic mass was a shallow, flat-bottomed glass petri-dish with a shattered cover: the petridish seemed to contain some kind of greengrey mildew. Lohman stepped back, mystified, wondered what all the fuss had been about. He had to admit, though, that there was a sinister aura around the box: it gave him a distinct feeling of unease. He flipped the lid: it closed with an almost inaudible sucking sound: he read the word STENDEC on top.

He turned his attention to the dead Tommy – at least, he assumed he was dead. From the back, he appeared to be a tall, unusually wiry soldier, with spindle legs and spidery arms. He was wearing a stocking-cap, and the same kind of hooded, sand-coloured smock that Caine and the other British commandos had been wearing. So this was the man who'd cleverly set the hidden charges, but had been too weak or wounded to use the machine-gun effectively. The odd thing was that he didn't seem to be wounded: there was no trace of blood.

The Totenkopf men had checked the face-down body for booby traps: now they were turning him over. Lohman squatted, interested to see the man the plump Tommy POW had called a *deserter*. He looked down, almost fell over in shock. *The face*: he'd never seen anything like it in all his years of combat. It was bloated and carbuncular, fungus-coloured skin split into a network of cracks like old porcelain. The eyeballs were popping out: the mouth was a swollen, gangrenous cavity: wormhole nostrils suppurated bile. The eyes, nose and mouth were distorted by transparent blisters like mouldering jellies – the blisters seemed to be swelling visibly. Some of them erupted as he watched, emitted a rotten-egg odour, squirted his men with viscid pus. Lohman staggered back in horror, saw that the Tommy's hands were covered in the same vomit-hued pustules: the joints between his long fingers festered with slime-green rot.

'*Get back*,' Lohman snapped: his men were already

371

backing off with cries of disgust, frantically wiping stinking pus off their faces with bare hands. More Totenkopf men gathered round, drawn by the commotion. '*Get away*,' the *Sturmscharführer* repeated. '*Don't go near it*.' At that moment the corpse moved: the fester of a mouth gaped, a putrefying tongue flopped out. Lohman saw the decayed lips working, heard a death-like rattle in the man's throat. '*The black box*,' the Tommy croaked. '*The . . . black . . . box*.'

Lohman cast a frightened glance at the box: had the soldier's horrific sickness come out of it? He shuddered, dekkoed his hands, noticed that there was a smear of pus on his knuckles. Just then, he heard the rumbling *doooommmmpppp* of a detonation from the direction of their leaguer. He swivelled round, craned his neck towards the higher ground, clocked fire and black smoke.

'*That's our transport*,' someone bawled.

43

From their position, Caine and Copeland couldn't see the Bir Souffra outpost: it was hidden from view by flaky grey protrusions of outcrop that pressed through the surface like dark vertebrae, alternating with open stretches, running in a broken curve towards the palm thickets. They were aware that shooting from that direction had stopped: Caine put it down to the fact that the Totenkopf men had broken off the attack. They waited five minutes before the Death's Head boys came into view, jogging in loose formation, chasing elastic shadows through the scrub.

There was a frenzied quality about their movements, Caine thought, as if they were being chased. He popped goosebumps. 'Wait till they're within a hundred yards,' he said.

The lorry-wrecks were burning out. When the Jerries slowed down to look at them, Copeland already had the point man in his crosshairs. He eased off the safety, hooooshed a breath, held it, took first pressure, tweaked the trigger. *Craaaaack*. The SMLE bolted a sear of flame: the round struck the Jerry in the solar plexus: he stood stock still for a moment, folded up with a graceful bow.

Caine switched to single shot, gripped the Thompson

underarm, brassed off three bullets with careful timing. *Blobbb. Blobbb. Blobbb.* He showed himself, paused a half-beat to make certain the Totenkopf men had seen him, hared off across open ground towards the next ridge, traileyed Copeland galloping after him on heron's legs. He dived into cover, whopped off another burst, saw that the Death's Head men had hit dirt. Rifles rumped, rounds squdged, richochets rollicked off rock with staccato screams. Copeland threw himself beside Caine, shuftied back to see that some of the enemy were up and coming after them in skirmishing pairs. He sighted up, watched a Jerry drop and roll, let the SMLE's muzzle follow his movement, blatted him out just as he came up into a firing position, heard a distant sigh.

Caine poised on the balls of his feet, ready for another run: he was panting: his legs were lumpen, the shrapnel scoriations on his arm had opened up. He felt as if he'd been dropkicked in the side: the ropeburns on his neck were acid fire. Copeland loosed another shot. 'You ready, mate?' Caine said.

He drew air deep, felt his lungs strain, forced himself out of cover: his legs worked sluggishly, his breath came in snags: every step was a minor hell. He reached the next sandpile, got down, watched Copeland zigzag behind him, almost forgot to fire. The Tommy-gun went *blammpp, blammpp*, as if someone else were shooting. Copeland threw himself down. 'There's something wrong with them,' he panted. 'They're falling off.'

Caine squinted towards the Jerries: he saw what Copeland meant. A few were still skirmishing, but the perfect precision he remembered from the el-Fayya fight had gone: they moved ponderously, almost reluctantly. *They look like I feel,* Caine thought.

He could see the outpost now. The tangled palm thickets cast bowbacked shadows on the desert, the dried palm fronds stood out like beaten gold. The sun was drifting home to the hills through pavilions of bloodedged cloud: the sky was cooling gunmetal. Each feature of the barren basin was cleanly picked out by the soft, liquid light: peppercorns of scrub, reaches of patinated limestone, clints and grykes of outcrops like the flaking fins of golden fish.

He tried to judge how far they had to go: he reckoned it was only another three hundred yards, but part of the way was without cover. There wasn't a peep from Fiske's position: there hadn't been since before they'd blown the wagons. Fiske might have been hit: he might simply have no idea what was going down.

They sprinted another stretch, then another, rolled in behind grass clusters that gave almost no cover from fire. Jerry slugs pipped air, dropped in sullen whinges out of the flint-hued sky. It was getting harder: Caine's limbs had a hot, weary, feverish feeling: his whole body was on fire. The outpost was only a stone's throw away but it felt like the end of the earth: they were down to a few rounds of ammunition. 'Last go,' Copeland gasped. 'We can make it to the trees in one run.'

Caine dekkoed him, caught a flare of blue lustre in the bloodshot eyes. 'See you on the ledge, Harry.'

'Yeah. You're buying the beers.'

Getting his body up was like hoisting a grand piano: Caine rocked to his feet, jammed the butt of his Thompson against his bicep, let the fingers of his left hand feel the foregrip grooves. '*Go,*' he yelled.

He zigzagged forward on legs like pincushions, dimly aware of Copeland behind him, hardly registering the blips of enemy fire. His lungs hurt, his heart pounded. The palm trees seemed miles away. He faltered, forced himself on, saw Betty Nolan rear up in his mind's eye: the thought of her boosted him. He dragged himself through a mire of agony: the palm groves were a paradise he'd never reach. Then suddenly the trees were rearing over him like a golden wave, and he was in among the cool sanctuary of their shade. He slumped down behind a knot of treeboles, rolled over, brought the Tommy up to cover Copeland. He blinked: Copeland wasn't there.

He scanned the area he'd just run over, saw, almost halfway across it, a pile gilded by the waning light. It was Copeland: Cope was down. He looked again, saw that the pile was moving. *He's alive: he's trying to get up.* Caine couldn't leave him there. He had to go back for his mate, but he'd used all his energy in the last run: he was drained. In the past three days he'd been hit by shrapnel, wounded in the side, caught in a bomb-blast, bashed with rifle-butts, hanged by the neck. He'd lost his entire patrol, including his closest friends. No one could take all that and keep going. The last run had been purgatory: he couldn't go back: he didn't have the strength. He surveyed the field again, saw that two Death's Head men were advancing towards his downed pal. They were a long way off as yet, and they seemed to be stumbling along erratically, but they were certainly heading in Cope's direction.

Caine sieved air through his nostrils. He'd promised that he would bring back his wounded comrades. He hadn't kept his promise in the case of Wallace and Trubman: even if it killed him, he wasn't going to let that happen to Cope. He raised himself on jellylegs, propped himself up against a palm trunk. He checked his magazine: his heart dropped. It was empty: he was out of rounds. He set the Thompson against the trunk, groped in his knapsack for Wallace's Purdey. It was still there. He hefted it in both hands: it wasn't much of a combat weapon, but it felt like a friend.

He launched himself out of the trees, gritted his teeth, overrode the torment, forced his muscles to sub-mit to his will. This time, he refused to heed the straining of his lungs, the ache in his muscles, the fire in his wounds, the swimming giddiness in his head. He was intent only on Copeland: he was going to get him out. He was running, turfing dust: it seemed as if he'd been running for ever. Miraculously, nobody was shoot-ing at him: he could still see two Huns moving towards Cope with a lumbering, manic gait. He was ten yards away, five: Copeland was trying to raise himself on one shaky arm, and a rifle-butt. Caine saw that he had been wounded in the calf: his trouserleg was soaked in blood. He crouched down, met Cope's eyes, saw the pupils dilated with pain. 'I've had it, Tom,' Copeland soughed. 'You get out of it.'

'Can't do it, mate.'

A sub-machine round fluepiped, chuzzled dust close to them. 'Don't get up,' he told Cope. 'We've got guests.' He flopped down on his stomach with a gasp, let go the shotgun. 'Gimme your weapon,' he said.

He took the Lee-Enfield, drew the stock into his shoulder. Copeland sucked rapid breaths, swivelled round so that he could see the enemy, trailed blood. Caine peeked through the sights, picked out the two Jerries. They were about a hundred and fifty paces out, coming on unsteadily without any attempt to use the ground: they were slightly staggered – a broadhipped, longlimbed Hun behind, and a shorter man with a triangular torso in front. Caine focused on the leading man. *Christ in Heaven.* It was Lohman, but not the same Lohman who'd strung him up not long before: his face was swollen, covered in vomit-coloured blisters: his mouth was a bloated purple gash: his eyes dark cherries almost lost in the diseased face. Caine gasped. He dekkoed the other trooper, saw that his features were distorted by the same rabid pustular growths. These Death's Head men were sick, badly sick, and whatever it was they'd got, they hadn't had it a few hours before. It must have come on very quickly: it hadn't been apparent when he'd scanned the battleground from the ridge. He was acutely aware that the sickness might be contagious. He didn't want any part of it: he'd rather face a bullet than death from disease.

The Jerries were swaying slightly but still moving. Caine wondered why they didn't shoot: he noticed that they were both carrying Schmeisser sub-machine carbines. They were about a hundred yards away now: near enough to hit him, but too far to be sure of a good shot. He lined up the sights: he couldn't allow them to get close. He had only a vague knowledge of germs: he knew that some could be passed on by touch, others through the air. He had no idea what distances were involved in airborne contagion, but the further away he kept the enemy the better,.

He chose the taller Squarehead, pinned him in the crosshairs, took a breath, pulled iron. There was a dry click. He cocked the handle, pulled again: nothing happened. 'Out of ammo,' he said disgustedly.

'Sorry, Tom: I forgot to count.'

'What about the pistol?'

Cope shook his head. 'Forget it. That's out, too.'

Caine swore, gave the rifle back to Copeland. 'Have a shufti,' he said.

He picked up Wallace's sawnoff: it was a close-quarter weapon with an effective range of only ten or fifteen yards. To hit anyone he'd have to let them get right up close, and by then it might be too late.

'*Jesus Christ,*' Cope ejaculated. 'Those boys are sick as pigs.'

Caine cocked the Purdey's hammers, came up into a crouch, levelled the barrels at the Jerries, aware that at this distance he could do no more than make a big bang: it might scare them off, though. '*Stop. Don't come any closer,*' he bawled.

The broadhipped Jerry seemed to spot him for the

first time, raised his weapon lethargically. He stumbled, doubled over, dropped the carbine, vomited copiously: then he tumbled face down into his own puke. Lohman glanced round at his fallen comrade, staggered, recovered himself. He fixed glittering goateyes on Caine, marched directly towards him. He was seventy-five paces distant – near enough for a Schmeisser shot: too far for the Purdey. Caine shivered, felt sweat break out on his brow. '*Stay back*,' he yelled. He was suddenly aware that other grey dots had popped up out of the shadows behind Lohman: just visible in the sombre purpled hues of late afternoon.

Lohman was sixty yards away. He wasn't slowing down: he looked like a clockwork mechanism that wouldn't stop until it was knocked over. The flush of clear sunlight illuminated the parchment-coloured papules on his face, trailed a monstrous shadow behind him like a dark cloak. *Fifty yards*: Caine's pulse sledgehammered, his breath came fast. He raised his left arm, swore at the pain, used his elbow to steady the twin barrels. He watched Lohman with both eyes wide, centred on the decomposing blur of his face, shifted to his fieldgrey chest. *Forty yards*. It was near enough: *too damn' near*. His finger tightened on the double-triggers, he paused, yanked steel.

The shotgun went *whommmmffffff*, shrivelled air, scattergunned an ironball spread. It had no effect on Lohman: the *Sturmscharführer* didn't falter. He strode on oblivious. Caine lowered the shotgun, saw smoke trickles become gold filigree in the dwindling light. He'd fired his last shots. There was nothing left but hand-to-hand, and Lohman would surely finish them both before he got that near. He felt suddenly tranquil, released from pain. He'd given it his best: he'd pushed himself beyond the limits of human endurance. He could do no more. He watched Lohman coming on, slowly raising the Schmeisser: he was close enough for Caine to see the raddled features, the quartzite glint in the eyes. Lohman halted abruptly, pulled the butt into his waist, then, as if in slow motion, sank down slowly to his knees with a stark, demented moan. He let his weapon drop: Caine saw that his whole body was shaking. The *Sturmscharführer* made a last attempt to raise his head: for a split second they looked at each other: Caine glimpsed jelly-eel eyes in sockets bulging with puce-coloured ulcers, like egg-yolks poached in fat. '*Caine . . .*' the *Sturmscharführer* wheezed. '*The blek box. The blek . . . box . . . ist Tod.*' His eyes closed: he crumpled into the desert floor and lay still.

44

Caine picked up his Tommy at the palm groves, stopped to bandage Cope's calf with strips torn from his smock. There was no exit wound: Caine was sure a bullet was lodged inside. The wound was agony, and they had no morphia: Cope could only just hobble with Caine's help. The Totenkopf boys didn't seem to be following them any more, but they were still about: Caine was acutely aware that if it came to a dingdong, he and Cope didn't have any ammunition. They had a bayonet, but Caine didn't fancy trying to take the Krauts down with that: not when it meant a chance of picking up that face-rotting lurgi.

They had about another forty minutes of light, he reckoned: there'd be less danger from the Huns at night. There were recognition panels on the landing ground, though: if a plane was coming in, it would be before dark. He had no idea who'd be on the plane or what their orders would be: he was ready to hijack the kite if he had to, but without loaded weapons wasn't sure how to manage it.

He helped Copeland to his feet: they limped through the underbrush with their arms around each other's shoulders, through tangled palm fronds draped in thick tapestries of light and shade. It was tough going: Caine was so weak from pain and exhaustion that he hardly knew who was supporting whom. They stopped to rest: Caine propped his friend against the broad, fluted bole of a palm. They had no water left: their mouths were thick with mucus.

'Did you hear what that last Jerry said?' Copeland panted. '*The blek box ist Tod.*'

Caine scratched his chin. 'That means . . .'

'The black box is death. Those Jerries were as sick as hell, and they weren't an hour ago. You were right, mate. There's some kind of germ-warfare agent in that box, call it *Holy Fire*, call it what you want. The Jerries must have opened it –'

'They must have overrun Fiske's position while we were blowing the lorries –'

'Or maybe Fiske had opened it already. Maybe *he* was sick. Maybe that's why his shooting was so off . . . maybe the Huns got the infection from him . . . but *Jesus*, it must spread like the clappers. I mean, they got it in minutes.'

Caine licked his arid tongue. 'There's no way that black box is getting out of here, Harry. Imagine what an infection like that would do in Egypt – it could wipe out half the population, let alone the Allied armies.'

Copeland made a visible effort to focus. 'What about the Krauts, though? If any of them gets away, they could spread it here. I mean, what if they were captured by our side?'

Caine pulled at his chinstubble. 'They can't get away: we put their transport out of action. They might try it on foot, but how far would they get in that state?'

'Disease affects people differently. Maybe some of them haven't got it yet. And don't forget, Tom, there's a jeep here somewhere. The one Fiske nicked. What if they get hold of that?'

Caine shook his head. 'We'll have to make sure they don't.'

'That's going to be dead easy with no ammo. Maybe we can use diplomacy, or you can finish 'em off with your clasp knife.'

'Fiske might have ammo . . .'

Copeland shuddered. 'I'm not going near Fiske. We don't know how close you have to be to pick up the germs.'

'We've got to at least have a shufti at his position.'

They found Fiske behind the broken wall of the disused well, slumped by the black box in a pool of his own vomit. His face was so bloated with blisters that he scarcely looked human. His head hung down on his chest: he lifted it as they approached, stared at them with eyes that were fevered dots in dark-jellied caverns.

'Don't come any closer,' he croaked. ' . . . It's spread by contact . . . I didn't know . . . Sears-Beach never told me what was in it . . .'

Caine was startled. 'Sears-Beach? What's he got . . .' Then he remembered – even Pickney had mentioned Sears-Beach.

Fiske didn't seem to hear him. 'Never told me . . . nor did Caversham or Maskelyne . . . maybe *they* didn't know . . . I opened it . . .'

'*You* opened it?'

Fiske's head flopped: Caine realized that he was hanging on to life by a thin strand. He was talking to himself now. 'Don't touch it,' he whispered. 'Don't touch anything. Don't let it get out of here. Get rid of it. You'd be doing the world a favour.'

Caine shivered. Those words had come in a voice that wasn't Fiske's: they were only subtly different from what he'd heard in the derelict aircraft. Fiske tried to lift his head again: the light caught the disease-blurred features and Caine froze. Behind the putrid mask of suffering, just for a second, he saw not Fiske's, but Maurice Pickney's face.

The RAF Blenheim came in twenty minutes before last light: Caine had guessed the time right, but hadn't expected to see a medium bomber. He and Copeland sat on the edge of the landing ground in a wreath of shadows, watched the big bird drift down through massed terraces of giltedged cloud: the embers of the sun burned firegold along the dark blade of the hills. The landing gear squeaked, the light played on the aircraft's glazed nose like splashed syrup, rippled along the tapered fuselage, the gun turrets – one on top, the other upside-down on her underbelly. Her wheels crunched on stones: she taxied towards them through billowing dusteddies: her twin Bristol Mercury engines boomed.

'Blenheims have a six-man crew,' Copeland rattled. 'How we going to deal with that?'

Caine winked. 'Like you said, mate, we've got two choices: clasp knife, or diplomacy.'

They watched the plane's grasshopper shadow

scorch to a standstill, caught the heady tang of aviation fuel, heard the propellers slew. The cockpit door yawned: an RAF pilot-officer jumped out, a gaunt figure in khakis and fleece-lined flying jacket, with a long chin, a fish-hook for a nose and a waxed cavalry moustache. He looked about nineteen, Caine thought. He poised loose-hipped in the plane's shadow, popped a pipe in his mouth, stared at them with mild surprise. 'Hallo,' he said. 'Anybody order a kite?'

Caine helped Copeland to his feet, aware suddenly what a sorry sight they must look in their torn, blood-caked uniforms, goresoaked dressings and filthy bandages, their faces gungy and powder-black, eyes like pissholes in snow.

'Captain Caine, 1st SAS Regiment,' Caine wheezed. 'This is Lieutenant Copeland.'

'Pilot-Officer Willington,' the RAF man said. 'I'm the driver of this kite.'

He put his pipe away, helped Caine support Copeland. 'I say, sir,' he said. 'Looks like you've taken some flak.'

'You could say that.'

Willington called a name: a robust-looking flight-sergeant with a pink blob of a face and grizzled hair jumped down and hurried to help. 'No, I'll do it, sir,' he told the pilot. 'I'll get him on a stretcher.'

The NCO helped Copeland through the door: other hands assisted from inside. Willington paused, turned to face Caine. 'I *was* rather expecting three parties – enlisted men,' he said. 'And there was talk of cargo. Something about a black box?'

Caine swayed: his head looped. He put a hand on the fuselage to steady himself.

'I say, sir,' Willington said. 'Perhaps you ought to be on a stretcher too.'

'I'm all right.'

'So what about this box thingamy?'

Caine shivered, wondered where to start, how to explain what they'd encountered back there: a derelict aircraft of a strange design, a deadly disease carried in a box that itself possessed weird qualities.

'Who gave you orders to pick up the black box?'

'Lieutenant-Colonel Caversham.'

'There's been a change of plan. The parties you were expecting are dead. The black box contains a deadly germ agent that's already infected a whole platoon of Huns. If it reaches Cairo there's no telling what will happen.'

The pilot looked at him with wide eyes. 'Are you *sure* you're all right, sir?'

'Perfectly.'

'You see, I have my —'

He was cut off by the sewing-machine buzz of a Schmeisser SMG. Caine wheeled round to clock a Totenkopf man in full battlekit and helmet poling out of the palm-grove shadows not twenty yards away. The man was snarling, lurching from side to side, laddering off rounds, kicking up dark traceries of dust. Willington drew his weapon, took a pace to the side, pointed the pistol at the swerving Jerry. Caine could clearly see the Hun's bared teeth, the suppurating scarlet chancre of

387

a mouth, the black beans of eyes lost in the raw, bubo-
ridden mass.

'*My God*,' Willington said.

'Shoot him, for God's sake.'

At that moment there came the *chackachack* of .303
rimfire, a javelin of flame from the upper gun-turret:
the Jerry crashed sideways, rolled into the deck.

The pilot lowered his pistol. 'That was our Flight-Sar'nt
Atkins, upper-turret gunner. Good shooting, what?'

'You want to have a closer look?' Caine said: he nodded towards the dead Jerry.

The RAF man holstered his weapon, cast a nervous
glance at the dead Hun. 'I rather think we should push
off, sir, black box or no black box. There may be more
of them out there.'

'Another dozen at least. If they get away, there'll be
shit on.'

Wellington set his teeth grimly. 'Get aboard, sir.
We've got a 1,000-pounder in the rack.'

Ten minutes later, the Blenheim was wheeling through
a sky of beaten copper. Caine sat in the glazed nose-
section, peered out at the aircraft's shadow flitting across
the smouldering reefs of the desert, like an angular
speck. The plane banked sharply, straightened as she
accelerated into her final run. Caine saw the sun like a
half-closed eye on the skyline, saw the ragbacked hills
go out of focus, saw knotfaults and rock jumbles form
long chains of darkness across the cobbled plain. The
Bir Souffra outpost came into view, the palm-forest like

a head of bushy hair sprouting from the leopardskin shoulder of the basin. Before the bombardier shouted *bombs away*, Caine thought he saw tiny figures scuttling about down there, like ants.

45

Celia Blaney sat at the wheel of a jeep parked, with the two other FS wagons, in the shadow of a butte overlooking LG101. Tonight, her magnificent red hair was invisible under a cap-comforter, and she was wearing a duffel coat over her battledress. The night was cool and inky: there was ambient light only from the glittering armadas of desert stars. Blaney could see Stocker standing about five paces away, watching the landing ground through binoculars.

The drone of aircraft engines was nearer now: Blaney had already identified the plane from the sound as a medium bomber. A few minutes earlier she'd seen the flash of an Aldis lamp from the airstrip: the aircraft was coming in, all right. Why would a bomber be landing on an airfield in Sinai designated for MO4 operations? The more she and Stocker had learned about Caversham's little outfit in the past few days, the more it seemed a world unto itself.

There was a gush of fire on the landing ground: petrol-tin flares bursting out in a double-chain of fire. Blaney stepped down from the jeep, moved silently to Stocker's side: even without binos she could make out ground crew moving among the flares, phantom shapes illuminated for a fleeting second before dissolving back into obscurity. The plane's engines dopplered: the aircraft touched down with a creak of wheels, her engines settled to a hum as she taxied forward, layering the night with the high-octane smog of aircraft fuel.

The flares were dim by the time the Blenheim came to a standstill: there was enough light to spot the dwarfish figure of Miles Caversham, and the scarecrow form of Jasper Maskelyne, hurrying towards the aircraft, followed by a group of BD-clad men. Stocker clocked another figure jumping down from the fuselage door, peered him through his field-glasses until the light failed.

'Good grief,' he said. 'It's Caine.'

Blaney's enquiries about MO4 staff had turned up some interesting data. Maskelyne was a hostilities-only officer – one of the so-called *Magic Gang* who'd masterminded the *Bertram* deception. Glenn was a professional soldier: both had been seconded to MO4 fairly recently. Caversham, though, was a different kettle of fish. He'd been in the army since the Ark, and had spent most of his time in Intelligence. He'd worked in Berlin in the 1930s and had made contacts with certain members of the German 'Defence Service' – the Abwehrdienst – who he thought might prove sympathetic to the British in time of war. It seemed unlikely, given Caversham's cut-glass background, that the tail was wagging the dog, but anything was possible, and, as Stocker had learned, the

Abwehr was a dangerous animal, capable of deceptions of the subtlest kind.

Meanwhile, Blaney's surveillance of St Anthony's had also come up with surprises. One day she'd spotted the umistakable form of the giant Trooper Fred Wallace, 1st SAS Regiment, being hustled into the monastery like a prisoner. Blaney was curious: she'd met Wallace once, and remembered he'd been in Tom Caine's crew on the *Sandhog* scheme. Shortly after, she was astonished to see another *Sandhog* survivor enter St Anthony's, apparently freely: it was the signaller Corporal Trubman, whom she'd also met. When, the following day, she'd clocked another slight acquaintance, Second Lieutenant Harold Copeland, getting out of a 3-tonner in the monastery forecourt, she'd heeded the saying that three times was enemy action, and reported it.

Meanwhile, Stocker had been investigating the provenance of the suspect communications from MO4. He'd been unable to read them because of the code, but their destination had intrigued him. A visit to the comms centre at GHQ had convinced him that, whoever the *Groot* was with whom Cavendish had been talking, he wasn't in Berlin at all. After reading Blaney's report, he'd also done some checking on the current whereabouts of Second Lieutenant Copeland: he'd been due to start an officer cadet course at OCTU in Palestine, but hadn't turned up. Strangely, both Wallace and Trubman were missing: Wallace had been in the MP lockup at Suez after a brawl, but had been removed without any paperwork. Trubman had vanished from the Transit Centre in the Canal Zone. When Stocker had discovered that Tom Caine himself had disappeared from a fleapit hotel in Ismaeliyya, an alarm bell started clanging. Wallace, Trubman, Copeland and Caine were the four male survivors of *Sandhog*: they had also incurred the wrath of Maskelyne and Glenn, two of the principal officers of MO4. Stocker had already worked out that the *highly reliable but confidential source* mentioned in the DMI dispatch must be a friendly mole inside Cavendish's section. If so, why had the source spilled the beans about Stirling, but reported nothing about Caine and his men? It could, of course, simply concern a top-secret mission that had been kept quiet even from most MO4 staff. The juxtaposition of Caine with Maskelyne and Glenn, though, had suggested something more worrying – especially if it were true that Caversham had already done for David Stirling.

It had been several days, though, before Stocker had decided to join Blaney in Sinai. He'd brought a section of Field Security NCOs with him, just in case. They'd watched the monastery after dark, seen Caversham and Maskelyne leaving in a jeep, with other ranks following in a 3-tonner. They'd tailed them to the landing ground.

Now the flares were out, Stocker could see nothing on the LG but the occasional weft of a torch-beam. He could hear raised voices, though: there was a sudden flash of gunfire: a single shot whamped. Both Stocker and Blaney jumped. More shouting. '*The blighter shot me*,' someone wailed. '*Put the cuffs on him, Corporal*,' bawled a basso voice.

Blaney looked at Stocker, her anxious eyes cupped in darkness. 'Do you think we ought to move in, sir?'

Stocker considered it for a moment. 'Let's hang on,' he said. 'Wait till we see where they go.'

46

'Please get Lieutenant Copeland to an aid-post,' Caine said.

He was sitting handcuffed in the same chair, in the same room, with its leather-bound books and devotional paintings, that the *Nighthawk* scheme had started: he no longer knew how many days ago that was. Caversham sat glowering at him with the same blackball eyes, through the same deep lenses, from the same sagging armchair: Maskelyne stood beside him, wagging his spring-laden head. He looked pale and irritated: a medical orderly was bandaging his wrist. Copeland lay slumped on the sofa, skin blanched, eyes glistening, too feverish to talk. Pilot-Officer Willington sat by the mullioned windows, looking almost as white as Cope. A corporal and two more enlisted men in BD and black berets had taken up a strategic position by the door: all three carried night-sticks and Sten sub-machine guns.

For once, Caine's speed had failed him: with the pain of his wounds and the accumulated fatigue, he'd been a fraction of a second too slow. Once he'd confirmed that Willington had orders to land at LG101, he'd managed to snatch the pilot-officer's weapon: he'd hated doing it, but he knew that if Caversham got hold of them unarmed, he and Cope would be for the high jump.

As soon as the Blenheim had come to a standstill, he'd piled out, confronted Caversham and Maskelyne: the look of astonishment on Caversham's face had almost been worth the whole scheme. Caine had been too close to them, though: he'd forgotten Maskelyne's speed. The ex-magician had whipped out a willowy arm, grabbed for the weapon. Caine had got off one shot, before the thugs jumped on him: Maskelyne had taken a graze in the wrist.

'Mr Copeland needs medical attention,' he insisted. 'Please get him to a hospital, now.'

'He's right, sir,' said Willington. 'The chap's in a bad way.'

Caversham ignored him. 'No one is leaving till I've discovered what's going on.'

He turned back to Caine, found him gazing at a spot on the wall over his shoulder. 'What in damnation are you staring at?'

Caine had been looking for the painting he remembered – *The Torment of St Anthony*: the one that had given him the clue to the contents of the black box. The painting was gone.

'That picture of St Anthony. It's not here.'

Caversham rolled his ballbearing eyes. 'Are you mad, Caine? There never was such a painting. What has it got to do with this anyway?'

'You told me St Anthony was known for curing a *bouquet* of plagues, collectively called St Anthony's Fire.'

'I never told you that. Your mind's playing tricks.'

'No,' Caine persisted. 'Those plagues were also called

Holy Fire. That's what was in the black box you sent us to get — plague, a deadly germ-warfare agent. A platoon of German soldiers is dead because of it. If you'd managed to get it here, it would have killed you all, and spread to every part of this country. It would have wiped us out.'

Caversham's fat lips formed an *O:* his eyes bulged, he hooted incredulous laughter.

'You *are* crazy, Caine. I sent you to Tunisia to blow a bridge. I don't believe I said anything about a black box.'

There was a rap on the door. Caversham looked mystified. He gestured to the corporal, who opened it. John Stocker stood there, a stout man in a patched duffel coat open over unkempt battledress, and a black beret a size too large: he was bespectacled and comfortable-looking, with an old pipe stuck in his mouth, yet to Caine he seemed to radiate authority and power.

'Major Stocker,' Stocker said. 'Field Security. May I come in?'

Caversham bristled. 'You have no right to barge in here, Major. This is MO4, and we are entitled to privacy.'

Stocker removed his pipe, surveyed the room: his eyes lingered on each person in turn. 'I don't think *you* have the right to arrest these officers, Colonel,' he said.

'Who told you they were under arrest?'

'Nobody. But this man' — he pointed at Caine — 'is handcuffed, and that one is clearly in need of medical attention. I would like to request that you release the one, and have the other taken to the sick-bay.'

The orderly had finished bandaging Maskelyne's arm. Caversham nodded to him. 'Take the lieutenant to the infirmary,' he said. 'One of these men will help you.'

'Very good, sir.'

Stocker stood back to allow them to manhandle Copeland out of the room. Caversham instructed the corporal to unlock Caine's handcuffs, watched Stocker with narrowed eyes. 'Oh, you might as well come in, Major. We've got nothing to hide. Do you know Major Maskelyne?'

'We've met.'

'And that is Pilot-Officer Willington.'

Stocker gave the RAF man a polite nod.

'Do sit down,' Maskelyne said.

'Thank you. I'd prefer to stand. Perhaps you wouldn't mind telling me what exactly is the problem.'

'The problem is this chap Caine,' Maskelyne said, holding up his spindly, bandaged arm. 'He shot me in the wrist. Only a scratch, but he'd have done worse if I hadn't snatched the gun off him.'

'That's why we had to handcuff him,' Caversham added. 'The man's an absolute menace. He's got a record of violence as long as your arm. He lost his commission in the Sappers for attempted murder, was locked up for beating an MP to a pulp, *and* shot a fellow officer in the knee.'

Stocker looked at Caine, noted that he was bloody, battlestained and seemed on the verge of passing out.

'Is it true that you shot Major Maskelyne?' he enquired.

Caine didn't look at him. 'It's true.'

'Why did you do that?'

'He and Colonel Caversham tried to have me and my comrades killed in Tunisia, by men under my own command. I knew they wouldn't be pleased to see I'd survived. It was self-defence, you might say.'

Caversham snorted. 'Major,' he said. 'Mr Caine is suffering from delusions. He's wounded and has lost the faculty of reason. The truth is that I sent him and six men on a secret mission in Tunisia, to blow a bridge. I can see that he's wounded and tired, but to claim that I somehow organized a mutiny within his ranks is preposterous. My mistake was in taking him on in the first place. I have documents proving that he's mentally unstable . . .'

Stocker raised an eyebrow. 'Yet you sent him into the field? A mentally unstable officer?'

Caversham wadded a stubby hand, made a gesture of despair. 'It was a vital job, and almost impossible to find special service troops.'

Stocker nodded, made no comment.

'Now, of course, he's come up with all manner of demented claims, rambling on about a black box that contains some sort of plague – *Holy Fire*, he called it – a germ-warfare agent. He says I was trying to smuggle it behind our own lines. Why would I do that? This is the stuff of delirious fantasy.'

Stocker fiddled with his pipe. 'Is this true, Captain Caine?' he asked.

Caine was having trouble keeping his head up: he tried to string his words together carefully, tried to get events into proper sequence. 'We answered a Mayday call. We found a derelict aircraft of an unknown type. No markings. There was a black box inside, with the word STENDEC stencilled on it. We took the box, but we were followed by a Jerry unit, who were also after it. We held them off at the el-Fayya pass, but one of my chaps did a bunk with the box. I'm sure he was under orders from Colonel Caversham, but I can't prove it. After the battle, Mr Copeland and I chased him to the RV, where he was to meet an aircraft, but the Jerries got there first. It was our chap who opened the box first, but they all got infected, and now, they're all dead.'

Stocker put the pipe in his mouth, took it out again. 'So where is this black box now?'

'It was destroyed. Mr Willington's crew dropped a bomb on it.'

Caversham shot him a furious glance. Stocker took a quick look at Willington. 'Is that so, Pilot-Officer?

The pilot fidgeted nervously. 'We did . . . drop a bomb, sir, yes,' he stammered, 'but as far as I know it was on a German unit.'

'Did you see a black box?'

'No, I didn't, but –'

'There you are, Major,' Caversham cut across him. 'There's no proof that such a black box ever existed, let alone some fabulous germ-warfare agent. There is only Mr Caine's word. Are we to take the word of a mental case, evidently out of his mind with battle exhaustion? I think not.' He turned to Caine, tilted his monkeyface to one side as if addressing a child. 'Captain Caine, did I give you orders to answer a Mayday call?'

Caine sighed. 'No, you didn't.'

'I see. Did I order you to bring back a black box?'

'No –'

'Good. Is it not the case that I instructed you to sabotage the el-Fayya bridge – that, and that alone?'

'Yes . . . but . . .'

Caversham smirked triumphantly at Stocker. 'I rest my case, Major. Even if there were a black box, it had no connection with MO4. I ask you, though, in the name of all that's rational, does it seem likely? A giant black aircraft with no markings? A black box carrying *Holy Fire*? Mr Caine's mind is delusional. That's why the medical officer wouldn't release him for active service. He imagines things.'

Stocker examined Caine's face. 'I've seen your medical record, Captain,' he said. 'Isn't it true that your sawbones wouldn't release you because you suffered from delusions?'

Caine gazed directly at Stocker for the first time: his eyes were bloodshot and distant. 'He wouldn't release me because I refused to believe that Elizabeth Nolan was dead. That wasn't a delusion. She's alive. That's how Colonel Caversham roped me into this. He promised to help me find her.'

'More nonsense,' Caversham chortled.

Caine's eyes were still on Stocker. He noticed that the Field Security officer looked slightly flushed. Stocker avoided his eyes, placed his pipe between his teeth, brought out a packet of Swan Vestas, lit one, spent several minutes lighting up. Everyone in the room watched him. He blew a ring of blue smoke, studied it intently, took the pipe from his mouth. He looked at Caversham. 'I have just one question, sir. After that, perhaps Mr Caine can go to the sick bay, and I'll leave you in peace.'

Caversham looked relieved. 'Certainly, what is it?'

'Just now you referred to a *giant black* aircraft with no markings. I just wondered why you said that. I don't recall Mr Caine mentioning that the hypothetical aircraft was either big or black. He referred to it only as a *derelict* aircraft.'

Caversham's thick lips goldfished. 'I . . . er . . . I don't remember. I'm sure he *did* say it . . .' He cast around for help, met Maskelyne's sparrow eyes: the ex-magician shook his head. Caversham bit his lip, blew his cheeks out. 'Well, I don't know where I got it from. Imagination, I suppose.'

Stocker blew smoke pensively, caught Caine's eye. 'Was this derelict aircraft you found big and black?'

Caine chuckled wearily. 'Biggest kite I've ever seen, sir. About a hundred and fifty feet from nose to tail: a hundred and twenty-foot wingspan. Four engines. And, yes, she was black: black as your hat: she was made of some black material, like resin.'

'Superb fantasy,' Caversham snickered.

'Did you tell Colonel Caversham about that? Anyone else here?'

Caine shook his head. 'Never mentioned it.'

'That doesn't prove anything,' Caversham scoffed.

'No, it doesn't, Colonel,' Stocker said placidly, 'but now I think of it, I do have a couple more questions. First, isn't it rather unusual for a sabotage team to be tasked by MO4? I mean, sabotage isn't your brief, is it?'

'We had orders from the DMO: I can prove that.'

'I see. The other question is' – Stocker pointed his pipe-stem in Willington's direction: his eyes didn't leave Caversham – 'why task a Blenheim bomber to go to Tunisia? You must have sent Mr Willington's crew to pick up *something*?'

Caversham's jaw tightened: his eyes behind the dense glasses were boreholes. 'To pick up the SAS patrol, of course.'

Stocker waved his pipe in disbelief. 'In a medium bomber? You'd surely have needed a troop-carrier for that?'

He raised an interrogative eyebrow at Willington: the pilot was out of his chair now, poised with his feet apart, his fists clenched. His eyes blazed: two rose-pink patches showed on his ivory cheeks.

'I say, I've had enough of this hogwash, sir.'

Stocker realized that the pilot wasn't talking to him: his gaze was fixed on Caversham. 'You claim the black box is Captain Caine's delusion,' he went on. 'Well, I said I didn't see a black box, and I didn't, but I *did* see one very sick Jerry with yellow pus-blisters all over his face, and so did my gunner. And if the black box didn't exist, why did you task me to pick it up? I risked my life and my crew's lives twice over for that damn' box.'

He turned to Stocker, yanked agitatedly at his moustache. 'Colonel Caversham ordered me to fly to Bir Souffra, in Tunisia, to retrieve a black box, sir. There were supposed to be three enlisted men with it. On the first run, the chaps didn't show. The colonel sent me back again, and I found two officers there: Mr Caine and Mr Copeland. They told me there'd been a change of plan: the black box contained a germ-warfare agent that had already infected a platoon of Krauts. I didn't believe it until I saw one of them with my own eyes – just before my gunner shot him.'

Caversham rose to his feet, whipped off his glasses, pointed them accusingly at the pilot. 'You fool, Willington. Don't you realize you've just given away classified information?' He swung round on Stocker: his bottle-top nostrils flared. 'You have no right to interrogate me about a secret operation. I want you out of here, now.'

He waved blunt fingers at the corporal by the door. 'See him out,' he ordered. The corporal hesitated. '*Celia*,' Stocker called.

The door flew open: a girl in battledress came in, bracing a Tommy-gun: she had cool, greyblue eyes, and a curly mass of flaming red hair. Behind her was a gruff-looking staff-sergeant and several other Field Security NCOs, all toting weapons.

'Sit down, Colonel,' Stocker said, 'and I'll tell you the real reason I'm here.'

47

'It was called STENDEC,' Caversham said: he had lost his bluster now: his voice was plaintive. 'It was a prototype electronic counter-measures device, capable of fooling enemy radar. It could have changed the whole course of the war.'

He sat hunched up on the sofa: Stocker had removed his duffel coat and beret: he perched on the edge of an upright chair, bending forward, his elbows on his knees, the pipe still in his mouth. Celia Blaney had cleared out the MO4 men, and escorted Maskelyne to another room, to be interviewed separately. The Field Security staff-sergeant was standing at the door, a Thompson slung muzzle-forwards over a beefy shoulder. Willington had gone back to his aircraft: Caine was in the infirmary with Copeland.

'So you knew about the derelict plane?' Stocker persisted.

Caversham stroked his orb of a head with a hirsute hand. '*Groot* reported that it was a new class of aircraft developed in Germany – a *silent aircraft*, it was called. It was invisible to radar, specially designed to carry the STENDEC device. It had apparently gone down in Tunisia on a test-flight.'

Stocker shoved his pipe into a breast pocket, buttoned

it. He removed his glasses, blew on them, began rubbing them hard with a piece of two-by-four. 'So you thought this STENDEC device worth sacrificing our own men for?'

Caversham gave a hollow sigh. 'There's always sacrifice in war, Major, you know that. In the case of Caine's patrol, it wasn't a great loss. I mean, half of them were hard cases from the glasshouse, and the others . . .'

'. . . were highly decorated, extraordinarily courageous soldiers.'

Caversham bared his teeth in a grimace. 'It's their job to take orders. It's not for the likes of Caine to reason why.'

Stocker felt an indignant flush seeping up his neck. He slammed his glasses on, stood up suddenly, stared down at the colonel. 'And what about David Stirling? Was it for the likes of *him* to reason why?'

Caversham's face seemed to sag. 'That was . . . unfortunate. Of course, Stirling was one of us –'

'Yet still you handed over our most brilliant special-service officer to the enemy –'

'That was . . . the agreement. It was the only way we could get the STENDEC device . . .'

Stocker saw red. 'There *was* no STENDEC device, you bloody imbecile. You were taken in by an Abwehr Trojan horse operation. The object was to get a germ-warfare agent inside our command centre. It could have destroyed us, and you fell for it lock, stock and barrel.'

Caversham's eyes dulled. 'But my contact, *Groot* . . .

he was a highly reliable double-agent . . . he was one of us. He would never have let me down . . .'

Stocker gasped in frustration. '*Groot* was compromised years ago. You weren't communicating with *Groot*, not even with Berlin. I checked the signals. They emanated from a local source –'

'Yes, but that was just a relay: the signals were passed on via *Groot*'s agent, codenamed *Cheshire Cat*, in Alexandria.'

'*What?*' Ice-cold feathers touched Stocker's cheeks: sweat popped his brow. He turned away, took a series of quick breaths. *Cheshire Cat* was Calvin, the man who'd taken control of the deserters. It fell into place with an almost audible *snap*. Calvin was a Nazi agent. He was organizing the deserters into an Axis fifth-column inside Egypt. At the same time, he'd put together this complex Trojan horse scheme, designed to wipe out Allied command. It was a one-man campaign, and Stocker had just sent Betty Nolan into the thick of it.

He grabbed his duffel coat and beret. Caversham watched him resentfully. 'Surely you're not leaving me like this? I acted with the best of intentions . . .'

Stocker pulled down his beret grimly. 'The highroad to hell is tarmacked with them, Colonel.'

'But come, come, Major, you're one of us, aren't you?'

'One of whom, exactly?'

'One of the ruling elite. People of good breeding.'

'Not really. My father worked on the railways: I got a scholarship to Oxford.'

He turned his back on Caversham, addressed the staff-sergeant. 'Throw this well-bred officer in the deepest dungeon this monastery has, Staff. If he tries to get away, shoot him.'

Caine sat with Celia Blaney by Copeland's cot in the infirmary: a small, clean ward with a handful of beds and bare stone walls. Cope was out for the count. The MO4 sawbones, a crop-haired youth with a permanent grin, had removed the bullet from his calf: the fever had subsided, and they'd given him a sedative. He was still pale, and his leg swollen, but the doc assured them he'd pull through. FANY nurses had washed Caine's wounds, disinfected the rope-burns on his neck, bandaged it. They'd thrown away his torn and bloodstained garments, found him a new battledress suit that almost fit.

The MO had instructed Caine to rest, but he was too excited. Blaney had just told him about the shooting incident during which she'd recognized Betty Nolan. He'd had to choke back tears. What Jizzard had told him was all true. Nolan had survived the crash. She'd lost her memory for a while but was now fine. She was working for Field Security among the deserters. Blaney had also told him that Angela Brunetto hadn't been an Axis plant after all: Stocker had devised that as a cover story. The truth was that Brunetto had also been deployed undercover among the deserter gangs, as Nolan's minder. Caine was so happy for Copeland that he had to be dissuaded from waking him up.

Blaney saw the euphoria in his eyes: she bit her lip

guiltily. She hadn't mentioned the fact that, only a few hours earlier, Brunetto had left an emergency message at the Field Security office: Nolan had been summoned to Calvin's HQ. It was the breakthrough they'd been waiting for, but Stocker was here in Sinai, and there'd been a delay before the message had reached him. It had come too late to dispatch an FS team to support her. They had to rely on Brunetto to keep tabs, and to maintain contact: since then, nothing had been heard.

Blaney had talked to Maskelyne for over an hour: the interview had been productive. The ex-magician had admitted that he'd wanted revenge on Caine and his men for their behaviour on *Sandhog*. He'd known about the STENDEC aircraft and the black box: he'd been in *Nighthawk* up to the hilt.

'It wasn't his idea to rope you in, though,' Blaney said. 'That came from another officer. Someone outside MO4.'

'Come on,' Caine said impatiently. 'Spill.'

'It was Lieutenant Sears-Beach.'

Caine almost fell out of his chair. Then he remembered: the dying Fiske had mentioned Sears-Beach: so had his vision of Pickney in the derelict aircraft.

'Sears-Beach knew about Captain Nolan,' Blaney went on. 'He knew she was living with the deserters, and that she'd lost her memory. He had her followed, had photographs taken of her . . . the ones they showed you.'

Caine's fists tightened. 'He *knew*? And he never reported it to GHQ? That *bastard* . . .' He swore to himself silently that one day he and Sears-Beach would meet again. 'Are Field Security going to pull him in?'

'That's not up to me to decide, sir, but he's certainly in this as deeply as they are. Maskelyne admitted that he approached Sears-Beach for commando-trained detainees to volunteer for *Nighthawk*. He came up with the idea of using you and the others. Maskelyne told him you might not be amenable: Sears-Beach proposed using his photos of Nolan to coerce you.'

Caine closed his eyes, took a breath, steadied himself. He tried to recall the faces of his men – the ones who'd died on *Nighthawk*, his mates Wallace and Trubman, who were missing, possibly dead. Sears-Beach had been partly responsible, but only partly. The decisions on the ground had been Caine's. There was no escaping that.

'Are you all right, Captain?' Blaney's voice was a gentle catpurr.

Caine opened his eyes. 'What about Maskelyne? What'll happen to him?'

'I don't know, sir.' She seemed cagey.

'He was in *Nighthawk* up to the hilt, you said.'

'There may be extenuating circumstances. Maskelyne is our mole in MO4.'

Caine's jaw dropped. '*Mole* – you mean informer?'

'Yes. He was the source of the DMI's information that Colonel Caversham had been in contact with the Abwehr, that he was involved in Colonel Stirling's capture. That's what put Major Stocker on MO4's track in the first place. We came here looking for Caversham, and we found . . . you.'

'I'm glad you did, but surely he's not . . .'

Caine was interrupted by the arrival of Stocker, looking unusually flustered. 'Celia, we've got to get to Alex,' he gasped. 'Get on the blower, lay on a Dakota to pick us up here.'

Blaney was already running.

Caine stood up. 'What is it, sir?'

Stocker caught his breath. 'I haven't been entirely fair with you, Tom,' he panted. 'Not with regard to Captain Nolan.'

A cold swill raced up Caine's back. 'What do you mean, sir? Miss Blaney told me –'

'You know she's alive,' Stocker cut across him, 'but she doesn't know you are. I told her you didn't survive the crash.'

'*What?*' Caine's senses groped. 'Why on earth did you do that?'

'I don't have time to explain, but I will. At this point in time, though, Nolan is in trouble. I've just realized from something Caversham said that the Nazi agent who set up the STENDEC scheme is the same man Nolan's been tracking for us, the man who's been organizing the deserters. And right now she's walking into the lion's den.'

48

They came for Betty Nolan in the late evening, about the same time Caine was landing in Sinai. They didn't take her, though: they took Angela Brunetto instead. Four goons in trenchcoats broke into the safe-house, battered Taylor unconscious with night-sticks, and marched Brunetto out to a waiting lorry. Nolan heard it all from her room. Her first impulse was to rush out and tell them that it was *her* they were after: she clenched her teeth, held back. She knew that Brunetto had understood the blunder, too. She and Angela were lookalikes: the thugs had probably just barged into the first room they came to, found a pretty blond girl, assumed she was the one. Taylor might have put them right, but they hadn't given him the chance.

Nolan paused for a few seconds to think: the crucial thing was to trace Calvin. That they'd snatched the wrong person didn't change that, as long as Nolan didn't lose track of Brunetto. They'd known this was coming for hours, ever since Taylor had arrived with the announcement *Calvin wants to see Maddy*. Nolan had repressed a shiver: this was the chance Stocker wanted, but she also recalled that, of the women who'd received such a summons, none had ever come back. Taylor remembered it, too. *Over my dead body* was his reaction.

From the sound of the beating they'd given him, it had almost come to that.

After the message arrived, Brunetto had managed to alert Field Security. Stocker had been out of the office, though, and there'd been no immediate reply. Nolan was aware that her job now was to follow Brunetto, hoping that they'd take her to Calvin's base, and that support would arrive ASAP.

She was wearing a one-piece black FANY overall and desert boots. She pulled on a cap-comforter, retrieved her Colt pistol from under the floorboards, grabbed the haversack she'd prepared. She ran across the ops room, stopped for a moment to examine Taylor. He was bleeding from the head: his breathing was regular. She wished she had time to help him, but told herself he'd be all right. She felt a wave of sadness: he'd done his best to stop this happening. She knew he'd been in love with her in his own gruff way. He'd kept on, hoping that one day she'd wake up and feel the same. *Poor Taylor. Loving someone who doesn't love you is like trying to catch a boat from a railway-station.*

When she emerged into the yard, the tail-lights of the wagon were just disappearing through the gate. There was no one else about. She jumped into the covered Willy's Bantam she and Brunetto had earmarked for the job, started her up, reversed on a sixpence, drove out of the gate in the lorry's tracks.

It was about one in the morning when she reached down-town Alexandria: the lorry was still in sight. It had taken a couple of hours to get there, but long stretches of the journey were lost to her: her senses had been focused on those red tail-lights, winking in front of her like rat-eyes. She remembered the occasional blink of gaslamps in silent Delta villages, the reek of smoke and nightsoil, dogs barking, the oily gleam of canal water, wedges of reed-forest, nightblue reaches of starfilled sky. The only tricky moment had been when she'd been stopped at an MP checkpoint on the outskirts of Alex. She'd talked her way through with false papers and a shy batting of eyelids at the young Redcap sergeant. For a moment she'd felt safe in the presence of that squad of solid British lads in battle-dress: she'd even considered telling the sergeant her real identity, asking him to contact Stocker's office. She'd rejected the idea, though: it would have taken too long to establish her credentials: her objective was to find out where Calvin was. Once she'd done that, all that remained would be to get Brunetto out.

She'd caught up with the lorry again near the har-bour, illuminated by a blaze of mulberry and orange lights. The fear of air raids had receded now: the war had shifted to Tunisia, the blackout was a thing of the past. The wagon turned left: she followed it along the corniche, tasted salt air, took in rainbow gleanings of light on the heavy waters of the Med. She shuddered: the waters reminded her of the last time she'd seen Tom Caine, the night they'd crashed into the Nile. Caine was forever creeping into her mind, no matter how hard she tried to keep him out. She was suddenly filled with a longing for him so intense it stifled her breath. Vivid images of that night flowed through her: the moment when she'd recognized the man at the driving wheel as Johann Eisner: the shock of discovering they were at the mercy of a Nazi spy who'd sworn to see her dead. She shivered again. Eisner was gone, but she'd never forget that face, nor the fact that he'd taken Caine from her.

She pushed the images away, focused on the lorry's tail-lights. She didn't know Alexandria well, but she was aware they were heading towards the royal palace at Ras al-Tin, a rambling labyrinth of colonnades and cupolas standing on the waterfront. She rounded the headland, saw the palace in front of her, lit up like a Christmas tree. About a quarter of a mile before reaching it, though, the lorry took a left up a blueshadowed lane. Two hundred yards further on, it turned right through a broken-down gate. Nolan switched off her lights, drove past, halted the jeep in deep blackness, further along the lane.

She slung her haversack, slipped out of the vehicle. Her stomach fluttered: she pulled the pistol from her pack, lodged it in the patch-pocket of her overalls. She padded as far as the gate along the base of lichen-covered walls with branches of dead trees hanging over their tops like bony fingers. The gate had been grand once: now its blocks were skewed and crumbling: sculptures of a griffon and an eagle that had probably once stood atop its great posts lay toppled in the dust.

Nolan squatted at the gate, peeked in. She clocked

a rubble-strewn courtyard, grass growing through paving stones, a collapsed ornamental fountain. The lorry was parked in front of what appeared to be the edifice of a ruined palazzo: she glimpsed creeper-covered walls, boarded-up windows, a sprawl of ramparts, turrets, protrusions, spreading over each other, merging with the night. She felt a spasm of uneasiness. There was no visible light, no movement, only darkness and tarblack shadow. Could this really be Calvin's HQ? No vehicles, no guards, no wireless antennae? Had she been drawn into a trap? Had they spotted her, led her to an abandoned building?

She heard voices, saw shadows bob, heard wagon-doors bang: the lorry's engine harrumphed: headlights reamed. Nolan pressed into a recess, waited for the vehicle to growl past. She got a glimpse of faces in the cab: no sign of Brunetto. She stayed where she was until the truck had turned right at the end of the lane, then took another shufti at the palazzo. They must have left Brunetto in there. Whatever the place looked like, this must be where the meeting with Calvin was supposed to take place. She felt a rush of panic. What would happen to Brunetto? The Italian girl had been taken in her place, and she hadn't done anything to prevent it. She felt the weight of the gun in her pocket: no matter how creepy the place looked, she was tempted to wade in right now. On the other hand, she'd found Calvin's base, or thought she had: that knowledge might be wasted if she didn't pass it on to Stocker.

How could she contact him? She had no wireless, so

it had to be by phone. Public phone booths were rare in Alex, but she remembered seeing one down by the harbour. She could be there and back in twenty minutes. In that time, though, anything could happen to Brunetto. Stocker hadn't been in the office when she'd called him earlier. It might take hours for a support unit to get here. One thing they'd taught her in training was *never go in without back-up*. She realized suddenly that she was wasting time debating it. She ran for the jeep.

She made it back in twenty-four minutes: she'd found the phone, got through to FS headquarters, only to be told that Stocker was still away. She'd left an urgent message, described the exact location of the palazzo in Alexandria, reported that she was going in to look for Brunetto. Stocker couldn't forbid her: he wasn't there.

She hovered for a long moment at the gate, drew her pistol with her left hand, took her torch in her right, slung her haversack over her backside so that it wouldn't impede her. She moved towards the *palazzo* as softly as a cat. Close up, she felt the presence of the building like a brooding creature, a dark beast with knotted skin covered in creeping serpents, dotted with orifices like haggard eyes. To look at, it was was mostly a black outline, though: Nolan took cues from the way the shadows fell to furnish it with gable-ends, lean-to roofs, turrets, fallen façades, bow windows, terraces and verandahs, broken-down steps with disintegrating balustrades.

There seemed to be no door in the cliff of decaying masonry, only a low-arched tunnel. She ducked under it: flying shapes whispered past – bats or ravens, it was too dark to tell. She found a stairwell, paused there, flashed a torch-beam, glimpsed fractured stone steps leading down into darkness. Her heart beat a devil's tattoo. She kept the torch on, worked her way down, stopped to listen every few minutes. There was a sepulchral smell: dried-out leather and rotting wet rags. At the bottom of the stairs it was as foetid as a tomb: she flashed the torch, found herself in a vaulted passage littered with mouldy fragments of basketry, yellow newspapers, cast-off chairs shedding their innards, tables with amputated limbs covered in dust. The walls were puke-green, scabbed with patterns of flaking paint, festooned with broken switch-boxes, nests of wires, disused light-sockets out of the Ark. There were many doors opening off the passage, rusted iron, with old rivets and enormous locks: she tried several, but they seemed stuck in place.

She switched off her torch, stood stock still, became aware of rustlings and scrapings, the drap-drap of water, the faint creak of what might have been ancient plumbing, and – somewhere far off – a child's sobs. The sobbing sound was the only sign of human presence. She couldn't be certain it was a child – even that it was really human – but it seemed to be coming from a narrow side-passage. Nolan hesitated, turned off the main corridor, headed towards the sound. She must have covered a hundred feet when she heard a door scrape. She stopped, switched off the torch, listened. Someone was coming up behind her in the darkness: she could hear footfalls and wheezing breath. She gripped her pistol, prepared to spin round, heard silence. From somewhere above her came a muffled cranking, like clockwork machinery. She waited: the mechanical sound stopped. Had she imagined the footfalls, the breathing? The darkness was a blank that your mind invested with all sorts of non-existent things. Now, she heard only the lubdub of her own pulse, the tattered edge of her own breathing. She moved on again: the footfalls returned. She halted once more, turned about, felt tempted to demand who was there. Again, she heard nothing. She bit her lip, carried on.

The sobbing was intermittent, but seemed to be getting closer. The direction was confusing, though: every few steps revealed new openings, doorways, side-corridors – the place was a sprawling underground maze. Then, the sobbing was replaced abruptly by a full-throated, high-pitched scream. Nolan froze, fought back a fresh frisson of fear. *That wasn't a child. It was a woman. Was it Brunetto? What were they doing to her?*

She stroked the safety-catch of her pistol, felt some comfort from the weapon. She hadn't imagined the scream: it had come from someplace nearby. She started off: the footfalls were with her again. They seemed to be approaching faster now. She stopped a third time, switched off the torch. The wheezing breath – she could hear it clearly. Suddenly there was a dry chuckle, so close that her nipples tightened in terror. Someone was standing right behind her. She swung round, extended pistol and torch together, the way they'd taught her in SOE school.

She flashed the torch: her finger went tight on the trigger. For a fraction of a second a face was engraved in the torch-beam, a face she knew, a face she'd last seen under a peasant's headcloth, seconds before their taxi crashed into the Nile. *Johann Eisner*. His unquiet eyes contracted in the blare of light, his jaw jutted like a knifeblade, his thinlipped mouth set itself in a vulpine sneer. Nolan pulled iron. The *DWOOOOMMMPPP-PHHH* was deafening in the confined space: the volcano of light blinded her, the gas-stench made her sick. A body blundered into her, knocked her flying, fell on top of her. She hit the wall, took the fall on her soft parts, felt hard male arms grope her, felt barbwire stubble rake her face. She rolled away frantically from the grabbing arms, fired again, heard the *whhaanggg-zzzzzssssttt* of a ricochet as the bullet shattered into fragments, bounced from wall to wall. She came up on to her feet, ran hell-for-leather into the darkness, half blind, ears ringing from the gunshots. She ran straight into a brick wall, staggered back, found a passage on her right, stumbled through it till she was in what felt like a wider space. It was pitch dark: she pressed herself against the wall, panting, strained through the chiming in her eardrums to pick up pursuing steps. She heard only the tom-tom beat of her heart. The shock of the encounter hit her like a rabbit-punch. *Eisner's dead. It looked like him, but it can't be. It was, though. You know it was. He's here, in Calvin's place. What's he doing here? Is Eisner Calvin?* Then she remembered Caine, and her terror was chased out by a hot tsunami of rage. *That swine killed Tom Caine.*

'*I thought you'd be here sooner or later,*' a disembodied voice growled, almost in her ear. Nolan jumped, raised the pistol, held her body rigid, eyeballed left and right. The darkness was impenetrable.

'*I've been expecting you, Maddy.*' It came from a different direction this time: Nolan swept the gun in a ninety-degree arc, saw only blackness.

'*Of course, I knew the other girl wasn't you. She looks like you, but she isn't in the same class.*' Again, a different place: Eisner must be cruising barefoot.

'*I've thought a lot about you since I discovered you were alive. I was angry at first, but then I realized that I felt something else. I was glad you were back. It's true, I swore to kill you. I no longer feel like that, especially since I realized that you had lost your identity. Neither of us is the person we used to be.*'

Nolan wasn't taking in the words: whatever Eisner said was a decoy. She was listening only to the voice itself. It was near: it seemed to be shifting constantly. She tried to pinpoint the movement, hoped to God she could get off a shot when he came in.

'*I talked to the deserters. I know they picked you up after the crash, that you lived with them because you'd lost your memory. That changed everything. Now I believe you could help me. I never felt that before.*'

A woman shrieked suddenly from a place not far away — a heart-rending squeal of agony that made the blood rush to Nolan's face. '*What are you doing to Angela, you . . . ?*'

She didn't even realize she'd spoken until it was too late. A hand closed on her wrist, held it with an iron grip, whipped her arm back so fast that the gun was wrenched out of her hand: an elbow grasped her neck in a vice. She yanked her gun-hand free, turned her head sideways, kicked down into his instep, tried to work the elbow off with both hands. She felt a finger-nail of curved steel touch her neck just below the ear, remembered the vicious little knife Eisner had used when he'd cut Mary Goddard's throat right in front of her. 'I don't want to hurt you,' Eisner whispered. 'Don't make me. That's better. Now, let me introduce you to Calvin. Perhaps I'll find out the identity of the impostor they sent in your place.'

49

It was half past one in the morning when Stocker, Blaney and the rest of the Field Security section took off from LG101 in pitch darkness, in an RAF Dakota. Caine was with them. At first, Stocker wouldn't hear of his coming to Alexandria. Caine was wounded and exhausted, he said. He'd done his bit and more: now he would have to do what the doctor ordered. Caine stuck his chin out. When Stocker looked as if he wasn't going to budge, he resorted to moral blackmail. He pointed out that, on his own admission, the major had lied about him to Nolan, causing her unforgivable distress.

'I had no choice,' Stocker protested. 'If I'd admitted you were alive, she would never have gone back to the deserters, and we'd never have found Calvin's location.'

'Steady on, sir. We still haven't found Calvin's location,' Blaney reminded him. 'We haven't heard from Brunetto yet.'

In the end, Stocker had caved in: he'd even told his lads to hand over some clips of .45 calibre ammunition for Caine's Thompson. Caine felt bad about leaving Copeland in the MO4 aid-post: the sawbones with the crew-cut told him that his chum would be moved to Cairo in the next few days. He didn't say goodbye to Cope: his mate was still out when he left.

It was a tense flight, though. Caine was still buzzing on Benzedrine and morphia, but he was terrified that something would happen to Nolan before he got there. She wasn't even aware that she was dealing with a top-flight Nazi agent rather than an Allied deserter-boss: from what Stocker had told him, Field Security had used her as bait. Last time they'd done that she'd been kept prisoner in a cellar for more than a week, and very nearly ended up getting done in by Johann Eisner.

The only good thing about it was that they'd sent Angela Brunetto as her minder. Angela had saved Caine's bacon more than once: for a girl, she was a damn' good man, he thought. He'd wanted to leave a note about Brunetto for Copeland to read when he woke up, but Stocker had vetoed it. Anything written down was a security risk, he said.

Stocker also spent a restless flight. He'd gone to tremendous lengths to plant Brunetto among the deserters: he'd trusted her. Since the signal that afternoon, though, he'd heard nothing. If they arrived in Alex without having discovered Calvin's location, everything would have been in vain. He didn't relish the prospect of telling Caine that the sweetheart he'd so nearly found again had once more been thrown to the dogs.

It wasn't until ten minutes before their aircraft was due to land in Alex that Blaney passed Stocker a signal from Field Security HQ: it had come through on the RAF wireless net. The text was a phone message originating in Alexandria some time earlier. It gave the precise address and location of the palazzo in which it was believed Calvin was based. Stocker sighed in relief.

'Well done, Signora Brunetto,' he intoned. 'I knew we could rely on you.'

Blaney raised a ginger eyebrow. 'You didn't notice, sir? That message didn't come from Brunetto. It came from Captain Nolan.'

Stocker sat up. Caine, dozing in the next seat, was suddenly wide awake. 'What's going on?' he demanded.

'Calvin's men made a mistake, sir. Apparently they kidnapped Brunetto instead of Nolan. Nolan must have shadowed her, discovered Calvin's location, and phoned it in.'

Caine and Stocker stared at each other. 'So where is Captain Nolan now?' Stocker enquired.

Blaney blushed. 'It's in the message, sir. She told our office that she was going into Calvin's HQ to extract Brunetto.'

'What? On her *own*?' Caine stammered.

Stocker looked worried. 'When did this message come through to the office?'

'At 1330 hours, sir.'

Stocker glanced at his watch. 'That's approximately an hour ago.'

'*Jesus*,' Caine swore. 'A heck of a lot can happen in an hour.'

50

'Two for the price of one,' Heinrich Rohde scoffed. 'Isn't that what the English say? "Two birds with one stone"?'

His voice was more effeminate than Nolan remembered, but no less chilling. It was as if a malevolent female spectre were speaking through his male body – or what was left of it.

Until Eisner had dragged her on to her knees in front of Rohde, she hadn't believed what he'd croaked in her ear out in the passage. *Calvin is an old acquaintance of yours. One you might not remember: Heinrich Rohde.* Even when she'd glimpsed the mass of scar tissue, the distorted features, the dark glasses like discs of polished obsidian, she wouldn't have recognized him. It was only the hand: those overlong fingers, writhing obscenely like tentacles – a hand that had once inflicted terrible pain on her. The sight filled her with such terror that she almost vomited. She could no more forget those fingers than she could forget Eisner's face.

Her hands were tied behind her back. A few feet to her right, Angela Brunetto knelt, sobbing. She was trussed up in the same way, naked from the waist up: her overall-top had been savagely ripped off. Her head lolled against her chest, spilling wild blond hair over breasts whose nipples were livid with vicious burns. Nolan had no doubt of the origin of the screams she'd heard outside. When Eisner had shoved her down next to Brunetto, they'd exchanged a fleeting look. Brunetto had betrayed no sign of recognition: Nolan was certain that the Italian girl hadn't talked. That gave her courage: Brunetto had as much reason to hate and fear Rohde as she had. She'd been tortured dreadfully, but Nolan guessed she wasn't in such a feeble state as it appeared: *always try to appear weaker and more stupid than you are.*

Rohde removed his glasses, leaned forward out of the shadow of his wing-backed chair. Nolan saw that one of his eyes was a vacant white pit, the other a narrow slot in a puffy mass of red tissue. She gasped. 'You find me repulsive?' Rohde enquired. 'Perhaps you recall the part you played in my disfigurement? Both of you – you and *Signora Brunetto* here – are responsible for this. I'm happy you're here. Before I dispose of you, you will discover the appalling cost of your action against me.'

Nolan had to exercise all the dramatic skills she'd learned in a lifetime to remain composed, to control the twitching of her face, to master the clinging dread in her belly. She'd been prepared for Calvin. Never in her darkest dreams had she imagined that she'd be facing the Nazi sadist she thought she'd seen blown to pieces six months earlier. First Eisner, now Rohde: two men she'd believed dead, who had more reason to do her harm than anyone else on earth. She fought to control her breath, to diminish the birdhouse shrill of fear in her ears.

She forced herself to focus. She had no hidden weapons: she doubted that Brunetto did either. There'd been two big men with pistols in the room when she'd come in: she guessed they were still lurking behind her in the shadows. The cellar was large and dimly lit: its walls were draped with faded crimson hangings. There was what appeared to be a signals booth to her left: she'd seen an enormous four-poster bed when she'd first entered. There seemed to be no windows – the cellar was underground, of course. There were several doors apart from the one she'd come in through: she'd counted five – three lining the wall to the right, one behind Rohde, and another to the left of the comms booth. Some might lead to auxiliary rooms, a toilet, others to passages or staircases. All in all, the chances of escape didn't look good. On impulse, she decided to rely on bluff.

The deserters knew her as Maddy – a girl they'd found wandering the streets, disorientated and unaware of her identity. She hadn't been listening to Eisner's words properly: now they came back to her. *I know they picked you up after the crash, that you lived with them because you'd lost your memory.* Eisner had also called her *Maddy*; *an old acquaintance of yours. One you might not remember*, he'd said of Rohde. It was a gamble, but right now it was all she had.

'Where's Calvin?' she demanded with a hysterical edge in her voice. 'I came to see Calvin. Where is he?'

Rohde's tonsils grated. 'You took me in once, *Miss Maddaleine Rose*. Not again. My friend Johann tells me that you are not the person you once were: that you have *lost your memory*. I was prepared to believe that until I discovered the signora here, who had been substituted for you. That seemed rather too much of a coincidence.'

'I don't know what you mean. I came here to see Calvin.'

'I'm aware that you're a good actress. I discovered that to my cost. I won't be caught again –'

'I talked to the deserters who found her,' Eisner cut in peevishly. He'd been standing in the shadows out of Nolan's vision: now, he moved noiselessly in front of her, stared at Rohde. 'They found her wandering around Cairo the night of our crash. She didn't know who she was or what she was doing there. She's been with them ever since. She's taken part in hijacks and shootings. Nobody's cover is that deep. How could she have known she'd be in an accident that night?'

'Even if that's true, doesn't it occur to you that the Italian bitch might have *told* her who she is?'

'That wouldn't necessarily make any difference. Not if her memory is blocked. She wouldn't *remember*.'

Rohde leaned forward again, allowing light to fall on his hideously deformed face. 'You see this? She is the same person who did this to me, whether she remembers it or not. She will suffer the consequences.'

He sat back, gasping for breath. 'I'm going to tell you about those consequences,' he said at last. 'You see, after I was maimed by you and others, I came up with an idea that would pay you out, and all your kind with you. Our germ specialists had developed a synthetic disease with the modest name of UB7. It was based on the fungus that causes ergotism. UB7 is highly infectious. It is passed from person to person by contact, and the symptoms show up within a few minutes. My idea was to have a huge dose of UB7 sealed in a black box, itself a clever device, with properties that might dissuade any casual observer from trying to open it. I had the box placed in the hull of a dummy aircraft, constructed to look as if it had crash-landed in the desert. All that remained was to leak to British intelligence that the black box really contained a prototype electronic counter-measures device that could deceive radar. Something they couldn't possibly ignore. The plan was so brilliantly conceived that our rivals, the SS, wanted it for themselves. They sent a unit to retrieve the black box. They were too late, of course. By now the box will be in Egypt. It may well have been opened. Even as we speak the plague may be spreading throughout Allied command. It won't be contained there. Many civilians will die. I tell you this so that you understand what your actions against me set in motion. Thousands will die horribly because of what you did.'

Nolan and Brunetto gaped at him. *He's mad*, Nolan thought. *He's stark, staring bonkers.* Rohde slipped out an automatic pistol, covered both of them. 'Normally, I give the females I invite here a choice. Either they can go to the palace to be fucked by any filthy Gyppo greaseball who wants them. Or they can play horse-and-jockey with Johann here. Most take the first choice.

In your case, though, I'm giving no such options. You will join Herr Eisner in his enjoyable games. Eisner loves horsy games, don't you, Eisner? As long as you are the rider, eh?'

Eisner blanched. 'What do you mean . . . ?'

Rohde's whispery voice was almost coaxing. 'You think I don't know about the vanishing girls? The ones who end up in shallow graves in the desert after you have sodomized them and slit their throats?'

Eisner's lips trembled. 'That's not me. I'm not responsible for that . . .'

'I see,' Rohde snickered dryly. 'So what is the purpose of that little knife in your pocket?'

'You don't understand,' Eisner stammered. 'The person who does that to those girls . . . it's not me . . . it's someone else.'

'I want you to get that little knife out and cut their throats.'

Brunetto let out a stifled scream. Nolan felt petrified with panic, tried to push it back by sheer will-power. *Whatever happens, you mustn't seem afraid.*

Eisner felt for his knife, brought it out. He looked at it, then at Maddy. She was facing death, yet she didn't seem scared. She was like a child, except that there were those eyes, deep, deep eyes, that seemed to draw you in. Eyes that seemed to be seeing another world.

'Eisner,' Rohde rapped. 'Do it.'

Eisner hesitated, caught in Nolan's beam like a rabbit. 'I'm not sure,' he stammered.

'I want to see you do it. You fouled up every single

attempt to kill her, you incompetent fool. Do her now while I watch. Do them both.'

Eisner stepped closer to Nolan, his knife ready. He lifted her chin gently, caressed her cheek, stroked her neck. She didn't flinch from his gaze. *She's not afraid. She's not afraid of me.* He remembered the time he'd been about to kill her in the Cairo house. That was what had made him hesitate then. Her refusal to show fear. *She's the only woman I've ever met who isn't afraid of me.* You could do anything to her, have her in any way you liked, and she'd never be afraid. He realized he wanted her more than anything: he wanted to do things to her until he finally saw the fear in her eyes.

'*Eisner.*'

Eisner let his hand drop: he raised the knife slowly. Then, with astonishing speed, he wheeled round on Rohde, sliced his neck with a single snick of the blade. Rohde's one good eye bugged, he choked, coughed, gurgled blood: gore and froth oozed from the severed flesh. His tarantula fingers twitched: he slumped sideways, toppled on to the floor.

Brunetto squealed, fought frantically at her bindings. Nolan heard deeper yells, half turned to see the guards advancing on Eisner with drawn pistols. He stood his ground, shot them both with Rohde's discarded automatic.

Rohde was lying face upwards in a puddle of blood, his hand on his throat, his slot of an eye blinking, making gurgling sounds in his throat. Eisner crouched over him, spoke in his ear. 'I know you can hear me,' he whispered. 'I wanted to tell you that it was me who informed SS command about STENDEC. It was me who gave the Totenkopf the location of the black aircraft. I realized long ago that the Abwehr was so riddled with double-agents and anti-Hitler people that it was no longer trusted by the OKW. You were right about one thing: I do like horsy games. That's why I changed horses in mid-gallop. I've been working for the Gestapo for months. So here's this for my incompetence.' He spat in Rohde's eye. 'I'm not going to finish the job. I'm going to let you lie here, bleed slowly to death, and ruminate on your *own* incompetence.'

He stood up, saw Brunetto trying to crawl away. He ignored her, dragged Nolan to her feet, started to sever her bindings. 'What are you doing?' she said.

He opened his wolf-eyes wide. 'I want you.' He paused, glanced at Brunetto. 'Your friend will have to go, of course, but not you. You're mine.'

There came a sudden spurt of gunfire from outside, screams, running feet. Eisner stood perfectly still, cocked his ears. At that moment Brunetto launched herself at him, shrieking: she was free of her bindings: she wielded in her hands the pistol she'd taken from one of the dead guards.

Eisner stepped back: his mouth gobfished.

Then the door exploded.

The cellar was full of fumes and shouting. Brunetto was sprawled on the floor with Eisner's little knife in her throat: Eisner was backing away with Nolan in a head-lock. His temple was blubbing gore where the Italian girl's bullet had winged him: he held Rohde's pistol against Nolan's neck. A broad-shouldered figure edged out of the murk: Tom Caine was there in front of them, his Thompson at the ready. For a moment Nolan thought she must be hallucinating. Caine looked different: his face scorched, his neck bandaged: there was a limpness to his left arm, a stiffness to his body. Then he said *Betty* and the bubble popped: it was Caine, Tom Caine, Thomas Caine, Thomas Edward Caine, solid, strong, as real as his stone-polished eyes, his blunt head, his freckled features. He was only yards away, yet it was infinity. Nolan tried to say something: words wouldn't come. Eisner dug the .22 pistol into her flesh, dragged her towards the green baize curtain behind Rohde's chair. His back came in contact with it: he elbowed it open, touched a button. Nolan heard the rattle of electric cascade doors: a *lift*.

Caine stared at them, frozen: a voice in his head shrieked, *This isn't happening. I've found her, and now Eisner is taking her away again.* His gorge rose like a tidal wave: he fought to keep calm, to ease the screeching inside. He needed a steady grip to make a headshot – a feat considered impossible with a hip-held Tommy-gun. *If I hit her that's the end. I couldn't go on, knowing I'd shot her. But if I don't, Eisner will have her. She'll be dead then, too.* He eased off the safety, felt the fingers of his left hand creep along the forward stock, touched the trigger-guard, shifted the muzzle slightly. He set his teeth: his boneground eyes fixed on a spot on Eisner's bleeding head.

Eisner was backing Nolan into the lift. '*Stop*,' Caine growled. 'Let her go.'

Eisner's wolf-eyes glowed. 'She's mine now, Caine. Mine to do what I like with.'

Caine remembered the words that had haunted him, so long ago, it seemed. If he'd been deluded then, his mind was now as clear as an icepick. They were almost in the lift. Caine's finger brushed the trigger. '*You can do it, skipper*,' a voice whispered. It was Pickney. '*Go on. It'll be all right.*'

Caine squeezed: the gun boomed, smoke belched, cordite blew. Eisner jerked, let go Nolan's head. As he fell back into the lift his pistol cracked. Nolan lurched forward, the lift doors closed: traction-cables rumbled. Caine fired burst after burst through the iron doorframes: he didn't stop shooting until Celia Blaney's fingers closed round his wrist. 'It's all right, Tom. He's dead.'

Whenever Caine thought about it later, what happened after that remained a hazy memory. He recalled seeing Brunetto on the floor, her naked chest heaving, her lips working soundlessly. He remembered seeing a one-legged, one-armed man with a horrifically mutilated face, gargling, as gore streamed through his fingers. Most of all, though, he remembered Betty Nolan – the pale features, the blood in the golden hair, the tiny entry wound in her head that seemed no bigger than a beesting. He remembered Blaney squatting at his elbow with a medical pack and a field dressing, recalled the graveness in her pigeoncoloured eyes. *She's still breathing, Tom. But only just.* Caine remembered the coldness that had gripped him then, how he'd staggered away, clutched at the wall, wailed inwardly *No. For Christ's sake. No.*

After that he remembered only how the sneer on Rohde's horror-mask face had faded when Stocker whispered in his ear that his STENDEC scheme had failed. He recalled the eldritch, oldcrone voice wheezing. 'You haven't defeated me, Caine . . . in Libya I gave you enough Olzon-13 to cause lasting nerve damage. Tell me . . . have you seen any ghosts recently?'

He recalled how the slot-like eye had burned, how the man had cackled, coughed, spluttered through his bloody phlegm, until the moment Caine had shot him in the head.

51

They walked down the corniche arm in arm, and sometimes Caine even forgot it was Celia Blaney beside him,
not Betty Nolan. For days after the incident he'd lain in
hospital raving in delirium – the result of wound-
trauma, battle-fatigue, shock: Blaney had sat patiently
at his bedside for hours on end. Later, as he'd begun the
long slog back to health, she'd been there for him whenever he'd needed her. They'd tested him for possible
nerve damage from Olzon-13 poisoning, but the results
had been inconclusive. Caine knew he'd experienced
some strange symptoms before and during *Nighthawk*,
but Maurice Pickney had paid him no visits lately, and
he realized that he would now never know if Rohde's
last words had been a bluff.

By the time the medics had passed him fit to return
to his regiment, though, everything had changed.
Montgomery had pushed the old Panzer Army far to
the north of Tunisia: Axis forces were hanging on there
by a thread. Even Hitler seemed to have abandoned
North Africa: Rommel had been recalled to Berlin.

There was another SAS Regiment, now, 2nd SAS,
based in Algeria, training for the invasion of Italy. 1st
Regiment hadn't really survived Stirling's capture: Stirling had made too many enemies among what he'd

always called the *fossilized shit* at GHQ. A desert raiding force wasn't needed any more, they pointed out. Word was that they were going to disband 1st SAS, and re-form it as an ordinary commando mob under Paddy Mayne.

Caine realized that they'd arrived at the place where the taxi carrying him and Nolan had crashed into the Nile, more than six months earlier. That had been the last time he'd spoken to her: now she'd been shipped back to Blighty, alive but in a coma. From the latest he'd heard, she was still unconscious, still in intensive care.

They shared a cigarette, watched Allied soldiers out taking the air, ogling the girls, arguing with vendors. The Nile waters were clay-brown and sluggish: a felucca with a sail like a white butterfly skimmed the stream.

'Any news of Wallace and Trubman?' Blaney asked.

Caine shook his head, took a drag, passed the cigarette to her. 'Officially declared missing in action.'

He steered his thoughts away, not willing to face that yawning chasm he'd looked into so often during his convalescence. 'Harry's doing all right, though. Been posted to officer-training at last.'

'He'll be happy about that.'

'Yeah. Over the moon.'

'Angela's OK?'

'Yep. They're still together.' Brunetto had been lucky: distracted by her shot, Eisner had struck her only a glancing cut. His knife had stuck in her flesh, but her windpipe hadn't been severed.

438

'You heard about Caversham and the others?' Blaney asked.

Caine raised his eyebrows. 'Surprise me.'

In the end, she told him, none of them had been court-martialled – not Caversham, nor his MO4 cronies, nor Sears-Beach. Caversham had been able to demonstrate that the DMO had ordered the op on el-Fayya bridge. Stocker guessed that the order had come in response to false int., supplied by MO4, that the Totenkopf objective was to hit the Kiwis from the rear, when in fact they'd simply been tasked to retrieve the black box. Stocker didn't believe that 164 Panzer Division had ever intended to cross the Matmata Hills. He couldn't prove any of it, of course, but if it were true, it meant that Caine's stand at the el-Fayya bridge had been a wasted effort. As for the black box, there was no proof other than hearsay that it had ever existed: Willington had never actually seen it, and the brass had preferred to believe Caversham, rather than Caine and Cope. Neither Stocker nor Blaney had been consulted. The Stirling affair had been swept quietly under the carpet. 'Insufficient evidence,' Blaney commented wryly. 'Otherwise known as *friends in high places*, Stocker says.'

Caine shrugged. It was no more or less than he'd expected. Whatever happened, it wouldn't bring Nolan back.

He stubbed out the cigarette, found Blaney looking at him with the gently expectant expression he'd grown used to. A smile widened her soft mouth.

'So what about you, Tom? What are you going to do now?'

He shrugged again. 'I don't know. Nothing's the same any more, is it? One thing I'm sure of, I'm not letting her go. Not while there's a chance she might come round.'

He saw a hint of sadness in her eyes, knew he'd been inconsiderate: it wasn't much of a reward for her devotion, to profess that his heart still belonged to another girl – a girl who might not even live. Was that how it would be for the rest of his life? he wondered. Would Nolan always be there, looking over his shoulder? He'd killed Eisner, but he'd failed Nolan: he'd been close, but not close enough. That was one wound that would never heal. The worst of it, though, was not knowing, not being sure.

He gave Blaney a peck on the cheek, slipped his arm through hers. 'Come on,' he said. 'I'll buy you a tea.'

Him and Blaney? He liked her. He liked the way the chip-bag cap sat jauntily on her fiery hair: he liked the soft, dove-coloured eyes, the peachy skin, the way the battledress clung to her figure. He liked her gentleness and her warm heart. She wasn't Betty Nolan, though: she never would be. But maybe she could be. He didn't know.